# A New Life

## Bernard Malamud

*Farrar, Straus and Cudahy*

NEW YORK

The author is grateful to the
Ford Foundation for a gift of time.

FIRST PRINTING, 1961

For Alex
and Bernadette

Lo, levin leaping lightens
in eyeblink Ireland's westward welkin!

ULYSSES

A New Life

S. Levin, formerly a drunkard, after a long and tiring trans-continental journey, got off the train at Marathon, Cascadia, toward evening of the last Sunday in August, 1950. Bearded, fatigued, lonely, Levin set down a valise and suitcase and looked around in a strange land for welcome. The small station area—like dozens he had seen en route—after a moment's activity, was as good as deserted, and Levin after searching around here and there, in disappointment was considering calling a taxi, when a man and woman in sports clothes appeared at the station. They stared at Levin—the man almost in alarm, the woman more mildly—and he gazed at them. As he grasped his bags and moved towards them they hurried to him. The man, in his forties, tall, energetic, with a rich head of red hair, strode forward with his hand outstretched.

"Sorry I'm late. My name's Dr. Gilley."

3

"S. Levin," Levin said, removing his black fedora, his teeth visible through his beard. "From the East."

"Good," beamed Gilley, his voice hearty. He indicated the tall, flat-chested woman in a white linen dress. "My wife."

"I'm pleased—" Levin said.

"I'm Pauline Gilley." She was like a lily on a long stalk.

"Let me help you with your bags," Gilley said.

"No, thanks, I—"

"No trouble at all."

He had grabbed both bags and now carried them around to his car, parked in front of the station, his wife and Levin hurrying after him. Unlocking the trunk, where two golf bags lay, one containing a brand new set of clubs, he deposited Levin's things.

Levin had opened the rear door but Pauline said there was room for all in front. He shyly got in and she sat between them.

"We were delayed at the golf course," she explained.

"Do you play?" Gilley asked Levin.

"Play?"

"Golf."

"Oh, no."

They drove a while in silence.

"I hope to learn some day," Levin said with a broken laugh.

"Good," said Gilley.

Levin relaxed and enjoyed the ride. They were driving along an almost deserted highway, in a broad farm-filled valley between distant mountain ranges laden with forests, the vast sky piled high with towering masses of golden clouds. The trees softly clustered on the river side of the road were for the most part deciduous; those crawling over the green hills to the south and west were spear-tipped fir.

My God, the West, Levin thought. He imagined the pioneers in covered wagons entering this valley for the first time, and found it a moving thought. Although he had lived little in nature Levin had always loved it, and the sense of having done

4

the right thing in leaving New York was renewed in him. He shuddered at his good fortune.

"The mountains to the left are the Cascades," Pauline Gilley was saying. "On the right is the Coastal Range. They're relatively young mountains, whatever that means. The Pacific lies on the other side of them, about fifty miles."

"The Pacific Ocean?"

"Yes."

"Marvelous."

The Gilleys laughed. "We could drive over to the coast some time before Registration Week," Dr. Gilley said.

He went on amiably, "Seymour shortens to Sy—isn't that right?"

Levin nodded.

"My first name's Gerald and you already know Pauline's. People aren't too formal out this way. One of the things you'll notice about the West is its democracy."

"Very nice."

"And we're curious about everybody," Pauline said. "One can't help be in a small town. Have you any pictures of your family in your wallet? Or perhaps a sweetheart?" She laughed a little.

Levin blushed. "No pictures, no sweetheart."

He said after a minute, "No wallet."

They laughed, Pauline merrily, Gilley chuckling.

"Oh, look there!" She pointed toward the eastern mountains.

In the distance, a huge snow-capped peak rising above the rosy clouds reflecting the setting sun, floated over the darkish blue mountain range.

"Extraordinary," muttered Levin.

"Mt. Chief Joseph," Pauline said. "I knew you'd like it."

"Overwhelming. I—"

His heart was still racing from the sight when Pauline said, "We're almost in town. Would you like us to drive through the campus?"

"Tomorrow," Gilley said. He pointed under the setting sun.

5

"That's Easchester we're coming to. The college is over there to the southwest. That tall building just over those trees is Chem Engineering. That one is the new Ag building. You can't see Humanities Hall, where we hang out, but it's in that direction there. We live about half a mile from the campus, about that way. You'll be living close in if you like Mrs. Beaty's house, about three blocks from the office, very convenient."

Levin murmured his thanks.

They were driving through downtown, and were, before he could get much of an impression, out of it and into a residential section of lovely tree-lined streets and attractive wooden houses. The many old trees and multitudes of green leaves excited Levin pleasantly. In a few minutes they had arrived in front of a two-story frame house, painted an agreeable brown, with a slender white birch on the lawn, its lacy branches moving in the summer breeze. What surprised Levin was the curb-strip planted thick with flowers the whole length of the house, asters, marigolds, chrysanthemums, he guessed; in his valise was a copy of *Western Birds, Trees and Flowers,* a fat volume recently purchased.

"This is our house," said Pauline, "although Gerald would prefer a ranch type."

"Someday we'll build," said Gerald. "She'd have a lot less housework," he said to Levin.

Though Levin liked the house, birch tree, and flowers, to enter a house after so long a time traveling slightly depressed him; he hid this as he followed Gilley along the flagstone path and through the door.

Pauline said she would whip up something for supper, nothing elaborate, as soon as the sitter had finished feeding the children in the kitchen.

"Care for a drink after your long journey?" Gilley asked Levin, winking.

Levin thanked him, no.

"Not even a short one?" he measured an inch with long thumb and forefinger.

6

"No, I really—"

"All right. Mind if I do?"

"Please, I—"

"How about beer?" Pauline asked. "Or if not that I can open an orange drink, or give you a glass of water?"

"Beer is fine," Levin said.

"I'd be just as happy to bring you water."

"I'll take the beer."

"There's a blue towel for you in the bathroom if you wish to wash."

She returned to the kitchen and Gilley drew the shade at the side window before he mixed martinis. Through the open blinds of the front window Levin admired a small purple-leaved tree in front of the house diagonally to the left across the wide street.

"Plum tree," Gilley said. "Pink flowers every spring."

"Beautiful." Levin, out of the corner of his eye, watched the man watching him.

When Pauline returned with the beer her husband raised his martini glass. "To a successful career for Sy."

"Cheers," said Pauline.

"Thank you." Levin's hand trembled as he held the glass aloft.

They drank, Levin drinking to himself before he knew he was doing it.

"Do you mind eating early?" Pauline asked. "It makes a longer evening. We've had to do that since the children."

"Please, as you desire."

He was sitting on the couch enjoying the beer and the room. It was a long room, tastefully furnished and curtained. On the wall hung a black and white print of a hunter shooting at a bird, and a Vermeer reproduction of a young woman. The shelved right wall was filled with books. On the kitchen side, the room was apparently for dining, and an old-fashioned round table stood there with three place settings and four chairs.

7

"TV?" Gilley asked. "The set's in my den."

"Later, Gerald," Pauline said. "I'm sure Mr. Levin has seen television."

"I didn't say he hadn't, but there won't be much time later. He's got to get settled."

"Don't have any worries on my account," Levin said.

"I'll drive you over to Mrs. Beaty's right after supper," Gilley said, pouring another martini. "She's got a good-sized room with a private entrance by way of the back yard. And there are kitchen privileges if you want them, Sy, damn convenient for eight o'clocks, which I can tell you you will have. She's a widow—nice woman, former grade-school teacher married to a carpenter; he died almost two years ago, I'd say—came from South Dakota, my native state. Funny thing, I spent my first week in this town, just eighteen years ago, in the same room she's offering you."

"You don't say," said Levin.

Gilley nodded.

"I'll be glad to have a look at it."

"If you don't like it you can come back here tonight," Pauline suggested.

Gilley seemed to be considering that but Levin hastily said, "That's so kind but I won't trouble you any more. The hotel is fine. You wrote me they have one here, as I remember?"

"Two—moderate prices."

"Fine," said Levin.

"Good. Let me freshen your beer."

"This is fine."

Pauline finished her drink and went into the kitchen.

"You're our twenty-first man, most we've ever had full-time in the department," Gilley said to Levin. "Professor Fairchild will meet you tomorrow afternoon at two. He's a fine gentleman and awfully considerate head of department, I'm sure you'll like him, Sy. He kept us going at full complement for years under tough budgetary conditions. Probably you've heard of his grammar text, *The Elements of Grammar*? God

8

knows how many editions it's been through. The department's been growing again following the drop we took after the peak load of veterans, though we've still got plenty of them around. We put on three men last year and we plan another two or three, next. College registration is around forty-two hundred now, but we figure we'll double that before ten years."

He smiled happily at Levin and Levin smiled at him. Nice chap, very friendly. He put you at your ease.

"We've been hearing from people from every state in the Union. For next year I already have a pile of applications half a foot high."

"I'm grateful for—"

"You won't miss New York? This is a small town, Sy, ninety-seven hundred, and there isn't much doing unless you get outdoors or are interested in football and such. Season tickets for athletic events are modestly priced for faculty."

"No, I won't miss it," Levin said with a sigh.

"Pauline's been talking for years about visiting New York City."

"Yes?"

"I wouldn't want to stay too long. I don't take to cities well, I get jumpy after a while."

"I know what you mean."

"You seem pretty glad to leave?"

"I lived there all my life."

"I should say. Eight million people, that's seven more than we have in the whole state of Cascadia."

"Imagine," muttered Levin.

"We're growing, though, about three thousand a year."

Pauline set glasses on the table, then came out of the kitchen, carrying a casserole.

"Tuna fish and mashed potatoes," she said apologetically. "I hope you like it."

"Perfect," Levin said. He was abruptly very hungry. They sat down at the round table, for which he felt a surprising immediate affection. Pauline had forgotten the salad bowl and went in to get it. When she returned she served the casserole, standing. A child called from the kitchen. Distracted, she missed Levin's plate and dropped a hot gob of tuna fish and potato into his lap.

He rose with a cry.

"I'm so dreadfully sorry." She hastily wiped at his pants with a cloth but Levin grabbed it from her and did it himself. The operation left a large wet stain.

"I'd better change," he said, shaken. "My other suit is in my bag."

"I'll get it," Gilley said, his face flushed. "It's still in the trunk."

"Everything will get stone cold," Pauline said. "Gerald, why don't you lend Mr. Levin a pair of your slacks? That'll be quicker."

"I'd rather get my own," Levin said.

"Let him do what he wants," Gilley told his wife.

"There's no need for him to be uncomfortable till we get his suitcase in. Your gray slacks will go nicely with his jacket. They're hanging in your closet."

"Please—" Levin was perspiring.

"Maybe she's right," Gilley said. "It'd be quicker."

"I'll change in a minute once I have my suitcase."

"Gerald's pants will be less trouble."

"They won't fit. He's taller than I am."

"Roll up the cuffs. By the time you're ready to leave I'll have your trousers spot-cleaned and ironed. It was my fault and I'd feel much better if you both please let me work it out my own way."

Gilley shrugged and Levin gave up. He changed into Gerald's slacks in the bathroom.

While he was there Pauline tapped on the door.

"I forgot about your shorts, they must be damp. I have a clean pair of Gerald's here."

He groaned to himself, then said quietly, "I don't want them."

"Are you sure?"

"Positive."

Before leaving the bathroom Levin soaped his hands and face, dried them vigorously and combed his damp whiskers. When he came out he felt momentarily foolish in Gilley's baggy pants but the food, kept hot, was delicious, and he ate heartily.

My first night in the Northwest, Levin mused, sitting in an armchair after dinner. Who could guess I would ever in my life come so far out? He began to think about the past and had to press himself not to.

Gilley looks restless, he thought. I'd better give him back his pants and find some place to sleep.

"Stay a while," Pauline murmured. She was arranging red roses in a Chinese vase on the table.

"Yep," Gilley said. He was scanning the Sunday paper, one long leg resting on a hassock.

I could be wrong, Levin thought.

Pauline shut a window and rubbed her goose-fleshed arms. "Gerald, would you build a fire?"

"It feels like fall," she said to Levin.

Gilley, grunting, got up. He stuffed several balls of newspaper under the grate of the fireplace, crisscrossed kindling, and topped the pile with two wood chunks with thick mossy bark.

"Burns most of the evening that way," he said to Levin. "The heat of each oak piece keeps the other going. That's the secret of it."

He lit the paper and the blaze roared. The operation was interesting to Levin, even moving. He had rarely in his life stood at a fireplace, never before seen a fire made in one. If the room Gilley had mentioned had a fireplace he thought he would take it.

A door by the couch opened and two children who had come downstairs with the sitter entered the room. They had been bathed and pajamaed, and when the boy saw the fire he ran to it. He was a red-head with a pale face. The little girl, blondish like the mother, had sores on her arms and legs. Though she barely toddled she carried a kitten.

"This is Mr. Levin, Zenamae," Pauline said to the sitter. "He's the new English professor. Zenamae Sonderson, Mr. Levin."

Levin blushed. "Hardly a professor—" Pauline paid the girl and she left.

The boy, turning from the fire, took a good look at Levin and began to cry.

"Bet it's the beard," Gilley said.

Levin picked up a magazine and pretended to read. The child stopped crying. Pauline led him by the hand to the new instructor.

"Mr. Levin, this is Erik Gilley. Erik, Mr. Levin is a nice man all the way from New York City."

He was grateful to her.

The boy said something that sounded like "Tory?"

"No," said Levin in surprise, "I'm a liberal."

Pauline laughed. "He wants you to tell him a story."

Gilley grinned. "Gave yourself away that time, Sy."

Levin, smiling in embarrassment, offered to tell the boy a story.

"Me," said the little girl, letting the kitten go and coming closer.

"She's our baby, Mary," said Pauline. "Does she look like me, Mr. Levin?"

"Something like," he said. "I'm no judge."

She smiled and kissed the child.

"Better not bother with stories just right now," Gilley said. "We'll be leaving in five more minutes."

"You promised." Erik had climbed up on Levin's knees.

"What kind of story do you want?"

"Funny."

Levin tried to think what he knew that was funny. Pauline,

with Mary on her lap, sat on the hassock, attentive. Gilley had drifted into his den and had the TV on.

Levin, scratching a hot right ear, began: "There was once a fox with a long white beard—"

Erik chuckled. In a minute he was laughing—to Levin's amazement—in shrieking peals. Levin snickered at his easy success, and as he did, felt something hot on his thigh. He rose in haste, holding the still wildly laughing child at arm's length as a jet of water shot out of the little penis that had slipped through his pajama fly.

Gilley came into the room. "Stop it, Erik!"

Pauline set Mary down, grabbed Erik and ran with him, his fountain streaming in a high graceful arc, into the bathroom.

Levin stood there in Gilley's pants, wet down his thigh, neither of them looking at the other. He felt desperate. I've got to get out before they hate me.

Pauline returned with wet mop and sponge.

"I guess you'd better change." She didn't look at him.

He nodded, depressed.

"I'll get your bag out of the car," Gilley said.

"There's no need to," said Pauline. "His trousers are dry. You can change in the bathroom again, Mr. Levin. Just drop Gerald's slacks down the laundry chute. I'm awfully sorry."

"Nothing serious." Levin went to the bathroom and began to wash up.

Pauline tapped on the door. "I have a pair of Gerald's French-back shorts for you. Yours are probably damp. They ought to fit if you use the third button."

"I don't want them," he said.

"You'll be more comfortable."

"No."

She burst into tears. Levin opened the door and reached out his hand. He took from Pauline a pair of her husband's striped shorts.

When he left the bathroom, once more wearing his own

pants, in a good mood and ready to go, the room was in order, high and dry, both kids upstairs in bed.

Pauline had pinned a rose on her white dress and was crocheting on the couch. Gilley was tying dry flies.

"Won't you have another cup of coffee, Mr. Levin?"

"Thanks, Mrs. Gilley, I'd better be off now."

"Please stay a little longer."

Levin glanced nervously at Gilley.

"Stay a while, Sy."

"If you say," he muttered. They were being polite out of embarrassment, he thought, and it annoyed him because he was worried about getting settled for the night.

But he stayed.

Erik wandered down the stairs and asked his father to go back up with him.

"All right," Gilley said to Levin. "And after that we'd better scoot over to Mrs. Beaty. She'll be wanting to get to bed."

"Agreed," said Levin.

Erik went to him and raised his arms.

"He wants to be picked up," Pauline said.

Levin, after hesitating, picked up the child.

Erik tugged at his beard. "Funny man."

"That's enough of that," said Pauline.

Gilley took Erik from Levin and carried him upstairs.

"There's no telling what next," she said.

"I had no objection."

She was silent. He inspected the book shelves and drew out a book.

She crocheted a while, then asked what he was looking at.

"*The American*, Henry James."

"Oh?" She got up, searched on the bottom book shelf, and came up with a reprint from an academic journal, which she handed Levin. Gilley's name was on the cover of a short article on Howells.

"He wrote it in graduate school," she said. "He was a teaching assistant and I was one of his students. Gerald was the only person of his year to have an article in *PMLA*, during his graduate career. I hoped he'd go on with scholarly papers but he says they're a bore."

"Is that so?"

She smiled almost sadly. "He's done a few textbook reviews here and there, but not much else. Gerald is an active type, too much so to write with patience. And there's no doubt he's lost some of his interest in literature. Nature here can be such an esthetic satisfaction that one slights others."

Levin instinctively shrugged.

"Life is so varied and what happens so often unexpected," Pauline said with a glance at him. "There's so much to do—to be done. I find myself—" She inspected the strip of lace she had crocheted, then went on, "If Gerald were among more people who were doing literary research and writing, I think he would too. Of course Dr. Fabrikant, in the department, is a scholar, but they don't take to each other for too many reasons to go into, and Gerald feels anyway that at Cascadia College—the kind of place this is—the emphasis should be on teaching. He's quite a popular lecturer."

"What kind of place—?"

"—He does many things and gets a lot of pleasure out of his life. He fishes—this is the country for it if you're interested; he's a wonderful dry fly fisherman, and I've seen other fishermen stop what they were doing to watch him. He also hunts pheasants and ducks and loves to watch athletic events. I never thought I would myself, but you'd be surprised how exciting these games can get. We generally have very good football and basketball teams, though not as high-powered as those in California. And Gerald is also an excellent photographer. He's very talented at candid shots and has won all sorts of prizes in almost every category. Last year one of his pictures won a first prize at the State Fair. Let me show it to you."

She slid open a door at the bottom of a bookcase and got out a thick picture album which she brought to the sofa.

I'm in for it now, Levin thought.

Pauline turned to an enlarged photograph of an old farmhouse that looked like an upended shoe box. " 'Pioneer Farmhouse,' " she read. "He's done a series of these all over the state. We go camping in summertime—I hate it but it's good for the kids—and he likes to hunt out these places and snap them. Gerald is in love with Americana. This is the sixth prize he's won with this particular subject."

"Very nice—"

She turned to the middle of the album. "Here he is with his sister when he was a boy in knickers in Abilene, South Dakota. Notice how alert he looks. Here's his father, a retired merchant. I take to the mother. They were here to see the children this summer."

She flipped back several pages, pausing at a portrait of a dignified-looking man with pince-nez and a grayish beard. "Papa," she said. "A wonderful man—very affectionate and maturely generous. He was a physician and literally lived the Hippocratic oath. Once when he was sick he got out of bed to attend a patient. The patient lived but poor Papa died. He was only fifty. It killed my mother."

"Ah—" said Levin.

"I lived afterwards with Papa's brother, in San Francisco. They're a wonderful family." She wiped one eye with a slender finger. He looked secretly but saw no dew.

On the next page, age twenty, she stood, in unearned innocence, on a hilly city street, shoulders touching a young man's with an expressionless face. She looked unhappy and wore a mousey fur coat and felt hat with an off-the-face brim.

"After your father died?" Levin asked.

"A year and a half. This was a boy I was engaged to for six months, before I married Gerald. He had won a Guggenheim and was off to Europe to study medieval history but I knew he was tired of me and I wouldn't see him again. I never did."

"He looks a little stupid to me."

16

"He was a nice boy. I guess I hadn't much to offer at that time. I'm one of those people who developed slowly."

She put the album aside, removed one shoe, then the other, and raising her legs drew them close to her body. She had pinned a rose to her poor chest. Why not two, he thought, one for each flat side? Was this why the medievalist had gone to Europe, to escape the American prairie? It did bother a bit, the observer conscious that nature had cheated where it hurt most. Yet she was attractive, he thought, with shapely legs if big feet, the long boats on the floor the indisputable evidence. And her face, compared to the girl's in the picture, was a mature improvement over age twenty. Studying her, though pretending not to, Levin thought her, despite her longness and lacks, an interesting-looking woman. She had large dark eyes in a small face, much helped by a frame of thickish straight blonde hair that touched her shoulders. The lips were well-formed, her nose, as if sniffing expectancy, touched on long and in flight. She was wearing pendant earrings; he realized she had put them on and changed her shoes, since coming home. Levin guessed she was for sure a good ten years younger than her husband. He had thought that when she told him she had been Gilley's student, but now the sense of her youth surprised him.

I was tired, he thought.

"And now that you know about me," she said, reaching for a cigarette, "what about you?"

Levin felt himself react against her question—had made no bargains. He was, besides, on edge to be settled and alone.

But her smile was innocent enough. "What I would like to know," she said, "is why have you come so far? Was it some special reason, or just that the job happened to be here?"

Resisting much there was to say, he replied truthfully. "When the offer came I was ready to go." Levin rubbed his hands with a handkerchief. "What's there to say that hasn't been said? One always hopes that a new place will inspire change—in one's life."

"Have you been to many places?"

"The opposite is true."

He cracked his knuckles as she fiddled with her rose.

He went on although advising himself not to. "My life, if I may say, has been without much purpose to speak of. Some blame the times for that, I blame myself. The times are bad but I've decided I'll have no other."

He laughed immoderately and stopped abruptly. After a minute's silence he went on, "In the past I cheated myself and killed my choices." Levin mopped his brow. "Now that I can—ah—move again I hope to make better use of—things.

"That sums me up." He got up and began to walk back and forth in the room.

"What better use?" she ultimately asked. Her voice seemed diminished.

"I've reclaimed an old ideal or two," Levin said awkwardly. "They give a man his value if he stands for them." He stopped pacing. "If you'll excuse me, that's about all I care to say on the subject. Too many abstract words make me self-conscious."

Pauline seemed to be listening to something going on in another part of the house. She asked, "How long have you been teaching?"

"Two years—in a high school," he confessed. "I was twenty-six when I realized I wanted to teach, a late insight. One day I thought, What you do for others you can do for yourself. Then I thought, I can do it teaching."

She yawned behind her fingers.

He was irritated by her long empty shoes on the floor.

"You remind me of somebody," she said.

Levin yawned too. "Excuse me—the long train ride. I didn't sleep so well."

"Gerald will be right down."

He nodded listlessly.

"I hope you won't be disappointed in us, Mr. Levin. In the College and the town. Easchester can be lonely for single people—I don't mean the college students, their world isn't

18

real. Someone from a big city might be disappointed here. You have no idea how sheltered we are, landlocked, and bland."

"Not me, I've had too much—"

She put out her cigarette. "I had a terrible time my first few years here. We miss a lot through nobody's fault in particular. It's the communal sin of omission. People here are satisfied. I blame it on nature, prosperity, and some sort of laziness, mine too, but for God's sake please don't quote me. Otherwise it's a lovely town, good will abounds, and there are many advantages for family living." She smoothed her skirt. "But for someone without a wife and children, maybe you ought to try San Francisco or Seattle."

"I've had my fill of cities," Levin replied. "For a change I want the open sky on my head."

"And the gentle rain?"

"It rains here?"

"It does. It almost drove me mad at first but I've learned to live with it. The trick is no longer to love the sun. Didn't Gerald write you about the rain?"

"No."

"About our community?"

"No."

"About the College?"

"A few words."

"He ought to have. It rains, for instance, most of the fall and winter and much of spring. It's a spongy sky you'll be wearing on your head."

"You can't have everything."

"To be fair I must also tell you the sun may shine for days on end in winter if a freeze sets in. At the same time it's not like Eastern cold, and Gerald wears a trench coat all year round. Many Cascadians want rain and warmth rather than sunlight and cold. But our summers, except rarely, are practically flawless. Even Californians come here then. There are people here, originally from the Plains states or the Midwest, who swear Easchester is paradise. Gerald is one of them. Wherever he goes he wants to come home."

A mild heaviness had settled on Levin's spirit. He felt he had talked too much about himself and was worried what she might repeat to her husband. Who could guess what a stranger would make out of his unguarded remarks about his past; he might already have endangered his career.

"I really must go."

Gilley came downstairs, yawning, his red head lighting the apple-green wall, one side of his face creased.

"Fell asleep in Erik's room."

"What did he want?"

"Company—he was a little scared."

"Of the dark?"

"Ghosts," Gilley said.

"Ghosts? That's new," she said.

"I guess we ought to go," Levin suggested.

"Sure thing," said Gilley. "I'll get my keys."

"Oh, my heavens, I didn't notice how late it's gotten," said Pauline. "Won't Mrs. Beaty be sleeping now, Gerald?"

Gilley held up his wrist. "By George, you're right, it's past ten. We'll have to make it tomorrow instead, Sy. My fault, I'm sorry."

"I'll go to a hotel," Levin said. "I had planned to anyway."

"Why waste five dollars?" Pauline asked. "We have a spare room, and in the morning Gerald can run you over to Mrs. Beaty's."

"I wouldn't want to bother you."

"You're no bother, Mr. Levin. It'll just take a minute to put a blanket on the bed." She ran up the stairs in stocking feet.

"Please—" Levin called after her.

"Give up, Sy," advised Gilley. "A woman's will. Drink?" he asked.

"No."

"It'll relax you."

20

"I'm relaxed."

"Good. Professor Fairchild'll love you. He doesn't touch liquor himself. His wife is first vice-president of the Anti-Liquor League. Mrs. Feeney's president, that's the recently retired dean's wife. Mind if I do?"

"Please—"

Gilley poured some Scotch into a glass and went into the kitchen for water. "Sy," he said warmly when he returned, "I bet you'll like the department and I'm sure we'll like you. We're a pretty nice bunch of friendly people engaged in the common endeavor. You'll find the comp staff particularly is nice—no false pretenses or such. Comp, as I wrote you, will be your program, plus one remedial grammar course which Avis Fliss will give you the dope on when she gets back next month. I will say this, that if you stay on here comp is what you'll be teaching till you get your doctorate—that's your union card if you want to stay in college teaching. After that you'll be given a lit class or two."

"I had hoped to teach literature," Levin sighed.

"I personally prefer teaching comp to lit. More satisfaction, I've found. You can just see these kids improving their writing from one term to the next, and even from one paper to the next. It isn't easy to notice much of a development of literary taste in a year."

"I suppose not—"

"We feel we make progress in composition. Morale is high, everybody works together—a nice bunch. You should see how we function getting finals out of the way and grades in. No problem children, if you know what I mean."

Levin nodded.

"The one or two we have around are in lit. I was very glad to be appointed director of comp some years ago and focus my attention on it. It's been an invigorating experience." He paused, seemed about to say more, then took a drink. "You'll like us all."

"I'm sure," said Levin.

"Good."

"Bad," Pauline said, coming down the stairs.

"Who's that?" asked her husband.

"Why didn't you tell Mr. Levin about the rain? I'll bet he came without a raincoat."

"No, I have one," said Levin, "and an umbrella."

"We have no more rain than you have in New York State," Gilley said, "only it's distributed more evenly. Anyway, it keeps Cascadia green."

"It's green enough," Pauline said. She put her arm around Gilley. He looked at her with affection.

Nice people, Levin thought, a real home. I shouldn't regret having to spend the night here.

"We'll get your bags, Sy." Gilley, putting down his glass, noticed the picture album on the table. "What's this out for?"

"I wanted Mr. Levin to see your prize-winning picture at the State Fair."

"Oh, that," Gilley said. He seemed momentarily lost in thought, then cheered up. "Got it with my Leica on a moderately bright day. I used Plus X on f11 at one one-hundredth of a second. Care to see my cameras sometime, Sy? Pauline bought me a Polaroid for my birthday."

"I don't know anything about them."

"Photography's not hard to learn. It's a satisfying and useful hobby. Come on, let's get the bags."

Levin went outside with him and almost cried out. In the amazing night air he smelled the forest. Imagine getting this for nothing. He drew in a deep wavering breath as he gazed at the stars splashed over the immense dark sky.

"There's your Big Dipper," Gilley was saying, "and that's the North Star. That way is Seattle, British Columbia, Alaska, and then the North Pole."

"North," said Levin, with a throb in his throat. "What profound mystery. You go north till there are no men. Imagine the silence, the cold, the insult to the human heart."

"You're a bit of a poet, Sy. The other way is San Francisco, and if you're interested, L.A."

Gilley unlocked the car trunk and got out the suitcases and golf bags. "We'll take one of each." He shut the trunk, paused a minute, then said to Levin, "Just this small matter, Sy. Do you always wear that beard?"

Levin looked at him in embarrassment. "I have for the past year. It's—er—given me a different view of myself." He laughed a little.

"Then it's not permanent?"

"I can't say just yet. It depends on how things work out—"

"I'll tell you why I mentioned it. I respect beards but some of your students may think you're an oddball. It doesn't take much to set them against a teacher."

"Some of my best professors wore beards," said Levin. "Americans have often worn them."

"Yes, but not so much since the safety razor. This is a sort of beardless town. No one on the faculty wears one that I know of. The administration is clean shaven. It's usually the students who will grow them. A lot of sophomores encourage whiskers for their spring carnival and they're a raggy, tacky-looking lot."

"I have a picture of Abraham Lincoln I could hang up."

"Well, suit yourself. I just thought I ought to mention it to you. The president's wife was saying only the other day every time she lays eyes on a beard the thought of a radical pops up in her head."

Levin guffawed.

Gilley beamed.

The new instructor carried in his valise and Pauline's clubs; Gilley, the suitcase and his new clubs.

Imagine me carrying golf clubs, Levin thought. Already he had done things he had never before done in his life.

In his room he removed Gilley's striped shorts and in the upstairs bathroom searched for the laundry chute to dispose

23

of them. He located it in the hall at the top of the stairs but the door was nailed fast, probably to keep the kids from falling in. In robe and slippers he went downstairs to the other bathroom and got rid of them there.

Levin brushed his teeth, took a quick bath, soaping himself thickly, and combed his beard to a fine point. On the stairs, through the slightly open bedroom door he caught a glimpse of the Gilleys, man and wife, embracing in their nightshirts.

Standing a moment later, at the curtained window of his room, Levin gazed at the moonlit mountains in the west, more frighteningly higher than he had remembered. In the back yard a birch tree leaned to the left, its symmetry spoiled by its bias. Levin was at first too excited to sleep, but even as he contemplated the possibilities of the future he fell into slumber. He heard Erik calling "papa" and tried to rouse himself, but then he heard a woman's steps coming up the stairs. He dreamed he had caught an enormous salmon by the tail and was hanging on for dear life but the furious fish, threshing the bleeding water, broke free: "Levin, go home." He woke in a sweat.

"I can't," he whispered to himself. "I can't fail again."

On the point of sleep he had the odd feeling he was being covered with a second blanket. Or maybe that was what she was doing to the children across the hall.

"God save us all," he muttered through his beard.

Levin saw himself fleeing with both heavy bags when he learned the next morning that Cascadia College wasn't a liberal arts college. Gerald Gilley gave him the news, one long leg, thick-ankled in home-knit argyle socks, amiably dangling over the arm of a chair in Levin's newly acquired room at Mrs. Beaty's, complete with fireplace and optional private entrance. The new instructor had waked at the Gilleys in despair, typical of him in a strange place (it often amazed Levin how past-drenched present time was) but when, as he was putting on his new-suit pants, he saw that last night's high-walled mountains had shrunk drastically—their vast height illusion, a trick of clouds massed above the peaks—his mood changed and he heartily enjoyed breakfast. "Come see us often," Pauline Gilley had waved, standing by the birch tree and lifting little Mary to wave as Levin and her husband drove off in his Buick. Afterwards Levin had liked the old landlady and the large light room she showed them, but Gilley's news disturbed him.

Though he tried to seem casual, Levin had risen from his chair. "Why I thought—I was positive—this was a liberal arts college."

"I guess you didn't stop to examine the catalogue I sent you," Gilley said.

"Did you? I never got—"

"That's too bad, probably reached you after you had left. I guess I sent it out late in the rush of summer school closing. Anyway, if you had read it you'd have understood, from the section in front about our history, that we are mostly a science and technology college. We were founded in 1876—next year we celebrate our 75th charter anniversary—as an agricultural and vocational community college, but after ten years the state took it over, and to the original schools of ag for men and home ec for women, added forestry, animal husbandry, every kind of engineering you can think of, and of course the pure sciences, and others. We also had the liberal arts here, beginning around 1880, but we lost them shortly after the First World War."

"Lost them?" Levin, feeling behind him, unsteadily resumed his seat.

"They were taken from us, Sy. I won't go into the whole long story but there's a history of some nasty pitched battles for funds between us and our sister institution, Cascadia University at Gettysburg. —That, if you have checked the map, is our capital city, a hundred miles north of here, where they still rib us as 'southerners,' to say nothing of 'aggies' and 'hay palace.' Politics get steaming hot every biennium when the state budget is in the works, and I guess some of our alumni took it into their heads that it might make things easier all around to bring CU right down here to Easchester—they're the younger institution, 1878, and we have a lot more land than they do—and incorporate us both into one big super-university

26

with one physical plant, which would, of course, have saved the taxpayers lots of money in the long run. Well, for too many reasons to mention, the plan didn't come off. Their alumni in the legislature raised a stink—they've always had the law and journalism schools and as a result can influence public opinion almost any way they want—and they got their own bill through, separating CC and CU more than we were in the first place. There was talk—as I've many times heard the story—of removing *us* to the Gettsyburg campus, but then they decided to settle for certain punitive measures, which in this case were nothing less than cutting out our upper-level courses in the liberal arts, which people here thought weren't so important anyway, so we'd be two absolutely different institutions and theoretically uncompetitive. To make it look fair, and at the insistence of some of our boys in the legislature and two or three influential lumbermen in town, they had to part with their upper-level science courses. Now the dirty part of the deal was that during World War II they got all their science back on the ground that it served the national interest, while we never did get back the liberal arts—"

"A dirty shame." Levin was on his feet again. "The liberal arts—as you know—since ancient times—have affirmed our rights and liberties. Socrates—"

"That's how these things go. It's best to be philosophical about it."

"Democracy owes its existence to the liberal arts. Shouldn't there be—er—some sort of protest?"

"I appreciate your attitude," Gilley said, "but there isn't much that can be done about it now. Due to the fact that our graduates land so many influential jobs in the state, and since our athletic teams are usually better than theirs, we have a larger student registration than the University, which annoys them no end. And they also haven't forgotten that during the Depression they lost a lot more staff positions than we did here, and we lost plenty, believe me. They still think of those days, though a lot of the old timers who have always hated us have died off. They're afraid if we keep on gaining at the rate we have since the end of the war, they'll lose out percentagewise in funds for buildings and faculty salaries, so you can bet your bottom dollar that as soon as somebody starts talking about bringing liberal arts majors back here they get hopping sore and start telegraphing the legislature. Frankly, it's a bread and butter proposition and you can't really blame them. We'd do the same in their place."

"But that's fantastic," Levin said, "—ah—isn't it? How can we—if you'll excuse my making myself familiar—teach what the human spirit is, or may achieve, if a college limits itself to vocational and professional education? 'The liberal arts feed our hearts,' this old professor of mine used to say." Levin laughed self-consciously.

"Don't get me wrong," Gilley said patiently. "We do have lower-level liberal arts courses here, though not many or in much variety. Still and all, there are departments of English, art, religion, history, speech, philosophy, modern languages, et cetera, on the campus. I will have to admit that the great majority of our boys and girls don't seem to be much interested in these subjects and take only what they have to. If they insist on more, they have to transfer elsewhere, usually to Gettysburg—and we don't go out of our way to encourage that. We have to handle it that way because the Higher Education Committee of the legislature just won't recommend an investment in a double liberal arts program in the two big state institutions of higher learning."

"But didn't you just say that full schools of science exist in both places?" Levin asked.

"They do but pure science has always been considered part of the liberal arts, and besides that's 'necessary duplication' because we have the Russkies to think about. What are you still standing for, Sy?"

"Excuse me." Levin sank into his chair. "I was just going to say—if you'll pardon me, I realize I'm a stranger—but I don't see how this situation can go on without weakening us

28

in the long run. Democracy is in trouble. How are our students supposed to—" His right ear, when he absently touched it, felt on fire. Levin ceased speaking and gnawed his beard at the lip.

Gilley, lifting his leg off the chair, sat back. "I like your enthusiasm, Sy, but I think you'll understand the situation better after you've been here a year or two. Frankly, though I agree with some of the things you just said, Cascadia is a conservative state, and we usually take a long look around before we commit ourselves to any important changes in our way of life. You might keep in mind that education for an agrarian society, which is what we are—the majority of our state legislators come from rural areas—is basically a 'how to work' education. And if you've been keeping up on your reading on the subject, more and more liberal arts colleges in America are going in for more and more vocational subjects."

"I think they're making a serious mistake—"

"That's not to say that we won't be making some changes here, but most of us at Cascadia agree there's no sense hurrying any faster than most people want to go. If you push too hard you arouse resentment and resistance, and the result is the changes you are pushing for are resisted too. We've seen that happen too often in the past. Also keep in mind that a lot of very fine upstanding people in this community don't give two hoots for the liberal arts."

The new instructor, though suspecting he ought to drop the subject, said, "Isn't that where—er—good leadership comes in?"

"I'd say we have just as good leadership here as you people have in the East."

Levin bit his tongue.

Gilley, after a moment, rose with a smile. "All I can say, Sy, is I hope you didn't write to the wrong place when you wrote us for a job. Some people get us mixed up with our Gettysburg adjunct, and vice versa."

Holy mackerel, Levin thought. He had written to both

Cascadia colleges and had probably confused the other, which had turned him down, with this.

"I'm glad to be teaching here," he said.

"Good," said Gilley. "Don't forget Professor Fairchild expects you this afternoon."

They shook hands and Gilley left by the outside stairs.

Levin sat long in his chair, tormenting himself for being the man he was. Why am I always committing myself before I know what it's all about? What's my fantastic big hurry?

"Anyway," he muttered as he began to unpack his bags, "it's a start."

Considering that he had just got his M.A. at thirty, and had only high school teaching experience to offer, Levin felt it was the greatest good luck that he had landed an instructorship in any college. Here if he watched his step and picked up two years of experience—the director of the N.Y.U. employment office had advised—and a couple of good recommendations, he shouldn't find it too hard to move on to a department where he could teach some literature, particularly if he began his Ph.D. work next summer. Wondering what Gilley would say if he knew his newly hired hand had been turned down, not only by the University at Gettysburg, but by at least fifty other colleges across the country, Levin felt a surge of gratitude to him for having given him, after so many failures and frustrations, an opportunity to begin his chosen career.

After a pleasant hour of wandering on the campus, Levin located Humanities Hall across the street from the Student Union at the corner of the college quadrangle. H-H, as it was designated in the catalogue, was a large gray clapboard structure with a huge leafy maple tree on its north lawn; it had been a women's dormitory before World War I, then had been converted into a "Museum of Pioneer Artifacts." After World War II it had been cleared out and rebuilt and now housed the English, speech and philosophy departments; English on the second and half of the third floors, according to the catalogue. Shortly before two, Levin went up the bannistered steps of the small, pediment-roofed porch, and slowly up a flight of creaking inside stairs. He dreaded interviews.

The long-halled second floor was divided into classrooms on one side of the stairs, and facing rows of offices on the other. Levin found the secretary's office but she wasn't there although a cup of hot coffee steamed on her desk. He waited five impatient minutes, then looked around to see if he could find her. Diagonally across the hall, at the very end of the building, he peeked through an open door and discovered Gerald Gilley. The director of composition was sitting in shirt sleeves behind an enormous cluttered desk in the center of a large green room loaded with bookcases and filing cabinets. He was cutting pictures out of *Life* with a pair of shears with blades a foot long.

Gilley glanced up at Levin absent-mindedly, placed him, and said pleasantly, "Come for your appointment, Sy?"

"I was wondering whether to go right into Professor Fairchild's office? The secretary seems to have stepped out a minute."

Gilley clipped a picture from the magazine, snipped four sides, and filed it in a thick folder.

"Future book," he told Levin.

"Illustrations?"

"Picture book of American lit." He cut into another page. "Like the idea?"

"Fine," said Levin.

"I thought the students would want to see what some of our writers looked like, the houses they lived in and such. Most of them can't tell Herman Melville from the Smith Brothers on the cough drop box."

Levin smoothed his beard. "Great stuff."

"Milly probably went to the ladies' room. She's been having trouble with her kidney. Come on, I'll introduce you."

He started directly across the broad corridor but in midstream changed his mind and asked Levin to follow him. Gilley tapped lightly on a door a bit farther up the hall, waited thirty seconds, then shook his head. "Guess he's not back yet. I had an airmail letter saying he might make it today from Carmel. This is George Bullock's office. He's a very sociable chap, city type like you, only he was born in L.A. George makes things happen instead of waiting for them to. He also has private means, which does no harm if you can manage it. You'll like Jeannette too, that's his wife, originally from Las Vegas, a real stunner. They give some lively parties."

He knocked again, to make sure.

"A dozen of our crew is up on the third floor," Gilley said, "instructors like yourself, most of them in their twenties. I like to keep them together because they have a lot in common, but everybody usually visits in the coffee room sometime during the day. Come on, I'll show you where it is."

They went across the hall to a doorless room that looked like a kitchen.

"Very convenient," Levin murmured.

In the open cupboard a long line of white coffee mugs hung from hooks, each cup with a name written on it in India ink.

"Sometime I'd like to put an espresso machine in here," Gilley mused.

Levin nodded, studying the man with interest.

"People drop in for coffee between classes, or when they're keeping office hours. It's just the thing when you need a break. Milly starts the pot boiling first thing in the morning. Professor Fairchild is a steady customer—comes in at ten, right after his Shakespeare, and again at three, after his nap."

"I prefer tea to coffee," Levin said.

"Let me show you where we keep the tea bags. Right here. Also cocoa. Milly collects a dollar and a half a month, and that's for doughnuts too. What beverage you drink makes no difference to us. Meeting here during the day gives us all a chance to visit informally and relax with each other. Now let me show you the comp room."

"Comp room?"

"That's right." This was, once more across the hall, a windowless cubicle lined with shelves divided into individual filing slots, each partly filled, Gilley showed Levin, with graded student themes.

"This was the boss's idea. Once we collect them, the students can't pass them around for their friends to copy. I suppose you've heard about fraternity files?"

"Couldn't they keep carbons of the compositions?"

"Most are too lazy to. Also, having this room, if you don't mind my saying so, sort of keeps the instructors on their toes, because they know Orville—that's Professor Fairchild—or I, can come in here and count the number of papers they've assigned. We ask for six the first term, and eight each, the second and third. We're on the quarter system here, three terms during the year and the fourth is summer school."

"What happens when the slots are full?"

"Milly clears them out just about this time every year, and Marv Beal burns 'em, then we're ready for fall term. Marv is janitor of this building and knows more about Cascadia's team performances than anyone around, including George or me. The only thing I'd warn you is he's very talky once he gets started."

Gilley pulled the door shut. "Opens with the common key. Remind me to give you one before you go. It works for all our offices on the second and third floors, with the exception of Orville's and mine." He glanced to the right, considered something, then said, "I guess you ought to meet Joe Bucket."

Gilley rapped on the door at the end of the hall before the stairs and listened.

"He was here about twenty minutes ago, picking up his mail. I guess he's gone home to his house."

"Excuse me?"

Gilley smiled. "He's been building it for years, a board here, a brick there. Makes you wonder if he'll ever get it done, or for that matter, his dissertation. That's come back three times so far for revisions, and he can't seem to get them right though he passed his orals first shot. Maybe it's his subject matter—Laurence Sterne." He shook his head. "They moved out of the shack they were in for years, camped in the basement of the new place another six months and now have the upstairs working, plus an additional bedroom because the kids keep coming—five, though they aren't Catholics. Anyway, the house is about done."

"That's surprising—an English professor building his own house."

"A lot do it here. Some of the married students start houses and never take their degrees. When they flunk out they sell the house and use the capital to start a business. Lucky for Joe he was one of Orville's good students, and Orville has sort of kept an eye on him. This past year he promoted him to assistant professor."

Levin sighed. "My two hands are practically useless."

"We'll get you doing things, Sy."

"Not a house. I wouldn't know where to begin."

"Maybe golf? We have a fine nine-hole course."

"Maybe fishing. I've enjoyed Izaak Walton."

"Good," said Gilley. "Let's go back to my office."

They walked down the hall and the director of composition hesitated at the office between Bullock's and his. "This is Dr. Fabrikant's. He's the senior man after me."

"The one who teaches the course in liberalism in American literature?"

"How'd you know that?"

"I looked at a copy of the catalogue in the library before I came up here."

Gilley knocked curtly and waited.

"Not in?" Levin whispered.

Gilley winked. "Hard to say," he whispered. "He's the department scholar. A bit of a hermit."

"Really?"

He knocked again. "He doesn't mingle much around the office. When he isn't taking notes or something, he's usually home riding his horse. Let's go."

34

Levin, concerned about the time, hoped they were going straight to Professor Fairchild's office, but the director of composition, without warning, reversed his field and walked quickly up the hall to a door opposite the comp room.

He fished a key out of his pants pocket. "We used this for storage last year but Marv has just cleared it and neatened it up."

The new instructor secretly looked at his watch as Gilley opened the door and snapped on the light. The office was a small one with a single window and was furnished with a new desk, file case, and two chairs. Through the window Levin caught a view of the long green quadrangle, and beyond that, above the fir trees at the edge of the campus were the western mountains.

"Beautiful."

"This is yours, Sy."

"Mine? Holy smoke, I—"

"Don't say a word," Gerald said. A muscle in the corner of his mouth flickered.

"Whoever expected anything so wonderful? I figured I would have to share a place with somebody."

"That's usually the case with a new man, but you're a lot more mature, especially with your beard, than some of our crewcut boys upstairs, so I thought I would keep you down here with us."

"That's very kind. I've dreamed for years of being a college professor. This is so—" He could say no more.

"Glad to help those dreams along."

Gilley remarked, after an emotional minute: "This office used to belong to someone by the name of Leo Duffy, and the less said the better, but you'll probably hear about him so I'll just say who he was. He was here for a year in '48-'49, a sort of disagreeable radical who made a lot of trouble. Among his wackinesses was the habit of breaking his window panes and I finally put one in of thicker glass which, you notice, he cracked anyway—don't ask me how or why. When he first came here, Orville took a shine to him and assigned him this office. He treated him like a son and for all his pains got headaches. I was more than thoughtful to him too." He had to work his throat clear of hoarseness. "After he left—by invitation, I should say—the only man this department has ever employed who got publicly disgraced, Orville had this office turned into a storage room, but he agreed to reconvert it when I told him how tight space was getting. Ferris Farper and someone else upstairs had their eye on it but I kept it for you." He handed Levin the key.

"I am most grateful."

"We want you to like it here."

"I know I will—"

"While we're at it," Gilley said, "your department assignment is you're chairman of the textbook committee. Bucket, Jones, Millard Scowers and Carson Fitch are on it too. I'll send you a memo next week."

"Me?" Levin said, uneasily. "Thanks very much but I—I really don't know the first thing about college textbooks. To perform—er—competently on this committee, I'll have to make a study of available texts in the field. Couldn't you for the time being make me just a regular member of the committee, and then after I get to know the books, why maybe then I could—"

"You're obviously conscientious," Gilley said, "and I wouldn't advise you to worry at all about the textbooks. You'll get to know them as you go along. The salesmen call and they'll send you what they hope you're looking for. What with *The Elements* and *Elements Workbooks*, Forms A, B, C, for regular, and D for remedial classes, in use, all we really have to worry about is a new freshman reader once in a while. We've kept *Science in Technology* as our reader for the last five years because it's been popular with the students. For the lit classes Orville usually picks the texts himself with an occasional assist by Bullock, Kuck, or Merdith Schultz—his is the office next door to yours, opposite Bucket's, but his wife has been seriously sick and he isn't around much more than he has to be. Anyway, if you take the time to examine the books that come in the mail—just thumb through them—you'll more than do your job."

"I will and thanks for everything." Levin looked at his watch. "Wow, it's ten after. My appointment was for two."

"Nothing to worry about," Gilley said calmly. "I told Orville I'd be showing you around first."

"I like to start out right." He tried not to laugh but did.

"You have. We'll go right away. Since talking with you I have confidence in your ability to do a good job. As I said, we're looking for people who can hold up their end of it and keep the department running smoothly. This is a fine place to start your college teaching, and if you're our type, it's a good place to stay. We don't pretend we're anything more than a typical American state college. The atmosphere is relaxed. There's no 'publish or perish' hanging over everybody's head. There are no geniuses around to make you uncomfortable. Life is peaceful here—people deserve that after all we've gone through in the last generation. We don't ask more than that a man does his work conscientiously—his share of it. What we don't want around are troublemakers. If someone is dissatisfied, if he doesn't like what we do, if he doesn't respect other people's intimate rights and peace of mind, the sooner he goes on his way the better. If he likes it here and wants to stay on, at the rate we're growing I'm sure we can keep him. We don't offer the best of salaries but we do advance people in not too long a time, and once you become an assistant professor you're on permanent tenure. If you're the type I think you are, Sy—and so, incidentally, does Pauline—you can be sure of a worthwhile career here. On the other hand, if you don't like the climate, let's say, and want to go elsewhere, the experience you get here will make it that much easier for you. That's up to you and all right with us."

He said in afterthought, observing his shoe, "We've got a new dean, the man who replaced Dean Feeney, and I guess he seems to want to make some changes here and there. Well, they may be good ones and they may not, but I've heard him say we'll need some first-class people for the responsible jobs."

Levin felt oddly wrung out. "Thanks, but could we go in now? I hate to be late—"

"Righto."

But in the hall, Gilley introduced him to a gray-haired man in coveralls, holding a broom. "This is Marv Beal. He'll be sweeping your office."

Levin shook hands with the janitor.

"He get his athletic season ticket yet?" Marv asked Gilley.

"No, not yet," Levin said hastily.

"He will, Marv."

To Levin, Gilley said, "I'll have a copy of *The Elements* and the workbooks for you when you come out. All you have to do is follow them more or less according to our syllabus, keeping an eye out for the d.o. That's the departmental objective final we always give the comp freshmen at the end of each term."

"STRANGERS ARE WELCOME HERE BECAUSE THERE IS ROOM FOR ALL OF THEM, AND THEREFORE THE OLD INHABITANTS ARE NOT JEALOUS OF THEM—" B. Franklin

The framed tapestried motto hung over Professor Orville Fairchild's head as Levin entered his many-windowed sunlit office, directly across the hall from Gilley's. Gerald had knocked and held the door open as Levin went in. The head of department laid down his galley proofs, fixed a cigarette in a yellowed ivory holder, lit it, and resting back in his flexible chair, examined Levin.

He was, secretly examined by the new man, an old one, meticulously dressed, with a flower in his button hole; he had a bit of a belly, bags under both eyes, and a halo of sunlight ensnared in his bushy gray hair.

He frowned as he puffed and Levin quickly warned himself not to let a foolish word pop out of his mouth.

The head of department shook out the lit match that had nipped his fingers, a gesture that eclipsed the flame. Snapping the burnt matchstick he dropped it into the metal wastebasket, at the same moment blowing a stream of smoke that partly hid a sigh.

Life, or my interruption? Levin wondered. In the direct path of the smoke, the new instructor discreetly coughed but did not avert his head, not to affront.

"Well," said Professor Fairchild, chuckling to himself, "how do you like the West?" A vibrant old man's voice filled space. With small blue eyes, when he looked it penetrated.

"What I've seen I like," Levin said. "I only got here yesterday."

"I myself am an anomaly here, an old man in a young country. What about you?"

Ancient, thought Levin. Not sure whether the question connected to the statement, he cagily answered nothing.

"What I meant to say, is what brought you out this way? We hear from all over, true, but rarely New York."

"I wanted a change—" Levin hesitated.

"From the city?—"

"That's right," he said with relief. "I'm grateful to you and Dr. Gilley for—"

"You've spoken to Gerald about the department, I take it? Our program and course offerings are limited. Have you examined the college catalogue?"

"I have, sir." He had discovered a glut of composition, bonehead grammar, and remedial reading, over about a dozen skimpy literature courses.

"What did he tell you?"

"He said the people around were nice to work with. He—er—also mentioned your grammar text."

"Did he say anything about the history and purposes of the department? We're pretty much service oriented. Our school, for example, is called The Liberal Arts Service Division. Did he go into that?"

"Not exactly, sir. But he told me about the liberal arts, that they were—"

"Our main function, as I always tell everyone we employ here, is to satisfy the needs of the professional schools on the campus with respect to written communication. In science and technology men must be taught to communicate with the strictest accuracy, therefore we teach more composition than anything else in this department. Our literature offerings aren't very diversified or extensive but they're adequate to our purpose."

"I was hoping to teach a lit course," Levin said, "—that is, if it were possible."

Professor Fairchild seemed not to have heard.

"There's talk, now that the new dean is on campus—his name is unfortunate, Seagram—that we may in the future be called on for something more than we're presently offering in the way of literature, perhaps even to produce English majors, but I've heard that false alarm several times in recent years and it hasn't come to a hill of beans. I don't put much stock in it, not because I don't want it to come to pass—I do—but because I know intimately and practically the needs of this community. Ours is a land economy based on forestry—the Douglas fir and ponderosa pine for the most part; and agriculture—grains, grasses, flowers and some fruit. Our fishing industry is important too. We need foresters, farmers, engineers, agronomists, fish-and-game people, and every sort of extension agent. We need them—let's be frank—more than we need English majors. You can't fell a tree, run a four-lane highway over a mountain, or build a dam with poetry."

He chuckled to himself, drawing on his cigarette holder. Levin bent to tighten a shoelace but the smoke blew in another direction.

"Certainly I'm for English majors—I was one myself—but there are other colleges in the state that do a good job of training them better than we can presently, with our orientation and limited resources. My own point of view is that we ought to take pride in doing well a task that has to be done, though I'm frank to confess there are one or two in the department who don't see it quite my way, but that's their problem."

He dipped the cigarette into an ash tray and left it smoking. The halo in his hair had faded, a trick of some passing cloud. As if conscious of that he ran a lacking hand through his hair.

"What was I saying? Well, I've made my point."

Levin nodded.

The old man picked up a ball-point pen and ticked off something he had written on a pink pad. He nearsightedly scanned the paper.

"Oh, yes." He turned to Levin. "Now I hope it won't unsettle you if I offer you a word of advice or two as a young man about to embark on his first college teaching venture. A word now may prevent future misunderstanding."

"Of course—"

"This department won't ask much of you in the way of research and the publication of small papers on matters of varying degrees of useless information—that's the headache of the big universities, to what effect I haven't been able to determine—but we *do* ask you to teach conscientiously and well. Get to know *The Elements* and give your students plenty of wholesome, snappy drill. You know," he said, "I've often wondered what we can expect of our American college graduates when so many of them don't even know the rules of syntax of their own language."

Levin agreed.

The professor scanned his pad and leaned back in his chair. "There are two kinds of people I deplore in the teaching profession. One is the misfit who sneaks in to escape his inadequacy elsewhere and who ought to be booted out—and isn't very often; and the other is the aggressive pest whose one purpose is to upset other people's applecarts, and the more apples, the better. We've had both types here, to our sorrow, and what's worse, sometimes in one and the same person."

The old man spoke sadly. "Leo Duffy comes to mind, a man no longer with us. Did Gerald tell you?"

"He mentioned him."

"He was—God forgive me—a nuisance of the thirty-second degree, irresponsible and perverse. He came here just two years ago—no, three." He coughed. "Two is correct, in '48. It was when Henry Wallace was running for president, something that shouldn't have been allowed to happen. That was a disastrous year. I remember my wife's brother, poor fellow, broke both legs in a tumble off his roof when he was erecting a TV aerial, the first in Easchester."

Levin, slowly stroking his beard, listened intently.

"Duffy was an ex-Catholic or something of the sort, from the South Chicago area. He was a handsome man in his way, with a wild head of Irish hair, intense eyes and a prominent jaw. He gave the impression of being thin and loose-jointed, maybe he was. When he appeared in this office my first thought was, here's an odd one now, get rid of him quickly; but his Gaelic charm was effectual and I neglected my warning to myself and later had to pay for it. He came to us very well recommended. Either he had forged his credentials, or he broke down here for causes unknown. In a short time he became a serious menace."

His eyes examined Levin, who, though he itched, forced himself not to scratch.

"His first term here—a terrible reflection on his teaching ability—he failed more than fifty percent of his composition students, and it gave us all a pretty headache before we could get that mess cleaned up. Luckily, my secretary called my attention to what he had done before we submitted the grades to the registrar, who would have been fit to be tied. In the end, after much frantic work we managed to reduce his failures to less than half the original number, though a figure still much above the department average of from three to five percent. For the moment at least we had managed to prevent a scandal."

Levin leaned forward. "Was he fired?"

"Not quite. Another characteristic of Duffy's was that he was unable to fit himself to the most elementary demands of a schedule and was constantly late to class, conference, meeting— you name it. Regularity, with respect to time, meant nothing to him. He graded papers, accumulated in a pile on his desk all term long, in one mad week at the end of each quarter, staying up nights with the assistance of pills; then returning hundreds of themes and quizzes in ferocious batches a day or so before the d.o., having deprived his students of the benefit of learning from previous papers what errors to avoid on later ones. I subsequently learned that he threw away, ungraded and unrecorded, more than one set of themes, because his dachshund, which had been trained to react on paper, wet on them. He apparently did his grading on the floor."

"Tst-tst."

"Where do you grade your papers, Mr. Levin?"

"Strictly at my desk, sir."

"That's as it should be. He wasn't a bad sort in his way but he became a problem with his numerous complaints against what he called, as if it were a dirty word, 'the status quo.' He wanted to reform us all in the shortest possible time—I'd say a week. I can stand legitimate criticism; as a matter of fact I invite it every time I prepare a new edition of my grammar, but the criticism of a man who is against you every minute of the day, who challenges everything you do, your ability and sincerity, even your purpose in life, without considering his own, eventually grates on people's nerves. Gerald—" he paused— "well, Gerald hated him."

"Was that why he was fired—if I may ask?"

"It all added up. I had a good deal of patience with him. He had, as I say, a certain charm. Still, there was no slowing him down or changing his erratic course. You thought you had repaired some harm he had done, and he promised to be careful and considerate, then a new incident occurred. For example, during the spring term—I beg your pardon, it was the winter—no, I'm wrong, it was the spring—after campaigning for Wallace he embraced another lost cause; but that was after a period of radicalism during which he asked his freshmen to write on the Moscow Trials, Lenin and Trotsky, the Lysenko theory and other controversial subjects I'm sure they knew nothing about. Some of the students who complained about him said he encouraged discussions of Marxism in his classes. Now I would like you to know, Mr. Levin, that I have no objection to an honest discussion of these subjects, though they certainly don't relate to our *Science in Tech* reader, but I'm sure you'll agree Marxism is specialized subject matter that ought to be confined to mature history or political science courses and not be intruded into freshmen composition. To give you some idea how far astray he went, Mr. Gallegher, our book store manager, called me one morning to tell me that Duffy had placed an order for one hundred and twenty-five copies of *The Communist Manifesto* as supplementary reading matter. I can tell you we soon scotched that."

The professor's cigarette ash dropped on the desk blotter. He blew it away and Levin sneezed.

"Don't you smoke?" the old man inquired. "Would you care for a cigarette?"

"I gave it up." Levin blew his nose.

"That shows will power."

"Not much, sir."

"Nevertheless," said Professor Fairchild, "towards the end of the academic year he was engaged in collecting funds on the campus for some radical group or other, I think they were called 'The Committee of Anti-Fascist Scientists' or some such name. You may remember that group, or one with a similar-sounding name, is on the Attorney General's list of subversive organizations. In fairness to all, I'll say I proceeded in this matter with the patience of a saint, because Duffy sometimes seemed to me to be like an overgrown boy challenging authority—but finally my patience wore thin."

He rubbed out his cigarette, detached it from the holder,

flipped it into the wastebasket and leaned back in his creaking chair. For a minute his eyes were shut.

Opening them, he said, "You'll have a good idea what I went through after I tell you the following incident, although it's embarrassing to me."

"Please don't, if—"

"One Sunday afternoon about a week before Commencement I was relaxing in my tub. My wife was entertaining Mrs. Feeney, our former dean's wife, at tea, when Leo Duffy rang the door bell and had the effrontery to solicit a contribution for his radical scientists' group, but of course Josephine refused. Apparently annoyed, he demanded to see me. She foolishly let him in. Spying Mrs. Feeney there, either out of perversity, or malice, he asked her for a contribution. Now this lady is nobody's fool. She was raised in New England and is head of our local Anti-Liquor League, where Josephine is the first vice-president. Mrs. Feeney told Duffy that if he tried to collect good American money for bad foreign causes he might soon find himself without a position at CC. This was nothing more than an informal warning; she obviously had no authority, either direct or indirect, since her husband was retiring, to cause him to be fired. Let's just say she was giving him a bit of motherly advice.

"But Duffy was infuriated. He said he wouldn't stand for that kind of talk from anybody. His gestures were violent, he was practically shouting. They were afraid he might physically attack them—that is to say, with his fists. Half asleep in my tub I was awakened by the commotion and thought the house was burning down—he was loudly repeating the word 'fired.' Naturally I jumped out of the tub, and before I had thought twice, ran out into the living room in my birthday suit—"

Professor Fairchild chuckled.

Levin brought out his nail file, wondered why, and quickly returned it to his pocket.

"Mrs. Feeney passed out. My wife, without thinking, threw

a cup of tea at me, the tea not the cup, and Duffy went into a fit of maniacal laughter, the like of which I had never heard before. I then determined he would thereafter laugh out of the other side of his mouth.

" 'Mr. Duffy,' I said as calmly as I could—I had by this time a bath towel around my middle, and Mrs. Feeney had been revived with Josephine's smelling salts—'I hereby give you notice that you will be asked to leave this college as soon as the Administrative Regulations permit.' Well, you should have seen his expression. I can't exactly describe it, though to this day I still clearly recollect it. It combined anger, haughtiness, and comprehension of defeat, although I will say he looked more deplorable a few days later when he was publicly discharged from his position by Dr. Marion Labhart, the president of this college."

Levin, on the edge of his seat, asked, "Because of the incident—?"

"That as well as others," said the old professor. "In the meantime he had apologized to me for these contretemps. I had reconsidered and wasn't going to report him, but Mrs. Feeney telephoned Leona Labhart, and she told the president what had happened at my house. Now Marion is a man with a temper—I've heard it blamed on his first name, but be that as it may he's a disciplinarian of the old school, and he immediately called me for a dossier on Duffy. I had Dr. Gilley compile it, and the very day he read it the president called a college-wide open meeting. The entire staff, more than five hundred strong, crowded into Sheffield Auditorium in the Dairy Building, and heard the president denounce Duffy as a fellow-traveling radical. He read aloud the long list of his indiscretions—which he had had mimeographed and passed out to the audience. It was a terrible indictment. After reading the document, Marion, whose brain literally seems to boil when he's angered, spoke directly to Duffy, who, although he had not been asked to, had risen from his seat as though hypnotized. The president told him in front of all that he was a disgrace to the institution and his contract would not be renewed. Duffy was, of course, on a yearly contract—so are you—all new people are; he made no attempt to reply, remained speechless, a broken man, the shadow of himself, quickly abandoned by all.

"After the president had stalked off the platform the audience dispersed, I one of the last to leave. Leo seemed physically exhausted; it was all he could do, after half an hour, to drag himself out of the building. Perhaps he had not foreseen this end for himself, although it is likely he may have, yet was thunderstruck by his fate. I felt sorry for him—the man was obviously a misfit—and I was afraid he would do himself some serious harm; his eyes were turned inward in a frightening way. Yet when I saw him the next afternoon he had recovered a bit of his brashness and even asked me for a letter of recommendation, which I could not bring myself to write, although I did offer some sound advice about the future which he preferred not to hear."

"So that's it," said Levin with a sigh. He had secretly loosened his necktie but the image persisted of Duffy standing alone in the auditorium, the weight of his disgrace on his cracked head.

"More or less. He afterwards raised a fuss in our local chapter of the American Association of Professors, and for a while Dr. Fabrikant, who was chairman of the Academic Freedom sub-committee that year, and a few others on the faculty, were defending him, but in the end they came to their senses and voted against submitting a complaint to the national AAP. Dean Feeney's last act in office was to write the letter notifying Duffy of his dismissal."

"Er—Was it true that he was a fellow traveler?" Levin asked.

"What would you say?" The professor looked with interest at the new instructor.

"It's hard to say from the evidence. As for myself," he went on hastily, "I am not now, nor have I ever been, a member of the Communist Party."

Levin laughed brokenly.

"Funny thing," Professor Fairchild went on, "despite all that had happened, the last time we met he begged me practically on his knees for a last chance—as if I could. He said he had learned from his errors, was a reformed man, had more reason than ever for wanting to stay on. I felt he had grown more attached to this place than he had realized and it was a bitter thing for him to leave. Or perhaps he sensed this was the end of his teaching career, as turned out to be the case. I had to tell him the matter was entirely out of my hands and advised him in that last emotional meeting that he wasn't truly meant to teach and we were doing him a favor to let him go so that he might find his true place in society. Yet for a while I felt as many fathers do after punishing their children. I had built up some affection for the poor devil, perhaps thinking of him as a sort of prodigal son, except that Leo Duffy never returned to the parental fold, nor was I, when all is said and done, his father. In the end he went his predestined way."

Levin drew a long breath.

"That's how these things go." Professor Fairchild gazed out of a window. "It surprises me how often an evil genius, in one guise or another, will raise his horns on a college campus."

He looked suddenly bored.

Levin rose to go, but the professor, glancing again at his pad, amiably remarked, "I think the administration would expect me to say something in passing on the subject of sex."

The new instructor sat down with a throbbing dry throat. "Did you say 'sex'?"

"Call it what you will. You're thirty, your application states. Without any intention to pry into your personal affairs, may I ask if you are presently considering marriage?"

"Only vaguely," Levin replied. "First I have certain plans I would like to carry—"

"Ultimately?"

"Absolutely, sir. I want a home and—"

"Some do, some don't. Too bad you aren't married now.

Easchester can be hard on bachelors. If you intend to stay on here I recommend marriage. It would pay to keep your eyes open this fall. Occasionally an eligible woman or two join the staff, but they are usually quickly spoken for so you will have to hustle if someone strikes you as especially fair. My own wife was teaching clothing design in home economics when we first met. I took her out of the hands of a professor of dairy products to whom she was considering engaging herself. However, the point I must make is that we expect you strictly to refrain from dating students, no matter what the provocation."

"I understand—"

"Nor is prowling among faculty wives tolerated."

"Yes, sir—"

"You might guess that Duffy would not respect these suggestions."

"You don't say?" said Levin, but the professor let it go at that.

He said, after a minute of reflection, "We once had a sad case of a nineteen-year-old student who killed herself when she became pregnant by her instructor—"

"You mean Duffy, sir?"

"No, this was long before his time. He was a young speech instructor, and when he denied responsibility, the poor girl cut her throat under his bedroom window outside the house he roomed in, the room in which he had led her astray. This unhappy incident occurred during the very first year I was here, or perhaps it was the year after—I'm not sure whether I was already married, I believe I was. Yes, I was. People still talk of the tragedy."

Levin shivered under his new suit. The professor ticked off a last item on the pad. I can go now, Levin thought.

But the head of the English Department, swiveling around so that he looked full in the new instructor's face, with no transition other than the mark he had made on his pink pad, said, "I trust you don't drink, Mr. Levin?"

Levin, breaking out in a sweat, answered loudly, "No, sir."

He had set himself for the question, but the shock of hearing it almost lifted him out of the chair. By an effort of the will he remained seated.

Good God, he thought, have I given myself away? He suspected his face looked ashen, black whiskers sprouting out of marble.

"I'm glad to hear that. You might keep in mind that this community—this part of the valley—was founded a hundred years ago by missionaries from the East, hard on the heels of the forty-niners; almost overnight they established temperance societies. I met Josephine at an Anti-Liquor League social."

To appear calm, Levin slowly stroked his beard.

"Mores are mores."

"Yes, sir."

"I bring this up," the professor said, lowering his voice, "because your appearance reminds me somewhat of Father's."

"Er—Whose father?"

"Mine. He wore whiskers remarkably like yours and had your color brown eyes. I have a photograph of him among my papers at home; and your beard, black and full, is the spit and image of his at about the time he was your age."

"Quite a coincidence, sir."

"Papa was a drinker."

Levin patted his brow with his handkerchief.

"Not that I am in any way implying that whiskers equate with drinking. One thinks of the Hebrew patriarchs and prophets. And we have our own abstemious Amish Mennonites in this country. All I'm saying is that you happen to remind me of my poor father, who at one time of his life—I make no secret of it—was an incurable drunkard."

Levin's handkerchief was by now moist.

"Papa was a harness-maker by trade. In those days we lived above his place of business in a retangular frame house in Kansas City, Missouri. My sister was eleven and I nine—no, we were twelve and ten, I remember detesting my fifth-grade arithmetic teacher—when Papa began to drink heavily for no reason that my poor mother could understand.

"Mama—a pioneer type—stood it for several years. At length, realizing the situation was not improving, she decided to leave Papa and move to Moscow, in the Idaho panhandle, where her parents were living. Before going she spoke to him in our presence—I still recollect her words. 'John,' she said, 'I'm taking the children to my father's for reasons you well understand. Nevertheless, I don't want to cut you off from your family if we mean anything to you. Father sent me fifty dollars to leave with you. I give you my heartfelt invitation to join us as soon as you can. If you will stay sober long enough to locate us, I believe you can conquer drink, and we will all live together again.'

"I recall my father wept. He told Mama that he loved her and the children dearly and would follow us to Moscow as soon as he was thoroughly sober, 'dried out' was how he phrased it. When we left he drove us to the train in his horse and wagon. He was, I learned later, true to his word, stayed away from the bottle and wound up his affairs. He sold what was left of his business, put on his Sunday suit, packed a bag, and set out for the railroad station. But he had rarely ridden on trains, and through some unfortunate mixup, was already in Chicago before he, or anyone, discovered he had been going the wrong way. He was so terribly disappointed he made straight for a saloon."

Levin softly groaned.

"Some kind person put him on the right train and Papa was off again on his journey. He had vowed, I was told, not to touch another drop; however he made the acquaintance of a tipsy drummer aboard the train, who persistently offered him a bottle. Papa said no often enough, but the drummer would not accept his refusal, so when the bottle was down to a mouthful or so, he said yes, apparently thinking he would take a last swallow and be forever done with it. However, his strategy proved impracticable because the drummer had a half dozen more bottles stored in his suitcases full of samples of ladies' underthings. The two of them managed to get as far as Omaha, where, because of their carousing they were ejected from the train.

"A few days later, eluding the drummer, Papa got onto another train going west, but he soon discovered he had lost his billfold containing what was left of the money Mama had given him and the sum he had raised from the sale of his harness and leather goods store. Unable to stand his profound disappointment in himself, he left the train at Pocatello, and having sold his gold watch and suitcase for a song, used the money to get impossibly drunk. He stayed in Pocatello for the rest of his life, which was not destined to be long.

"Many years later—it was shortly after the birth of my eldest son—he's a mining engineer in New Mexico—I set out one summer in search of Papa. Employing a private detective, I traced him first to Omaha, then Pocatello, and a man we located there, a merchant who owned a feed and seed store where Papa was employed for a time, told me what had happened. Papa had in truth sworn off liquor not long after his arrival in Pocatello, but he was, as I understand it, ashamed to face us, penniless. The feed and seed merchant told me that each year of the four he lived in Idaho before he died, both at Christmastime, and in April, a few days before Mama's birthday, Papa made plans to go to Moscow, but for one reason or another he never got there. I presume he died trying. At any rate, none of us ever saw him again after the day we said goodbye in Kansas City. His life was wasted, but at least it taught me how to use mine."

Levin rose unsteadily. He got out, "I promise never to touch a"—before he clamped his jaws tight.

Professor Fairchild stood up and warmly shook his hand. "'I greet you at the beginning of a great career.'"

The sun flared in his hair and he looked like a saintly old man amid his books. Picking out a volume from one of the shelves, he handed it to Levin. "*The Elements of Grammar,* revised, thirteenth edition."

Levin at last relaxed. "Thank you. Dr. Gilley is giving me a copy."

"Keep both, should you lose one."

"I'm much obliged."

"Tell your students the book will be very useful to them. Funny thing," the professor chuckled, "they may hate it in the beginning but they'll love it in the end. More than one of my former students have returned to tell me that mastering English grammar was the turning point of their lives."

Levin held a nervous hand on the door knob but the old man was still talking.

"You'll like it here, Mr. Levin. This is wonderful country. If you don't mind the rain you'll like the climate. We have a friendly department—no strife to speak of, although there is sometimes an honest difference of opinion. Gerald Gilley is a good man in composition, you can learn a lot from him. The work is interesting, the students easy to deal with. It's a blessing to teach. I've been at it for nearly forty years and have never regretted my choice of profession. I'm nearing the end of my stewardship here and look back upon my work with satisfaction. I've fought the good fight. *The Elements* was born here. The department, in my time, grew from three to twenty-one. Yet the path was not always without thorns: We've had hard times, when the administration gave us almost nothing to live on. I scrimped to save. I had to pare down salaries, occasionally causing friction, I confess; still, what had to be done had to be done. The first duty of a good leader is to carry out orders. I did as I was ordered. At one time I ran about the cheapest department on the Coast, and frankly I was proud to help keep the college solvent and functioning during times of crisis. Dean Feeney felt as I did. He's also a careful man with a dollar. We have to be—we're not a rich state. The dean and I saw eye to eye. I have in my papers at home a letter from him commending me for my efforts in the college's behalf. I'm proud of it. I admit it troubled me to discover later that not every department head always followed the letter of the law. A few, during the Depression, had bought almost no supplies and kept salaries slightly higher—not by much—than some of us were paying. One man did his own secretarial work and divided the secretarial fund among his staff, but he had a very small staff. Maybe I should have tried something of the sort, but it didn't seem honest to me. At least I gave employment to another mouth. In general, when I think of what I would change if I had my life to live over, I doubt I would change much."

He was still talking, the light fading in his hair, as Levin left.

What new with Levin in the September weeks before classes began?

His world—inside he was Levin, although the New Levin, man of purpose after largely wasted years. For Mrs. Beaty, an old widow alone with her roomer in a bulky two-story white frame house, he performed chores he hadn't conceived doing before, in exchange for something off the rent. Levin mowed lawns front and rear—the health of the grass was amazing, it sprouted overnight and every week he had to cut. On a shaky ladder that left him with nervous knees he gathered yellow pears, shying away from the bees sucking the sweet wounds of fruit. The cherry tree had yielded, thank God, at the end of June, and the walnut wasn't due till late October. The landlady had eight trees on her hundred by seventy-five, including an orange-berried mountain ash, new to his eye.

Three weeks after he had arrived, after a night of rain Levin raked off the front lawn the first enormous leaves, fallen like wet rags from the sycamores in front of the old houses across the street; he had thought, until the old woman told him no, that they were from some Bunyanesque species of maple tree.

A truck dumped a backbreaking load of practically orange sawdust in the alley, and Levin slowly shoveled it through a window into the cellar—working up respect for the shovelers of the world—where it gave off a Christmas-tree fragrance that all but levitated the house. Mrs. Beaty demonstrated how to light the sawdust furnace and Levin agreed to keep it hot when the weather got cold, load the hopper twice a day, and every month vacuum the dust filters in the heat blower. He learned a sickle was not a scythe when he laboriously cut down and dug up a weedy flower garden she could no longer take care of, and discovered last season's walnuts and acorns, six varieties of worms, a soggy doll, and thickly-rusted screw driver from yesteryear. The past hides but is present. Watching a robin straining to snap a worm out of the earth Levin momentarily thought of himself as a latter-day Thoreau, but gave that up—he had come too late to nature. He whitewashed cellar walls until his beard dripped like the brush he was using; hosed the clapboard front of the house; again on a ladder, dug leaves out of rain gutters; changed washers in water taps; and though it worried him to work with electricity, even replaced wall switches where old ones were broken. Levin was surprised at all an inexperienced hand could do with only a slight loss of blood. He seriously considered taking up hunting and fishing, and planned to visit Seattle and San Francisco as soon as he had a few dollars in his pocket.

Mrs. Beaty lived and let live, a woman of sixty-nine, gone half deaf; she wore a gray comb in her gray hair and a hearing button in her left ear but rarely turned it on except to answer the phone when she "felt" it ringing, and to talk with Levin when he ate in the kitchen—this was their major involvement. Sometimes when he avoided her he realized she was avoiding him. She went to bed at eight each night, except on the rare nights she entertained; and early the next morning, wearing galoshes to protect her shoes from the wet grass, was already snipping flowers, or poking into the shrubbery around the house. She lived unself-consciously in the presence of her dead husband's cabinetry, rocking chair, pipes; his tools were still hanging above his workbench in the cellar. She had, she sometimes said, nothing against the world, and Levin envied her a little. She actively cleaned, baked, canned and sewed; she cooked well and was generous with food although careful with a dime. The cat got scraps. Levin did better; more than once she insisted on adding something to his inexpensive meals. And to make things livelier she promised another roomer soon, a graduate student from Syria. She took in only a gentleman or two, she said; ladies were too hard on hot water, the telephone, and the gentlemen. She said she was a minister's daughter and then remarked how nice it was to have a "scholar" in the house. For a full week she called him "Dr. Levin," but he denied it until she reverted to "mister." Once or twice, apropos of nothing, she said she knew Dr. Gilley quite well. Her husband had worked for him more than once and they had gone fishing together. She was not well acquainted with Mrs. Gilley but had heard about her from mutual friends.

Levin enjoyed the run of the house; never before had he lived where inside was so close to out. In a tenement, each descent to the street was an expedition through dank caves and dreary tunnels. He enjoyed the cherry tree reaching its knotty, mildewed branches to his back window. At the side he had a view of the wooded hills, changing shape and color as the clouds did. He could see the mountains from three windows. Not locking doors when he went out was new to him and he worried things might be stolen but soon stopped locking his doors. He noticed bicycles and toys left on lawns overnight and was pleased this could be done.

Levin's large room, next to the smaller one awaiting the Syrian student, was lit in sunlight during the afternoon. It grew hot for a while but sea breezes cooled it at four. At night he slept under two blankets, another kindness of nature. His white metal bed was an old-fashioned double— he suspected it had been Mrs. Beaty's marriage bed; he slept on its right side, on his right; he dreamed too often on his left. The desk he used was a good-sized walnut table built by the carpenter; it stood at the window with a view to the hills. Levin sat there often during the day writing in a thick hard-covered notebook he had used years ago as a commonplace book, and had recently revived. He wrote in it summaries of books he thought highly of, copying out passages. One section of the notebook was for "insights," and a few pages in the middle detailed "plans." He often read over sentences he had copied, such as "To change intention changes fortune"— Montaigne; "Important principles may and must be inflexible" —A. Lincoln, and was lately writing them into short essays he tried his hand at. Among Levin's "insights" were: "The new life hangs on an old soul," and "I am one who creates his own peril." Also, "The danger of the times is the betrayal of man" —S. Levin. He exhorted himself to "keep the circle broken." He was a conscientious becomer but worried that it had taken him so long to get started. The future burned in his head. Time not converted to good use tormented him; he liked having his new alarm clock around because it helped, in a primitive way, to organize him. Sleep loosened the nuts and bolts of his defenses, but time used to good purpose tightened them. Sitting at his desk, he studied *The Elements*, did the workbook exercises, and read all the essays in *Science in Technology*, taking notes from which to develop class lessons. He wished there were a poem or two in the book.

Levin warned himself to get out of the room more often. The warning was urgent so he walked. The country was conveniently fifteen minutes in any direction; if through downtown, then across a white plank bridge over the Sacajawea

River. He tramped for miles along dirt roads, wherever they led, usually from one farm to another. For weeks the blue sky was cloudless but lately huge white masses drifted in from the Pacific, floating toward the east. He wore his raincoat and carried a large umbrella; he did not like to be caught in a storm and soaked. A city boy let loose, Levin took in all the sights, stopping for five minutes at his first row of rural mailboxes. He enjoyed the variety of aging and ancient barns. In bright sunlight the stubble of grain- or grass-harvested fields looked like snow on the ground. One farm had a green scrub oak at its center that seemed to be growing in snow. The illusion created pleasure. He watched farmers burning the harvest stubble and afterward the fields were black, a sight he had never imagined. One day, as he walked past a black field, a visible funnel of wind whirled over it and headed for him. Levin wildly wondered whether to run, grab a fence post, or lie still in the road; then the little twister turned and blew another way. Within a week men on tractors were harrowing the burnt fields, and the rich brown earth looked newly combed and awaiting planting. The sight of the expectant earth raised a hunger in Levin's throat. He yearned for the return of spring, a terrifying habit he strongly resisted: the season was not yet officially autumn. He was now dead set against the destruction of unlived time. As he walked, he enjoyed surprises of landscape: the variety of green, yellow, brown, and black fields, compositions with distant trees, the poetry of perspective. Without investment to speak of he had become rich in sight of nature, a satisfying wealth. In the past he had had almost none of this, though in winter he had tenaciously watched the frozen city trees for the first signs of budding; observed with reluctance the growth of leaves; walked alone at night close to full-blown summer trees; and in autumn followed dead leaves to their graves. Now he took in miles of countryside—a marvelous invention. He had never seen so many horses, sheep, pigs across fences. The heavy Herefords (he had looked them up) turned white faces to the road as he went by. He had never seen one in the open before, or black Angus; they had never seen a Levin.

The image of autumn was already in his eye, but he did not compel it, as he had in the past compelled every flower and tree, to solace, or mourn with, his spirit. He saw almost the moment when strings of white birch leaves faded from green to yellow; and under the green skirts of maples, bunches of leaves flared gold. Except for a scarlet vine on a fence there were few reds—this into October, a green and yellow autumn, less poignant than his last year's. Except on warm days it took a sharp sniffer to unearth its bouquet, for an almost monotonous freshness of air dampened the effects of odor. He missed the smell of change and its associations, the sense of unwilled motion toward an inevitable end, of winter coming and what of one's life in a cold season? What most moved him was memory. Yet when the autumn day was momentarily cloudless, blue-skied, still to the point of a dog's bark miles away, it sometimes burdened the heart.

One afternoon after a long lonely walk, a mood induced, he thought, by the odor of wood smoke in the air, Levin stopped off at the Gilleys.

Pauline, coming to the door in tight violet toreador pants and a paint-smeared shirt, drew back when she saw him.

"Oh, you frightened me," she laughed in embarrassment, "I wasn't expecting anyone. That is, a guest."

"Excuse me," Levin said. "Is your husband home?"

"Why no," she said, controlled now. "He's downtown doing something at the bank. After that he was planning to go to the hardware store to buy a toilet seat for our split one in the upstairs bathroom—the kids slam them down so hard. Would you care to come in? The house is a mess, I've been painting chairs."

But he saw from her distraction she wished he wouldn't. Levin said thanks and moved away. He said he would see Gerald in the office. The screen door slammed behind her.

" 'Come see us often,' " he mimicked her.

Unwilling to be enticed by old habits of loneness, in late September Levin went to call on Assistant Professor Joseph Bucket. On Gilley's advice he had previously telephoned George Bullock, but he and his family, after returning from Carmel, had taken off for the coast. Bucket already interested Levin because of what he had heard about him. Mrs. Beaty knew the mother, the widow of a logger killed in the woods when the son was fifteen. He had transferred, after two years at Cascadia College, to the University at Gettysburg, then had served a year in the army, been discharged for an asthmatic condition, and after three hand-to-mouth years at graduate school in Arizona, Bucket had returned as an instructor in English at the College, his Ph.D. uncompleted. He had come back with a pregnant wife and three children. Since they were too poor to buy a house, and to rent a decent place at that time was impossible, Bucket borrowed as much as he could and began to build. Besides teaching and working on his house, he carried on odd-jobs all over town. Now, four years, two more kids, and a promotion later, he was still building, and still writing his dissertation. There was about this man's experience, as Levin had heard it, a quality that made him think they could be friends.

Bucket lived on the worn side of town, just over a twisting fork of the Sacajawea, a narrow arm of the river at times laden with logs floating down from the hills to a lumbermill at the southeastern edge of Easchester. One afternoon, Levin, wandering past the squarish two-story gray house, sporting a porch much too large for it, discovered the assistant professor on his hands and knees on the steeply-pitched high gabled roof, hammering nails into loose shingles and replacing others.

"Excuse me," Levin called up, "Professor Bucket?"

"Speaking." Bucket glanced down to see who it was, then turned cautiously, supporting himself against one of the two-by-fours temporarily nailed down. He was a long skinny man, about thirty-five, with a narrow face and meaty ears, and he wore large horn-rimmed glasses.

"Maybe I came at the wrong time?" Levin apologized. "I'm the new instructor in the English department. I happened to be passing by and thought I'd say hello."

Bucket, in cement-stained levis, large army surplus shoes, and a loose, thick home-knit green sweater, rested his hammer and can of nails behind a two-by-four, and still on hands and knees, examined Levin.

"That's kind of you. Sorry I can't talk just now. I'm not inhospitable, I'd like you to know, but I have to settle a leak that's been plaguing us, before it gets too dark to work."

Levin remained stationary in disappointment.

"Registration Week begins Monday, and since, as I understand it, we have offices on the same floor, we'll not be without opportunity to converse."

"With pleasure," Levin replied. He had harbored a sneaking hope that once they had got started talking Bucket would invite him to come back that evening.

The assistant professor may have sensed some such thought. "You're not from the West, Mr. Levin?"

"From New York City."

"New York?" He slowly slid down the roof and set himself cross-legged a few feet from its edge, worrying Levin that he might fall.

"How has it been coming along—your house?" he asked.

"I gather you've heard?" Bucket said. "If it strikes you as nearing completion, that's an illusion. This house—and, I might add—my dissertation, are as long in the making as Tristram Shandy in being born, or mine Uncle Toby in curing his military wound, a blow from a stone at the siege of Namur. If you happened to glance over the laurel hedge as you turned the corner, no doubt you noticed, in what was at one time part of our back yard, a bedroom I added last year; now Algene and I have decided that a playroom for the children is a necessity if we are to preserve what we have already built. As Tristram puts it in another context, '. . . such a building do

I foresee it will turn out, as never was planned, and as never was executed since Adam.' In the meantime there remains a good deal of interior woodwork finishing, and I've also had to install an additional half bathroom—we're eight in the house —my mother resides with us—and to reinforce the foundation at the rear. Sometimes I think my life follows that pattern of events Sterne calls the 'sad vicissitude of things.' " He laughed at that—it was almost a cackle, over in a minute yet exhaustive.

"Ah, too bad," Levin murmured. "Would you," he asked, "be interested in resting from your labors by going to the movies tonight as my guest? I understand the film they're showing is fairly good."

"Awfully nice of you," Bucket said. "A bit of entertainment is not uncalled for but most of my evenings are spent at the office. I referred to my dissertation a moment ago, 'Disorder and Sorrow in Sterne,' in reality a study of his humor. It has, unfortunately," he said without shame or bitterness, "come back to me for the third time, and I am presently engaged in a new rewriting. What I'm really doing, I shouldn't be too surprised, is waiting for the chairman of my committee either to retire or expire, although I would prefer retirement if only he'd hurry. Though, if pressed, he will not deny that my scholarship has merit, he doesn't seem to care for what he calls my presentation and style, and I haven't in any of my attempts been able to satisfy him. Although my own mentor, my sponsor on the committee, is loyally with me, the chairman is influential and the paper has come back each time with new criticisms and requests for additional alterations. I'm now sending it in chapter by chapter but haven't got past the second of eight. I've many times been tempted to abandon the project but mustn't or there'll be no advancement beyond my present rank and a salary I find it impossible to live on."

"Tst-tst."

"Had I the courage of my convictions I would twist my committee chairman's nose till he passed me, but I know it would end up with his twisting mine. As Sterne puts it, 'They order these things better in France.' "

"I wouldn't know," Levin murmured. "This is as far as I've been from where I was born."

"What brings you to this knot of the woods?"

"My fate, I suppose—"

Bucket cackled. He got up carefully on his hands and knees. "I mustn't delay any longer, if you'll pardon me."

"Have you got another hammer by chance? Maybe I could help you?" Levin said.

"My heartfelt thanks, but I don't carry liability insurance and the roof slopes somewhat too acutely."

Levin, reluctantly about to depart, thought of something. "I'm sort of curious about this Mr. Duffy you had around here the year before last. In short, could you tell me what he was like?"

Bucket looked down at Levin with new interest. "Who told you about him?"

"Who not? In particular Professor Fairchild."

"What, specifically, would you like to know?"

"I was told he was a radical of some sort, but I'm not clear what kind. That is, was he a crackpot or somebody with a liberal idea?"

The assistant professor contemplated Levin's beard.

"I can't say positively but there were elements of a philosophy that may be defined as liberalism."

"You're not using the word pejoratively?"

"Not I—personally."

"Was he a communist?"

"I strongly doubt it, although there were some who thought so."

"A fellow traveler?"

"I've heard that too."

"What did Dr. Gilley mean, could you tell me, when he characterized him as a 'disagreeable radical?' Was it the political connotation he had in mind or the oddball?" Levin hesitated. "I might have asked him, but being new I thought it best not to."

"I can understand your discretion."

Bucket continued to gaze down and Levin to crane until the back of his neck grew stiff.

"Nice people—the Gilleys" he said, to adjust a possibly wrong impression.

"Yes."

"Pauline—Mrs. Gilley, that is—they're both nice. Very hospitable. He has many interests. She showed me some pictures he—"

Bucket lost his hold on the roof and slid forward. Levin, fearing for the man's life, rushed toward the house to break his fall, but the assistant professor managed to dig his heels into the gutter, stopping himself from going off the roof.

"Holy cow!" He looked sick.

"My fault," Levin said, disturbed. "Sorry I bothered you. I'm on my way."

"My own inexcusable carelessness," Bucket gasped. "I should never come up here without crampons." He drew a deep breath, righted himself, and crawled back to the security of a two-by-four.

"I'll say goodbye." But Levin turned at the gate. "Excuse me," he called, "could you direct me to Dr. Fabrikant's house?"

"Fabrikant?"

Once more with the big eyes, Levin thought. What's so strange about every question I ask? "C. D. Fabrikant, in our department."

"I wanted to be sure you hadn't confused him with Carleton Fabricius in entomology. I once courted his daughter Imogene."

"Not that one."

Bucket pointed west with his hammer. "About half a mile past the college barns. His house is the first you'll come to."

Levin lifted his hat.

"Nice to meet you." Bucket crawled up the roof and was again banging nails into shingles.

Poor guy, Levin thought. 'Sad vicissitude of things.'

On his way along the county road the new instructor peeked through the door of the voluminous red college barn at the pedigreed black bulls in pens, marvelous beasts, but when they bellowed at the sight of him he quickly left.

Coming to Dr. Fabrikant's mailbox, under a chestnut tree, Levin followed a graveled driveway to an old blistered-green house, set back about a hundred feet from the road. The house was of wood with broad tower-like structures on both sides of the façade, not what Levin had expected to see. This seemed to have a New England quality, the little he knew of New England after a three-day pilgrimage wandering in the vicinity of Boston.

It was an odd place and creaked in the breeze, he thought, until he discovered a thin-faced woman watching him from her rocker on the porch. Lifting his startled hat, he went to her. She was shelling beans in a pot on her lap.

"Good evening," said Levin. It was still afternoon. She was straight-backed and meager, her black hair grizzled, at the tight hairpinned bun.

"Looking for somebody?"

"Please," said Levin. "Is Dr. C. D. Fabrikant home?"

"You're not a student, are you? I don't see so well without my glasses."

"No, ma'am—a teacher, new instructor here. I don't want to bother him if he's busy. I was just out walking."

"He's not at his desk," she said, still rocking slowly. "I think he's out to the melon patch on Isobel—that's his mare. I'd go look for him but I just got over my sciatica, and the fields are more than is ripe for me just now."

"Don't think of it," Levin said. "I'll be glad to wait a bit if you don't mind." He sat down on the doorstep.

"Doorstep's dirty, why don't you take the chair there?"

The chair on the porch held books that Levin didn't want to disturb; he said he was all right on the step.

"You say you're at the college?" she asked. "Do I know you? Not that I get around so much but after a while you know names and such."

"No ma'am. I'm the new man in the English department."

"Oh? Where from?"

"New York City."

She placed the pot on the floor. "I'd better call CD. He'll want to meet you. He got his Ph.D. at Harvard, in the East."

"You don't say," said Levin. "Maybe I'd better not disturb him."

She walked to the far end of the long porch and searched the weedy field, her hand shading her eyes. Then she came back to the rocker.

"My father sent him East. It was before the Depression and he was having some good years. He was a farmer in Montana. There were six of us kids, I being the eldest and CD right after me. He was the smart one right off. Read him something out of a book, even when he was a shaver, and he would rattle it right back at you in the same words. After his A.B., CD got three or four years of business experience, but he didn't like any of it, so Father sent him to Harvard, and he had a fine career there in A grades and all sorts of honorable mention. This professor he had—he was sort of a world authority—said CD showed remarkable promise and would have a successful career. He would have had for sure if the Depression hadn't come along.

"I guess you heard how hard things were then? I remember seeing pictures of bread lines in New York, hungry men, some with coats, some without 'em or even a hat, standing in the snow for a doughnut and coffee. We didn't have it that bad but we had it bad enough, partly on account of the drought we had in the state at that same awful time. Wheat was fifty cents a bushel, if that, and you couldn't get enough to pay for fixing your machines to harvest it. One year Father put in a hundred acres of flax, but though the clouds stayed low there was no rain and he cut less than three, not enough to pay back the cost of the seed. We used to mill a little wheat for breakfast food and bread, and we had some stock so no one starved. But our clothes were shameful and would come apart if I rubbed too hard on the board. And to make things worse our poor mother died. She didn't say how sick she was, although the doctor would've come for nothing if she had called him a few months before. Anyway, after CD had graduated with his doctor's degree he taught for two years in a real old college in Maine, but then it had to close down and he was out of work. He came back to Montana and after about a year took the first job that opened to him, in a country school near Bozeman. I knew it was a terrible trial to him with all his education. He never said much—CD isn't that type—but you could tell by looking at him what it meant not to be doing what he was fit to."

She began shelling her beans again.

"After a year of that, there came this letter from CD's professor at Harvard—the one I told you about that liked him—that Professor Fairchild, out here, was short a man because somebody had died, and he advised CD to apply right away. To make the story shorter, CD did get the place, but as fate had it, Father took seriously sick and CD had to help me care for him because we were the only ones around by now, and I was already on and off with my sciatica. Well, that winter Father died. In the meantime, some lady teacher on the staff here got herself married and quit so there was another opening, for which Dr. Gilley was hired. He came in September, 1932, just before the winter CD could come, and so he beat CD in by three months and has had seniority over him ever since by that one term, although in some of the departments of the college, CD found out later, the man with the Ph.D. generally gets the seniority over the one who hasn't got it if they come in close together. Dr. Gilley got his degree years later but that didn't seem to make any difference to Professor Fairchild. Just by that one term, after the two or three older men had retired, Dr. Gilley got his promotions and raises first, including his full professorship. CD is still an associate, though

68

he had many times been promised his advancement. I admit my prejudices, but I have my own doubts that Dr. Gilley really deserved advancement over CD. He hasn't got CD's intellect or his list of publications, but that's Professor Fairchild for you.

"When my brother came here he was paid sixteen hundred dollars a year. Of course he's doing financially all right now, since he's single and has me to help him, or we couldn't have bought this property—the house and twenty acres—but to tell you the truth, though he doesn't complain about it, I'm sorry for all the years he has stuck it out here. I wish he had taken a chance to move to a university where a man of his background could have had the kind of authority and courses he was entitled to by his education and writing. He didn't want to move, because once he had his assistant professorship and we had bought this farm, he got attached to it—we're all close to the land—and he said he'd rather not move to any place that might turn out worse than this. Even now I still advise him to look around for a change to a better college where he could get the respect he deserves, but he's fifty now and hasn't got the energy for that kind of a move. Besides he's disgusted with what he's been through in his life, though I can't exactly say I blame him for that.

"Personally, I still wish he had gone back East sometime, he'd have been better off for opportunities. He's the only one of the whole department here who will take the trouble to read up on an idea and write it out. He's had more than twenty different articles and essays published and some day hopes to have them all in a book. He has long since deserved his advancement, but I told you about this seniority business, and besides, the old dean who has just retired, Dean Feeney, was a tight-fisted man, and so for that matter, though I'm not trying to prejudice you—he has his virtues but he has his faults —is Professor Fairchild. They could have advanced CD as far as he is entitled, but they said the department wasn't big enough to hold three full professors. CD says they don't like his plain talk is why they haven't given him his due. He's an outspoken man and isn't afraid to call a spade by name. Last June CD blew up when he didn't get his promotion, and he told Professor Fairchild a thing or two. He promised to see what he could do this year. Please don't go around spreading that—it's nobody's business but CD's."

"No, ma'am, I won't."

"Well, he's promised before, but I guess Professor Fairchild feels it's no nails in his pants if CD doesn't get what he ought to. Which is worse than it sounds, because he's always had it good with those textbooks that CD wouldn't, as a scholar, lower himself to write. And there are others around here whose names I won't mention who are jealous of him. CD says they have average minds at best, and he tries to stay away from them so they don't waste his time. I've heard him wonder if some of the professors here have a college education themselves. Of course that really isn't so, but CD says there's an essay by William James—he's also from Harvard—and it's called, 'The Social Value of the College Bred.' The whole point to it is, if you have read it, that the reason for getting a college education in the first place is so you can tell a good man when you see him, and that's what nobody seems to be able to do around here."

Levin listened, holding his hat in his hands.

"You're getting impatient," she said. "I'll help you find CD."

"Kindly don't trouble yourself," he said, rising and dusting his raincoat. "Not after your sciatica. I'll look myself."

"Watch out for Lady Macbeth. She's our cow and has a frisky tail for strangers."

He followed her directions—going around the back of the house and across a weedy pasture. He crossed a dirt road he wasn't sure was part of Dr. Fabrikant's property—trespassing made him uneasy—went through a stand of poplars and as they thinned out, found himself confronting a hefty, big-uddered white cow, Lady Macbeth, without doubt, and God help him if her lord were around. Horrified by the immensity of the beast, he retreated, his hat slapped off by a poplar branch. As he tried to sneak up and snatch the hat from the ground, Levin stepped into a recently deposited cow pie. Cursing, he wiped his shoe on some dead leaves. Lady Macbeth approached, mooing. Levin grabbed up his hat and retreated through the trees. On the road he heard the sound of hoofbeats, and as he looked up, saw a horse galloping towards him. He jumped wildly aside. The startled rider managed to pull the animal to a halt; Levin knew at once he was Dr. Fabrikant.

Gripping the reins short as he calmed the frightened mare, Dr. Fabrikant, a cigar butt clamped between his teeth, the pupil of a gloomy left eye enlarged over that of a sober right, under heavy eyebrows examined the intruder. His sister had said he was fifty but the associate professor looked older, his face seamed by many lines; he sat stiff on his horse, giving an impression of unease. Stocky, short, on top of his small mount, wearing an old camping hat, he resembled U. S. Grant, but Grant lacking something, maybe his whiskey barrel. Though he looked like an outdoor type in khaki pants and jacket, with field boots laced to his knees, Dr. Fabrikant appeared to Levin, conscious of his prior knowledge of him, an inside man momentarily out.

"I'm terribly sorry," he explained. "I got lost looking for you."

"I don't permit salesmen on this property," said Dr. Fabrikant. "That's tacked up on a tree in front of the house."

"I'm not a salesman—not any more, a month finished that. S. Levin is my name—I'm sorry to disturb you. I was passing by and thought I'd say hello for a minute if I might. Your sister—Miss Fabrikant, told me you were out this way, and on account of her sciatica I went to look for you myself. I'm the new man here."

"What new man?"

"In the English department I should've said. I heard about you and came to pay my respects to a fellow liberal."

Dr. Fabrikant, shifting his weight on the horse, studied Levin.

"I also heard from more than one source that you're the leading scholar of the department."

The associate professor, removing his cigar, laughed in two short syllables—engine and caboose. "That's not saying much."

"I hope to read your articles sometime."

Dr. Fabrikant bowed, finally seemed pleased. "Nice of you to come."

"The reason I mentioned liberal is I happened to notice the title of one of your courses in the college catalogue. I also heard you were an outspoken defender of—ah—Mr. Duffy."

The horseman's expression was at once wary. "What did you hear about that?"

"Not much, really, except you had been sympathetic to him —for a while at least."

"Duffy was a damn fool."

"You don't say? I'm sorry," Levin was disappointed. "I had hoped he was worth defending."

"He was—up to a point."

"He seemed to me, when I heard about him, like a sympathetic person."

"Did my sister tell you about him?"

"Oh no, sir. Some other people did, including Professors Fairchild, Gilley, and Bucket."

"You've met them all?"

"I've been here almost a month."

"Where are you from?"

"New York City—Manhattan, to be exact."

Dr. Fabrikant dismounted and they shook hands.

"What satirical wind blew you hither?"

"I came for the change you might say."

"It's more than change, it's transmogrification."

"I know I'll like it once I make a friend or two."

Fabrikant lit a match and sucked in the flame, at the same time continuing to look Levin over. He thrust the burnt match into his pants pocket. "Woods are very dry about now." He gazed at the trees, puffing his cigar.

"Well, I guess I ought to be going," Levin said. He had hoped to stir up an invitation to stay a while, but the associate professor extended none.

They walked together, Fabrikant leading his horse, till they reached the road that led to town.

"Enjoying a place depends a lot on the people you meet," Levin was saying. "I already like Mr.—Professor Bucket, and I'm fond of Dr. Gilley."

Fabrikant grunted. "If you're fond of him I don't think you'll care for me."

Levin, off balance, did not know what to say.

The associate professor mounted his horse, then came an edict: "Gilley and I may be in a contest for department head-ship after Fairchild retires. If you're a liberal, you may be called on to prove it."

He galloped back in the direction he had come.

The Syrian graduate student Mrs. Beaty had been expecting turned out to be Mr. Sadek Abdul Meheen, from Damascus, and Levin made his acquaintance the day he arrived. He was a short young man with a fluff of curly black hair on a balding brown skull, and a delicate Semitic nose that sniffed in the direction of vagrant odors. His moist black eyes were gently popped. He was respectful of Levin as an instructor, and although he spoke English well, consulted him in matters of usage. Levin tried but was not much taken by the man, hidden as a person and fanatic about hygiene. The fumes of Lysol stank up the bathroom for a half hour after he had been in it; he rubbed everything he touched—before, not after—with his personal bottle. He was majoring in sanitary bacteriology and taking courses in rat control and the bacteriology of sewage. But he played chess better than Levin and talked entertainingly of the Middle East.

Although they were uneasy with each other the two men

restlessly roamed the Easchester streets together. The town, though attractive, was much of sameness. It had grown in a semicircle around a bend in the Sacajawea and now extended thinly to the western and northern hills; surrounding the long rectangle of green campus and red-brick college buildings. Downtown was a treeless grid of boxlike store and small office buildings, unimaginative and verging on abstraction. The goods in store windows supplied its only color. Around the business district were many old-fashioned double-pediform houses, mainly carpenter-built on small plots of ground, squeezed together; some were redeemed by gardens, shrubbery and trees, whose apples, plums and walnuts often rotted on sidewalks as Levin walked, evoking in him guilt for the waste. Farther out, past the campus, appeared the modern ranch houses with picture windows; tilted roof types; and split-levels climbing the hills. The fraternity and sorority houses were the most magnificent of the community. During the day, Levin enjoyed the town though it seemed entirely contemporary, without visible or tangible connection with the past. Nature was the town's true history, the streets and park barren of fountain spray or sculpture to commemorate word or deed of any meaningful past event. Lewis and Clark had not slept here, nor Sitting Bull, Rutherford B. Hayes, nor Frank Lloyd Wright. After the covered wagons apparently little had happened that was worth public remembrance except a few serious fires and the expulsion, not hanging, of Leo Duffy. But what Easchester lacked in communal memory and imaginativeness, it made up in beauty of natural setting, trees and clouds, cleanliness and quiet. Roses and ivy grew up some of the phone poles; and automobiles by law stopped at street corners when pedestrians crossed. This was civilized. Not since New York had any harried driver called Levin dirty names as he hurriedly crossed the street. There were no harried drivers. The new instructor's spirit was eased. He did not mind the smallness of the town. Had not Concord been for Thoreau a sufficient miniature of the universe?

But at night remembrance of New York City struck him like a spear hurled across the continent, adding weight to his body and years to his age. He walked with the map of the city underfoot; sometimes he thought of it as a jeweled grave to fall into, or a wound at his side. At night he missed the movement and mystery of people in dark city streets. The anticipation of adventure next block—walk one more and meet your fate among strangers—a bag of thousand-dollar bills dropped at your feet, or a wise and beautiful woman waiting for you at the corner. In Easchester, an hour after supper, although lines of cars were parked tight along the downtown curbs, the streets were weirdly deserted. Sadek and Levin met almost no one unless they entered a beer tavern or movie; these were usually two-thirds empty, more lonely than the streets. Levin had heard that the fraternal lodges were crowded, but at ten P.M., the town, from river to hills, except for a few scattered lights signifying human existence, was dead. Still they wandered, Sadek regretting that "a poor scholarship student" could not afford a car, Levin, who couldn't drive, not planning to learn. For want of something more exciting to do they walked out into the country; nature, except for the luminous furniture in the sky, hiding in the dark. Peering into the night, Sadek restlessly sniffing, they sought something it never seemed to offer. They were, Levin knew, on the prowl for a woman, who if she miraculously appeared, would run if she saw them—the bug-eyed Syrian who had smelled her out with his conjuror's nose, and the black-hatted, bearded Levin, unwed instructor, famished for love and willing to marry.

Several days before registration the college students began to arrive in town. Levin, though excited by their coming, was a little afraid of them for their looks and youth, whereas he was old at thirty and knew too much they didn't. The girls were mildly attractive, often hefty, not many truly pretty ones but the few who were, could make him ache. More could than could not. On Friday night before Registration Week Levin sat with Sadek in a booth in a tavern they had taken to coming to at the end of the evening. The tavern was barnlike, with a short blunt bar at which a few men with inexpressive faces dawdled. They drank with little talk, or quietly played shuffle-board. It surprised the new instructor how vast yet still the place could be. Most of the students left before eleven except for a married couple or two who sat around till midnight. This night Sadek and Levin were sitting in the rear booth, close to where the waitress stationed herself when she had nothing to do. She was a big-boned girl with a thinly pretty face. Her frame lacked flesh but her legs were good and her small hard breasts tantalized Levin.

She had served beers in a booth up front and was presently leaning against the wall, Sadek engaged in wooing her in a manner that had caused Levin astonishment and embarrass-ment the night before, when the Syrian had first demon-strated his attack. His method—was *this* the lore of the Levant? —was to turn his face to the girl's hips, where she was standing at rest, lean forward and address an incantation directly to the confluence of her anatomy. He crooned in an unknown tongue, his sensitive nose not more than a inch from her body. The waitress, after an amazed stare, squirmed, but then found it funny and broken into a nervous giggle, although she blushed when her eye caught Levin's. When she left to take an order, Sadek, as if his performance were nothing out of the ordinary, pared his nails with a small penknife, unmoved by Levin's sharp warning to behave. After the girl returned and took up her relaxed position against the wall, he again directed his plaint, or crooning, to her midpart. This occurred once more before they left the tavern. Tonight, as the Syrian repeated the ritual—it took less than thirty seconds and no one but Levin seemed to notice—the girl looked into the far dis-tance but her eyes were tender.

As her affection for Sadek visibly bloomed, Levin, although irritated by the odd lovemaking, fought a growing jealousy of him, for the Syrian had developed a system that the new instructor envied. When Sadek left the table to relieve himself in the back alley—the toilet facilities of the tavern horrified him and he preferred not to do a major Lysol job there—on these occasions Levin talked to the waitress and learned her name was Laverne. He had told her he was Levin but she showed no interest. He wished he had the nerve to move up close and attempt to deal directly with the consumer, but this flair, or means of incitement, was beyond his talent and timidity, although the torment of his unexpected desire for the girl was now something to contend with.

It grew late—towards one. The college students had gone; only two silent drinkers stood at the bar, the bartender-boss on a stool near the cash register, glasses on, scanning a newspaper. The booths, except for Sadek and Levin, were empty. Laverne, dreamy-eyed, hugged the wall close to where the Syrian sat. He spoke to all of her now and she responded with smiles and laughter. At midnight Sadek had turned to Levin and asked him to leave, but Levin coldly replied he ran his own business. He sat in the pale beyond their acceptance, greedy for the girl and contemptuous of himself because of her indifference. Sadek got up and they moved away from the booth. The Syrian spoke quietly, she answered in low tones. Levin, straining to hear, grew tense with frustrated desire. He struggled to free himself from this degrading emotion but sat as if will-less. Sadek returned to his seat, not glancing at Levin, his dark face serene as he fondled his beer glass. Levin considered dashing out of the place to gulp fresh air but couldn't move because something he had often wished might happen to him, had happened instead to this freak. He longed to know from Sadek if he had made a date with Laverne, thinking that if he had he would accept the inevitable and depart, but he could not bring himself to ask, because he knew the answer. Sadek impassively scraped his nails. At closing time the girl changed her shoes and put on her coat as the Syrian, having drained his beer glass, ducked through the back door into the alley for a quick one.

Ten minutes later, as the bartender was putting out the window lights and the girl was standing impatiently by a clothes tree near the phone booth, a young policeman entered the back door and seeing Levin, spoke to him.

"Say, are you a friend of Sadek A. Meheen?" He read the name from a small black notebook.

Levin cautiously admitted he had heard of him.

"If it's all the same to you," said the cop, "would you want to come around to the police station and talk to the assistant chief? We just caught this guy committing a nuisance in the alley behind here. He was pissing against the wall, and my buddy issued him a summons returnable in Municipal Court tomorrow morning, but then this guy, or whatever his name is, got sore and called us some pretty filthy names, so we drove him to the clink to cool his ass off. The assistant chief wanted to call the dean of men and tell him what happened, but he don't like to be waked up past eleven, so when this guy said a friend of his was here and you were a professor at the college, the assistant chief sent me over because your friend might throw a fit if somebody don't calm him down. I'm telling you because if he keeps on acting this way he might get himself bounced out of college. Also we are worried because he's a foreigner and everybody is touchy on that subject nowadays."

Excitement boiled up in Levin as he foresaw adventure, although he warned himself not to be tempted. The battle he fought was short, nor would he admit he had lost, for adventure was adventure and how much of it had he had in his life?

"I'll drop in if I can," he said.

The cop answered, "It's no hair off us if you don't. We wanted you to know where your buddy was, and what for."

"I'm much obliged."

The policeman left by the back door.

Laverne, who had been standing near the bar with the boss, both curiously looking on, approached Levin.

"What happened to your boy friend?" she asked.

Levin reached for his hat. "Let's talk outside." His throat was tight.

The girl followed him into the quiet street as her boss put out the last light and locked the door. Under a dim street lamp in front of the tavern Levin told Laverne that Sadek had got into trouble and was now in the police jail.

"What'd he do?" she asked sullenly, as if he were to blame.

"He committed a public nuisance."

"What's that?"

"Frankly, he urinated in the alley."

"What would he want to do that for? We have a gent's room."

"You know these foreigners." Levin shrugged.

"Are you American?"

"American citizen, born and bred in the U.S.A."

"How come you have that big beard?"

"Out of respect for the dead."

"Oh."

"Look, Laverne," he said thickly, "I like you a lot. It would give me great pleasure to be with you tonight. You're very attractive."

"I bet you say that to make me like you."

He admitted every man had his own language.

"I've never done it before with a guy with a beard."

"It won't bother you."

She tittered. "We were going to my brother-in-law's barn, three miles out on Route 5 by the river. Have you got your car?"

"No, but why don't we go to a hotel?"

"Have you got six bucks for a double?"

"Frankly no, now that I think of it. All I have on me is four dollars and change."

"They won't give you a room for that. Your friend was planning on a cab out to the barn."

"In that case let's do the same—but how will we get back?"

"I don't know for sure. We didn't talk about that."

"Could you call a cab from your brother-in-law's house?"

"No. He don't know I use his barn or he'd tell my sister. Anyway, they don't run cabs after half-past two. Have you got a friend of yours who could pick us up?"

"No." Levin looked at his watch. It was one-twenty. "What we could do is walk home," he suggested. "It shouldn't take us too long to walk three miles if you know the way."

"All right," Laverne said. She linked her arm with his and they went through the deserted streets. He tipped his hat as they passed the police station.

The taxi took them out to the country, to Levin the pitch-black middle of nowhere. Somewhere along a road with a wire fence on one side and bushes on the other, Laverne told the driver to stop. Levin paid the fare and the cab disappeared in the dark.

"Duck under this wire," she whispered, "and you better be quiet."

"Are there any dogs around?"

"Just one in the house but that's down a ways."

"Which is the barn?"

"Straight ahead. You'll see it when your eyes get used to the dark."

"I see it now."

He followed her over harvested ground. Laverne rolled open the barn door. She snapped on the overhead light, found an oil lamp, lit it and set it on the ground in an empty stall. She then switched off the overhead light. At the far side of the barn several cows were sleeping on straw. The warm, fecund odor of the animals and the sweet smell of the hay and grain stored in the barn, filled Levin with a sense of well-being. It was overwhelming how his life had changed in a month. You gave up the Metropolitan Museum of Art and got love in a haystack.

"My first barn," Levin murmured.

"I'll get the blanket and then we can lay down," Laverne said.

"In front of the cows?"

"They won't wake up."

"Why not in the hayloft? Nice and soft."

"The hay prickles my skin and makes me laugh in the wrong places. I'll be right back with Buster's blanket. You better be getting your pants off."

"Is Buster your brother-in-law?"

"No, his horse."

"There's no chance of anyone coming in on us?" Levin asked. "Farmers get up early."

"At four he gets up. We'll be home long before that." She found the blanket and returned. Levin was still waiting.

"Why don't you take your pants off?"

"It's cold here. Have you got a blanket to cover us?"

"No, just this one to lay on."

"In that case I'll keep my jacket on."

"But take your pants off or they'll get crinkled."

"Why can't we take one of the blankets off a cow?" Levin asked. "We'll put it back later."

"If you look good you'll see the cows don't sleep with blankets on them. They'd get sick if they did."

Laverne spread the horse blanket on the ground, and standing on it began to undress. She was neat with her clothes, folding each thing and putting it down on a hay bale nearby. Levin placed his hat, trousers, and shoes stuffed with socks and garters, next to her things. He kept his shorts on.

Watching the girl undress in the shadowy light of the lamp in the stall, Levin felt for her an irresistible desire. Ah, the miraculous beauty of women. He considered falling in love with her but gave up the idea. He embraced Laverne and they kissed passionately.

"Your breasts," he murmured, "smell like hay."

"I always wash well," she said.

"I mean it as a compliment."

"It ain't so bad here, is it now?" she said softly. "The cows make it warm."

She knelt on the blanket and Levin got down beside her.

"Blow out the light," she said.

He did and crawled back to the blanket.

In front of cows, he thought. Now I belong to the ages.

"Do you love me any?" Laverne whispered, lying beside him. "Your friend said he did."

"I love your body. I love your breasts and am grateful to be near them."

She laughed, seeking him with her hand.

"Now," she said languidly. Levin rose to his knees and was about to be in her when a noise stiffened him. The barn door rolled open and a light flashed on them. Laverne screamed. Levin rose in panic.

Someone entered the barn, snatched their clothes off the hay bale and ran out.

"Sadek," Levin called. "Come back, you bastard." He chased after him but the Syrian was faster. He popped through the wire fence, dropping something but escaping with most of the clothes. A taxi was waiting in the road. The door slammed and the car drove off. Levin furiously shook his fist.

At the fence he found one of Laverne's shoes and her brassiere. He found nothing else there but near the barn he stepped on cloth and was overjoyed to pick up his pants.

Laverne had the lamp lit and the horse blanket around her.

"Sadek," Levin said. "They let him go and he probably got the same cab we had to bring him out here. He grabbed everything except this couple of things of yours I found and my pants. Would there be something around to wear?"

"Not that I know," she said, "but let's finish what we were doing and maybe by then he'll bring our clothes back."

But Levin, afraid he had waked someone with his shout, wanted to leave. He worried how to get Laverne home with only a blanket around her, and himself without socks or shoes. If they escaped freezing to death, suppose a cop stopped them in town? He could then kiss goodbye to his unbegun college teaching career. The thought gripped him by the hair.

"He won't bring anything back," Levin said. "Couldn't you

possibly borrow some clothes from your sister? We'll surely get picked up if a cop spots you in that horse blanket."

"No," she said sullenly.

"Look Laverne, I'm sorry about the way this has turned out. I didn't plan it this way, I assure you, but we'd better do something sensible or we'll both land in trouble. We'd better start out for town right now, before the moon comes up, if it's going to, or dawn begins to show. In the dark we have a chance."

"You sure are some fine flop," she said acidly. "It's what I get for picking you instead of waiting for the one with guts."

He felt bad but answered nothing. Levin got his pants on, and she fastened her brassiere and slipped on her shoe. When she had the blanket wrapped around her they left the barn and got through the fence. They followed a rutted road, then a graveled one that butchered Levin's feet. He picked his way along the road, each step painful. Laverne limped along on one shoe but after a while took it off and flung it into the bushes. Barefoot, she walked without trouble.

"How far to the highway?" he asked.

"About a mile."

In ten minutes her teeth began to chatter.

"Cold?"

"My ass is frozen."

Levin, after a minute, stopped and removed his trousers. He handed them to Laverne. She stepped into them without a word, knotted the belt around her waist and rolled up the cuffs. They trudged along the dirt road till they came to an asphalt highway. Laverne wanted to thumb a ride but Levin asked her not to. When a car or truck approached they hid behind trees or lay down in the open fields. Then they went on again, neither speaking.

Stars peppered the sky but Levin's astronomy was the astronomy of fear, in particular, of losing his job. If he could get rid of the girl and her horse blanket he might make it, with or without pants sneak into town and quickly be home. He saw himself noiselessly jogging through the streets, as if training for a long distance race. He could ask her to put his pants in a bag and he would pick them up at the beer tavern the next night.

A dog appeared from off the side of the road and began to follow them. Levin considered tossing a rock at it but didn't want to antagonize the animal. The dog came closer, its eyes glowing in the dark. Levin was thinking of shinnying up the next tree but what would Laverne do? She bent for a stick and flung it at the dog. It took off with a whimper.

A truck approached from the rear. "Come on," urged Levin and ducked behind a tree, but this time Laverne continued walking. As the headlights hit her, to Levin's dismay she was jerking her thumb for a ride. The truck slowed down, then someone pitched an empty beer can at her, hitting her with a pong on the rump. Levin found her crying.

"Don't cry, Laverne."

"Bullshit."

They walked on. Once Levin went off the road into icy water in a drainage ditch. And Laverne tripped over half a rubber tire and skinned her elbow. He tied it with his handkerchief.

It seemed to Levin they had walked half the night before they finally entered Easchester. Under the garish highway lamps he was at his most anxious, fearing the police prowl car, tempted every minute to say goodnight and sprint home.

But he couldn't leave her because he considered it partly his fault they were in this mess, and he felt for her a certain tenderness for having for a minute lain under him.

They passed the lumber mill and a few minutes later he recognized Bucket's house. Laverne led him into a long alley, across a bridge and through a small park, where the icy grass froze what was left of warmth in his blood. A milkman stared at them from his truck. Levin urged her to go faster but when they turned the next corner she said they were home.

He was immensely relieved, at the same time fatigued and

chilled. Only his overworked nerves had kept from him how bad he had been feeling. But on the porch, as Laverne took off his pants, the sight of her body aroused his desire.

"I'm grateful to you in more ways than one, Laverne," he said haltingly. "Couldn't we meet sometime—under better circumstances, and—"

She kicked his pants off the porch. "No, you bastard, don't ever let me see you again in your whole goddam life. Don't think those whiskers on your face hide that you ain't a man."

This broke Levin up.

Levin woke with a sob from a dream of wrestling Leo Duffy, who when last seen, riotously tarred and turkey-feathered, was riding a rail out of town. Et tu, Brute? He shook his bloody fist at the new instructor. Levin leaped out of bed, indignantly shook the alarm clock, a new piece of junk, and pitched it out of the window. He hopped into his pants, fumbled with shoe laces, hurried into shirt, tie, jacket—everything thoughtfully laid out last night. Thank God he didn't have to shave; the beard paid off. Holding to his inexpensive broad-brimmed new brown hat, he ran on an empty stomach in a drizzle from Mrs. Beaty's house to Humanities Hall. Although it was only five after eight on the first day of fall term, the quadrangle was deserted, not a solitary soul visible. His students were already in class but Levin wasn't so he galloped to get there, his first hard running in years, heart whamming, throat parched, rain-coattails flying in the breeze. Bounding up the steps into the old wooden building he went two at a time up the inside stairs. On the second floor he shot a glance down the office side of the hall—luckily all clear, every door shut. Sneaking into his office, Levin dropped his damp hat and raincoat on a chair and grabbed books and papers. He hastened to class, running a broken comb through his whiskers. When for some unexplained reason he looked back, Professor Fairchild and Dr. Gilley, huddled together near the water cooler at the far end of the hall, were watching his progress.

A hush rose like a noisy fog as Levin entered the classroom. Confronted by sixty eyes exploring from the upturned soles of his shoes to his hairy face, he was momentarily panicked, wanted to fly—flee across the continent and hide in someone's cellar. But he said to himself, For shame, kiddo, with your experience! So he sat at the desk calling the roll in last year's voice, ashamed to have been late to his first college class; and to tell the truth the students seemed embarrassed too. But Levin recalled how certain of his old profs had habitually been unable to be anywhere on time, for which nobody he knew blamed them, so why exaggerate molehills? Tomorrow he'd be punctual as usual and a bad beginning would be forgotten. If Professor Fairchild came to work at seven-thirty A.M. he would see Levin long since at his desk.

Having finished with attendance, still wobbly within, as if he hadn't yet caught up with what time it was, or had forgotten something he shouldn't have, although he hoped not, Levin wrote out on the board his name and office number and considered saying a few words of welcome, he the host so to speak. But since he was carefully following the mimeographed instruction sheet, he listed, first, texts, then described the course this was, namely freshman composition via formal grammar, a study he commended after a moment of silence; it clarified writing, that of course was the big thing. "A man who can clearly write an idea is one who can invent one," was Levin's good word for the day. In ten minutes he had gone through the fifteen items on the sheet and was vaguely considering dismissing the class—what could he teach them the nervous first day?—when by luck his eye fell on a line at the bottom of the page: "N.B. DO *NOT* DISMISS YOUR CLASS BEFORE THE END OF THE HOUR, G.G., DIR. COMP." Sweating over the error he might have made (he pictured both of them in the hall waiting for his class to let out before the bell rang), Levin got up and demonstrated on the blackboard types of sentences, as the students, after a momentary restlessness, raptly watched his performance.

Silence thickened as he talked, the attentiveness of the class surprising him, although it was a college class—that made the difference. He had expected, to tell the truth, some boredom— the teacher pushing the tide; but everyone's eyes were fastened on him. Heartened by this, his shame at having been late all but evaporated, Levin, with a dozen minutes left to the hour, finally dropped grammar to say what was still on his mind: namely, welcome to Cascadia College. He was himself a stranger in the West but that didn't matter. By some miracle of movement and change, standing before them as their English instructor by virtue of his appointment, Levin welcomed them from wherever they came: the Northwest states, California, and a few from beyond the Rockies, a thrilling representation to a man who had in all his life never been west of Jersey City. If they worked conscientiously in college, he said, they would come in time to a better understanding of who they were and what their lives might yield, education being revelation. At this they laughed, though he wasn't sure why. Still if they could be so good-humored early in the morning it was all right with him. He noticed now that some of them turned in their seats to greet old friends; two shook hands as if to say this was the place to be. Levin grew eloquent. The men in the class—there were a few older students, veterans—listened with good-natured interest, and the girls gazed at the instructor with rosy-faced, shy affection. In his heart he thanked them, sensing he had created their welcome of him. They represented the America he had so often heard of, the fabulous friendly West. So what if he spoke with flat a's and they with rocky r's? Or he was dark and nervously animated, they blond, tending to impassive? Or if he had come from a vast metropolis of many-countried immigrants, they from towns and small cities where anyone was much like everyone? In Levin's classroom they shared ideals of seeking knowledge, one and indivisible. "This is the life for me," he admitted, and they broke into cheers, whistles, loud laughter. The bell rang and the class moved noisily into the hall, some nearly convulsed. As if inspired, Levin glanced down at his fly and it was, as it must be, all the way open.

Pauline Gilley had telephoned Levin to invite him to the department potluck, held customarily on the evening of the first day of classes, at the river park.

"I've heard 'potluck' before," Levin said, "and think I know what it means but I like to be sure."

Pauline said, "Don't tell me you've never been to a potluck picnic?"

"Not that I remember by that name, though we used to bring sandwiches to Van Cortlandt Park on P.S. 111 field day."

"Stop, Mr. Levin, you'll make me cry." Instead she laughed. "It's a picnic supper where everyone brings some dish or other to share. Gerald says it kept social life alive in Easchester during the Depression."

"I'll bring a bakery cake," Levin said.

"Just bring yourself, bachelors are privileged."

He thanked her warmly.

"How do you like our department?" Pauline asked.

"Fine," said Levin.

"I'm so glad."

So Levin arrived empty-handed at the river park at 3:30 P.M. on Monday, feeling shy, a useless emotion returned from childhood; also foolish in new suit and sweater, since most of the men were in slacks and sport shirts. The park, thick with fir and spruce, redwood picnic tables strewn among the trees, was damp from the morning drizzle but no one seemed to mind and Levin was glad he had resisted the impulse to bring along his hat and raincoat. The number of people present surprised him, including many kids who set the park in motion. As the wives unloaded cartons and picnic baskets and laid the food on the tables, the men who weren't making the fire swung swings, played catch, and two or three fished with some of the older boys on the riverbank.

Levin attached himself to the Buckets. Algene was an awkward, long-necked, pretty woman. The five little Buckets, serious children, stayed together, Joe carrying the youngest on his arm.

He never lets up, thought Levin.

"Joe never complains," Algene said. "His motto is: 'Labor, sorrow, grief, sickness, want and woes are the sauces of life.'"

"Sources?"

"Sauces."

"From Sterne?" Levin asked.

"What else?"

Pauline, in skirt and sweater and wearing pendant earrings, found Levin and insisted on introducing him to the department wives. These ran from plain to healthfully pretty; several looked like girls, two pregnant, the wives of Ed Purtzer and Wayne Sprinkle, instructors on the third floor. The other women ranged from young middle-aged to Mrs. Fairchild, old. Pauline said that among them were ex-grade school teachers, librarians, a nurse or two and some former secretaries. Several, married in college, had supported their husbands through M.A. degrees. None was without a suggestion of experience in the world and glad to be done with it—whatever their experience had been, the world outside Easchester, the unmated life. "We've settled in, all family," Pauline said.

Levin said he envied them.

"Do you envy Bucket?"

"Him, no."

She disappeared to round up her children, then returned to finish introducing him. Like their crewcut husbands whom he had met during the last week, the wives were hospitable and friendly. Despite his worrisome clothes, and bushy beard, which some of them scrutinized with interest, and one woman apparently could not abide, among them Levin felt more or less at ease.

Pauline saw to it that he got plenty to eat, his appetite inspired by the variety of food, the fresh air, and piney fragrance of the park. He sampled at least a dozen dishes, then, uneasy at all he had put away while contributing nothing, wandered from the table while Pauline was getting coffee. He met Gilley roaming around with a Zeiss Ikon, and watched him snapping people at random, responding happily to requests to take more. Gerald measured with a light meter what was left of daylight, screwed his eye to the view finder, patiently adjusted subject with object, then signaled hold it, and popped the shutter. A memory was fixed forever on shiny paper. Pauline and both kids came out of the heavier woods surrounding the park, Erik sobbing, and Gilley, to divert the boy, handed Levin the camera and asked him to shoot one of the family. He had set the instrument, balanced one kid on each shoulder, and moved close to Pauline. Levin, enjoying the novelty, snapped. Gilley invited him to pose with his wife but Pauline said it was too dark.

After everyone had eaten and the tables were cleared, the fire in the pit was built up within a semicircle of benches, and Professor Fairchild, in mackinaw and old hat, rose and stood at the far side of the fire, facing the picnickers. His wife, the Anti-Liquor League V.P., a gray-haired lady with two chins and rimless eyeglasses reflecting firelight, sat nearby on a portable chair, bulkily bundled in cloth overcoat and fur cap. In the ordered silence that descended, the children miraculously restrained, the professor spoke:

"The president and new dean have formally welcomed you, and I know Dr. Gilley has for the department, but I usually reserve this informal occasion to say hello to you and your happy families at the beginning of the academic year, and to announce what is new with us. I greet you, refreshed, I trust, by the long and peaceful summer—a priceless time of relaxation and pleasure, and, I sincerely hope, of reflection and the gathering of resources. I have no doubt you are looking forward to the duties of the new term, and the enjoyment and rewards of teaching.

"Let us at this time welcome back Dr. Leopold and Mrs. Alma Kuck, recently returned from Leopold's sabbatical year and the successful completion of his doctoral work. Leopold is now, and has been since June, the possessor of a doctor's degree in English from the University of Wyoming—his native state. A copy of his dissertation on *Piers Plowman* is now on file in the college library, and I urge you all to have a look at it. A lot of work goes into these papers and we ought to do everything we can to keep them alive. Well done, Leopold, and I hope this will be an inspiration to some of you younger men to consider your professional advancement. The Ph.D. is our conditio sine qua non, and everyone who has not yet acquired the degree should be working for it, no matter how rigorous the course.

"Once he had been awarded his doctorate, Leopold, with Alma and their two children, Mickey and Joanne, embarked on a well-deserved six-week vacation tour of the British Isles. Leopold tells me he has returned with twelve-hundred color slides of literary and historic interest, to entertain us during the coming winter. At my request he is also preparing a ten-page summary of the high spots of their trip, which I shall have Milly mimeograph and place in your boxes next week. We can't all get out into the world and are gratified when some of you bring it to us.

"Dr. Kuck." He pointed across the fire that reddened his face, and a man with gaunt features and prematurely gray hair got up and nodded to a sprinkling of applause.

"We also welcome back Avis Fliss, after a spring-term leave

of absence without pay to attend her ailing mother in Louisville, Kentucky. Mrs. Fliss has benefited from her daughter's care, and we hope she is well along on the road to recovery. We've missed you, Avis, nice to have you back again."

He pointed into the dark. Again handclapping. Levin looked around but no Miss Fliss evolved. Apparently she was shy and the professor did not urge her to stand.

"I would like now to announce that Dr. George Bullock has recently been notified of the acceptance, by Koch and McCook, publishers, of his anthology *American Short Stories for College Use*. No doubt we'll be adopting it here in the near future for our 'Survey of Literature' class. And while I'm on the subject just let me say to you men"—he peered across the fire— "that I hope some of you will look into opportunities for writing or editing textbooks. The rewards aren't stupendous, but I can tell you from my own experience that the satisfaction in ordering one's thoughts and committing them to paper is greater than some of you young people seem to realize. We ought all to be expanding our horizons. George, I congratulate you on your usual energy and initiative."

George Bullock, a sharp-faced handsome man with light hair plastered tight on a long skull, bowed amiably, sitting on his hands.

"The department of vital statistics," the professor went on with a chuckle, "has no engagements, weddings, or births to announce presently, but we have acquired a new bachelor, so that we may be said to retain a stake in the future."

He said, after the momentary laughter, "I now take the opportunity to welcome among us Mr. Seymour Levin, a native of New York City, New York; B.A. from New York University, New York, 1940; and M.A. from the same institution, 1950. He comes to us at Cascadia College as an instructor in composition. We are happy to welcome him and hope he will enrich us from his experience in the East. There he is sitting with the Gilleys. Would you mind standing, Mr. Levin?"

Levin stood limply, with a bob of the head acknowledging the polite applause.

"Hooray," piped Erik Gilley in the aftermath of silence, and everyone laughed. Levin quickly sat down. When his color diminished to cool he noticed that Pauline's face still retained an embarrassed glow.

When Levin tried to think across the continent to a New York autumn his rainy thoughts no longer let him. They stopped at the drenched mountainside forests of the Cascades. He had cut himself off, he had discovered, from longing for the East. Without regret. If Levin regretted anything it was not long ago having escaped the city. In Easchester he felt comparatively at peace with himself, more than for years. To stay at peace he let days go by without opening a newspaper or turning on a broadcast. He knew what the news was and preferred to forget it: The cold war blew on the world like an approaching glacier. The Korean War flamed hot, although less hopelessly for America. The country had become, in fear and self-accusation, a nation of spies and communists. Senator McCarthy held in his hairy fist everyman's name. And there were rumors of further frightening intercourse between scientists and atomic things. America was in the best sense of a bad term, un-American. Levin was content to be hidden amid forests and mountains in an unknown town in the Far West.

His alarm clock, retrieved and repaired, woke him in the dark shortly after six. He dressed in the cold, his senses like lit candles, and went down to the cellar to load the sawdust hopper with six pailfuls. The heat blew up in minutes. He fed Mrs. Beaty's white cat, then himself. Levin ate leisurely, reflecting that much of his enjoyment of Easchester was relief in having escaped the city's nervous hurry. After washing his few dishes, when the sky brightened he snapped off the kitchen light and sat in the morning dark. Afterwards he read for fifteen or twenty minutes in the front room, looking up from time to time at the ticking clock on the mantel—he was, after all, Levin—and left the house at seven-twenty. He walked to work, the streets deserted; fifteen minutes later the flow of students on foot and in cars, began. At seven-twenty Levin could still be the first man abroad in the world, another refreshment.

If it was raining he went under his blooming black umbrella. Usually the morning was overcast between wettings, the moving sky continuously surprising. Overhead the clouds roiled dark; ahead thinning through shades of gray to an accident of gold. To the north above the dark green hills, a moody blue. In the west white steam shrouded the mountain tops. Depending on the direction he looked, above could be gold, black, silver, gray. He had never in his life gazed so long at sky, probed so often the places of light, threads bursting, spoonfuls burning, webs of glowing caught in trees. Around noon, if it was going to, the sun poked its steaming eye through the mist, and clouds broke into rivers and lakes, creating blue afternoons. Marvelous.

Teaching was itself sanctuary—to be enclosed in a warm four-walled classroom. Levin taught twelve hours a week, a thankful reduction of the more than twenty of his high school program. Bonehead grammar was all daily drill, *The Elements*, plus workbook D; but Comp 10, the regular freshman course was a little more civilized. Although *The Elements* again prevailed, with workbook A constituting two-thirds of the instruction, here at least were six themes, based on *Science in Technology*. These, with frequent quizzes, produced a heady pile of paper which the instructor, with Duffy in mind, labored to stay abreast of. He was told that in English 11, next term, he would teach writing. "It's more a college course," Gilley said. "First we have to teach them what the high schools didn't." Though disappointed in the subject matter, Levin taught with passion although it came out grammar. But the students respected what mystified them, so he enjoyed teaching it.

He was independent—no supervision nor direct official inquiries, though Avis Fliss, Gilley's assistant in remedial courses, gave tactful advice here and there. She had materialized as a not-bad-looking woman of about thirty-five, with a breathy voice and fluttery eyelids, the one who had looked away from his beard when Pauline had introduced him. Her taut, flexible neck was a surprising instrument, it seemed to Levin she might see behind her if she tried. Among Avis' assets were a well-stacked bosom, and behind like a hard head of cabbage in a tight skirt. Her scent was a warm mixture of orange blossom toilet water and tobacco smoke; Levin found it interesting. For a while she was ill at ease with him, not knowing whether to confront his whiskers head on or peek around or under to uncover a fugitive from justice. Her eyelids fluttered as she spoke to his left shoulder. But he waited for her to come to grips with him and before long she did. Her flutterings diminished, the voice took heart, and though coy, she addressed him to his eye.

Between classes he appreciated his private office—*his*—the first he had ever had, an unbeatable institution for someone who lived much alone. During two daily office hours Levin saw his students and "counselees"—ten, whose programs and performance he had to keep an eye on—did what he could for them, and sent them on their way. Once his hours were over he kept his door shut and graded papers, or read, a privilege during the working day. Yet when someone knocked, his impulse was to hide the book. Some of the other men, Bucket for one, gave unlimited time to their freshmen, and Levin uneasily thought he might be cutting it too short but finally figured he taught conscientiously and was available when he was supposed to be. After that he had work of his own and wasn't, like some of the boys on the third floor, whose voices he heard in the hall as he passed their offices, interested in discussing at length the World Series or the latest football scores. Being new at the business he needed time to himself. Not that he used every minute earning his salary. Often he stood at the window —the cracked part resembling a tree in the glass—watching the clouds drifting eastward. He gazed at the green-lawned, thickly-treed quadrangle, liking its order and beauty as he recalled the stone skyscrapers in which he had gone to college. And he was fascinated by the casting classes across the street, men and women with fishing rods, flipping weighted lines at colored hoops in the grass, for two college credits. A new world, Levin.

People visited informally from office to office. His coffee mug preceded George Bullock through doors, then he emerged. Avis, wandering, loved to sit on people's desks; her legs were fair. Others Levin met in the men's room, but the crossroads of Humanities Hall was the coffee room. Before hurrying to the lavatory with her weak kidney, Milly Womack, the secretary, about twenty-five, with harlequin glasses, set the forty-cup percolator going for the first morning round. Soon Gerald's practiced ear picked up the sound of bubbling and he called down the hall, "Water's boiling." Then the daylong trek began. Whenever Levin came in for his daily cup or two of tea he was sure to meet someone, if not a crowd.

His colleagues, gathered for coffee, were amiable people, sociable, unpretentious, several well-educated but no one eager to show it. On a dark day one might be momentarily invisible against the wall. Every man, no matter his rank, was every man's assumed equal, very relaxing. Competitiveness, if it existed, was hidden: no visible back-biting or in-fighting, promotions came when they came and nothing could be done about it. No jackdaws crowed, though Bullock's wit produced a mild vaudeville, a Californian among Westerners. Despite their degrees or progress toward degrees, their pipes and casualness, the professors looked like the Rotarians downtown, with cheaper suits. But they wore their clothes without self-consciousness, and those whose haircuts were the work of wives with Sears Roebuck clippers, were proud of it. Saving money was a serious entertainment. The upstairs young men were of the same friendly breed, livelier, with more colorful jacket and slacks combinations. About five of the dozen were addicted to flattop crewcuts and occasional jive talk, though not much beyond conservative otherwise. They were, as Gerald put it, "very normal people," and Levin liked them, except Ferris Farper, a heavy-faced man with eyeglass frames too tight for his head, who glowered at him whenever they met until Levin grew uncomfortable. Farper would not forgive him for acquiring Duffy's office. Levin controlled his feelings until he discovered that Farper, after using the toilet for whatever purpose, did not wash his hands; he then returned him dislike for dislike. During October the instructor was invited home by Millard Scowers, O. E. Jones, and Dave Fitznogle, all from upstairs.

With the exception of Levin, CD Fabrikant, and Avis Fliss, everyone in the department was married. Some had been at fantastically young ages, and Levin envied them the years of loneliness they had escaped. There was much talk of domestic matters: kids, houses, the high cost of living. In self-defense a surprising number of men were expert at fixing any mechanical apparatus—cars, washing machines, flush toilets, hi-fi sets. Courtney Haddock, Maurice White and Gene McElfrish teamed up to clean a blocked sewer, pour two yards of concrete, and install a twenty-five foot television antenna. They discussed these jobs with theoretic and practical knowledge that made the instructor feel he had been born on another planet. Gardens were carefully kept up. Leaves were raked—speared almost as they fell—into piles on parking strips for the town truck to haul away. No wonder Levin missed the odor of burning autumn leaves—it wasn't allowed. Lawn mowing went on and on. Let the sun shine a minute and Ed Purtzer, whose house was two blocks to the college side of Mrs. Beaty's, changed into shorts and sweatshirt, rolled the mower out of the garage, oiled and adjusted it, then shaved his lawn, raked the cut grass, edged and combed the one-inch turf until it resembled his own stiff haircut. If a shampoo for grass were on the market he would have used it.

Most of them were specialists at saving money—of necessity on their salaries, although Levin felt one or two went above and beyond the call of duty. Dave Fitznogle could quote from memory the latest *Consumer Reports* ratings on anything from baby diapers to Piper Cubs. John Cutler, another upstairs man, was fanatic about auctions. He attended those in Marathon on Tuesday nights and bought things at bargain prices. One night he bid a dollar for a case of corn flakes and to his surprise, got it. Cutler couldn't stand cold cereal so he gave boxes of it away to colleagues and neighbors. Thanks to his generosity Levin enjoyed two weeks of inexpensive breakfasts.

During the fall the men in the coffee room talked about flying saucers, five percenters, TV, Ben Hogan's golf comeback last June, hunting, fishing, their army experiences, and the graduate school ratrace. There was talk about the weather; they congratulated themselves on its mildness. Although books were mentioned they were rarely discussed, and Levin continued to confide his thoughts of what he had read to his notebook. At ten and three, when Professor Fairchild appeared in the coffee room, there was standing room only. The old man, his cup in hand—he never seemed to drink—discoursed humorously on politics. His subject usually was creeping socialism, where it crept, the tyranny of the New Deal, which Easchester had four times voted against, and the evils of federal aid to education. No one questioned his argument or contradicted his facts. Even after he left, controversy did not begin. If there was a mild discussion it ended in agreement. The men or the times? Levin wondered. He had been told there had been "some hot arguments" when Duffy was around. If there was no visible fear in the department—no one spoke the word—Levin presumed an innocence or vacuum he did not inquire into. He was afraid to.

Gerald Gilley often sat alone in the coffee room. Levin, on his way to Milly's office or the water cooler, saw him on the bench, long legs comfortably crossed, his finger on the loop of a half-empty coffee mug dangling down his knee, eyes reflectively lit; or the cup full and thoughtfully rising to his puckered lips. Seeing the instructor going by, Gilley would lift his arm in greeting; most often he seemed not to know who was passing, involved with his coffee, the sipping so satisfying he smiled as if the brew were bewitched to some useful purpose. Levin envied him his particular cupful, the same brand he tried at night when he had a set or two of themes to knock off before tomorrow, only it didn't jazz up his dreams. If Gerald, examining the interior of his coffee mug, saw a vision of the future, it seemed to please him.

He was, as director of composition, cordial and generous. He never stopped giving Levin things, ordered for him a Webster's dictionary, S. LEVIN lettered in gold on the cover, brought in a flowered tin wastebasket, desk calendar, red-ink ballpoint pen, handy for grading; and he predicted the arrival of a foam rubber backrest for the instructor's chair, and a replacement, soon, of the cracked window that split the campus scene. "You're too kind," Levin said humbly, and Gilley blew his nose. It could truthfully be said he didn't know who next to give what. Levin wondered what the secret of his good nature was—constitution? the woman he had married? Maybe it was the years he had lived in small towns, his nervous system protected from city pressures, city grind? Maybe a combination of these things? Levin was curious about Gerald's experience—his life seemed to have gone along evenly—and he wondered if he had ever been ecstatic or miserable. And with wondering Levin wished him continued good fortune.

One morning Gerald knocked on his door. "Coffee, Sy? I mean tea? We could go across the street to the Student Union for a change?"

"Thanks, Gerald, I just had my cup." He nodded at the mug on his desk.

Gilley shut the door quietly and sat in the visitor's chair. "I've been thinking we could drive out to the coast tomorrow, if you're agreeable, and do some salmon fishing. There's a river

I fish that gives up some good catches on eggs and flashbait. The fish are beginning to color—they get bruised up by this time of the year, but they're still in good condition. I've more than once taken Chinooks out of the water weighing thirty or forty pounds. What I do is bring my outboard motor and rent a boat. There'll be plenty of room for you, George, and me. I could lend you a spinner and a couple of lures. The regular license is five dollars but maybe we could get you a one-shot visitor's permit for a dollar, or skip it altogether. I haven't seen a warden all year."

"If we went I'd better pay," Levin said. "I get socked when I try to get away with something." He thanked him for the invitation. "I would like to go, Gerald, but frankly, I happen to be loaded down with papers just this week. Maybe we could make it some other time?"

"Sure," said Gilley, "we'll do it in the spring." He didn't seem too disappointed. Still it was nice of him to ask, Levin thought.

Gilley looked absently out of the cracked window, then at Levin. "How's it been coming, Sy? Your work and all that? Do you like it here?"

Levin said he did.

"Good deal."

Gerald after a minute asked, "I was wondering if you had heard of Professor Fairchild's impending retirement next summer?"

"Only that and no more."

"Orville's had a distinguished career here. He's known all over the state. Still," he said, "there's a lot to be done in the department." He had lowered his voice. "He's a little on the old-fashioned side and that's hindered us a bit. I say this loyally, you understand?"

"Yes, of course." Levin felt his throat tighten.

"I hear the new dean has a change or two in mind for us. The right sort of thing, I hope, because change just to change

102

is senseless." He sounded moody. "Wouldn't you agree with that?"

"Sure," said Levin.

Gilley brightened. "If I were head here there are a few things I'd be inclined to start off with. First, I'd ask for at least five additional positions. Comp, as you know, is running thirty to a class, about five too many, ideally ten, but who has money for the ideal? And some of our lit sections go up as high as sixty. If I could bring them down to thirty–thirty-five, we might have some class discussions instead of concentrating on lecturing. This is confidential, Sy, but Orville's a little tight on budget matters. He prides himself on keeping costs down, and I'm for that myself, a hundred percent, but with a little more depth on the bench we'd be a better department."

Excited, Levin thought. This is his vision.

"Would you agree with that?"

"Certainly."

The director of composition wet his lips almost invisibly.

"If you happen to have any suggestions of your own for improving anything I'd be happy to hear them."

Good of him, Levin thought, but I'd better lay off.

"I'm really serious about that," Gilley said.

"In that case," Levin said with a thick tongue, "maybe I ought to say I think English 10 is a good place to begin teaching writing. I hate to mention this, Gerald, but some of the freshmen think a paragraph is a new invention. And I'm not against grammar but I'm against—I don't care for only grammar. For the boneheads it's torture."

"Bonehead is bonehead, Sy," said Gerald. "That's why they're there, to get the drill they didn't get before. As for paragraphing in English 10, that's an idea, but some of the men would shoot anyone who suggested more paper work in that course."

"The continuous workbook stuff is deadening."

"You've got your reader."

"We could stand one for the bonehead course, something

with a little variety to it. I respect science and technology but it's not enough for growing boys and girls."

Gerald smiled. "I'll say this, I've thought of some of the things you're talking about, but frankly, Orville swears by the course as it's given. Still and all, whatever ideas you have for improving comp I'd be glad to listen to when the time comes. I like suggestions given in a friendly spirit by people who are aware of what the practical problems are and how long it took to build Rome."

Levin decided he had said all he was going to. He stroked his beard, twice yawning.

"Anyway," Gerald said, "I have no doubt that we see eye to eye on the important things."

Levin nodded.

"And I can count on your support?"

The instructor left off pacifying his whiskers. "Support?"

"What I have in mind," Gerald said, "is that I would like us all to work in harmony after Orville retires, to make this the kind of department it ought to be."

"I'm for that," said Levin.

"Good." Gerald extended his hand and Levin took it. "Every man counts."

The instructor, without knowing why, blushed.

Gilley, looking at his shoe, then at the mountains in the distance, said, "Maybe you've heard there might be some sort of contest between Fabrikant and me for the department headship? Have you talked to him yet?"

"A little, is about all I can say."

"He's a Harvard graduate and all that, good scholar but stiff as a board. I have seniority over him and I think Orville would like me in after him. That's just between us, please. It's not favoritism either. Years ago Orville offered CD the directorship of composition but he turned it down, so I got it. I've been doing the dirty work while CD has sat behind a locked door, writing his literary papers. That's why Orville favors me."

"In that case, why worry?"

"I'm really not, but we do have this new dean and, frankly, people in power are just plain unpredictable. If he starts calling department members into his office to consult them about a choice, I want them to know what I stand for, although I admit it's embarrassing going around talking to everyone. Pauline doesn't like it either."

Levin shrugged. "Practical politics."

"I'm glad you understand, Sy."

Gilley was getting up but sat down. "By the way, would you want a phone of your own put in here so you won't have to be running to Milly's office when she buzzes? I got George one two years ago."

"Who would I call?" Levin asked.

"That reminds me," Gilley said. "Pauline has been talking about having you over but there's been a million things and the kids already have colds. Erik starts off hacking and then little Mary picks it up."

"Spsssh," said Levin. "Plenty of time."

"I just want you to know we've been keeping you in mind. Pauline finds it a little hard to get started entertaining after the summer. She says the town is over-organized—just too many things for everybody to do and she's in a lot of it, though I've been begging her to cut down. Tires her out. She's on the Library Committee, the Community Chest, and the Women Voters—they're trying to do something about the sewage and she goes to more damn meetings till all hours. I try to get her to ease up but she says it's all worth while, so she wears herself out. We've been a little snowed under but we expect to see more of our friends soon."

Levin thanked him.

Gilley got up. "One last thing. One of the textbook salesmen is after me to do a freshman reader. Would you care to lend a hand? It'd be mostly finding suitable articles and writing up a few questions and notes. After paying off contributors we could expect a yearly five or six hundred apiece for about half a dozen years. After that we could revise without too much

trouble and the thing could go on and on. Nobody gets rich—
Orville's sales are unusual, but the money is nothing to sneeze
at either."

"Thanks, again," Levin said, blowing his nose. "Maybe
sometime, but you know how it is on a new job. You have to
work at it for a while before you have any spare time on hand."

Gilley grinned. "I think you work too g.d. hard, Sy. You
ought to have more fun. I'm getting worried about you."

Levin, on the verge of cracked laughter, peremptorily cut
it out.


Over the week-end, in blasts of wind and rain, the walnuts
began to fall in the backyard, plopping down on dead leaves
and sopping grass. When Levin saw what was happening he
ran out with Mrs. Beaty's big aluminum pot to collect them.
The nuts were large, their shells glowing orange when they
fell from the broken pods. He greedily cracked one open and
tried eating it but the meat was rubbery. When he brought
the loaded pot into the kitchen, the landlady set aside those
with broken shells and scrubbed the others with a brush. She
showed Levin where to put up an old window screen, on
pipes above the furnace, for the walnuts to dry out on. All day
Levin went often to his window and when he saw any nuts on
the ground, ran down the stairs with the pot. In bed, for hours
he heard the nuts socking the wet earth in the dark. At dawn
he quickly gathered them up, not at peace until all the walnuts
were in and drying, and the tree was bare.

Leaves fell in the rain in droves, multitudes, refugee mil-
lions—maple, oak, chestnut, walnut, pear, cherry, mountain
ash, and the large alien sycamore leaves from across the street;
like a soggy blanket they covered gutter, sidewalk, lawn, backyard, bushes and alley. Levin resisted raking them until he
could no longer stand his resistance. One afternoon after class
he began to work. He raked first the front lawn, then the sidewalk and swept it clean, carrying wet bunches of dripping
leaves to the piles on the curb-strip. He raked under each shrub

and handpicked the bushes clean. Although it was soon dark and he was tired he continued to gather leaves. By the light of the street lamp he scraped up those along the curb, and then in the light from Mrs. Beaty's kitchen window, raked the backyard. He raked wearily, without thought, both palms blistered, arms and back aching. The landlady, through her window, begged him to stop but Levin raked to destroy all dead leaves. He went on in a misty drizzle, stacking the back-yard leaves on the mulch pile behind the garage. When he was through, at an unknown hour, the grounds around the house were neat and clean yet he regretted not having got at the leaves in the gutter.

The instructor was thinking of going to Gilley to make it clear to him that he wasn't committing himself to anyone for head of department until he knew more than he did about both candidates. Instead, on impulse late one afternoon, Levin knocked on Dr. Fabrikant's door down the hall. Though he had passed the scholar in the hall more than once, his white socks visible as he walked, his bachelorhood unyielding, they had not talked since the time Levin had visited his farm.

He was in, Levin heard him cough. He waited until something that sounded like a bolt was withdrawn. Fabrikant stared out at him.

"Excuse me, I—"

But the scholar held the door open. "Come in." Off his horse he looked less formidable. And he turned out to be, without a hat, bald, yet in need of a haircut around the pelted head.

His office, as Levin had expected, was overrun by books, including loose-paged piles on the window sill, radiator, and spare desk in the corner of the room. On his desk he had laid out rows of note cards, thickly scribbled; these ran onto the floor. Levin, envying work in progress, would have liked to know what the scholar was doing, but he had heard from Bucket that he was secretive about his research. Feeling with both hands among the paraphernalia on his desk, Fabrikant located a cigar butt, lit up, shaking the match out over his head, then pointed with the smoking stick to a chair. Levin, after stepping gingerly over the cards, removed half a dozen books from the chair and seated himself.

"I would hate to interrupt something important."

Fabrikant puffed his cigar butt without comment. "How are you coming along?"

"I can't complain."

"I can and do." The scholar laughed his two syllable laugh. "Do you like the West?"

"Yes, I do. Everybody's friendly."

Fabrikant, regarding him, grunted. "I wouldn't live in the East again if they offered me the mint. I've often thought if the capital of the United States were located out here we'd have a lot more sanity in our national life."

"I left New York on my own accord—"

"It was sensible."

"—seeking, you might say, my manifest destiny."

"This corner of the country was come upon by explorers searching for the mythical Northwest Passage," Fabrikant said, "and it was opened by traders and trappers in their canoes trying to find the Great River of the West, the second Mississippi they had heard of. Then the settlers came, fighting the Indians, clearing the land, and building their homes out of their guts and bone."

"Marvelous," Levin murmured.

"'There were giants in those days,'" Fabrikant said moodily. "Their descendants are playing a defensive game. Their great fear is that tomorrow will be different from today. I've never seen so many pygmies in my life."

"That's very interesting," said Levin. "It reminds me what you said last time: that if I was a liberal I might be called on to prove it. Those were your words and would you care to elaborate a little?"

Though his butt had gone out, Fabrikant still puffed. He

puffed and said nothing. Levin grew uncomfortable. In his mind he began to search for an exit.

"Did I say that?"

"Something of that nature."

"I was annoyed. Frankly, I didn't like the circumstances of your hiring."

"Me?" Levin had partially risen.

"Yes," said Fabrikant. "The arrangement is for the three senior members of the department—Fairchild, I, Gilley—to look over applications for positions and make a choice. I wrested this morsel of democratic procedure, together with a course or two, out of them some years ago, but in your case my approval was omitted."

"I'm very sorry."

"It's true that there was an emergency when the man we had hired in the spring reneged in summer and a new selection had to be made in a hurry. Fairchild was in Walla Walla at his daughter's, and Gilley, without consulting me, acted on his own. He later contended he had tried to get me on the phone at my house but couldn't. My answer to that was he ought to have driven over to the farm, because he knew my sister was in the hospital with her sciatica and I am usually on the premises. He didn't bother and made the selection alone. He hired you."

"Ah—I'm sorry."

"No fault of yours."

Levin felt low. Once in his life he hoped to be somebody's unchallenged first choice.

"After talking to you," Fabrikant said, "I was satisfied Gilley had blundered into a suitable appointment. Nevertheless, I have to insist on the few prerogatives I have here."

"I understand," Levin said. "What I was referring to before is that since there seems to be a contest of some kind developing, I thought I ought to inform myself what your ideas are for running the department, if I may ask."

Fabrikant was deathly silent.

My God, have I jumped the gun again? Levin asked himself. "I—er—hope the question is not out of order?"

"No," said Fabrikant, "but I'll answer only if it's understood I'm not politicking. I don't care for that."

"Of course."

"If I become head of this department," Fabrikant said, "I'll change plenty." He gazed gloomily at the book-lined wall. "But this is all premature. I don't know that I'm even remotely considered as a possibility. There's been talk that the new dean may want—but that could be no more than rumor. At any rate whoever they may or may not have in mind for the job, I'll say without false modesty that I am at all odds the logical choice. They can't match my educational background, nor my research and publications, granted that they mean something in this institution, which I won't grant."

"I have heard that you were being considered—"

"Possibly. This is strictly confidential, but the administration hasn't always been happy with me. I've espoused more than one unpopular cause in the past."

"Like Duffy, for instance?"

Fabrikant grimaced. "Let's forget him."

"Excuse me—"

"I've been too independent for them. I haven't made friends or influenced people. Gilley has made a career of that. He's always washed Fairchild's dirty drawers so the old man could be free to potter with his textbook. Such devotion is not for nothing."

"Does Mrs. Gilley approve of that?"

"I have no interest in Mrs. Gilley," Fabrikant said. "Since you've brought this matter up I'll tell you what I would try to accomplish in the department. First of all I'd ask this new dean to do something drastic about salaries. Fairchild is stingy, so was Dean Feeney, a conjunction of two constipated stars in the same constellation. For years they kept us dancing in our bare bones; as a result, this department is the lowest paid on the campus. If Fairchild had gone bellowing to the president

110

that he employs human beings, Labhart might have done something more than throw the poor dog a bone."

"Tst-tst."

"Before I brought it to a stop Fairchild wasn't spending the pittance we were allowed for a library allotment and was turning part of the money back to Dean Feeney, who assigned it to those departments who were overdrawn on theirs."

"That's too bad—"

Fabrikant drew on his dead cigar. "By the way, what are we paying you?"

"Me? Three thousand a year."

"That's scandalous. You should be getting thirty-five hundred, at least."

"Without college teaching experience? I taught for two years in a high school."

"Even so you're ridiculously underpaid."

"Dr. Gilley said he would have given me more if I were married."

"What's that got to do with your ability to perform your task? I'm not married and proud of it."

"I'm just saying what he told me."

"We have a few good men here, most of whom I've insisted ought to be hired, but their efforts are frustrated by those who came to teaching to hide their ignorance. I'll name no names. I'd throw them out if I could and bury the rest in composition."

"Could I ask what you'd do in composition—to improve it?"

"I'd throw out *The Elements.*"

Levin gulped.

"He's got stinking rich out of that atrocity."

"Er—What is your position on the liberal arts issue? Would you try to bring back English majors?"

"One couldn't unilaterally," Fabrikant said. "That's a political football and would have to be worked out with our idealistic friends at Gettysburg. Of course I'd plug for the return of the whole liberal arts program, but keep in mind that this situation

111

has existed for thirty years and nothing's going to change it overnight. I don't think the majority of this faculty is interested in a good liberal arts program."

"But some are?"

"Very few and that includes those in our own division. They've lived in the graveyard so long I doubt they'll ever come back to life. I'm frankly pessimistic and don't foresee any change in the situation during my lifetime. It takes fifty years to grow a tree and that sort of thing influences people's ideas around here."

"Shouldn't we start propagandizing—working, that is, for the idea, to recover what we once had? With the right leader we—"

"There's only one leader at Cascadia College and that's Marion Labhart. What he wants is what we get."

"Couldn't it be suggested to him?—"

"It has been, but it won't do any good until he falls over it himself. One has to be careful with that type."

Levin imagined the scholar hadn't been.

Fabrikant dropped the cigar stub into the wastebasket and rose. So did Levin.

The scholar fixed him with his gloomy eye—it was almost without iris. "I'll have to caution you again to be discreet about our talk. In my position a man has to think along more than one track. If Gilley should be chosen over me I'd still have to live with him."

"I won't say a word." Levin stepped over the note cards on the floor. "Thanks, I've—ah—learned a lot."

Fabrikant lifted his shoe to strike a match, then realized he had discarded the cigar butt. He shook out the match and tossed it into the wastebasket. In afterthought he poured half a glass of water into the basket.

Levin had the door open but shut it. "Do you happen to know how much Mr. Duffy was paid?"

"Thirty-seven hundred."

"I guess he had more experience?"

"He had never taught before."

"You don't say? Er—Would you know any special reason or circumstance why I was chosen over other applicants for the job? Was I the only one who was willing to take three thousand?"

"As I told you, Gilley didn't consult me."

"Thanks anyway." Levin left.

A minute later he was back. "Sorry to bother you again. This popped into my head but I forgot to ask you. They're showing a good film downtown tonight and I wondered if you'd be interested in seeing it? We could have some coffee after—that is, if the idea appeals to you?"

"Thank you, no," Fabrikant said. "I don't go to the movies, too darn much sex."

Levin guffawed.

The instructor had discovered a rich night life on the second floor of Humanities Hall. He found not only Bucket at his lamplit desk—door wide open for he felt it unnatural to work in silence after living with five kids—but also George Bullock, usually with a half dozen six-footers sitting around his desk; and Avis Fliss typing or mimeographing objective tests for her remedial classes. Levin heard from her that Gilley popped in once in a while, and it was rumored Merdith Schultz also came in but no one tried to prove it.

Levin had several times spoken with Bucket, but only in passing, for the assistant professor was one of the few genuinely busy men in the department. When not in class he had one or more students in his office, who came early and stayed late. At night Bucket banged away in a fast hunt-and-peck on the latest revision of his dissertation. He worked in the same cement-stained levis Levin had seen him in on the roof, and in socks, his army shoes on the floor. Since he was always so busy Levin preferred not to bother him, but one rainy night in early November, shortly after his talk with Fabrikant, after twice wandering past Bucket's open door without attracting his attention, the instructor knocked on the jamb.

Bucket hastily covered the papers on his desk with a folder and swiveled to face his visitor.

"Could I see you for a few minutes?" Levin asked.

"Please come in."

"I won't stay long. I know what your time means to you."

Bucket cackled. "I've meant to visit with you but you know my situation."

"Tst," said Levin.

"It could be worse."

"I admire your patience."

" 'Tis known by the name of perseverance in a good cause,— and of obstinacy in a bad.' "

"Sterne?"

"Touché."

Leaning back in his chair Bucket rested his shoeless feet on the desk. He reconsidered and withdrew them.

Levin sat with his handkerchief in his hands.

Bucket glanced covertly at the typewriter but waited patiently.

Levin sighed. "I've been teaching here five weeks, half the term, without a feeling I'm accomplishing much. I'm up to par," he went on quickly, "according to the syllabus, but short on satisfaction. Maybe you can advise me?"

Bucket glanced out into the hall. "You might keep your voice down."

Levin peered through the door but saw no one. "If you'll pardon me for saying so, I'm so busy with *The Elements*, trying to cover what I have to for the departmental objective, that there's very little time for much else."

Bucket nodded.

"The themes I've been getting are short on ideas, and I've had to take time off in self-defense, though the syllabus doesn't call for it, to teach how to organize and develop a topic. I know they're supposed to know—"

114

Bucket nodded.

"Er—The *Science in Tech* essays, when we do get to them are something less than inspiring, for which I blame not the subject but the selection. I blamed myself until I read them again. Believe me, I can understand why Duffy ordered outside readings."

Bucket, poking his head into the hall, quietly shut the door. In afterthought he snapped the lock. Stepping into his shoes, he polished his glasses and sat back in the chair.

"The way the world is now," Levin said, "I sometimes feel I'm engaged in a great irrelevancy, teaching people how to write who don't know what to write. I can give them subjects but not subject matter. I worry I'm not teaching how to keep civilization from destroying itself." The instructor laughed embarrassedly. "Imagine that, Bucket, I know it sounds ridiculous, pretentious. I'm not particularly gifted—ordinary if the truth be told—with a not very talented intellect, and how much good would I do, if any? Still, I have the strongest urge to say they must understand what humanism means or they won't know when freedom no longer exists. And that they must either be the best—masters of ideas and of themselves—or choose the best to lead them; in either case democracy wins. I have the strongest compulsion to be involved with such thoughts in the classroom, if you know what I mean."

"I do," said Bucket, "but if we all did that who'd be teaching composition?"

"That's what I tell myself but it doesn't help much."

"Take my advice and don't introduce any extraneous text into the course without Professor Fairchild's express permission."

Someone knocked on the door.

When Levin realized he was looking for a place to hide, he composed himself by smoothing his beard.

Bucket, after a quick glance around, got up and turned the lock.

George Bullock was standing in the hall, blinking at the

light, his hat and trench coat soaked. His sharp nose and narrow cleft chin inclined him to hatchet-faced.

"Raining," he said.

"So?" said Bucket.

"I heard voices. Thought Gerald might be here." His glance fell on Levin.

"Sorry," Bullock said to Bucket.

Bucket shut the door, he seemed uneasy.

"Was he listening?" Levin asked.

"Sh." The assistant professor kept his ear to the door until they heard footsteps going down the hall.

"Don't you like him?" Levin asked.

"That's a difficult question."

"Excuse me for asking."

"We're not friendly, a case of mutual disapprobation." He put his ear to the door again, then sat down.

"What does he do here at night?"

"He tutors athletes twice a week."

"Athletes?"

"Bullock seems genuinely concerned about them as under-privileged people. Sometimes he has more than a half dozen a night who are having trouble in composition or literature, or both."

"Is that an assignment?"

"As I understand it, no official source has commissioned this particular occupation. Bullock apparently thought up the idea on his own and no one opposes it. At first it was a completely voluntary, and, I suppose, generous act on his part, but then the Physical Education department heard about it and insisted on paying for his services. I've heard no complaints about it. I understand that Leroy Davis and someone else from upstairs, have pitched in now and then, at George's request, to help. He's a popular figure with the athletes. Last Christmas Eve the football and basketball squads serenaded him and Jeannette on their front lawn. They held white candles and sang carols."

"Why would a Ph.D. in English be so interested in athletes?"

"The breed has infinite varieties." Bucket cackled.

"Is that sort of thing cricket?"

"Some say no."

"Er—Shouldn't something be done about it?"

"Possibly—under the right circumstances."

Levin pondered his remark. "You mean if the right person gets to be head?"

"I'll say no more."

"I'll go now."

"You needn't rush."

"I've wasted your evening."

Bucket denied it. "I'll be revising this accursed paper forever."

"Then one more question: I've lately talked to Fabrikant and Gilley—I've heard that either one or the other may be the next head. They're different types, that's sure, but both very conscious of the limitations of whatever powers they might have in the future—in other words, what they can hope to accomplish here. I'm a little more favorable to Fabrikant, I like his point of view, but I like Gerald too, as a person. I have no illusions that my support, or the lack of it, will mean anything much to either of them but just so that I know what I'm doing, who's the better man if you don't mind saying?"

Levin put away his handkerchief and Bucket pulled his out and mopped his brow.

He said in a low voice, "My own considered preference is for CD over Gerald."

"Aha."

"That of course is strictly confidential."

"Of course."

"Gerald, in his way, can be an efficient administrator. He may someday be dean of something or other, but CD, in my opinion, is more truly interested in literature and literary scholarship and would be more effective in raising our standards. Although I agree with your observation that there'll be few daring innovations under either man, yet what comes with CD will come with increasing value."

"I didn't mean—"

"When I say 'raising our standards,'" Bucket hurried on, "I speak without disrespect for Professor Fairchild, an old and much-liked teacher of mine. I've often thought it a shame that he did not devote himself entirely to teaching. I'll testify he does it well."

"Does Fabrikant have a chance at the job?"

"Your guess is equal to mine. I understand the situation is fluid. No one I know quite understands the preference of the new dean in all this. One hears all sorts of rumors."

"Is Gilley at all liberal? His wife sounds as though she might be."

"I wouldn't judge him by her."

"He was dead set against Duffy?" Levin asked, one hand investigating his beard.

"That describes it."

"And Fabrikant defended him?"

"At the outset."

"Something happened between them? Was it some sort of fight?"

"I don't think I'd care to go into that."

"Were they ever friends?" Levin asked.

"I believe they respected each other but that's as far as it went. They were both very independent people and tended not to attract one another." Having said that, Bucket stepped out of his shoes.

"I'm leaving now," Levin said, "after this: When Fabrikant dropped Duffy's defense in the AAP, wasn't there anyone else to take it up?"

"He had become universally unpopular."

"Was he, with you?"

"I personally liked him, though I can't say I liked everything he did."

Levin rose at last. "Thanks for your time."

"Think nothing of it. I rely on your discretion." He said it with an inquiet laugh.

"Have no fear," said Levin.

He tried grading papers but could not keep his mind on it and left the office. Downstairs he waited on the porch for the pouring rain to let up, thinking of his talk with Bucket.

Whatever's happening here, he thought, I'd better not get involved.

The door behind him opened, George Bullock. "Want a ride?"

Levin looked at the night. "Thanks."

"Wait'll I get the wagon," Bullock said. "No use both of us drowning."

In a few minutes he drew up to the curb in a mauve station wagon and Levin ran down the steps and ducked in. He noticed at once a whiskey odor, and Bullock, as if sensing it, lit a cigarette. He was an intense man and drove with his head thrust forward, his sharp face like a ship's prow directed against the saturated night.

"I'll take the Bay Area winter fog to this soup anytime."

"Is that so?" said Levin. "I heard in the coffee room you had recently turned down an offer from a college in Frisco."

"Nobody but Easterners say Frisco."

"Excuse me, San Francisco."

"Your information was correct. My wife loves her mother. I figure better us alone in Cascadia dew than mama living with us in the California sunshine."

"Aha," said Levin.

"Now that we're sharing confessions, and without meaning to be personal, I didn't know you were palsy walsy with Bucket."

"Er—Shouldn't I be?"

"Who said so? I have nothing against the guy even if he does talk like the *New York Times*, but what makes me uncomfortable is the futility he gives off. Of all the people to write about: 'Laurence Sterne: a long digression.'"

"What's wrong with Sterne?"

"That immoral twerp."

"You don't say?"

"Have you read Thackeray on him?"

"No."

"You should." Bullock shook his head. "What were you two boys doing with your heads together? I bet Bucket played up CD Fabrikant for head of department?"

"His name was mentioned," the instructor said warily.

"Bucket overrates him, take my word. CD is a fair-enough scholar but starched like my granddaddy's collar."

"I hear he's had a hard life?"

"Who hasn't."

"You've had?" Levin asked.

"At fourteen I was crippled by polio. The doctor said I would never walk again."

"Tst-tst."

"So much for medical science. In college I ran a hundred yards in eleven seconds."

"Wonderful," Levin murmured.

"Have you read any of his stuff?" Bullock asked.

"Fabrikant's?"

"Yes."

"I expect to."

"Be sure to go over it with a vacuum cleaner."

"It's dusty?"

"You'll die sneezing."

"No good insights?"

"They were decrepit when he came on them."

"Ah, too bad," said Levin. "I like the thought of having a good scholar in the department."

"Goddam, imagine bibliographing Civil War fiction." Bullock snickered.

"Is that what he's doing?"

"That's what he told Avis. She drops in to see him every once in a while and he looks at her legs. That's the only time he keeps his office door open, to show he's not seducing her. What kind of head of department would he make if you have to get to him with a crowbar?"

"More important," said Levin, "is does he have qualities of leadership?"

"Who leads behind a locked door?—unless it's Casanova, which he's not."

"Sometimes the door opens and out comes a man with a sword."

"If you think so he's your baby."

"I've heard some of the men speak of him with respect."

"Maybe so, but they know Gerald is the better choice. He gets along with everybody, and don't think that's so easy. He plays pinochle with Labhart and they golf together. When the chips are down I'll bet lox to bagels that Gerald will get more for the department than CD ever could with his history of antagonizing the administration."

"Are you referring to the Duffy case?"

"No, that time he was safe on base."

"When he dropped the AAP defense?"

"Yes."

"Would you happen to know why he did?"

"Didn't Bucket tell you?"

"No."

"Maybe Duffy pissed on one of Fabrikant's Persian melons. Or the old boy finally discovered what everybody else knew all along, that Leo was a fake. Up to then they had a sneaking admiration for each other as members of the maverick's union. What Fabrikant liked about Duffy was he did what *he* didn't dare to. Leo was the oddball's oddball, he hit the wall with his head. CD is a Milquetoast Quixote."

As they turned onto Levin's street, Bullock said, "I'll tell you what let's do. Let's shoot over to my joint and see how much comes out of the rum bottle when we squeeze. Jeannette's a sociable girl and would be happy to have you."

"Thanks," said Levin, "but I'm behind in themes."

Yet when the station wagon stopped in front of Mrs. Beaty's house, he lingered.

"What I don't understand," Levin said, "is why everybody is choosing sides. Will our advice be so important to whoever makes the choice?"

Bullock shot his cigarette out of a window he had lowered. "It was an appointive job at one time but may not be now. Gerald was a shoo-in until they dug up Seagram from the cornfields of Iowa. This former buddy of mine who teaches where he did, wrote me the dean had done a study for some foundation or other on the new rage—departmental elections. Charlie says he's bugs on the subject. Well, whatever the method is, appointive or elective, I have my dough on Gerald. He's the logical choice."

"An election?" Levin felt excitement.

"Nobody knows for sure, but nobody's taking chances." He winked in the glass. "Realpolitik."

The instructor, with the door half open, had another thought. "Ah—when did Gerald first get wind there might be an election?"

"I told him last spring after I heard from Charlie that Seagram was coming here. Why?"

Levin shrugged. He pulled the door shut and went with Bullock.

On days the rain let up Levin still walked on country roads. Once he passed a barn where he thought he had been with Laverne. He thought of her with desire, up to when Sadek entered. After weeks of rain he thirsted for color, the eye seeking it in whatever light. White birches stood in baths of tiny yellow leaves. Elms had golden hair and naked black bodies. Chestnut trees in strong sunlight wore orange impasto. Vine maples, the only adventurers, flared yellow, red, and purple around green at the core. In the setting sun maples turned bronze, and oaks red. Toward Thanksgiving, except for willows, flaming vine maples, and a few tenacious birch and oak, most of the trees that had leaves to lose had lost them, bare except for patches of soggy brown rags and abandoned birds nests.

It seemed to Levin that just when he was about to take the

loss, the yearly symbolic death of nature, to heart, he discovered that many of the recently harrowed fields were touched with bright green grass that turned out to be winter wheat. Bread growing in the harvested field—this went against pathetic fallacy. One day as he was walking outside a forest trying to persuade himself (against the NO HUNTING, FISHING, TRESPASSING warning) to enter and explore, he heard strange noises in the sky, and looking up, beheld for the first time in his life a flight of geese. The fluttering, honking formation of birds was like a ship borne by the wind into the high invisible distance. Levin's ear burned all night, as if soaked in pitch and set on fire. He wondered what omen the flight held for him and hungered for a victory over nature.

Leaving Humanities Hall late one Friday afternoon, the instructor skidded on a wet leaf on the porch and his books and papers took to the air; he landed on the wet walk, whacking his head. Star clusters popped in his brain. For a second he thought he would remember everything in his life and braced himself not to. The rain drizzled on him but he was too hurt to move. He was vaguely conscious some students, possibly his own, were passing by, but either he was invisible or they were in a hurry. I am a man alone, thought Levin. It seemed a long year but only minutes had gone by before he dragged himself up, found his soiled new hat, collected wet books and papers, and hobbled home.

Levin lay on his bed with Mrs. Beaty's ice bag tucked under the egg at the back of his bruised and aching head. After twenty minutes' freezing his brain he got up and stared out the dark window. None but the lonely rain. The instructor riffled through a wet set of quizzes, then thrust them into a drawer where he kept his bird watcher's guide and a pair of cheap binoculars he had recently bought to follow things in flight. Supper, Levin? He had planned just a Swiss cheese sandwich and a cup of tea but decided he could not stand Mrs. Beaty's mental health in the kitchen tonight. Sadek, the clothes snatcher, was long since gone with his Lysol bottle, and the landlady, possibly because she realized she was ageing, had not attempted to rent his room; which suited Levin fine. But he longed for company tonight and considered calling Avis Fliss, though not with great enthusiasm. He was disappointed at how lonely he still was after almost three months in Easchester. Was the past, he asked himself, taking over in a new land? Had the new self failed? He had had invitations here and there, but as Pauline and others had told him, it was tough to be a bachelor in this town. Without a family you were almost always left out. Even Bucket had never invited him to his house. Levin wanted friendship and got friendliness; he wanted steak and they offered spam. Each day his past weighed more. He was, after all, thirty, and time moved on relentless roller skates. When, for God's sake, came love, marriage, children?

Opening a book, he looked down a page without reading, then tossed it aside. In the cellar he filled the sawdust hopper and left the house. Levin walked in the cold rain, the wettest, dreariest he had ever been in. The town was tight around his shoulders, the wet streets long and dark, street lights obscure at corners. A man could drown mid-block and nobody would know. It was after eight but half the houses he passed were totally dark. On rainy nights people went to bed; it was, after all, a diversion for the married; another was the small blue images of television he occasionally glimpsed through drawn curtains. Levin listened, as he walked, for a human sound and heard himself walking in the rain. He stood for five full minutes at the next street corner, not knowing which way to go, finally wandering toward the Gilleys.

Half heartedly he rang the bell. A light in a glass barrel went on over his head and Gerald opened the door. When he saw who it was he seemed embarrassed.

"I was passing by," Levin explained. "But if you're busy or otherwise occupied, I'll make it some other time."

"We're late getting the kids to bed," Gilley said. He glanced back into the house. "Come on in if you can stand the mess."

He spoke without welcome so Levin held back.

"I'll make it some other time."

"Was it department business?"

"No, I was just walking by—" He looked at the rain.

Gilley peered out. "Better come on in." He held the door open.

Levin, relieved, entered, and Gerald hung up his soaked raincoat and hat.

Pauline, in her violet pants, came out of the kitchen with an armful of diapers. Seeing who it was she let out a little shriek and darted up the stairs. Levin was nervously having a beer with Gilley when she reappeared in a green woolen dress. Five minutes ago in pants, uncombed hair, flat chest, she had all the appeal of a pine board. Now, with the same apparatus, the green dress, her hair brushed, she seemed to glow. She knew how to use what she had, not a bad talent.

"Excuse me for coming without phoning—"

"Excuse *me*, Mr. Levin. I hope I didn't scare you out of your normal growth but I hate to be seen in my pants."

She giggled at the way she had put it, Gilley mildly eyeing her.

"Gerald," Pauline said, "please stack the dishwasher while I get Erik out of the tub before he goes down the drain. Excuse me for one minute, Mr. Levin."

"I came at the wrong time," he called after them.

A few minutes later, Erik, in bunny pajamas, waddled in from the bathroom and went through Levin's beard with both hands.

"Any bugs in it?"

"Butterflies."

The boy tugged at the whiskers, then ran with a little cry to the kitchen. He pushed open the swing-door and Levin saw Gerald and Pauline facing each other across a table loaded with dirty dishes.

126

"We've got to get started entertaining again," he was saying with emotion. "It's hurting me in the department."

She grabbed the butter dish and flung it at the wall. It hit the electric clock. The butter stuck to the face of the clock as the plate crashed to the floor.

Gilley yanked Erik into the kitchen and the door snapped shut.

Levin put down his beer and got into his wet raincoat and hat. He was headed for the front door when Pauline, flushed, entered the room.

"Oh, you're not leaving yet, Mr. Levin? We haven't exchanged a word."

"I've got this headache," he explained, removing his hat and showing her his bump. "I slipped on a leaf and hurt my head. Tell Gerald thanks for the beer."

She touched the bump gently with cold fingers, Levin conscious she smelled like a flower garden. "I'm awfully sorry, can't I get you some ice?"

"I've had some." He moved towards the door.

"Try us again soon," she called after him through the open door. "We'd honestly love to see you."

He hurried away.

The rain had thinned to mist, and a part-time moon wandered amid the broken pieces of sky. Walking on the campus, Levin was drawn to the Student Union by the sound of dance music. He watched a dance through the barred ballroom window. The girls were prettier than they had ever been, the men with more possibilities than that morning in class. He stood there for a half hour, envying them their looks, their youth, their future. His own was imprisoned in the old Levin. Where is my life? What has become of me? he asked himself. Ancient questions. Once more the music began, the same he had heard in another time, in another world. Though Levin made no sound, his shoulders shook.

My youth, my lost youth.

After recovering from Levin's beard Avis Fliss took to visiting him in his office to discuss the tactics of teaching remedial grammar, sometimes staying so long he grew restless. Her virtue was her unique fund of information concerning department and college routine; she always knew what was due when, and usually had it in first. And she seemed to know the activities and accomplishment of everyone in the department. On a more primitive level his eye was drawn to her bosom and ungirdled behind. Whenever in her presence he found himself thinking of her as a woman, he sensed a response but wasn't sure. What bothered him about Avis was that as soon as she came close to revealing something personal, her eyelids fluttered autonomously, her voice took flight, and when it returned she launched into a long digression addressed to his shoulder. He had, however, learned she had stopped off at Easchester several years ago, after a summer school vacation in Alaska, to surprise an old friend. The friend had been married and was gone, but Avis, possibly inspired by the event, had stayed on where it had taken place. Although she had only a bachelor's degree, she had taught in a well-known private girls' school, and Professor Fairchild, with Gilley's vote —despite Fabrikant's lack of enthusiasm, "though not against the lady personally although I don't like having too many around"—had put her on in the flourishing remedial program. Fairchild, therefore, was a "dear," and the director of composition, whose unofficial assistant she was, "tops." She praised him as an able man with a lovely little family, although she said once in passing that his wife was not entirely suited to him.

"Really?" said Levin. He asked her why she thought so.

"Well," she said, with a hesitant laugh, "she strikes me as the sort of person who can't always be depended on to strengthen a man's rear when he's on the march."

"On the march?"

"Advancing careerwise."

"His rear?"

"Figuratively speaking. Please don't misunderstand me, Seymour, I have nothing against Pauline. She's been nice to me, especially when I first came to Easchester, kind with invitations to their house, though I suspect Gerald had to ask her to ask me. What I have reference to is that she gives the impression of being dissatisfied in the midst of plenty, and I imagine some people wonder whose fault that is and unjustly blame Gerald. She can also be absent-minded about her social responsibilities, which rather disturbs him."

"What do you mean 'in the midst of plenty'?"

"What any woman would consider herself lucky to have."

"To me they look like people who generally get along. I could be wrong."

"Oh, they do," Avis said. She seemed worried. "Please don't quote me."

One Saturday night, Levin, with nothing to do, drifted up to the office. Down the hall Avis' door was open but apparently no one else was around, Levin wondering if Bucket were sick. He began a letter to a second cousin, a lady in Cleveland who sometimes wrote to him, when Avis knocked. She was looking for a match, but when he had none, discovered a last one at the bottom of her purse. She stayed to smoke, resting one buttock on his desk. They talked of this and that, then books, then poetry, and were soon reading aloud to each other from an anthology. Levin read several stanzas from "The Eve of St. Agnes," and Avis read Tennyson's "Flower in the Crannied Wall." One poem led to another, and soon Levin, taking Avis' bashful hand, gently drew her down upon his lap. A blessed thing, poetry.

They kissed, Levin suffused in her orange blossom and tobacco aroma, then kissed again more deeply.

"Your whiskers tickle," she laughed, her bosom heaving. "You ought to cut them off."

"Never."

"For a person who isn't handsome, Seymour, you act as though you were."

"Ha ha," laughed Levin.

After another breathless kiss Avis suggested they go for a drive.

"Fine," he said. "Where's your car?"

"I was thinking of yours."

"I have none."

"Oh, too bad. Mine's in the garage having its valves ground."

"Tst-tst." To test what she had in mind, he said, "We could walk if you don't mind the rain."

She coughed bronchially.

He was considering his room. They could sneak up the back stairs, only Mrs. Beaty was tonight entertaining some club ladies. If sex was approaching Levin wanted it without the worry of visitors.

"What about your place?" he asked.

"I daren't. The landlady's teen-age daughter sleeps in the next room to mine."

He was weighing other possibilities when Avis hopped quickly up out of his lap.

"What was that?" She listened tensely at the door. "I thought I heard footsteps."

He listened. "Nothing."

Levin was aroused. They kissed at the door. He felt for her nipple. Avis pushed his hand away.

An old maid, he thought, I'd better not.

"Would you rather go to a movie?"

"Would you?" Her eyelids moved like a bird's wings.

"Then let's be honest," Levin said. "Will you come with me to a hotel?"

"Not in town. We'd be recognized as faculty people. I know I would. So would you with your beard."

"We could take a cab to the one in Marathon. It wouldn't be too expensive."

"The night clerk in Marathon is one of my former Grammar Z students," Avis said. "Couldn't we stay here?"

"In the office?"

"Might we?"

Levin seized a practical suggestion. "Gladly. I'll spread my raincoat on the desk."

"The desk?" She hesitated. "It seems sacrilegious."

"I hate to mention the floor but what else is there?"

"I have a blanket I keep in my office for football games," Avis said.

"Marvelous. Shall I go get it?"

"You'll find it in my closet."

Levin went for the blanket. When he got back she had her dress and shoes off and was in brassiere and half slip. He folded the blanket lengthwise on the floor, then removed his jacket and tie.

As they were undressing they heard unmistakable footsteps coming up the stairs. Avis frantically stepped into her slippers and pulled on her dress. Levin got his shirt partly buttoned, and tie on, knotted badly. He helped her zip her dress.

A knock sounded on the door.

"Sy?" The voice was Gilley's.

Levin shuddered. The danger was if he said nothing Gerald might open the door with the common key.

Avis frantically gestured: answer.

"Here," Levin said. He said, "Avis is with me."

There was a pause. "Could I see you?"

"Why not?" He heaped the blanket and kicked it under the desk. Avis had seated herself and poked her dead nose into a grammar text. Her poor neck was rigid.

"I saw the light under your door," Gilley said. He had a mackinaw and boots, and was holding a hunting cap.

Avis smiled dimly. "Hello, Gerald." She looked a wreck.

Gilley's eyes roved uneasily but Levin's glance assured him the blanket was invisible.

"Avis has been helping me in Grammar Z. She says I'm trying to cover too much in an hour."

"Good," said Gilley. He said he had come up for a book for Pauline. "George and I are taking off for some early shooting.

We usually snooze in his wagon and are right on the spot when the ducks fly in. Pauline hasn't been sleeping too well lately and she wants something by Hardy around. All we have home is *The Return of the Native*, which she reread recently. Have you got something by him in your bookcase, Sy, maybe *Far From the Madding Crowd?* Maybe you have, Avis?"

"No, Gerald, I don't care for Hardy."

Levin searched his shelves. "Here's *Under the Greenwood Tree* in paperback."

"I don't think she's read that. Could I give either or both of you a lift?"

"Not me, thanks," Levin said.

"Nor me," said Avis. "I promised to return a set of quizzes Monday. Now that Seymour has his lessons in shape I think I'll go back to my office and finish grading my tests. I hate to work on Sundays. Good night, gentlemen."

"Good night, Avis," Gerald said.

"Good night," said Levin.

She walked quickly down the hall.

"Thanks for the book," Gilley said. "Don't work too late, Sy."

"I'll quit soon." Levin yawned. "Got a letter to my cousin to finish up."

Gerald lingered. He doesn't believe me, Levin thought.

"Give my best to Pauline. I hope she sleeps tonight."

"She has these periods." He said after a minute, "I'll make a note to have this window Duffy cracked, replaced."

"I would appreciate it."

Gilley said, "Listen, Sy, you might as well know the boss is very strict about the separation of the sexes in offices. That's why he's never allowed a man and a woman to share one."

"You don't say?"

"I just want to give you an idea how he thinks."

"I'm much obliged."

Still Gilley stayed. "Avis is a very nice gal, but if I were you I'd keep in mind that women her age who aren't married can be upset pretty easily. Well, so long."

"Good night, Gerald. Tell Pauline I hope she sleeps well."

"She will. She has these periods on and off."

When Gilley had gone, Levin rested his head on his arms on the desk. His galloping heart slowed down to a fast trot. He finished his letter and was thinking of leaving.

But then Avis was back, freshly made up, her orange blossom renewed.

Her eyelids throbbed. "Shall we—go on?"

Levin peeled his jacket, snapped the lock, and again spread the blanket.

"This time we'd better put out the light," she said.

When her brassiere came off, her breasts, handsome under clothes, hung like water-filled balloons from her chest. Levin shivered a bit, that splendid bosom formless. Still, for a starving man—

Once more they embraced, Levin in white shorts, Avis in pink panties.

He snapped off the light. Again she stopped his hand when he touched her left breast. "Not that one, it hurts."

"Hurts?"

"Feel this." Her fingers guided his. He felt a long scar on the underside of her breast.

She said she had once had an operation. "It was a benign fibroma. Now I have another and the doctor says it's the same thing but I'll have to have it out anyway, I imagine during the Christmas vacation. Here's what hurts when you press."

He felt a hard spot under his fingers.

Levin snapped on the light.

"Why, what's the matter?" Avis asked.

"I'm sorry for your breast."

"Don't worry about it. You may fondle the other."

Poor dame, he thought. She has little, why should I make it less?

He wavered indecisively, then reached for his pants and drew them on.

"I don't understand," she faltered. "Aren't you—aren't we going on?"

"When we have a better place, when you feel better," Levin said. "I don't want to hurt you."

Avis dressed quickly, grabbed her football blanket and left furiously.

To escape occasionally from town and loneliness, Levin, after much debate with himself—having consulted Bucket and Courtney Haddock, who knew about second-hand cars, bought himself one. He had arranged with a student of his, Lyman Myler from Los Gatos, another expert, a former hot rodder now majoring in automotive engineering, to accompany him to a used-car lot. Almost everyone of his freshman could drive, and most of them owned cars, usually new, but not Levin. Lyman helped him settle on a 1946 Hudson, a brown, two-door, five-passenger sedan, which though it sagged a bit in the rear, was in decent shape; and Levin agreed to pay three hundred and fifty dollars, a sum it made him nervous to owe anybody. He later learned he had bought ex-Dean Feeney's trade-in for the latest model. The Hudson didn't look like something he had dreamed of, but at least it moved on wheels, and so might Levin. He knew the town and a mile or two beyond, but not much more. It was time to venture forth.

Lyman drove the Hudson home and parked it in Mrs. Beaty's garage. The next day he gave Levin his first driving lesson. The instructor fancied he would learn fairly quickly but found himself less apt than he had expected. He couldn't understand how it was possible to shift, accelerate, turn, while watching direction, signs, and traffic—a confusing task for a mind that was non-mechanical or had come too late to mechanics. At the same time he felt a useless anger against himself for not at once mastering this carapace of tin over box of oil-soaked nuts and bolts. Two weeks later he knew the operation of the car but still overshot corners and skidded against curbs when pulling to a stop. He was uneasy in traffic, especially when making left turns off busy streets. What bothered him most was that he was careless in ways he would not have predicted: momentarily lost in thought he could forget stop signs, and which was one way in a one-way street. Twice Lyman had to grab the wheel to prevent a mishap. As a result, Levin had his fears of the car and said so. Lyman said, "We all have to die sometime sooner or later."

"Better later," Levin muttered. "I have not yet begun to live."

Lyman said Levin would feel better once he had passed his test and driven a hundred miles alone. However, Levin seriously considered giving up the car and going back to walking. He was at best a bus and subway man. As for loneliness, better than a car was a girl; he would look actively now.

A few days later he failed his driver's test and went home humiliated, convinced he must part with the car. Lyman offered to see if one of his frat brothers was interested, and Levin agreed to sell for three hundred dollars. He was ashamed of himself and mildly depressed. But after supper that night he sneaked downstairs, and backing the Hudson out of the garage, took off alone, a feat to begin with. It was of course raining and he felt a throb of satisfaction when he turned on the windshield wiper and it worked. Levin drove slowly in the rain, his heart beating thickly over the illegal thing he was doing, at the same time thinking he had never before so clearly seen raindrops falling into light. He felt intensely the danger of the adventure, pictured himself blundering into accident, arrest, being forbidden to drive in Cascadia, possibly sent to jail. It would all get into the paper, and everybody, including his students, would know him for the fool and lawbreaker he, by nature, was.

Bent over the wheel, peering into the dewy gloom, he drove in the emptiest part of town, practicing turns from street to street, and later—heart high and dry—drove downtown. Almost at once he saw the police car coming his way and felt paralysis of arm and leg; but when the car with its spinning blinker passed him, neither of the cops giving him so much as a glance,

Levin headed for the main highway out of Easchester. He drove for three miles at his fastest speed ever, a breakneck forty-five—then not to tempt fate, turned at a gas station and drove back. Behind him on the misty light-studded highway lay San Francisco, ahead Seattle, cities he longed to see. He pictured the U.S.A. as a structure of highways and freeways, Levin at the wheel, embarked on one leading to another, speeding up hill and down in his trusty Hudson, his lance at his side, driving through a series of amorous and philanthropic adventures. Home safely, though his legs trembled when he stepped out of the car, he was all in one piece and marvelously elated.

After passing his driver's test and getting his license, Levin was giving some thought to calling Avis Fliss, if at all feasible, when an attractive girl in one of his classes, Nadalee Hammerstad, began to haunt the surprised forefront of his mind. One day as they were sitting together in his office, discussing her latest theme—she had come in to ask about her grades—Nadalee, imperceptibly leaning forward, nuzzled her hard little breast against Levin's lonely elbow. He moved his arm as if bitten although somehow managing not to be abrupt, at the same time considering the touch unintentional—someone else wouldn't have noticed. He continued talking about her paragraphs, and although he could almost not believe it, the breast again caressed. To test whether this was his imagination overworking, Levin kept his arm where it had been, and the girl for the third time gave him this unmistakable sign of her favor as he droned on about her writing, his thoughts in the wild wind. Two minutes later she thanked him for his criticism and left with a happy smile, not the vaguest sign of a blush on her, although Levin glowed as with high fever.

He had noticed her more than once, a slim girl with short dark-brown hair, pretty, with greenish eyes, mature face, and shapely figure. Although her lower lip was thin and she used eyebrow pencil a bit smearily, she had a way with clothes. Whereas the other girls in her class were contented with skirts and sweaters of pastel shades, or blouses, Nadalee fitted into tight dresses and favored bright colors, a blessing on rainy days. The freshman girls smelled of body heat and talcum powder, but she wore a spicy perfume, which when it touched Levin's nostrils, never failed to interest him. When she slid into her seat in the second row he knew it without looking. There was about her a quality of having been and seen, that made the instructor feel he could talk to her. And she wrote well, sometimes imaginatively. He felt let down when she was absent. Still, he paid her no special attention, and had given her not much thought after class until her visit to his office. After that she was in his mind so tenaciously it wearied him.

Nadalee took on a private uniqueness, a nearness and dearness as though he were in love with her. Although he told himself he wasn't, she had in a sense offered love, and love was what Levin wanted. Though he tried diligently to cast her out of his thoughts, she sneaked back in with half her clothes off to incite him to undress the rest of her. He tried to figure out how to achieve an honorable relationship with the girl. If they were elsewhere in another season—if let's say, in the Catskills in July or August, he might with comparatively undisturbed conscience have taken a bite of what she offered. But here in Easchester, at Cascadia College, English 10, Section Y, 11 A.M. MWF, she was his student and he her instructor, in loco parentis, practically a sacred trust. Levin determined to forget the girl, but his determination was affected by hers. Nadalee appeared in class, the day after the time she had upset him in his office, in one of her prettiest dresses, a thickly petticoated affair, white with wine stripes encircling hips, belly and breasts. She crossed and uncrossed her slim young legs enhanced in nylon stockings. On her narrow feet she wore black ballet slippers in which, without much trouble, he could see her on her toes in *Swan Lake*, himself the evil magician.

Surely, he thought, this dressing up isn't for me; and though he went on in class as if he knew what he was doing, he could not keep from desiring her—to consume and be consumed. Afterwards, alone in his office, his chest palpitating as though he were contemplating murder, or flying off on a roaring drunk, Levin reread her themes and in one came across a biographical bit he couldn't understand why he had forgotten. When she was eighteen she had spent a summer on her uncle's ranch in Northern California. In the afternoon when it was hot Nadalee rode her horse to a small lake surrounded by pine trees, tossed off shirt and bra, stepped out of levis and underpants, and dived into the cold blue water. Though Levin's legs cramped after a too hasty immersion in cold water, he jumped in after her and spent most of the night swimming with Nadalee.

The next day the sight of her skirt clinging to her thighs was enough to upset him. After once glancing at her, every line lovely, conscious of his relentless consciousness of her he vowed not to look again, and managed not to that morning, but it was worse later when he was alone. Desire butchered him. He beheld his slaughtered face in the mirror and stared at it, wretched. How escape the ferocious lust that enflamed and tormented his thoughts as it corroded his will? Why must Levin's unlived life put him always in peril? Why obsessively seek what was lost—unlived—in the past? He had no wish to be Faust, or Gatsby; or St. Anthony of Somewhere, who to conquer his torment, had nipped off his balls. Levin wanted to be himself, at peace in present time.

He tried various means of self-control: exhortation, rationalization, censorship, obfuscation. One trick was to think of the girl as his daughter. He was her old man and had watched her grow from a thing in dirty diapers. At twelve she was menstruating; on her eighteenth birthday Levin married her off to a successful lawyer, to whom she bore seven children in six years, all boys. Her father, ever a man to be tempted by every damned temptation—life had plugged him full of sockets and it took only a slight breeze to make a connection—was safe and sound in her invasive presence, until by a dirty stroke of fate (try as he would Levin-père could not reverse it) the lawyer expired of a heart attack from overwork. But Nadalee was financially provided for, so Levin went off to Europe to live, traveling from country to country this side the iron curtain. It couldn't be said he didn't enjoy his life, though where exactly was home? Several years later, in Sevilla—he was then fifty-five going on fifty-six—half drunk on val de peñas one festival night before the corrida, he met this masked beauty at a costume ball. One tango led to another, the dance to a sense of fundamental intimacy—what, after all, is a dance? So, whispering together—Levin confessing most of his sins, including advancing age, the señorita saying nothing of importance—they left for his suite at the Hilton. First they ate. George, the fine waiter, served wild asparagus, a plate of cold meats, manchiego cheese and some dry white capri, iced in buckets; after coffee a bottle of anis del mono, which tasted like licorice and warmed all the way. Then they made love. The masked beauty refused—despite the inconvenience, which she argued was tit for tat for his grizzled beard—to remove her disguise until it was unalterably too late. When he looked at her true face at dawn, he groaned at the misery he had committed. Levin thereupon put out both eyes and threw himself off a high cliff into the shark-infested sea.

He argued with himself: I have evil thoughts, expensive to my spirit; they represent my basest self. I must expunge them by will, no weak thing in man. I must live by responsibility, an invention of mine in me. The girl trusts me, I can't betray her. If I want sex I must be prepared to love, and love may mean marriage. (I live by my nature, not Casanova's.) If I'm not prepared to marry her I'd better stay away. He exhorted himself: teach her only grammar, the principle parts of verbs, spelling, punctuation—nothing not in the syllabus. He would not let the casual brush of a girl's breast against his sleeve seduce him into acting without honor. The self would behave as it must. She would not make a fool of him, much less a worm. He would, in denial, reveal the depth of his strongest, truest strength. Character over lust. By night, after these terrible exertions, including two cold showers, Levin's mind was comparatively calm—he had bludgeoned desire, and though exhausted, beaten half to death by the bloody club he carried against the self, felt more or less at peace.

About a week later, Levin encountered Nadalee, one morning, in the college bookstore. He had been wandering among the book tables and looked up, experiencing overwhelming relief to find her by his side, for he had at once seen her as she was—diminished from a temptress into a nice kid. Levin observed with interest the errors of her face and figure, the thin underlip, too heavily penciled brows; her legs less than slim although not actually skinny, and her childlike ballet-slippered feet. Objectivity, if it did less for her, did more for him. It was her youth that moved me, Levin thought. Also her unexpected favor. He desired those who found him desirable, a too easy response; he must watch this in himself.

Nadalee said she was looking for an entertaining novel and could he suggest one: "It's a gift—a birthday present for guess who?—me, I'm twenty today."

Levin congratulated her. "Twenty, did you say?"

She explained why she was two years older than most freshman. "You see, I worked in a bank before coming here." But the bank had bored her, so she had quit and registered, with some financial assistance from her father, at Cascadia College. All this was news to Levin, though he tried to sidestep the impression it might be good news. Could good news be bad? Her age, perhaps, explained her maturity. Yet twenty was not too different from eighteen. Before he could decide how different, if different, or where or why different, he hastened to think: she's still too young—ten years between us—a kid. Just look at her feet. Besides I'm her teacher.

Levin found her a novel, tipped his hat, and left for lunch.

Later, to prove he trusted his strength he telephoned her to ask if she liked to walk. "Madly," Nadalee answered. Since she honestly interested him, he had made up his mind it would be better for his nerves if he saw her now and then, in a Platonic relationship. A walk, a bit of a drive here and there, at most a movie in a neighboring town. Company, talk—a blessing under the right circumstances.

They met in the park by the green river. She came in cardigan and skirt, carrying a poplin raincoat; Levin had his on. They wandered along the bank of the Sacajawea. The morning had been gray but this afternoon was blue, infused with light of the invisible sun.

"Don't you just love the day when it's like this?" Nadalee said.

"Very much."

"Look at those clouds in the west. How would you describe them?"

"Vaporous, toiling."

"Tempestuous, like some people's emotions?"

"Whose, for instance?"

"Yours."

"You are observant," he said with a sigh, "mature."

"I'm glad you finally noticed."

Levin bent for a stone to scale on the water but it sank with a plop.

"If you had any idea that I am a little-innocent," she said, watching the ripples in the water, "well, I'm not, if that's what you're worried about. I was once engaged to be married."

The wall he had so painfully built against her, against desire, fell on his head.

He asked in hidden anguish, "Why do you tell me that?"

"Because I am a woman and wish to be treated so."

"By me?"

"Yes, if you must know."

"But why me?" he asked.

"I guess you know I'm different than most of the other girls in your class? I'm tired of college boys. I want real companionship."

"But why me?" Levin said. "There are other men around, graduate students, instructors, some handsome."

"I bet you'd be better looking without your beard."

"No, I wouldn't."

"Anyway, the answer is you happen to appeal to me. I've always liked the intellectual type. I like the way you talk, it's very sincere."

He was humbly grateful to her. They were standing under a tree and impulsively kissed, her young breasts stabbing his chest. They kissed so hard his hat fell off.

Levin said, as they went on, hands locked, "I don't have to tell you Nadalee, the need for absolute secrecy? Many people would not understand or approve this. It could make trouble."

She said she had thought of that and had a scheme for them to spend some time together alone if he agreed. He agreed. Her aunt, Nadalee said, owned a little motel on the coast. She was planning to visit her daughter in Missoula next weekend, and whenever she left she closed up and lit the no-vacancy sign. There wasn't much business at this time of the year, only occasional tourists and some hunters or fishermen. Anyway, Nadalee had promised to look after the place and they could have it to themselves. "We could walk on the beach and the dunes, and picnic and ride around, and just sort of relax. My aunt won't get home till late on Sunday."

Levin resisted every sentence but his imagination was whipped to froth. Who could resist Eden?

Came Friday. He was resolved to go but not necessarily to collect. The fun was having a place to go, companionship, not something he could unfairly get from the girl. He was obliged to treat her responsibly. He would explain this when he got there—she had left by bus that morning but he had a one o'clock to teach; it had been decided they were not to go or come back together. Let's be friends, Levin planned to say. If we can honestly be, later we may think of sex. It will come more pleasurably to friends—a two-fold blessing. That he had reached this conclusion satisfied him. After trimming his beard a half-inch around he drove out of Easchester in a marvelous mood.

For the first time in his life Levin was on the road alone in a car—his own—carried along on his own power, so to say. Three cheers for the pioneers of the auto industry; they had put him on wheels to go where he pleased! He thought with pleasure of the many things he had learned to do in his few months here: had mowed frequent lawns, the grass still green and growing in December; raked a billion leaves, fifty percent from neighboring trees; gathered walnuts in October; picked yellow pears; regularly attended and even cleaned Mrs. B's rumbling sawdust furnace, and so on and what not. Last week he had washed and waxed his car. Levin the handy man; that is to say, man of hands. And here he was with both of them solidly on the wheel, miraculously in motion along the countryside, enjoying the compression of scenery. Heading towards unknown mountains in voyage to the Pacific Ocean, world's greatest. Imagine, Levin from Atlantic to Pacific—who would have thought so only a few years ago?—seeing up close sights he had never seen before: big stone mountains ahead, thick green forests, unexpected farms scattered over the hillsides, the ghostly remains of forest fire, black snags against the sky. Something else new: a little too close for comfort he passed a log truck, surely half a block long, pyramided high with enormous tree trunks, heavily chained, thank God. Here and there millponds were afloat with brown logs, to be fished out and cut into boards. He whizzed past a smoldering, tree-tall furnace shaped like a shuttlecock, a black slash burner that consumed wood waste, its head ablaze at night. He was discovering in person the face of America.

And the weather was better than the newspaper had expected. For short intervals warm sunlight—through thick clouds breaking into sky streams—lit the fields; some harboring sheep, a few with starlings on their backs, picking a living out of the wool. At times the clouds massed darkly, yet the day managed to be cheery, and the bright green winter wheat yielded hidden light. Levin guessed the temperature was around fifty, and this they called onset of winter. It said so on the calendar, and Mrs. Beaty was airing her winter undies and talking of Christmas. Who immersed in Eastern snow and icy winds could guess at Cascadia's pleasant weather? Here, Bucket had told him, spring came sometimes in midwinter; autumn in the right mood might hang on till January, and at times spring lingered through summer. A season and a half they called it but Levin would not complain. Only a week ago he had caught the odor of a white rose in the best of health on somebody's front lawn. So what if they paid in wetness for the mild climate; the warmth made up for rain, and wasn't it wonderful to be riding to the beach in December? Who but a polar bear would indulge in the Bronx?

He saw stone ascending and discovered himself doing the same. "Holy Moses, I'm up a mountain." As the road turned, his startled sight beheld below a vast forest of pointed conifers, and as he emerged from a corkscrew curve, a mass of peaks— rocks and shadow—extended into the dim distance. "Alps on Alps arise." His heart leapt at the view but when he realized how narrow the ledge he was traveling on, how sheer the drop if he dropped, his heart settled with a wham and he found himself toiling at driving. WARNING, SHARP CURVES. He was sweating to master them as his tires screeched, rolling the wheel as if fighting a storm at sea; to stay on the road yet keep from hitting anything that might come zooming around the bend—ahead invisible till he got there; also to move fast enough to satisfy the irritable pest behind him, sprung up from nowhere and blasting his horn till Levin had a headache. He was doing twenty and considered crawling at ten but didn't dare with this madman behind him. He tried to signal the fiend to stop with the horn, or quell him with a dirty look in the mirror, but no signals worked and he had to keep his eyes glued ahead for fear of losing the slightest sight of the perilous, tortuous road. Another blast of the horn filled him with rage and dismay. He considered stopping and getting out to grapple with his nemesis, but luckily the road widened a few feet, and Levin pulled hard against the side of the cliff to let the monster pass. He furiously shook his fist as a dilapidated Chevy squeezed by, the pee-wee driver with a snip of black mustache, more Chaplin than Hitler, offering a thumbed nose. His dusty license plate read New Jersey—too small world. With no further stomach for tight curves, Levin considered giving his breath a rest, but since no one any longer fastened onto his tail he went his winding way, conscious of abysses deeper than those in dreams, worried that a momentary lapse of attention might send him hurtling into the murderous maw of the forest below, dead, destroyed, never to be seen again. Yet he negotiated each curve as it came, some bent into such unpredictable tormented arcs that it flashed on him he knew for the first time in his life what "straight" meant; and this insight carried him down the mountain onto a peaceful road.

Peaceful for a short happy while, then the grade rose again and his eyes widened in the dusty windshield. But Levin got used to it: Steeplechase, you did what the bear did. There were many mountains and you took them one by one, paying no attention to the rest of the family. Soon the worst seemed over. Descending, Levin was surprised to sail through a momentary hamlet, a cluster of jerry-built, long-unpainted houses around a general store with a dirty gas pump in front. Here too America; you learned as you lived, a refreshing change from books. Out of the townlet and embarked on a broadly winding level road, he hypnotically watched a puff of smoke float up from his radiator and evaporate, Levin at once apprehensive of trouble although he couldn't call it by name. He wondered whether to drive back to the gas pump, but the narrowness of the twisting road made a turn impossible. And he didn't like going back once the plan was to go forward. It was getting late, he was slow, Nadalee was waiting. He studied the hood at intervals, and seeing no more smoke, vowed not to stop until the first service station he hit. By the merest chance his eye caught the progress of the needle of the temperature gauge. It was flirting with HOT. "What'll I do now?" Levin asked himself, trying to recall what the manual that came with the car said, but remembering only confusion. So he drove on till he again spied smoke. The red needle had struck HOT. Fearing fire, he quickly brought the Hudson to a stop on the road and shut off the ignition. A cloud of steam rose from the radiator. Levin, agitated, lifted the hood. He burned his fingers trying to unscrew the water cap, then managed to turn it with a folded handkerchief. A hissing stream of steam and bubbling brown water spilled over, a pox on ex-Dean Feeney. Levin remembered having read about this under BOILING OVER.

Two hours later he was on his way again. The sun was sinking and he was very late. He had been pushed by a pickup truck to a small gas station in a logging village not too far away, whose owner-and-mechanic-on-duty had "gone home for half hour," it said on a stenciled strip of cardboard on the gas pump. Levin fretted as he waited, because he had only twenty dollars in his pocket and Friday was going fast. When at last the man had appeared, he recommended a reverse flush, and though this sounded like a bad poker hand it suited Levin if somebody who knew said so; but the operation took more than an hour, the man wandering off every so often to attend his pump or sell something. Levin walked down the road and sat on a rock watching time hurrying by and nothing he could do about it. He considered trying to call Nadalee to tell her what had happened but gave it up as too complicated. He had estimated—she had—that they would be together by four, but four had come and gone, and with it went some of the beauty of the day and the pleasure of anticipation, because he liked things to work out as planned, time and all. He seriously wondered whether to take this incident as a warning of sorts, yet cheered up when the car was ready, paid twelve dollars courageously, and was again en voyage with a full gas tank and recommended change of oil, although he had changed it last week. He warily watched the temperature gauge, suffering when the needle went up and rejoicing when it settled back. Since the coast was only thirty-five miles away, he gave himself at the very most an hour to get there, counseling calm, the fun was yet to be, Nadalee will wait for me. The road was presently good and he clocked five miles in six minutes. Although the sun had sunk, and shade arose in the fields, a golden-green glow hung in the sky. He enjoyed the stillness, each tree still, the timbered hills multiplying silence. With some misgiving he climbed a new rise. At the first turn of the road a log truck, like a fat worm pulling itself out of a hole in the earth, rumbled forth hauling the largest, most terrifying hunk of wood Levin had ever seen; it looked like a threat to humanity. He pulled the Hudson quickly to the shoulder of the road, holding his foot hard on the brake until the long truck puffed by. When Levin was ready to move he discovered he couldn't, his right rear wheel sunk in a ditch.

"I'll die," he muttered after twenty minutes of struggling to free the wheel. Not one car had come by. He pictured himself frozen to death in the Hudson during the night. In the morning they would haul off a stiff corpse; he had read of these things in the paper. Levin desperately figured he had to do something, but the right rear wheel had no respect for reason or will. He was wondering why he had come on this impossible journey when a tractor rattled around the bend and wobbled towards him. It was an old machine, the farmer driving it a wizened man with a small leathery face. He wore a wilted straw hat, and sat up on a high seat, swaying as he sat.

To Levin's astonishment the machine passed by, the farmer lost in thought; he had to yell to get his attention. With a clank the tractor came to a halt, the driver gazing back at Levin as though he couldn't understand where he had risen from.

"Excuse me for bothering you," Levin explained, "but I'm stuck in this ditch."

The farmer in silence got down from the seat, dug a length of rope out of his tool box and knotted it to Levin's front bumper. In less than a minute the Hudson was out of the ditch. It had happened so fast he could hardly believe it.

"Three cheers for the American Farmer!"

The farmer smiled wanly. "Say," he said, "could you give me a hand with some trouble I been havin' of my own?"

"Gladly," said Levin, "although I have an important engagement."

He stepped out of the car. The farmer fished in his tool box and came up with a pair of needle-nose pliers.

"Got an achin' tooth here at the back of my mouth. Could you give it a pull with these pliers?"

Levin's muscles tightened to the point of shivers. He saw himself trying to pull the tooth, breaking it, not being able to get it all out, as the man bled, and it ended by his having to drive him to the hospital. Yet he wanted to show his gratitude to the farmer for rescuing him from the ditch.

"Couldn't I drive you to a dentist?" he said. "I'm on my way to the coast."

"Can't stand 'em," the farmer said. "An' I got thirty head of Angus to look after. I'm alone by myself since the missus died."

Opening his mouth he touched a gnarled finger to the offending tooth, a discolored snag.

Levin tried several times to get the pliers gripping the tooth. "Is this it?"

"Feels like. I ain't sure."

He withdrew the pliers from the farmer's mouth and handed them to him. "I'd only hurt you without doing any good."

"Sure hurts anyway," the man said. He tossed the pliers into the tool box and climbed up on his high seat. The tractor rattled down the hill.

"God bless your tooth," Levin called after him. Failed again, he thought.

He started the Hudson and stepped on the gas. "Nadalee, I'm coming."

It was almost six. I've got to make time. He sped along the mountain road, wondering why it was so dark, then hurriedly switched on his lights, gasping as the beams flew forward and were trapped in pools of fog. A sense of doom infected him and he fell to brooding. Where is the fog, in or out? He had slowed to a crawl, every minute convinced he would the very next go shooting into space. Should he stay rooted? If he stopped where he was and escaped being smashed in the rear, he would have to stay put until the fog lifted, if it did, in the morning. If he went on how would he know if he was on the road or off—levitated in space before the ultimate crash, decapitation, dismemberment—what sort of terrible end for a man who had lived through so much in his life and had so many plans?

He drove on with droplets of mist in his beard, at ten miles an hour, and could see only as many feet ahead, frightened by awesome crags that loomed up before him and the fragments of bare rock over his head. Every few seconds he braked, sounding his horn like a wail as he went, by the greatest good luck skirting half-hidden boulders and grotesquely twisted tree trunks whose crowns were shrouded in fog. He had endless visions of disaster, monotonously called himself "idiot" for having invented this purgatorial journey. Levin promised himself he would celebrate if he got out alive.

It seemed to him, his nerves pricking through his skin, that he had journeyed for years on an abandoned road, had started as a child but was surely by now somebody's grandpa, his hair turned bone-white, although the face, when he caught a reflected glimpse of it, looked hauntingly dark. He felt he had crawled on for hours, without confidence that he knew which road was presently which, and after a while, with a sense of not much caring. He went where the road went, because it was there; where it ended he would.

He saw then, lit in his headlights, a horse—could it be?

—No, this was a mule standing immobile in the road, gazing at something in the night. It slowly came to Levin, for he was worn out, that the mule was not a nightmare; it was real and he was staring at it from a distance of thirty feet; and that the fog had broken into moving patches; the sky glowing with stars, amid them the moon. Yet even as he sighed in unbelievable relief at the lifting of the fog, the mule, like a stone statue, stood broadside on the road, impassable at either end. Ten feet from the animal Levin stopped the car and got out to see what he could do about moving it, offering first a Life Saver, gingerly holding it a foot from the mule's nose, hoping it might mistake the candy for sugar, but its nostrils didn't even mildly twitch. Levin, walking down the road in the glare of his headlights, tore up some wet ferns. He tried holding out a handful but the salad did not tempt the animal. In exasperation he hunted for a rock to bounce off its bony back, but as he was looking, gave up the thought. In the car he cradled his head on his arms folded on the wheel. The horn blast startled the mule. It gave a frightened whinny and took off in an unknown direction.

The moonlit road stretched ahead for visible miles and Levin made fast time. But after he had traveled another twenty-five and still saw no end to his journey, continuing doubts tormented him. Was he on the right road or headed for Mexico or Canada? Would he get there tonight? Would she still be waiting? With these worries he drove through a covered bridge, and as he emerged, saw headlights rising in the distance. Levin pulled to a hasty stop several feet beyond the bridge. After two minutes a car approached. Stepping out of his Hudson, Levin waved both arms and succeeded in flagging down a Dodge of ancient vintage, the driver braking to a screeching stop.

"If you'll pardon me," Levin said, "I'm looking for the coast. How far to go would you say?"

The driver, an old man wearing a large hat and rimless glasses, peered at Levin's limp beard.

"You a Mormon or somethin'?"

"Just a citizen."

"Live in Cascadia?"

"Yes."

The man lifted his hat, and with a finger of the same hand, scratched his veinous bald cranium.

"Beats me," he muttered. "Ain't it t'other way?" He pointed back over Levin's shoulder.

A minute later his car disappeared into the covered bridge.

Levin, about to collapse, tried to figure where he had gone wrong. He guessed in the fog. Somewhere in it he had missed a turn and taken the wrong direction. It served him right for his evil intentions.

As he drove aimlessly on, in sadness contemplating all the failures of his life, the multifarious wrong ways he had gone, the waste of his going, he sniffed a sea smell. Whirling down the window, he smelled again and let out a cry.

The ocean! Either the old geezer hadn't understood his question or was lost himself; maybe he had suspected Levin was a Russian spy.

He beheld in the distance a golden lace of moonlight on the dark bosom of the vast sea.

Ocean in view, oh the joy. "My God, the Pacific!"

He saw himself as stout Cortez—Balboa, that is—gazing down at the water in wild surmise, both eyes moist.

Some minutes later he asked at a service station the way to Nadalee's aunt's place. Though it was about nine when he got there, the motel was dark, no sign lit. But Levin knocked on each cabin door until a light went on in one, and the door fell open.

There stood Nadalee in a sheer nightie.

"Mr. Levin—I mean Seymour."

"Nadalee—I got lost." Before he could say where or why, she had shucked off her garment and her gloriously young body shed light as he hungrily embraced it.

In the past, Dr. Fabrikant had told Levin, Professor Fairchild, to uphold standards of efficiency and purity, had locked the composition instructors—mostly ladies then—in one large classroom as they collectively graded departmental objective exams. Although with advancing age he had changed some of his ways, under Gilley other curious customs prevailed, for instance the competition among instructors and those assistant professors who taught comp, to get done with d.o. finals on the very day they were given. Gerald said he did not encourage the race for itself, though he enjoyed races, but he liked to have comp grades in well ahead of the registrar's deadline, so he asked all possible speed in correcting papers, tallying scores, and submitting term grades. Though Levin functioned poorly in a rush, he feared being left out of things, so he raced along with the others for hours without pausing to drink or pass water.

Each exam paper consisted of two hundred short-answer questions on eight mimeographed pages, and the instructor had one hundred and fourteen students, including Grammar Z inmates, who had their own objective tests, made up by Avis. Levin hurriedly counted correct answers, making little red check marks down the margin of the page, later changing to economical dots. He totaled aloud, wrote the number of right answers at the bottom of the page and hastily flipped to the next sheet, once in a while taking a few seconds to work his fingers against cramp. He fidgeted and sweated when he heard people running up and down the stairs and hall, worrying that they might be turning in their scores while he sat with a great stack of uncorrected papers in front of him. Though the coffee room was open for business, and he thirsted for tea, he didn't dare go in, fearing to fall farther behind. Avis was the talented one at this game and usually led the pack; at the very worst she came in second to Bullock, another speedster. Her flushed joy in victory matched Gilley's beamish approval of her deed; he liked a winner.

Try as he would, Levin was no match for the professionals, although he began to like the competitive hurry and the pleasures of simple arithmetic; but he finished third from last. Gerald afterwards ribbed him and Farper, who had come in after him, for holding up the making of the departmental curve for an hour. This was the Bell graph of grade scores, which Gilley, according to set percentages, divided into letter grades. As each instructor had handed in his tally sheet, Gerald and Milly had transposed the figures to a master tally. When the statistics were in, the director of composition retired behind his locked office door and working with a slide rule he was fond of, carefully plotted the curve and divided it into segments, indicating the number of A's, B's, etc., that would be permitted. He hoped someday to have an IBM machine that would do the job, grading and all, in a jiffy. Milly then typed the statistics of the curve on a stencil, which she ran off like a newspaper extra. Gerald grabbed up these papers and strode down the hall, handing one to each man who taught comp. Ed Purtzer, formerly a track star, distributed a pile to his colleagues on the third floor.

With this latest information, the instructors were able to inscribe letter grades on each exam paper. Once they had this done, they arrived at term marks by averaging the d.o., with class quiz, and theme averages, the latter two having been figured out during the previous week by all but the hopelessly disorganized. Levin thought the competition would end at this point, since it was late in the day, dark outside, but many of the comp people returned after supper to complete grades and transcribe them on two sets of cards so they could hand them to Milly first thing in the morning. Once all grades were in, working again from the individual tally sheets, Gilley drew a bar graph in colors to show how each man had fared in d.o. results. Avis again excelled; she had the longest red bar, signifying highest number of A's, whereas Levin had a medium-size bar. Hers was twice as long as his, a fact that made him feel momentarily ashamed. He tried to find out who the man with the smallest red bar was, hoping to befriend him, but Gilley wouldn't say. Later Bucket confessed it was he.

"I never teach directly for the d.o.," he said. "These tests are distasteful to me."

"Aha," said Levin.

Levin found himself thinking about the girl Professor Fairchild had told him about during their meeting in August, the one who had cut her throat outside her instructor's bedroom window. She often popped into his mind as he was running the subtle course between encouraging Nadalee not to expect very much more of their lovemaking and pretending he wasn't. It had been a mostly happy weekend for Levin until he had left her; only then would he admit he had felt no true affection for the girl, and that was enough to undo in aftermath some of his pleasure. This reaction was an old stock-in-trade of his and did not help endear him to himself. Why he should feel no genuine affection for Nadalee after his previous hot desire for her, he blamed to some degree on the disappointment of his trip through the mountains, and also on the fact that he had perhaps too severely previously subdued his ardency for her; or if it wasn't exactly that, certainly affection had been overlaid with a fear that troubled him all along, not that she would slit her throat under the cherry tree in the backyard; but that if news of their affair leaked out, it would end his career at Cascadia with a backbreaking thump. Levin worried she might give them away by a changed attitude, or sign, however unconscious or unwilling, that the teacher-student relationship had shifted to something more personal. It turned out that for the remaining few days of the fall term there was no serious change in her, except that she pretended nothing had gone on between them, and Levin was afraid her pretense was visible. He also worried that someone might have seen them on the coast—Bullock and Gilley, after ducks—or that she might, humanly enough, say something to her roommate about her new boy friend—tickle me and I'll tell you his name—a bearded member of the English department, ravished by her charms. The roommate might, in moments of passion, carelessly blow about this information, till it landed in Professor Fairchild's lap, whose wrath Levin feared most. He wondered if the fun he had had was worth it.

But after not too long he convinced himself the girl could be discreet. She had her own reputation to protect; and suppose news of the non-paying guest got back to the aunt who owned the motel, an affront to business? Levin learned with relief that neither Gilley nor Bullock had been out for ducks that weekend. Gerald had been on a recruitment trip to high schools in North Cascadia, while the University at Gettysburg —it said in the newspaper—was working southern pastures, practically a lost cause, since most of the kids there patriotically favored the southern college. And George, according to Bucket, had been busy tutoring his athletes for the finals; he had had them working last year's d.o's. Yet when Nadalee, looking most attractive, appeared in the instructor's office one afternoon not long after their recent intimacy and suggested another fling before finals, Levin, clearing his throat, said he didn't think it would be a good idea until maybe the Christmas or Easter holidays. He also advised Nadalee to take next term's English 11 with another instructor, and she intelligently saw the point.

"But we will meet now and again, won't we, Seymour?"

"Now and then," Levin said. "We might go for walks along the river."

She looked at him curiously. "Is something wrong? Did I do something you didn't like?"

"Oh, no," he said, "nothing of the sort. It's just that we have to be very careful, I told you that."

"Then when during Christmas will we meet? I could find an excuse to stay on at the dorm and maybe we could go to your room sometime, or something like that if it could be arranged."

"That would be nice but I may be going to San Francisco during Christmas," Levin said.

"Oh, swell! Wouldn't it be nice if we could go together? I'd pay my own way, of course."

He said it would be except he had promised a colleague he might go along with him, in the other's car.

"Oh," said Nadalee.

Though they talked longer, she seemed, when she left, to have grown cool to him. He observed this with regret. He was treating her badly.

A week later, two days after the English 10 final, she was in his office again, upset, angry, on the verge of tears. It was a dark mid-December morning, the rain blurring the wet world. She was herself drenched, her raincoat and poplin hat thoroughly wet, and Levin had hung them above the radiator, to dry. She had on a pair of tight red culottes, a white sweater that cuddled her hard little breasts, and white fur-trimmed boots on her childlike feet. Levin had serious second thoughts about the wisdom of so soon having called it quits with her,

156

and even assembled a temporary plan for reclaiming her friendship, but this, on reflection, he abandoned. Yet he felt regret for the reduction, for whatever reason, of his former interest in her, and her feeling for him. If I were only in love, he thought.

She had come, it turned out, to protest her English grade. At her request Levin had mailed Nadalee her mark ahead of the official transcript, and she was clearly unhappy with the C she had got. She said, with moist, hurt eyes, she surely deserved at least a B and accused the instructor of having leaned over backwards in grading her.

"What do you mean?"

Her voice broke. "Aren't you punishing me because you did something you shouldn't have?"

Levin went to the door and listened. He listened at the walls.

"Please, Nadalee, keep your voice down."

She tightened her trembling lips as he, after a minute, spoke. "This I'll say: your term mark had absolutely no connection— it wasn't in any way influenced by my conscience, or any other feeling relative to our relationship, which I look back on with gratitude to you—if that's what you mean."

He showed her how he had worked out her grade. "First of all, we're all directed to grade the same way in comp, one-third each for class quiz, and theme averages, plus d.o. Now, going into the final, you had B plus in themes and only C plus in quizzes. I was hoping you'd hit at least a B minus in the d.o.—I was hoping for more than that, but at least a B minus to give you a B minus average for the term, which the registrar records as a straight B because he doesn't—as I understand it— like to monkey with plus or minuses because that means more clerical help. Anyway, to my deep disappointment—and I'm very sincere about it—you pulled a D for some strange reason, and that made your average C plus for the term, which is what I gave you, and that was the reason for the registrar's C. I will also admit I considered raising you to a B anyway, because, as I just said, I feel a lot of gratitude to you. But the truth of it is that what happened to us, as you must understand, has no connection with your grade and I can't give it any. I thought it wouldn't be fair to mark you on one standard and everyone else on another. Do you see what I mean, Nadalee?"

She gave up her struggle to conceal contempt. "I see there were things you could bring yourself to do when they suited you."

Levin was shaken. "If that's honestly so, and there was nothing more to it than that, then I regret it."

She began to cry. She sat in the visitor's chair and wept in her hands. He pulled a tissue out of his drawer but she wouldn't take it.

"I had the curse when I took that final. I never do well then."

"I'm sorry, Nadalee."

"You don't know how much this means to me. I was banking on at least a B."

After a while she dried her reddened eyes and renewed her lips. Though he was tempted to ask her not to say or do anything rash, he managed not to. When she left she had regained a certain composure, but not Levin.

He was uncomfortable for hours in bed that night, trying to decide what to do. Had he marked her fairly? Possibly he had gone off a bit in grading her work in class, yet that might have been to her advantage as well as not. On the other hand, since she was a better than average writer in a comp course, why not raise the C plus to a B minus and let it go at that? Damn the small difference. He would not swear in the light of eternity and/or Second Law of Thermodynamics that his B minus meant a better performance than his C plus. Who was Gilley with his iron law of grade averages, God almighty?

Bullock had once said in the coffee room that he tended to upgrade the work of girls with good figures. Levin, on his part, was inclined to favor a petitioner. A student could arouse his sympathy by saying, "Look, Mr. Levin, I'm working extra hard this term. I have reformed and hope you'll notice it." Or by telling him his father had recently died and the widowed mother was entirely dependent on the son's grades. If his "objectivity" had been influenced before, why not now for her who had slept with him? He owed her more than he had owed the others.

I can't, he thought, as he stared out into the wet night. It's the principle of it.

He had resolved nothing. When he managed to fall asleep he woke after an hour and thought of what he had thought before.

She appeared in his office again the next day. Her pale face was without lip rouge or eyebrow pencil; and without perfume her body odor was bittersweet. She looked, Levin clearly saw, like no one he particularly knew, which he blamed on himself.

"When I spoke to you before," she said, "I didn't tell you why I needed the B, because I was ashamed to. But I have to have it because I found out I have flunked my math. I need the B in English to keep from being put on probation. If that happens in my first term here, Daddy said he would make me leave and go back to the bank. He's very strict about everything, Mr. Levin."

Now she tells me.

"I can't do it," Levin sighed.

"Doesn't how close we once were mean anything at all to you?" Nadalee asked.

"It does, but not to make me dishonest."

She looked at him bitterly. "Weren't you dishonest in sleeping with me?"

"How so?"

"To your obligations?"

"Yes."

"Then would it make you any more so to raise my grade just a teeny, to a B minus?"

"Yes."

Her eyes brimmed. He found her a tissue but she flung it away, shot him a cold look, and left the office.

Levin was afraid of the worst: When her father yanked her out of college she would take him along for the ride—the end of his short careless career as a college instructor. Ah, if I could begin all over again, he thought.

That night he was back at his desk at the office, reading through Nadalee's d.o. Possibly in the mad rush he had made a mistake. Levin first went through her paper to see that he hadn't skipped a page or marked any right answers wrong. He hadn't. Then he checked the count on each page—correct— and totaled the eight page scores. He added them three times and got three different figures, one twenty-two points higher than that on her paper. He flung down his pencil.

He hurried across the hall to Bucket, who obliged by doing the addition on Milly's adding machine. It came out twenty-two points higher than the original score. Referring to the grade distribution sheet, Levin saw she would easily make a B minus, giving her the B she needed. He was elated yet irritated by his carelessness.

"Something wrong?" Bucket asked.

"What do you do if you've sent the registrar a wrong grade?"

"I suggest you ask the secretary for a 'change of grade card' and say a prayer."

"Really? What for?"

"The registrar doesn't like to change grades."

Levin, in his office, kicked himself for not having checked his additions. He took his pile of exams to Milly's desk and sat there re-adding scores on the machine. By one A.M. he had uncovered three more errors. One wasn't serious—did not affect the student's letter grade; but three of the four were. Nadalee must, of course, be raised. A veteran in her class had to go up from B to A minus; and a girl in another section had to have her grade lowered from B to straight C. The instructor held his head.

Early that morning, the Friday before the vacation began, he asked Milly for three "change of grade" cards. She handed

160

them to him, concerned behind her harlequin glasses. "They're hardly ever used, Mr. Levin."

He filled them out on her desk, writing "error in addition" for "reason for change," and then took them across the hall for Gilley's signature.

Gerald's face slowly flushed.

"For Pete's sake, Sy, three? Why, the registrar will go right through the roof. You have no idea of all they have to do right now. They'll be working through Saturday and Sunday and all of next week while the rest of us are loafing on our vacations. Each of these cards means half a dozen different changes for each student. It's a mess of clerical work, and they just can't spare that much time. The worst of it is it's entirely possible this girl you want to drop to a C may already have her transcript. Now what do you think she's going to feel like to get notice of this change?"

Levin, his beard prickly, was apologetic. "I'm sorry, Gerald, but a mistake is a mistake."

Gilley studied the three cards. "I'll tell you what we could do. Why don't you just turn in the two grade raises and never mind the other one? The girl will have a fit if she finds out her mark has been reduced. She could make trouble not only for you but for the department. Her father or some relative might call the president's office and the next thing you'd be sweating on his carpet, and we'd be hearing about it."

Levin, mopping his face, answered, "I would show him the evidence."

"It would still reflect on our good name."

"Still," said Levin, "if two changes are going to be made, why not the third? It's only logical."

After reflecting another minute, Gilley, his face resembling a lightly boiled beet, glumly gave in.

"But for crying in the sink, be careful in the future."

Levin promised and hastily left. Later he telephoned Nadalee and told her about his error.

"You mean I had B minus all the while?"

He admitted it.

"Then thanks for nothing."

She hung up hard but he felt comparatively clear in conscience.

During the long winter vacation it rained continuously, the sky a low thick motionless raincloud, the warmish wet-cold season without dry corner. After daylong rain it rained all night, the dark, liquescent, dripping from trees. When he woke in the night to heft his life, he listened to the rain as natural history, the Pacific extending itself over the land. Huge sopping clouds floated over breakers threading the beaches and struck against mountainsides, rain pouring from an armada of smashed hulls, drenching the craggy crawling forests, drowning green hills black, soaking the grasslit fields. In the dark Levin remembered the rain of his childhood, blown in wind against the faces of tenements, engulfing the leafless backyard tree in foaming bursts; but when it had ended—after a day, three, a week—it had ended and enter light, the worshipful sun. Here was no sense of being between rains; it was a climate, a condition, the water burbling, thick, thin, fine, ubiquitous, continuous, monotonous, formless. Once in a while he saw two rainbows in the same sky but after rainbows it rained. Wherever Levin went he went in rubbers, raincoat, umbrella; the only other man he saw with an umbrella was Professor Fairchild. Students stood bareheaded in the pelting rain, talking leisurely, even opening a book to prove a point. Meanwhile Levin had grown neither fins nor duckfeathers; nor armorplate against loneliness.

Bullock had invited him to drive to San Francisco with him, Jeannette, and the kids, and Levin was willing, but at the last minute George had to change his plans. Levin considered attempting the drive—for experience—in his Hudson, but he had tormenting visions of boiling over on every mountain top, being stuck in innumerable ditches, breaking down in snow, having to be towed and repaired until he was bankrupt.

So he stayed home without much to do, though there were one or two little invitations, and he was looking forward to Bullock's apparently annual New Year's Eve shindig that Gerald had been rubbing his hands over. He read a lot, sometimes putting down his book to think of Nadalee, often with desire. One night he went to the tavern to see if Laverne was there but she had quit. He thought of the barn with nostalgia. The new waitress did not interest him so he left after one beer. During the week he visited Millard Scowers and O. E. Jones, and on Christmas night saw four hundred of Dr. Kuck's color slides. All eight Buckets—he had phoned several times and knocked on their door twice—had apparently left town. Levin thought of telephoning Avis but remembered her operation. The town had little to offer of entertainment. One night the instructor drove ninety miles to see a foreign film. The next day he drove two hundred, coming and going, to inspect the University at Gettysburg. While in the art gallery there, he bowed his head for the return of the liberal arts to Cascadia College. In the evening he searched the pages of the Easchester *Commercial Budget* for some local cultural event to attend, but what were Zonta, Daughters of the Nile, Men's Loyalty Club? He was too young for Let's Be Forty but considered dropping in at a meeting of You and Me because he had heard boy met girl there. Before he could go, Levin was sick in bed.

He had caught a miserable cold. His throat burned, sour nose dripped, head ached, and he sneezed in bunches. Sleep was hard to come by; when he dozed, his raspy breathing woke him. Bullock called to say Jeannette had the flu and they were canceling out for New Year's. Levin felt himself grow depressed. He thought of Nadalee endlessly, had got her without deserving to—fruit for teacher—a mean way to win a lay. His escape to the West had thus far come to nothing, space corrupted by time, the past-contaminated self. Mold memories, bad habit, worse luck. He recalled in dirty detail each disgusting defeat from boyhood, his weaknesses, impoverishment, undiscipline—the limp self entangled in the fabric

163

of a will-less life. A white-eyed hound bayed at him from the window—his classic fear, failure after grimy years to master himself. He lay in silence, solitude, and darkness. More than once he experienced crawling self-hatred. It left him frightened because he thought he had outdistanced it by three thousand miles. The future as new life was no longer predictable. That caused the floor to move under his bed.

Levin fell into sadness, an old kind; this lonely man remembering this lonely man in the dark of a dirty room. So it went for ages, too long to think about. After came apathy; a rock with a cold in the head lay in bed, his own monument. But apathy he bore on the edge of shrieking; in iron desperation he concentrated on the sad golden beauty of a fifth of whiskey. The vision made him terribly thirsty. He reached for a bottle and found himself staring into a pair of brown eyes. Levin shuddered, no one had entered, was he already drunk? Then he saw Pauline Gilley watching him through the glass top of the back door, something like pity in her eyes. When she knocked, he craftily kept his mouth shut, but she had turned the knob and was already breathlessly in the room, naming, as she placed them on the table, what she had brought him: "Nosedrops, anti-histamine, vitamin C, a lemon for your tea, and some oranges and cookies. Excuse me for coming in the back way, but Gerald said Mrs. Beatty naps in the afternoon, and I didn't want to ring the bell."

She had removed her coat and was unknotting the black scarf on her head. Talking all the while, she picked things up, hung up his clothes, straightened the papers on his desk, saying as though it mattered she would have come before but Gerald hadn't told her until today that Levin was sick. "I had asked about you and he said George had said you had a bad cold. I'm terribly sorry."

He answered nothing, beard clotted, hair matted with sweat, the sick waste of a man. Whatever she thought she must do, let her do it and go.

Then she was sitting in a chair by his bed, facing the mess

he was, knitting an obscene gray sock. "I wish you had phoned me." Her voice was at times inaudible. It made no difference.

"There's no need for you to be alone when you're sick. My father used to say that did more harm than the illness. Would you like me to read to you? I've brought *The Woodlanders,* a book I like very much."

He waited with shut eyes for her to go. It was a matter of time. She had stopped talking. Now he heard, as he stared at the ceiling, the click of her knitting needles. When the sound was gone she would be. He waited for that so he could take up his thirst.

"The children aren't our own," she was saying. "We adopted little Mary last year and Erik the year before, after being childless since we were married."

Levin waited with cunning patience and after long silence she put away the needles and got up. The rain had stopped. Under golden clouds the setting sun flooded the room. In the light she was knotting her scarf and then he no longer saw her. Afterwards his nose bled and he could smell the lemon and oranges she had left.

Levin got up and dressed. He pulled on rubbers but omitted the umbrella. Going out the back way, he walked along wet streets, sunlight glistening on the branches of black-trunked trees, to where the houses ended and he could see the sunset over the fields. The sun had sunk behind the mountains but the sky flamed rose. Clouds in surprising shapes and colors floated over his head. One looked like a fat red salmon. Another was a purple flower. One was a golden-breasted torso out of Rubens. His thirst was gone; everything was wet, trees, puddled roads, the grassy evening earth. His misery had exhaled itself. He was once more the improved Levin.

It was that goddamned cold, he thought. If I had kept that in mind I could have saved myself pain. He regretted not having said a kind word to her; but he felt like a man entering a new life and entered.

He returned to class still dissatisfied with his teaching. English 11, "more a college course," Gilley had described it, though an improvement over last term's course, still depended too heavily on *The Elements*. Sometimes Levin interrupted drill in Workbook Form B, to speak of a good novel or read aloud a poem, the only poem some of them would hear in college, possibly in their lives. Sometimes, between a comma and semicolon, he reformed the world. But since that was irrelevant to the subject matter of the curriculum, he felt uneasy. Who am I anyway, the fourth Isaiah? And he failed more papers than he had last term. He lectured his students for the thinness of their themes, for their pleasant good-natured selves without a critical attitude to life. Then he was conscience-stricken for not patiently teaching.

A few people disappeared from his classes. When he got their withdrawal slips he assumed they had dropped English or left college, until he learned they had been in to see Gilley, who had arranged their transfer to other comp courses. Gerald admitted this to Levin once when they were alone in the coffee room. "Better take it easy, Sy. These kids have every right to be treated with respect."

"That they have," said Levin, secretly incensed, "—to be respected as people. But don't they have to earn my respect for their work?"

"You can't go lecturing them like high school kids. That's why they wanted out."

"Wouldn't it—er—have been better if you had advised them to stay with me? Since the issue was the quality of their work, if you transfer them out of my classes, aren't you really kicking my standards in the pants? Maybe you should have asked them to talk to me first?"

Gilley rinsed his cup. "My experience is that once a student has no further use for his instructor the best thing is to separate them both."

Though Levin denied the worth of the tactic, the loss of his students confirmed his fear he wasn't teaching well.

One wet January day, with Professor Fairchild present, sucking his yellowed ivory cigarette holder, Gilley convened a meeting of the composition staff to discuss the increase in plagiarized papers. Since October, the director of composition said, Avis had turned in three clinkers, he had lit on one, Farper one, and now Jones thought he had another. Gilley was sure others, as yet undetected, were around. He advised stricter scrutiny of all compositions, and consultation with colleagues if any seemed suspect. Avis had a flair for spotting work that had been copied. "Try her, Dr. Kuck, or me," he said. "Though the comp room does a good job of holding down the number of cribbed papers, some do get by us. If you suspect a theme— if it hits your eye wrong—that's a sure sign to watch out. If you can't spot its source right off, as I say, bring it to one of us. I've nailed quite a few of these tin potatoes in my time and will be glad to help you."

Levin asked what happened to a student who got caught.

Professor Fairchild removed his cigarette holder to reply, but Gilley spoke first. "Once we have certain proof, or a confession, the student is brought before the Student Dishonesty Committee. His or her instructor and I are the complainants, and he or she is advised as to his or her rights by the dean of men or women. Usually he or she fails English and is suspended from college for the rest of the term. If the case is very serious—if we have proof and he or she won't confess— we may expel him or her.

Professor Fairchild, nodding between puffs, added, "That's right. And once you've got a clear-cut case of cribbing, don't take the responsibility on yourself for judging or not judging guilt. Avoid false pity and turn the guilty one in to either Dr. Gilley or me. Preferably Dr. Gilley. It's the only way to stamp out this thing."

"That's right," Gilley said, but the old professor, with a chuckle, had begun a story: "About a year after I'd come here" —he scratched his eyebrow with one finger—"I guess it was closer to five, but no matter. At any rate, I had in one of my classes a boy I rather liked. I thought he was a gentleman until he handed me a paper I recognized at once as part of a magazine article I had recently read. You know, I had a chat with this young fellow—he came from a good family and readily admitted his error. He said he had been loaded down with engineering studies and hadn't any time left to do his English.

"I said that I'd forgive him his first offense and not take any drastic measures if he would turn in a makeup paper that same day. He did, that afternoon. It was a good paper. The boy was a competent writer—I knew that from a previous theme he had written in class, and I think I gave his makeup paper a grade of B or B plus, most likely B. But something about it didn't quite sit right with me. I woke up out of a sound after-lunch nap and began to wonder about the second paper. Something smelled fishy in Denmark. I spoke to Dr. Femur, in political science—he retired after we lost liberal arts degrees—and after some research he located the contents of the composition in an address by Theodore Roosevelt. I immediately wrote the boy's father, a successful shoe merchant, who came from Portland, Oregon, to see me. We had what amounted to an emotional session. The young man, in tears, swore on my wife's Bible that it would never happen again. I took his word, and so, may I add, did his father.

"Well, the boy handed in a third paper, but I was forewarned, and forewarned is forearmed. I asked Dr. Fabrikant— I think it was Fabrikant—" he looked around the room but Dr. Fabrikant was not present "—to read it over. He gave me the clue I needed and I located most of the contents of the third paper in the writings of John Stuart Mill. Needless to say, the boy was expelled from college. As an amusing postscript, I will add that the father wrote me an angry letter, in which he doubted my competence as a professor because I had given Teddy Roosevelt a grade of only B, or B plus, whichever it was."

He laughed to himself. "I cite this little story to show how they will take advantage of your good will, Mr. Levin, if you aren't alert and on guard. I've been hard to fool since then."

The meeting broke up, Levin pleasantly excited.

With him, to name an evil was to encounter it. In a few days he read a theme he was suspicious of. His suspicions made him nervous because one of his own painful memories was of cheating on a math final in college; he had copied from a paper a friend had slipped him—at Levin's request. But the instructor felt he had the right to judge his own students' honesty. It was the way of society: the reformed judging the unreformed. Better that than the other way around.

He compared the paper to two others the boy had written, one in class at the start of the winter term. The theme in question was a four-hundred word essay he had entitled, "Build Your Own House and Like It." Levin found this paper to be without any of the writer's usual weaknesses of structure and content, and with a kind of humor he hadn't encountered in his previous work. As a matter of fact, it was unusually good. The author of the paper, Albert O. Birdless, nineteen, from Marathon, Cascadia, was majoring in vocational education. His build reminded Levin of a young tugboat. He was stocky, with a short neck, heavy shoulders and legs, and stubby feet in square-toed shoes. His longish crewcut appeared to have gone to seed. On his head he usually wore a freshman beanie. Birdless was the exception to the almost universal rule of cordiality on the campus; his eyes were blue unsmiling marbles. He was a writer of less than average skill who did not attempt to hide from Levin his opinion that composition was a waste of time.

Since he sat in the last row it may have seemed to him that Levin paid no attention to him, because he sometimes put back his head and sneaked off a quick catnap during the hour. Levin had by now got over feeling very much annoyed with those who fell asleep on him; yet he had once or twice with a look tried to get Albert to resist boredom, and Albert had flushed and turned away. As he began to snooze one morning after a poor recitation, Levin asked him to snap out of it. He was then annoyed by the boy's scowl as he shifted his shoulders and reluctantly sat up, but the instructor suppressed a wisecrack and the incident was over. Later, passing each other in the hall, they exchanged cold glances. To some extent this bothered Levin, for there was little enough good feeling in the world and he did not like to add to the bad. Yet it seemed to him that those you chose to dislike had by some rule of economy in nature chosen you, so that narrowed ill-feeling.

Albert's average was a solid D plus when he handed in his spectacular theme. Although Levin's suspicions were at once aroused, after reading the paper he considered giving it an A under a remark that the improvement was miraculous and would he do the same next time they were writing a theme in class. But he was angered at the boy for trying to pull this on him. O. E. Jones, who had given Albert a D last term, shook his head over this paper. After some hesitation, Levin handed it to Gilley, who took in page one in a swoop, and said with a throb in his voice, "No doubt about it, Sy, this is a professional job. You've caught a rat."

Levin's throat went dry. "Are you sure? Where would it be from?"

Gilley, leaning back in his chair, reflected, one eye aimed at the ceiling. "I guess some place like *Reader's Digest* or *Coronet*. Also try *American Home* and one or two of that kind. Just thumb through the back issues of the last couple of years. Freshmen, as a rule, are too lazy to go too far back, only so far that the instructor isn't likely to pick up that same issue in the dentist's office. I don't think you'll have much trouble locating it."

"Should I ask him about it first—if he did crib it?"

"I have no doubt he did but I leave that up to you. Some ask questions first. Some would rather not until they have the evidence. Avis has a knack of going straight to the *Readers Guide*, looking over the titles of articles on the cribbed subject for a couple of years past or so, and just about right away putting her finger on the one she needs. Her last incident she had this student nailed dead to rights an hour and a half after she read his theme. We had him suspended by his dean and off the campus before five o'clock of the same day."

After class the next morning, Levin, still uneasy, asked Albert to drop into his office during the afternoon.

"What for?" he asked.

"We'll talk when you come in."

"Okay." He popped on his beanie and left.

He didn't show up till after five. Levin had his coat on but sat down.

"Anything wrong—sir?"

"Would you mind taking off your cap?"

"Yes, sir." He was able to look at Levin without meeting his eyes.

Levin asked him to have a seat. Albert, placing his books on the desk, sat on the edge of the chair. When he thought about it he sat back and crossed his well packed thighs.

"Could I smoke?"

"Yes."

But he was out of cigarettes and Levin had none to offer him.

"I'll make it short," he said. "This last theme you gave me— this on my desk—is a very skillful job. It's so much better than anything you've so far handed in that I have to ask you if it's your own work?"

Albert's unsmiling eyes were steady after a quick glance at his theme.

"You weren't helped by somebody, directly or indirectly?"

"Who says so?"

"Some students don't quite understand where citation ends and cribbing begins. Sometimes they will copy material from a magazine or book and forget to acknowledge the source. Did you happen to do something like that?"

"Every word on that paper came out of my own head," Albert said.

"Every word?"

"Some came out of the dictionary."

Levin nervously stroked his beard. "But how do you account for such an unusual improvement in your writing? Usually—you have to admit, and this holds for your last term's themes which I've also looked at—you have at least one sentence fragment in every paper. Your ideas are presented with difficulty and without humor, whereas in this everything is lucid and the humor is really funny. Your paragraphs, Albert, if you don't mind my saying so, are generally badly built. After a short elaboration you pay no attention to the topic sentence, in the rare cases where you have one. Your first two themes, with indulgence, came to D. This, though, is a first-rate A. Suppose you were the instructor, what would you think?"

"If you don't write so good, that doesn't mean you're a failure."

"I never said so. All I ask is how you can explain this practically flawless piece of work?" He handed Albert the paper.

The student opened his mouth to let in air. His voice was emotional. "I worked twelve hours on that one theme. Isn't a guy entitled to a good grade once in a while? It just so happens I know about house construction. This last summer I helped my uncle who's a builder. And if this one sounds so funny that's because there are some things that happen to be funny, so why shouldn't I write that way?"

He was staring with a wet-lipped grin at Levin's hot ear.

Levin stood up, buttoning his coat. "I guess that's all."

Albert was also on his feet. "I bet you don't believe me."

"In this case I frankly don't see how I can. This paper is the work of an educated man."

"There's more than one way to be educated."

"This is educated in only one way."

"So you think I'm lying?"

"I don't think you're telling the whole truth."

"That's what I thought," Albert said sullenly. "I know damn well you never did like me. I'm not the only one that has your number. There are a lot of other guys who don't like your class."

"You've taken a poll?" Levin inquired.

"I hear people talking. They say you never give anybody a break."

Levin denied it but Albert did not stay to hear.

The instructor could hardly wait to get to the library, after supper, to find the article Albert had copied from. His hand trembled as he thumbed through a volume of magazines. Finding nothing that night, he returned the next morning during a free hour. Albert sat at a nearby table, watching Levin over the top of an open book that covered his face to the eyes. Levin imagined a disembodied smirk hanging behind the book.

Once or twice his heart raced as he thought he had the article, but it turned out no. The third day, impatient to get the unpleasant job done with, he gave the whole afternoon to the search. Nothing doing. Every night that week he read in the main reading room, adding other periodicals to those Gilley had suggested. Albert was almost always present in the vicinity, sitting behind a stack of books around which he peered from time to time, a sight Levin, to his surprise, found mildly pleasurable. Yet he was annoyed at all the time this was taking, angered that Albert knew what he wanted to know and so far couldn't. Amazing how denial creates doubt. He was out to destroy that doubt.

Twice Gilley came over to lend a hand; and Avis, now wearing bangs, although still cold to Levin—he had heard from Gerald the poor breast had been successfully operated on—pitched in for a full evening, together with Dr. Kuck. Though there were occasions they all felt they were approaching a definitive find, nothing came of it. One night after closing, as Levin was going down the stone steps of the library, Albert, a few steps behind, made a noise that even in Cascadia sounded like a Bronx cheer. Levin ground his teeth.

He extended his efforts, despite papers to grade and his own reading piling up; giving every spare minute to the hunt, and some not so spare, devouring volumes of up to fifteen years ago. He read with murderous intent, to ensnare and expunge Albert O. Birdless. Levin saw himself as a man-eating shark cleaving with the speed of a locomotive through a thick sea of words, Albert, a tricky fat eel hidden among them, only his boiling blue eyes visible through the alphabet soup. Levin, in fast pursuit, caught nothing in his toothy mouth and began to doubt he would catch anything. But Gilley cheered him on, though by now Levin was playing with the idea that Albert's theme had been the work of a talented friend, although how he would rate such a friend was a question. Gerald pooh-poohed the possibility.

In class Levin had given up calling on Albert, even avoided looking in his direction. Then one morning, about ten days after Levin had read the allegedly plagiarized theme, happening to meet the boy's eyes, the instructor saw they were soiled with worry, and his face had taken on a yellowish cast. Levin felt bad: he had created a victim. Albert might be guilty; if so he had got to where his guilt, by some trick of human drama, rubbed off on his prosecutor. Levin hadn't the heart to go to the library that day.

He sat in his office trying to decide what to do. If Albert was guilty he ought to be punished, but Levin, though almost positive he hadn't written the theme, couldn't prove it. Not having been able to prove it in a reasonable time—reasonable defined by the state of Albert's sagging nervous system, not to mention ten wasted days for Levin—wasn't it better to drop the whole business? He could forever go on investigating and finding nothing, creating a perpetual indictment. I've got to be quick with a reasonable doubt. He wasn't excusing Albert but had to stop torturing him.

Levin decided to call it quits. He considered reducing the theme grade to C but couldn't logically. It was, as a paper, worth A, and once he dropped the matter, A is what it would

174

get. Albert would recover his contentment, but it was his contentment.

Levin made up his mind over the weekend. On Monday he called the boy to his desk after class. Albert popped on his lid as he approached. He stood near the desk, dully, swaying the slightest bit, not looking at Levin. His breathing was heavy, his breath bad.

Levin spoke through a constricted throat. "Albert, I haven't been able to prove your composition was copied so I have to assume you're innocent. Still, if you're really not, maybe you ought to say so? If you admit it, I'll drop you from the course without a grade. If you don't I'm forgetting the matter anyway, and you can stay on in the class without prejudice. The theme will go down for an A."

Albert's eyes were lusterless, as a smirk, a skull and cross-bones rising on a tugboat's halyard, by degrees took possession of his face.

"I have no confession at all to make," he said in a quavering voice. "You tried to make a damn fool out of me and made one out of yourself instead."

He was about to cry and turned not to be seen, but Levin, unable to confront his image in Albert's eyes, had turned from him.

That ended it, he thought, until Gilley, seeing him in the hall, called Levin into his office.

"How's it going, Sy?"

"What?"

"The paper Birdless cribbed. How are you coming along on that?"

"Oh that," Levin said, scratching his cheek through his whiskers, "I couldn't prove anything so I dropped it."

"What!" said Gilley. "Dropped it?"

"I couldn't prove anything," Levin explained. "The boy was punch-drunk and turning yellow—his skin, I mean. I thought I'd better drop it."

"If he looked guilty," Gilley fidgeted, "that's because he was. He should have been tracked down and exposed."

"I tried, you know I did. I neglected everything else."

"In that case, why don't you leave his paper with me and I'll give it some more attention in a day or two?"

"Thanks, Gerald," Levin said, "but the case is closed."

"What grade did you give him?"

"An A."

"Are you crazy?" Gilley stared at him sternly.

Levin was startled. Yet when he looked again, the director of composition was smiling.

"Sy, do you remember what Professor Fairchild told us all in the last monthly meeting? About the procedure to be followed in a case of this kind?"

"Wasn't it in a different context," Levin asked, "referring to what to do after guilt was proved? I didn't prove anything."

"He said to avoid false pity and stamp this thing out. You and I know that boy is guilty. He should have been nailed or he'll do it again. I wonder if you have any idea what we're up against in cheating these days? Not only cribbed papers but all kinds of cheating. Students break into offices for exams. They steal Milly's wastebasket regularly to see if there are any copies of tests she might have mimeographed; I've had to change her lock twice this year. They cheat by every means you can think of. Girls pin notes under their skirts which they modestly lower when a proctor comes along. They hide answers in their brassieres. Some of the boys come with sentences diagrammed on their palms and definitions printed all the way up their arms. They keep notes in their cuffs and socks. One kid even had a kind of invisible ink he used to write with on his shirt cuffs, and a pair of dark glasses he could see the writing with. It's a regular industry and the only way to lick it is to stamp it out without mercy wherever we find it."

Levin agreed. "Still, if you'll pardon my saying this, Gerald, isn't it—er—partly our fault? I've never heard so much talk about grades as I have around here—including the coffee room.

It's as though grades is what everybody graduates to after batting averages."

"Oh, come off it, Sy. Let's not get into complaining about the grading system. We have to have standards. And I'll bet you'll find just as much cheating in the liberal arts colleges as we have here. Let's stick to Birdless' paper."

"When I saw how he was beginning to look," Levin said, "I said to myself a good teacher is a liberator."

"Sure, but let's be relevant. You can't liberate a thief. Once you do he'll steal again. That was pretty clear from the story Orville told us. That boy cribbed three times in a row. If they didn't throw him out he'd still be doing it."

"I said to myself, You can't indict without evidence, and you can't indict in perpetuity."

"You could have got the evidence."

"I tried very hard."

"All this disturbs me."

"It disturbs me too."

"Then why don't you let me take the paper over for a couple-three days and ask Avis to finish the job?"

"No, I couldn't do that." Levin excused himself and left.

An hour later he met Gilley, in good humor, in the men's room. "Sy," he said, "something a lot more pleasant. Pauline asked me to invite you to dinner for Friday night. Can you make it?"

Levin tried to think of a way out but couldn't and accepted.

"Fine, I'll tell her. By the way, I've transferred Birdless out of your class. Avis agreed to take him. You'll get the drop notice in a day or so."

Levin, shaking in his clothes, tried to steady his voice. "Did you—ah—transfer him to get at his theme?"

"No," said Gilley, rubbing his hands with a paper towel, "he came in and asked to be taken out of your class. I did it because, as I said before, there's no point in perpetuating bad feelings between students and instructors."

"Don't you see," Levin said, "you are destroying my authority?"

"Now take it easy, Sy. I've done nothing of the kind. I respect your point of view but it's psychologically a bad thing to have a kid in the class of an instructor he says he hates. The student shows his disrespect in his attitude. He might spread all kinds of rumors or lies about you and it would be bad for class morale. You're well rid of a troublemaker."

This man is my enemy, Levin thought.

He laughed brokenly.

At the Bullocks' for cocktails Levin wandered restlessly from one group to another. He listened for a minute with half an ear, then moved on, wondering what he thought he might find in one bunch that he wouldn't in the next. The house was a stylish split-level on a fashionable western hill, whose large wood-paneled living room could hold thirty without trying and did this Sunday evening in the middle of January. Despite the crowd, with the exception of Avis there wasn't an unmarried woman around, and Levin thought that grim fact accounted for his dullish mood. People were pairing him off with her, he had noticed, and this explained, he thought, his recent popularity, if not with Avis. The beard seemed to help, making him in some people's eyes a person he wasn't. They could have it.

After a short stretch in the garden at sunset, Levin, a mouthful of martini held aimlessly in his hand, sat on the sofa between Alma Kuck and Jeannette Bullock, Alma again going on about the British Isles, and Jeannette deathlessly attentive, that rare thing, a beautiful woman who managed to be uninteresting. Pauline said she had never got over the fact she hadn't been to college. Levin noticed that although her legs attracted wherever she sat, she spent five minutes trying to hide them under her skirts, a pity. But she had constructed a lovely garden amid the oaks and fir trees on their property and was said to send everyone a birthday card on his birthday. As Alma talked and Jeannette listened, Levin, escaping from a yawn, had both eyes on Pauline Gilley across the room, standing partly turned from him amid some of the younger wives. She was attractive in a tight black dress. A small veil floating before her eyes from a wisp of hat created a mystery where none had been before. Who was the masked lady? Amazing what entices, Levin thought. Yet when she happened to glance in his direction, her thin-stemmed martini glass like a flower in her fingers, he pretended to be inspecting his new brown shoes. Secretly he continued to watch her. Alma diverted him with a question, and when he got up a minute later and went to Pauline she was gone.

Bullock appeared with his flowing pitcher, dispensing a boffo with every shot. The contents looked like innocent water but packed a hard wallop. People at the party were gay, they enjoyed Bullock's daring pitcher, a departure from the town's mores. Some were beginning to dance, a rarity in faculty houses. To dance, Levin had been told, one usually joined a social dancing club. There were dances the last Friday of each month, with extras for holidays. If Professor Fairchild or ex-Dean Feeney was present at a party, soft drinks and sweet green punch prevailed, but none of the older people having been invited, the host freely poured firewater, an empty glass seeming to threaten his security. Surprising the instructor without a glass, Bullock handed him one and aimed the spout, but Levin, worried by the man's unthinking prodigality, said he had had enough.

"I thought this was a party," George said. When he was drinking he breathed through a half-open mouth, both eyes verging on vacant. But a sweetness descended on him, and he loved on Sundays those he tolerated weekdays. Levin felt that neither of them took to the other. Bullock invited him because he sensed Levin disliked him, and he came because he couldn't afford to turn down an invitation. He got none from Bucket or Fabrikant, whom he liked, nor were they ever present at Bullock's.

"It is," answered Levin, "but I've already had two."

"That was my last batch. This will dissolve the rust on your gonads, if not the gonads. Have three."

Figuring he would abandon the glass, Levin let him fill it. "Nice party."

George blinked. "Think so? We were late getting off the ground this fall. By now we've usually had three or four big blasts, but Jeannette hasn't been up to it lately—flu plus miscarriage (keep it quiet) et cetera. I also blame the late god-awful football season, let it rest. There's nothing like a consistently losing team to put a damper on your entertaining instinct. It depressed Gerald too."

"Is that so?"

"Yep. Everybody expected a bang-up season. *Look* predicted a possible Rose Bowl for us, then the roof caved in. We won three out of ten with some of the best material on the coast. The alumni are sore as hell at Lon Lewis, the head coach, and he'll probably be traded for somebody with a T-formation. I know most of the boys on the squad and I'll tell you it was no inspiration to see their hangdog pusses in class on Monday mornings."

"They're all in your classes?"

"Some are. They have their free choice of instructors."

"I didn't mean they didn't—"

"Anyway," Bullock said, "exit football, enter basketball. We've copped the first four games and look like a shoo-in to take the coast conference. Bought your season ticket?"

"No," said Levin.

"Tough titty. Keep it in mind for next year. Saves you thirty percent. To the future champs." He raised his right hand, crossing fingers.

Levin lifted his glass. Remembering the red bumper-strip on Bullock's station wagon: "Keep Basketball King at Cascadia College," he drank to a better world.

Like raw gin. He had visions of being picked up drunk in town and fined a hundred dollars and costs.

"Gerald is also affected by a losing team?" Levin asked.

"After some of the rough ones he can't talk for an hour."

"Really? Pauline too?"

"She has her moments. Jeannette gets listless."

"Is that why the Gilleys didn't entertain much this fall?"

"It wouldn't surprise me. They like to have people in after a game but didn't do any of that after the shellacking we got from Cal, right off. He's the fan, though she keeps him pretty steady company at the big games. Both she and Jeannette say sports take their minds off their worries, whatever the hell they are. Pauline can be a moody dame, and I suppose having two kids all of a sudden is no picnic. Gerald did some lousy duck shooting in December. I've never seen him so bad. He's been worn out."

"She wears him out?"

Bullock winked. "I didn't say so but she helps, though last year the kids' colds knocked them both for a loop. Erik gets everything in the book plus some unidentified bugs. That was on top of the fact that Gerald hadn't recovered from L'affaire Duffy, the year before."

"It was that bad?"

"He bore the brunt for more than one reason, one being that Orville folds up his tent and goes home at the first sniff of scandal."

"It was really a scandal?"

"It amounted to one. Excuse me," George said, "the place is going dry." He lifted the spout but Levin withdrew his glass.

"Before you go," he said to Bullock, "have you seen where Pauline went?"

George looked vacantly around. "Try the upstairs bedroom. When she gets high she sometimes lies down."

Levin searched the bedrooms and daylight basement but she wasn't there. Back in the party he saw Avis eyeing him. He headed for the kitchen, slipped behind some people, and sliding open the opaque glass door, walked down six steps to the patio.

Levin sighed at the stars and was at once unexpectedly emotional. An odor of flowers assailed him. Because of the season he thought it was pure imagination, the result of more liquor than he should have had. I'm back in summer, Levin thought, or that far forward, why nobody knows. But he knew that even if he were living in another time he would be wishing for another time. The view in the dark, stars through bare-branched oaks, and the lights of the town below affected him as though he were listening to music. For the first time in years he thirsted for a butt.

Smelling smoke, he looked abruptly around.

In the dim light reflected from the interior of the house he made out Pauline Gilley standing between fir trees with a cigarette in her hand.

"Did I frighten you, Mr. Levin?" She had been watching him.

He went across the lawn to her. "I was looking for you, Mrs. Gilley."

He told her he felt bad about that time she had come to see him. "Excuse me, I was sick."

"Don't you like me?" Pauline asked. Her scent in the cool air was warm. He wished he could see her eyes through the veil.

"On the contrary—"

She waited.

"—I like you," Levin said.

"Then why didn't you come to dinner Friday night?"

He nervously fingered his beard. "Would you—er—keep it confidential?"

"I'm awfully good at that."

"Gerald and I had a disagreement and, frankly, I didn't feel like accepting his hospitality just then."

"It was my hospitality too."

He admitted it.

"What were you annoyed with Gerald about?"

"I would rather not say, some department thing."

She dropped her cigarette in the grass, stepping on it. "That was a mistake. Now I'm dizzy again."

He was eager to help. "Can I do something for you?"

She said in a throaty voice, "I should never let George get near me when he's loose with that pitcher. I can't keep track of how many I've had because he refills after every mouthful."

"For the sport?"

She gazed at the house. "Doesn't it look like a ship from here, and here we are, you and I, on an island in the middle of the sea? Or am I high? Are you?"

"I'm not."

"Excuse me for mentioning it but have you graduated to cocktails? The night we met, you wouldn't have one."

"Just a sip or two for sociability. I'm always saying no."

"Why?"

"Habit."

"What do you do for sin, Mr. Levin?"

Levin guffawed but came to quickly.

Hugging her arms, Pauline looked down at the lights of Easchester. "I should be home now, little Mary was running a temperature when we left, and I know Erik will have something by tomorrow. Have you seen Gerald?"

"No," said Levin. "Why don't you stay a little longer?"

"Should I?"

"There's a bench in the rock garden."

"Just for a short while, I have to get back to my children. I told Zenamae to have them tucked in by seven-thirty but I know they won't be. Erik gets up after he's been put down and goes exploring."

He was surprised, as he followed her across the patio, at her figure from the rear, so much better than he had noticed. The tight dress helped. Her shoulders, long waist and can were very good. Although a bit unsteady she walked with grace.

Where were my eyes? Levin thought.

"Don't be surprised if I fall," said Pauline.

"Let me help you." Levin took her arm and led her to the wooden bench in the rock garden. They sat in the dark, tall trees behind them.

"You look cold." He offered his jacket.

"I'll get my coat."

"I'll get it," Levin said. "You stay here."

"You won't know where it is. I'll be right back, you won't lose me, Mr. Levin," Pauline laughed.

She walked across the grass as though concentrating on not falling.

Five minutes later Levin was certain she wouldn't return. He was staring glumly at the stars as she came across the lawn with a coat over her shoulders.

"I'd've brought yours if I knew where it was," she said. "Why don't you go in and get it? I wouldn't want you to catch another cold."

"I've had this winter's cold."

"Do you plan everything, Mr. Levin?"

"What I can, I plan."

"My plans come to not much."

"Is that so?"

She touched his beard. "Does it keep you warm?"

She's high for sure, Levin thought. The veil irritated him. It hid as much as it revealed.

"I did have another drink," Pauline said. "George sneaked up on me when I was inside. I was feeling better and my defenses were down. I hope I'm not really drunk, Mr. Levin, because when I am I get sick. I don't want to be sick, please."

"Sit here till you feel better."

"My impression of your whiskers that day we met—it was my fault we were late, I was trying to get up my nerve to meet somebody new, would you guess that?—was they were coal black. But they're really a dark shade of brown. Do you know that beards bring out the quality of a man's lips and eyes? You have sensitive lips and kind eyes, Mr. Levin."

"I grew it in a time of doubt," confessed Levin. "When I couldn't look myself in the face."

"Should I become a bearded lady? Unless this veil does the trick. Does it hide me? At least my beastly nose?"

"Ah, but you're a lovely woman."

"How sweet of you. I'm not really lovely but I grow on people. I'd be nicer if I were less superficial and more accomplished. Oh, there's Gerald."

The glass door had opened and Gilley appeared on the veranda above the patio. He stood there for a wavering minute, a red-headed owl peering into the dark.

Levin sat silent, on the verge of disappointment.

But Gilley, probably affected by Bullock's powerful pitcher, blinked without seeing them although staring in their direction. He disappeared into the house.

They were motionless until she spoke. "I'll have to go now. Gerald wants me." Pauline got up but unsteadily sat down. "I feel like hell."

"Sit till you feel better."

A light went on in an upstairs room. It went out, and on in another. They watched it until it was out.

"What did he do that you didn't like?" she asked.

"It wasn't important."

"I'll bet it was."

Levin shrugged.

She did not pursue it. After a while she said, "I remember your saying, the night we met, that you hoped to make better use of your life here. Have you?"

"It's what one always has to do."

"Tell me what you want from life?"

"Order, value, accomplishment, love," said Levin.

"Love last?"

"Love any time."

"Pardon me for asking, but are you unhappy, Mr. Levin?"

"Why that question?"

"That day I came to see you—"

"Not as I have in the past known unhappiness."

"I sensed that."

"What about you?"

Pauline smiled. "I too am conscious of the misuses of my life, how quickly it goes and how little I do. I want more from myself than I get, probably than I've got. Are we misfits, Mr. Levin?"

Looking at her veil he thought, Take it off.

"Gerald suffers from my nature," she said, "though he's a patient man. With a woman more satisfied with herself, less critical and more appreciative of his good qualities, maybe he would have been a different person." She went on half absently, "Through the years I've known him he's substituted a series of minor gratifications for serious substantial ones. He's partly affected by what he thinks people expect of him, and partly he's reacted as he has because I've urged the opposite. Lately he's developed an intense ambition to follow Orville in as head of the English department."

"Wasn't it always what he wanted?"

"Not so much until the last year or so."

"Ambition is no crime."

"Not if you're strong."

She quickly said, "I wouldn't want to leave the impression Gerald is weak. He isn't, Mr. Levin, I assure you. He's always been an excellent provider, wonderful to me and the children. If you knew him better I'm sure you'd like him."

"I don't dislike him."

Pauline yawned. "Excuse me, I had a restless night."

189

Levin rose. "Shall we go in?"

But she sat there. "If you're a married woman past thirty you have at that age pretty much what you're going to have. Still, I blame myself for my compromises, and I resist the homogenization of experience and—if I may call it such—intellect. I wish I could do more for myself, I really can't blame Gerald for not wanting to make a career of shoring up my lacks."

He listened with interest, finally sitting again.

"Poor Mr. Levin, you came out for a breath of air and I've told you all I know."

"We could all do with a cause."

Pauline said, "Leo Duffy used to say, 'A good cause is the highest excitement.' "

Levin copied it on a piece of paper and slipped it into his pocket. "People talk about him but don't say much. Was he a friend of yours?"

He thought for a minute she would raise her veil but Pauline sat with quiet hands. "What have you heard?"

"Not much—that he livened things up."

"Yes, he did. Leo was different and not the slightest bit fake under any circumstances. He was serious about ideas and should have been given a fair chance to defend his. People were irritated with him because he challenged their premises."

"That I guessed."

"I had the highest regard for him."

"I have his office now."

"So I've heard."

She gasped as they were drenched in glaring light. Bullock's garden spotlights had been turned on.

"That's the end of the party. George flushes the garden with those lights." Pauline rose, swayed in her tracks, and again had to sit down, her face so white the veil looked blacker.

"I feel deathly sick. Please, Mr. Levin, call my husband before I pass out."

"Couldn't I get you some coffee?"

"Just get Gerald."

"Let me take you in where you can lie down."

"Tell Gerald to come take me home."

Levin hurried into the house. The party was over, the room deserted except for Leopold and Alma Kuck in overcoats, talking quietly to both Bullocks.

"Pauline isn't feeling so well," Levin said. "Where's Gerald?"

"He'll be down in a jiffy," George said.

"She's in the garden and wants to go home."

The Kucks left. Jeannette saw them to the door.

"The dope is," Bullock said to Levin, "Gerald's in the upstairs head. I understand they both ate something that didn't agree with them. Maybe I ought to drive her home?"

"You're in no condition to, George," Jeannette said. "I will."

"Don't bother," Levin said. "I will."

He asked George where the toilet was.

"First to the left upstairs. There's another down here if it's for your use."

"Not for mine," said Levin. He raced up the stairs and knocked on the bathroom door. "Gerald, this is Sy. Pauline doesn't feel so well. She wants you to take her home. If you can't, can I?"

Gilley, after a minute, tiredly spoke. "Why don't you do that, Sy? This has caught me by surprise, but I'm sure it's something we ate last night, some Italian stuff with red peppers and olive oil. Plus too much vino. We both got up queasy this morning. Tell her she can expect me soon."

Levin hurried down, found his coat, and returned to the garden. George and Jeannette were there with Pauline.

"I'm awfully sorry," she was saying.

"Some food she ate," Levin said. He helped her to her feet. "Gerald asked me to drive you home."

She felt his beard and giggled. "For a minute I thought you were somebody else."

"Who, for instance?" George said.

"None of your business," said Jeannette.

191

"I'm awfully sorry, Jeannette," said Pauline.

"It's not your fault."

Levin threw Bullock a dirty look but missed. They left by way of the garden. He helped Pauline into his Hudson and quickly drove off.

She rested her head against his shoulder.

"How do you feel?" Levin asked.

"Awful, but sexy. Do you think George wants to seduce me, Mr. Levin? He pours me such big drinks."

Levin laughed although he felt a headache coming on.

"My one talent," she said, rubbing her head against him, "only lately developed, is that I know people. I know you, Mr. Levin."

"What do you know?"

"Who you really are. And you know me, don't you?"

"I'm not sure."

She sat up. "I've told you about myself but not about my children."

"Later," said Levin.

"At first I didn't want them because I was ashamed a big girl like me couldn't have her own. When we were first married I had some menstrual trouble and the doctor noticed I had a tipped womb. All along I thought that was the reason why, but years later we were both examined and it turned out Gerald had no seeds. He had had the mumps and enflamed testicles when he was twenty-two."

"I don't want to hear about his personal troubles."

"I know I'm drunk, it makes me talkative."

She fell asleep with her head on his shoulder and awoke when the car stopped in front of her house. Pauline sucked a mint before she got out. He attempted to hold her arm as they walked up the flagstone path to the door but she wouldn't let him. In the house while she was paying Zenamae she showed no signs of distress but when the girl was gone she collapsed on the sofa, her hat awry, the veil crawling up one eye.

"Stay with me and hold my hand."

192

Her dress had risen above her knees. The legs were exciting though the long black shoes were like stiff herrings aimed skyward. Her chest had the topography of an ironing board.

"I'm suddenly terribly hungry. Could you make me a scrambled egg, Mr. Levin?"

That goddamn veil, he thought. On impulse he tried to pluck her hat off but Pauline clasped both hands over her head. "Stop, it's my only defense."

I'd better not start anything, Levin thought.

Upstairs Mary cried. Erik called, "Mommy."

"Mr. Levin," said Pauline, "I entreat you to look after my poor babies." Her head touched the sofa and she sat bolt upright.

"I married a man with no seeds at all."

She fell asleep, her stomach gurgling.

Levin went upstairs to the little girl's room and turned on the light. She stopped crying and stared at him. Her bottle was in the crib so he fed her part of it.

In the next room, through the open door he saw Erik sitting up in his bed. "Who're you?"

"Mr. Levin—the funny man."

"I want a drink."

He went to the bathroom and got the water. Erik drank and lay back. As Levin was covering him the child raised his head and kissed him under the eye.

Mary was asleep. Levin put off the light and listened to the children sleeping. The poor orphans. He burst into tears.

A warm, sunlit day exhaling pure spring startled Levin at the end of January. He had been forewarned of this, but the long habit of Eastern winter kept him from believing the season could go without once punishing by blizzard or lacerating freeze every dweller in its domain. He felt unsettled for it seemed to him the unused winter must return to extract a measure of revenge for dying so young, so little of it had there been: a few months of darkish rain, a week of soft wet snow (crowning the mountains and drawing the hills closer), gone quickly to slush then gone forever; the returned rain broken by nine days of sunlit cold—never below twenty degrees, afternoons warming—which exhilarated Levin although his students complained. Maybe a reluctant icicle had hung for a day or two from the roof of Mrs. Beaty's porch. Having as a kid, nose and feet burning, waded many times through snow-drifts, and often worn an overcoat into mid-April, Levin felt now as though he had been reprieved by prestidigitation, not entirely trustworthy, from ice, snow, and wild wind. If winter were already dead it left him with some guilt, as though he had helped murder it, or got something for nothing when they read the will, rare in his life. Yet the thought remained that to be alive was a short season.

Pessimism was momentary. Better enjoy the changes that had taken place with or without his knowing. Primroses, Mrs. Beaty had showed him, were in flower, had been all winter. At Christmastime, as Levin lay gloomily in bed, daffodil shoots were a stiff two inches above the ground; crocus under January snow. On New Year's day naked jasmine in the backyard by the cherry tree touched the dark world with yellow light; forsythia performed the same feat a few weeks later. Camelias were budding in January; quince and heather in flower, petals touching the stillest air. After the snow Levin had come upon a cluster of violets behind the garage. Rain was lighter, moodier, giving way to broken sunlight. And he enjoyed the lengthened day, seven A.M. now six-thirty. There was as yet little of spring to smell, either because early spring odors were still too subtle for his city-built nose, or the Northwest cool cheated scent, the throb of emotion in the wake of warm fragrance. If this was spring, Levin knew it because he eternally hunted for it, was always nosing out the new season, the new life, "a new birth in freedom."

On this reasonable facsimile of a late March day, a Thursday when Levin had no afternoon classes, although he had planned to return to the office after lunch and grind away at technical reports, the weather tempted him to a country walk to see what nature across the bridge had been busy at without him; and to feel the sun's beneficent hand on his head. He got out of his bureau drawer, where they had lain all winter, his binoculars and *Western Birds, Trees and Flowers*. Since he had read in last night's paper it might rain, he carried his trusty umbrella; and with this armload, tramped to the distant wood rising to the hills. He went by a route he had not tried before, a country road lined with old pussy willow trees, their sticky budding branches massed against the sky. Although Levin rejoiced at the unexpected weather, his pleasure was tempered by a touch of habitual sadness at the relentless rhythm of nature; change ordained by a force that produced, whether he wanted it or not, today's spring, tomorrow's frost, age, death, yet no man's accomplishment; change that wasn't change, in cycles eternal sameness, a repetition he was part of, so how win freedom in and from self? Was this why his life, despite his determined effort to break away from what he had already lived, remained so much the same? And why, constituted as he was and living the experience he engendered, he had not won anything more than short periods of contentment, not decently prolonged to where he could stop asking himself whether he had it or not? If I could only live as I believe, Levin thought. How often have I told myself happiness is not something you flush out in a planned expedition, a hidden complicated grail all at once the beholder's; that it's rather grace settled on the spirit in desire of life. We're here for a short time, often under the worst circumstances—possible that man may someday be blown off the tips of Somebody's Fingers; the battle lost before we knew what we were about, yet how magnanimously beautiful even to have been is. I have many times in differing circumstances told myself this, so why can't I quit worrying if happiness comes and how long lasts, if it does either? Discontent brings neither cold cash nor true love, therefore why not enjoy this tender marvelous day instead of greeting it with news of everything I haven't got?

He was still a distance from the hills when he approached a large wood—call it a forest—that he had come upon before by other routes. On impulse Levin left the road, hopped over a ditch, and crossing a field, entered among the evergreens. Once in the wood he was not entirely at his ease because he was trespassing, and as he went quietly along he worried about possible bears or maybe a snarling cougar or two, though he had heard of none in the vicinity; if there were any he had only an umbrella to defend himself with. Mostly his uneasiness arose from the thought that his life had been lived largely without experience of very many trees, and among them he felt a little unacquainted. Yet to be alone in the forest, this far in, was already a feat for a born city boy who had never been a Boy Scout. Levin took heart. He walked on soft ground among dark conifers, giants and dwarfs, and a large scattering of leafless other trees; but now he recognized fir, cedars, in green skirts touching the ground, blue spruce, and even hemlock, the trees in profusion, their branches interlaced, the forest gloom broken by rays of sunlight dappling the ground. The wood, as he walked, pungent with levitating coolness, suggested endless distance and deepest depth. Levin began to be worried about getting lost if he wandered too far in, and to avoid circular confusion, considered marking his way with bits of torn paper. The mystery of the wood, the presence of unseen life in natural time, and the feeling that few men had been where he presently was, (Levin, woodsman, explorer; he now understood the soul of Natty Bumppo, formerly paper; "Here, D. Boone CILLED A. BAR") caused him to nudge aside anxiety and continue to venture among the trees in shade and sunlight.

As he came out of the woods into a clearing, a yellow-green, rich grassy meadow sloping downward, a flock of robins— from Canada, he had been told, while the Cascadian species was vacationing in California; you were dealing with strangers who looked like friends—scattered noisily over his head. From the wood across the field a bird hidden in a tree screeched at the world. Levin's head was immersed in silence deepened by a drumming in the wood behind, a woody tattoo. After a short bafflement he located with his glasses a bird drilling away near the top of a dead fir. Hurriedly searching for his bird guide, he read with the greatest satisfaction that he had spotted a red-headed woodpecker, never before seen so clearly. The bird spied Levin and flew into the forest. A moment later he turned pages hastily to identify first a Seattle wren, then a very blue, graybellied blue jay, exciting color; and a chickadee, the first he remembered looking at and naming; also a yellow bird he couldn't identify, whose flight above the treeline Levin followed with pleasure until it disappeared into light like a light gone out. Who sees this in Manhattan Isle? None but the gifted. Here the common man rejoiced in what was naturally visible. But being where he was not supposed to be continued to trouble Levin; he turned as if forewarned someone was in the wood behind him; expecting, if not a boot in the pants, at least the forester's hard hand and gruff get the hell off private property. He would run like mad. Instead, he saw Pauline Gilley watching him from amid trees.

She looked like someone he had never expected to see again, or was the thought a trick on himself to protect what was left of unused virginity? Pauline approached as if unwilling, an expression he attributed to an embarrassment of remembrance; then as though she had made peace with herself in mid-voyage, she looked up, smiling at his astonishment. Her raincoat unbuttoned, he took in blouse, gray skirt, long blue socks and walking shoes. He also quickly calculated what she had on underneath, an innovation in their relationship.

Her hair shone in the sun. "I'm sorry I startled you, Mr. Levin. I'm just as surprised to see you."

Levin explained his umbrella; the paper said rain. She smiled at his armload. "Let me help you."

"It's nothing much." Her presence in the wood aroused a renewed momentary sadness, as if he had come too late to the right place, familiar situation of his dreams.

197

"The day turned out so springlike I left the children with a sitter so I could walk," Pauline said.

"You've been here before—in this wood?"

"Yes, haven't you?"

"No."

"I didn't know you watched birds."

"If you can call it that. Most get away before I know what I've seen."

"You were engrossed when I saw you."

"When I was a kid I used to look out of the window at sparrows on telegraph wires or hopping in the snow."

"I haven't seen you for weeks, Mr. Levin," Pauline said.

"About two, I'd say. Time flies."

"I talked so much at the Bullocks. I don't think I've been that much affected by liquor in years."

"No need to worry, I've forgotten what you said."

"Please don't."

They weren't looking at each other. When their eyes met, although he obsessively expected a veil, there was none, and Levin beheld an expression of such hungry tenderness he could hardly believe it was addressed to him. Enduring many complicated doubts, he dropped his things in the grass. They moved toward each other, their bodies hitting as they embraced.

"Dear God," Pauline murmured. Her kiss buckled his knees. He had not expected wanting so much in so much giving.

Levin warned himself, Take off, kid, and in their deep kiss saw himself in flight, bearded bird, dream figure, but couldn't move.

They parted, breathing heavily, looked at each other as though seeing were drinking—he could have counted twenty —and after mutual hesitation to the point of pain, embraced.

"My darling."

"Pauline." He kept himself from crying love.

Levin clutched at her chest, and seizing nothing, ran his

hand the other way. She gripped his fingers, then let go, embracing him tightly.

"Where shall we go?"

"Anywhere."

She took his hand and they went into the woods, Levin glancing back to see where his things were. "Here," she said in the green shade. The evergreens were thick, the ground damp but soft with fir needles and dead leaves.

"Spread your coat." She spread hers over his, then stepped out of her shoes. She removed a black undergarment, the mask unmasked. Lying on the coats, Pauline raised her hips and drew back her skirt, to Levin the most intimate and beautiful gesture ever made for him.

He hung his trousers over the branch of a fir. When he knelt she received him with outstretched arms, gently smoothed his beard, then embraced him with passion as she fixed her rhythm to his.

He was throughout conscious of the marvel of it—in the open forest, nothing less, what triumph!

As she was combing the needles out of her hair the woods turned dark and it began to rain. They waited under Levin's umbrella under an old lichenous elm. If he expected uneasiness after the fact, he felt none. When he searched her eyes for guilt he was distracted by their light and warmth. He held the umbrella over their heads, his arm around her waist. They were resting against the tree trunk, her head on his shoulder. He felt, in gratitude, peace, and tried not to think of what he didn't have to, namely the future.

When she spoke he wished she hadn't. "Please don't worry about anything."

"Worry?"

"I mean if you have any regrets you're not bound to me. There are no obligations. You can leave this minute if you wish."

Levin pictured himself leaving her under the tree in the rain. Later he returned to see if she were there.

"Why speak of regrets? I have none."

"Your eyes seem sad."

"The fix of habit. I'm happy."

"What were you thinking of just now?" she asked.

"Oh you, your quality. I never had it this way before."

"You haven't had many women, have you?"

"Not many."

"I know you've been in love."

"Often—with the wrong kind. One or two made hash of me."

"I'm so sorry."

"My own fault, but that's in the past."

"Poor boy, did you have to connive for sex?"

"Not connive but pleasure never came too easy."

She was silent a minute. "Did this?"

"This is good."

"You respect me?"

"Of course."

"Mrs. Gilley, mother of two?"

"I respect you, Pauline."

They kissed again. She rubbed her head against his. "I'm hungry to know everything about you."

"I've had my bad times."

"Tell me what happened."

Levin was reluctant to speak about the past.

"You never do. I won't ask again."

He said, thick-voiced, half his face crippled, "The emotion of my youth was humiliation. That wasn't only because we were poor. My father was continuously a thief. Always thieving, always caught, he finally died in prison. My mother went crazy and killed herself. One night I came home and found her sitting on the kitchen floor looking at a bloody bread knife."

Pauline leaned her face against him.

"I mourned them but it was a lie. I was in love with an unhappy, embittered woman who had just got rid of me. I mourned the loss of her more than I did them. I was mourning myself. I became a drunk, it was the only fate that satisfied me."

She moaned; Levin trembled.

"I drank, I stank. I was filthy, skin on bone, maybe a hundred ten pounds. My eyes looked as though they had been pissed on. I saw the world in yellow light."

"Please, that's all."

"For two years I lived in self-hatred, willing to part with life. I won't tell you what I had come to. But one morning in somebody's filthy cellar, I awoke under burlap bags and saw my rotting shoes on a broken chair. They were lit in dim sunlight from a shaft or window. I stared at the chair, it looked like a painting, a thing with a value of its own. I squeezed what was left of my brain to understand why this should move me so deeply, why I was crying. Then I thought, Levin, if you were dead there would be no light on your shoes in this cellar. I came to believe what I had often wanted to, that life is holy. I then became a man of principle."

"Oh, Lev," she said.

"That was the end of my drinking though not of unhappiness. Just when I thought I had discovered what would save me—when I believed it—my senses seemed to die, as though self-redemption wasn't possible because of what I was—my emptiness the sign of my worth. I denied the self for having denied life. I managed to get and hang onto a little job but as a person I was nothing. People speak of emptiness but it was a terrifying fullness, the soul has gas. It isn't exactly apathy, you have feeling but it's buried six feet. I couldn't respond to experience, the thought of love was unbearable. It was my largest and most hopeless loss of self before death."

Her eyes were shut.

"I felt I had come to something worse than drunkenness. This went on for how long I can't say. I lived in stone. My only occasional relief was in reading. I had a small dark room in a rooming house overrun by roaches and bugs. Once a week I burned the bedbugs with a candle through the bedsprings; they popped as they died. One Sunday night after a not otherwise memorable day, as I was reading in this room, I had the feeling I was about to remember everything I had read in my life. The book felt like a slab of marble in my hands. I strained to see if it could possibly be a compendium of every book ever written, describing all experience. I felt I had somewhere read something I must remember. Sensing an affirmation, I jumped up. That I was a free man lit in my mind even as I denied it. I suddenly knew, as though I were discovering it for the first time, that the source of freedom is the human spirit. This had been passed down to me but I had somehow forgotten. More than forgetting—I had lived away from it, had let it drift out of my consciousness. I thought I must get back what belongs to me; then I thought, 'This is how we invent it when it's gone.' Afterwards I experienced an emotion of well being so intense that I've lived on it ever since."

He said no more. Pauline rubbed her wet eyes against his shoulder. "I sensed it. I knew who you were."

"I felt a new identity."

"You became Levin with a beard."

"What was new were my plans for myself."

"I won't interfere with them," she said fervently. "We shan't meet again."

Pauline smoked as they watched the rain let up. "I'd better be getting back."

Levin, gathering up his things, tucked the umbrella under his arm, and they went through the wet woods. He called it a miraculous forest but she laughed and said it was the property of Cascadia College, where they trained foresters.

"Then it's no miracle you came here today?"

"I've often been, on picnics with forestry friends, and sometimes I come alone to walk in the woods."

It worried him they might have been seen, but she seemed

unconcerned so he was content. Whosever forest it was, he had gone into it, met her, and they had made love in the open, marvel enough for Levin.

On the road to town, although the sun shone brightly through broken clouds, he opened the umbrella over their heads.

In his room Levin laughed one minute and groaned the next. Breathing heavily, he paced back and forth for hours. Or he stared out of an open window, lost in profuse memory. Sometimes he silently celebrated his performance in the open—his first married woman, sex uncomplicated in a bed of leaves, short hours, good pay. He was invigorated by the experience, one he would not have predicted for himself. A few minutes later he was soberly conscious of this figure within—an old friend with a broken nose warning him against risking his new identity. The new life was very new. Yet he wondered what he could be with her. Could he, with Pauline, be more than he was? Levin thought in terms of experience with her, not necessarily commitment. Hadn't she herself denied he was obligated to her? This could only mean she wanted no serious tie to him. Yet he was glad he had told her about the past; it was a relief to share that with someone.

By night the forest had taken on a dreamlike quality. Was there such a forest? Were the trees still standing? Were they real? Was it Pauline he had met there? He asked himself, Who is she? Extraordinary thing to have been in a woman and not know her. Could he trust her? What did she want from him; why, for instance, Levin? Because her saintly papa had worn whiskers—beard as totem? Was there perhaps some design in her choice of him (Had she purposely followed him into the woods? Impossible!) or was their lovemaking the more or less accidental end of a discontented woman's desire? If not, if she had in one way or another sought him out, what could he offer her, a man at thirty still running after last year's train, far behind in the world? Nothing. To be involved with a married woman—danger by definition, whose behavior he had no way of predicting was no joke. Who could guess what grade *she* would want changed; or what she might whisper to her lawfully-wedded spouse in a moment of tenderness, or hurl at him in hatred. If she threw Levin up to Gilley, farewell Levin. He feared his fate in her hand. Yet if she were concealment itself he knew his relationship to Gilley was changed for all time. This bothered him. Since he disliked him he wanted it to be for a just cause, to wit, Gilley, not because Levin had stolen from him—the primal cheating, result, oppressor hating oppressed. The thought that haunted him most was that the slightest revelation of the act under the tree would mean the worst disaster he could think of: end of future.

During the week, though she was often in his mind, Levin felt he didn't miss her, and probably vice versa. She could never be interested in a man with his kind of past. As he mulled this, he could not be sure he was right—she had seemed more than sympathetic to him, had practically wept. Probably it was closer to truth to think she had wanted the distraction of an affair, had had it, and quits. Or maybe she's now ashamed of it. She's the one with a husband; thank God I have no wife. So fare thee well. Yet too bad, for what's good deserves repeating. He had been thinking it was impossible to live on memory of sexual pleasure, no matter how satisfying. The better the pleasure the more useless the memory.

This was his mood one rainy night, the week after the forest, as he sat in his room. The fire of unseasoned applewood had sizzled out after nine, and Levin, tired of reading, had rebuilt it. He went back to his book but found it hard to concentrate; had to nail down each sentence before he could move to the next. The alternative was to shut the book and think of her. Let me be honest with myself, he thought; if I have her again I must keep romance apart from convenience. Love goes with freedom in my book. He had less than a minute to test his reflection, for there was a sound on the back stairs, and through the blurred glass he saw Pauline about to tap with a key. He rose hastily, his impression that she had been observing him, questioning what—his existence? worth? good sense? Levin momentarily thought of disappearing, but went instead to open the door where she stood. Could a man do less on a rainy night?

Pauline entered quickly. "Did you want me to come?" Her eyes hid from his.

If he said no it wasn't yes, but Levin said yes. Still, it was yes without pain, unless pain could be present without one's knowing, an unlikely procedure.

They kissed and at once parted as if there was much to say, or at least get straight, before they could kiss again. Her face and hands were cold, she had shivered as he held her. Levin hung up her wet raincoat. Pauline stood before the fire in the green dress he remembered from the night he had banged his head. She wore pendant earrings.

"Just let me get my breath back."

But breath she had. What was missing he wasn't sure. She seemed troubled, said little. Levin guessed what it probably was—the difference between last time and this. Their meeting in the woods was accidental. Tonight she must have lied to Gilley when she left the house. There was, in any case, that house to leave and this to come to.

For a half hour they watched the fire. She offered no explanation for her mood and he made it a point not to ask. He had disappointing visions of a short sexless evening. At length Pauline sighed and gave him her hand.

She looked around. "Is there anyone else on this floor?"

"Nobody. Mrs. Beaty sleeps downstairs."

Pauline plucked off her earrings and dropped them into her purse. She stepped out of her shoes and began to undress. He did the same though nobody had asked him. The contract was in the prior act, there in the forest.

In her lace-bosomed slip reflecting the fire she looked at him with a half-sad smile.

"Do you like me in this?"

"It's a poetic garment."

"You've never seen me naked."

The fact surprised him.

She drew the slip over her head and was naked. Her hips were slim. She was long waisted, the legs and trunk gracefully proportioned, her arms and shoulders lovely. Naked, she looked unmarried.

But her chest was barren, the flowerlike nipples only slightly fleshy. He had almost looked away.

"Shall I keep my slip on? Would you like that better?"

"No." He had to watch himself with her.

She pressed down the mattress to see if the bed creaked.

"Are you afraid?" he asked her.

"Dreadfully. I'd die if anyone heard us."

He took her in his arms. "Don't be afraid. The landlady's deaf when she's asleep. She's asleep now."

She was suddenly passionate, bit his lip. In bed she met him with open mouth. He thought what he must do for her but there was hardly time. "Take me." She came quickly, at the end half singing out as she had in the woods, a sound that sang in him. At its onset he had taken it for sobbing—regret for what she was doing—but it was a halting cry of pleasure. She took him with her before he thought it time to go. He laughed at the ease of it.

Afterwards she asked, her face lit in the glow of a cigarette, "Does 'My young love's rip'ning breasts' mean so much? Does my flat bosom bother you?"

"If it did it doesn't."

"At least I have symmetry," she said. "My roommate in college had a bigger right breast than left."

He was for symmetry.

"And I've never worn falsies, would you want me to?"

"You're not the type."

"What type am I?"

"The type that doesn't wear them."

"Please always be honest with me," Pauline said.

He said he had to or got mangled.

She asked if he always taught himself lessons from experience.

"Almost always."

"My poor Levin."

"I don't like to make the mistakes I've made."

She said, after putting out her cigarette, "What will you teach yourself from us?"

"Something good, I think."

"Something lovely, perhaps enduring?"

He said he thought so.

"Do you think you could fall in love with a woman without breasts?"

"I've never tried."

She said, suddenly, "I shouldn't really be here."

Pauline was at once out of bed. "Gerald's in Marathon tonight. The children are alone because I couldn't get a sitter. I feel like a heel."

But she swept off the bedsheet and tightened it under him. Emptying the ashtray into the fireplace, Pauline aired the room, dressed, and left. Levin was at once asleep.

She visited him not often but often enough. One of her "meetings" was a good enough excuse for a night out. And Gilley assisted by teaching a winter-term weekly extension course for teachers, in Marathon. Usually Pauline walked the dozen blocks to Levin's. When she had the car she parked it about two blocks from the house. Gilley was home from Marathon by eleven. She had left Levin's room at ten-thirty, short but sweet. He could read afterwards without a stray thought, a great convenience. He envisioned a new Utopia, everyone over eighteen sexually satisfied, aggression reduced, peace in the world. Once she came for an hour after Gilley had fallen asleep, worrying Levin. She was no longer dreadfully afraid; the change in her had escaped him. She said she sometimes slept on a couch in Erik's room and Gilley was a heavy sleeper. In the unlikely event he awoke he would not miss her. But Levin asked her not to take chances. She promised, then went frankly on record in extenuation of the chances she took. "Gerald can sometimes be indifferent to me for weeks. He began to be after we found out the true reason why we couldn't have children, although I will admit there are times when it's my fault, when I just don't have the energy."

What a waste, he thought.

The next time they were in bed, after Levin had dozed and waked, she brought up Gerald. "Why don't you like him?"

"I never said I didn't."

"Tell me what happened in the department."

"I told you we didn't agree about some things."

"Be patient with him," she said. "He has good will towards you."

"Let's not talk about him," Levin said.

"He's really been very sweet to me. Sometimes I'm a moody bitch, but he's usually patient and I'd like to be grateful."

He said nothing.

"We weren't doing so badly at first," Pauline said, "then we began to have some nasty spells. He disappointed me in certain ways, some not his fault. I know I disappointed him. We had

209

a very bad time just before we got Erik but it's really been better since the kids came. They've made me as nearly happy as I've been in recent years. Gerald does a lot for us. Lately I've been thinking I'd like to be in love with him again. It was very nice when we first were. Do you think anybody can bring past love alive or is it gone forever once it goes?"

"I don't know."

"Sometimes I've thought that if I were having an affair he might sense I'm being attractive to someone, and it might awaken more of his desire for me. If that happened maybe I would respond. Do you think that could happen?"

"I doubt it," he said.

"So do I," said Pauline.

He interpreted this to mean she wanted pleasure, solace, a momentary change, but no serious involvement with him. Her marriage, deficient as it seemed to him, apparently meant something to her. The situation suited him. If it made their relationship seem less consequential than it might be, on reflection so much the better. If his affair with Pauline inspired Gilley to respond to her, and she to love him for responding, so much the freer Levin's conscience. It wasn't easy to be helpful while enjoying the fruits of another man's wife.

He anticipated her visits, the tap of her key on the glass. They embraced ardently, her hand going for his fly. Levin guessed this was new for her, probably a new way she saw herself. It was new for him. Off came her earrings, then her clothes, without embarrassment. Breasts or none, her woman's wealth satisfied him. When he touched her nipples the effect was electric. She could be a little wild in bed. "Your fingers are fires." He enjoyed her long body, the cool flesh, sex smell, fragrant hair. He enjoyed the possession and adventure, her intensity with detachment. In bed he rarely thought of her as Gilley's wife. If he did he countered conscience with the thought he could break it off by spending the summer in San Francisco. In the fall he could find some excuse not to see her. He could say he had fallen in love and was thinking of getting married.

The forest had shrunk to a double bed. In bed they lived, in bed explored their bodies and history. She often asked him about his life, what he was like at ten, seventeen, twenty.

"A romantic," Levin said.

"That's still in you."

He shrugged. "Almost gone."

"Don't you like it?"

"I've lived too much on air."

"I like that in you."

Then she said, "Is love air?"

"Too often it was."

When he asked about her she asked: Did he find her attractive? Did he like her hair long? Did he like her legs? "I have such big feet." "I'm not pretty, am I?" She said once she didn't think she was interesting. "I've had so few experiences. My life was so prosaically different from yours. It's almost as though I wouldn't go the extra step to make something happen, and not much did."

"You are an interesting woman," Levin said.

"Do you mean as a person or sexually?"

"As a person with sex."

"Is that part of me strong, the sex?"

"Yes."

"I wish I had been more that way when I was young. If I had been confident of myself I might have had a lover or two."

"Didn't you?"

"I was a virgin when I was married."

"After that?"

"I was interested in men but I've never had the sort of relationship we're having."

A minute later she asked, "Tell me what you hear about me?"

"In what way?"

"Any way."

211

"Jeannette says you're a very fine person."

"She's a very fine person. What does George say?"

"Nothing I remember."

"Avis?"

"She thinks you could do more to help your husband."

"She's right," said Pauline. "Is that all she said?"

"Yes."

"She's had a crush on Gerald for years."

Levin said he had thought so.

He fell asleep. She woke him. "A woman my age is too old for a man yours. Wouldn't you really be better off with a girl of twenty-three or -four?"

His thoughts were scattered and he answered nothing.

She said wearily, "I'd be afraid of intense love now."

She dressed and went down the back stairs.

He expected her nightly all the next week but she didn't come. One day they met by chance on a downtown street.

"Did I say something wrong last time?" Levin asked.

"No, I haven't been myself."

"Not my fault?"

"I've been nervous, nothing new, an effect of periodicity."

"When can you come again?"

After a while she said she would soon.

Pauline reappeared the next night. Usually she was at once affectionate but tonight she sat at the fire, chain smoking. They talked but not about themselves. When he looked directly at her she seemed to look away. Levin assumed she felt guilty and foresaw the end of their affair.

"Suppose we were to break up?" she said.

"It would depend on you."

It grew late. Pauline got up and put on her coat. She looked lonely. Levin, exploring an insight, lifted her and carried her to the bed. She stiff armed him. "You don't dare." He pushed her down.

Afterwards she grabbed his frontispiece. "I'll never let you go, Mr. Micawber."

The next time after making love, Levin experienced a fiery pain in the butt. He broke into a cold sweat and lay apart from her, his body stiff, pretending to be asleep. He shoved his face into the pillow to keep from crying out. For ten brutal minutes he was in torment, then the pain gradually eased. He felt sickly limp but relieved, thankful for his good health. Less than a week later he felt the same agonizing, flaming pain. Though tensed to misery Levin managed to hide it from her although the torture was worse than any he remembered. It moved up the side, then to the scrotum, then back to the butt, a harrowing embarrassment after sex and shameful way to be vulnerable.

After another such spasm he began to dread going to bed with her. At the same time he was disgusted with himself—pure Levin reaction, for every pleasure, pain. He thought of telling Pauline what the trouble was, but for a lover it was a too vital weakness to confess, one which might, if it continued, waken contempt. When she appeared the next time he suggested going for a drive or maybe to a movie in another town. Pauline seemed touched by the suggestion, sweetly agreed, but in one womanly way and another—although he sensed her puzzlement—enticed him into a performance. Levin paid the price of emission, a fiery pain in the ass.

"Aren't you well?" she asked after minutes of silence.

He said he was.

"I feel you haven't been enjoying yourself lately, I can't quite describe it. Has my breath been bad?"

"No."

"Would you like me to come less often, or not at all?"

"No."

She left it at that, perhaps afraid to ask more, obviously worried. When the pain was gone, although they talked affectionately, he saw her watching him. Before she left she clung to him.

On the night of Gilley's next class in Marathon, Levin tried hiding from her. After supper he went to a movie and later drank beer until midnight. She had left a note: "Sorry I missed you." He slept badly, dreamed his whiskers were on fire. It seemed to him he had just fallen asleep when he was awakened by footsteps coming stealthily up the back stairs. These weren't her steps. Levin listened, nailed to the bed, his heart thundering. The steps stopped. He jumped up in wet sweat, fumbled for the light, fell over his shoes, sprang up and flung open the door. Nothing. Rain in swirling light. Someone wandered up the inside stairs. Levin hastily got into a robe before Mrs. Beaty knocked. She stood at the door in her flannel robe, her earpiece in, holding the battery box in her hand. He said he had had a nightmare and fallen out of bed. She said to be careful, she knew a man who had broken his back that way.

Fearing something serious—kidney, bladder, rectal—possibly cancer—and because he was making Pauline so jumpy she went two moody visits without looking at the bed, Levin decided to see a doctor. He had hoped the pain would go without treatment but it was as bad as ever when they went to bed again.

One afternoon he drove to Marathon to someone recommended by Joe Bucket; he didn't want anyone in Easchester to know his business. The doctor, an old man, examined him elaborately with every instrument he could think of except forceps. He made various tests, then pronounced his judgment.

"Tinsion is all I can find."

"My God, what's that?"

"Some sort of tinsion is causing rectal and other spasms, though possibly it's the prostate, but I can't find any evidence. Have you felt like going to the toilet when you have the pain?"

"I've gone."

"Does it help?"

"No."

"No relief or relaxation?"

"Isn't sex supposed to relax you?"

"It is and it isn't. It does and it doesn't." The doctor scratched behind his ear. "Is the lady your wife?"

"Yes," he lied.

"Are conditions favorable for intercourse?"

"Yes."

"You aren't worried about your business or any such worries?"

"No."

"Beats me, I'm afraid," said the doctor, "unless you don't like your wife."

Everyman's Freud, thought Levin.

"You might rest up a week."

"I've rested, it comes back."

The doctor wrote out a prescription. "Take one of the little green pills before intercourse. If that doesn't work, take the white pill afterward. The first is a relaxant for your tinsion, it's an anti-spasmodic. The other is a pain killer. If neither of them work come back and I'll give you an antibiotic."

In the street Levin tore up the prescription and scattered the pieces.

Levin afflicted by mystery: What was the painful egg the rooster was trying to lay? In the middle of driving home a thought he had had but never particularly valued, stalled the car. He was asking himself what he was hiding from: That he too clearly saw her shortcomings and other disadvantages, and was urgently urging himself to drop her before it was too late? That he was tired of the uneasy life, fed up with assignations with the boss's wife, sick up to here with awareness of danger and fear of consequences? Here was truth yet not enough truth. After mulling these and related thoughts, Levin tracking an idea concerning Pauline, fell over one regarding himself: the dissatisfaction he had lately been hiding from, or feeling for an inadmissibly long time, was with him for withholding what he had to give. He then gave birth. Love ungiven had caused Levin's pain. To be unpained he must give what he unwillingly withheld. It was then he jumped up, stalling the car.

Once home, he didn't know what to do with himself. Run twice around the block. Stand on his ear? Dig hard head into concrete sidewalk? Kiss the mirror or hit it with a hammer for imaging the dark-bearded one who ever complicated the infernally complicated? And Einstein, it said in the papers, used the same cake of soap to shave and bathe. Levin sat in his chair, momentarily slept, started while dreaming, bounded up to spend hours staring out of the open window at nothing he particularly saw. He lay on the bed, then rose up as if the sheets were on fire. He left his room to hurry somewhere—anywhere—and awoke to find himself standing on the back stairs. Above the tops of budding trees he watched the flaring, setting sun, wanting to abolish thought, afraid to probe the complexion of the next minute lest it erupt in his face a fact that would alter his existence. But nature—was it?—a bull aiming at a red flag (Levin's vulnerability, the old self's hunger) charged from behind and the Manhattan matador, rarely in control of any contest, felt himself lifted high and plummeted over violet hills toward an unmapped abyss. Through fields of stars he fell in love.

... Love? Levin eventually sighed. Is it love or insufficient exercise? Escape, perhaps, or excitement born from the tension of secrecy, wrongdoing? Love? How at all possible if the proposed lover had such profound reservations concerning the game, rules, even players? Consider once more, for instance, her lank frame, comic big tootsies, nose flying, chest bereft of female flowers. He mourned that motherless breast, the lost softness over the heart to pillow a man's head. He had once in frustration nipped at her nipple; she had socked his head with both fists. Levin had never imagined such as she his, her insufficiencies, discontents. Consider too the burden of her ambient: prior claimant, husband-in-law; the paraphernalia of her married life—love her, love her past. With her possibly take kids and their toys. Not for me, he told himself. He wanted

216

no tying down with ropes, long or short, seen or invisible—had to have room to move so he could fruitfully use freedom. If, ecstasied out of his senses he let down his guard—was leapt on by fate—Lord help Levin!

But if he loved her why loved he her? You are comely, my love. Your self is loveliness. You make me rich in feeling. You have grace, character. I trust you. He loved because she had one unforgettable day given herself to a city boy in a forest. And for the continuance of her generosity in bed (was he less generous?) abating desire as she made it grow, taking serious chances (did he not chance as much?). Or was he moved to love because her eyes mirrored Levin when he looked? Or, to drag truth closer, because he was compelled by his being to be in love with her open, honest, intelligent, clearly not very happy self? (Why do I feel I have chosen her because I am her choice?) The catechism made little difference, for he knew fait accompli when accomplished. Who was he kidding, or what pretending to delay or dress in camouflage? "The truth is I love Pauline Gilley." His confession deeply moved him. What an extraordinary only human thing to be in love. What human-woven mystery. As Levin walked the streets under a pale moon he felt he had recovered everything he had ever lost. If life is not so, at least he feels it is. The world changed as he looked. He thought of his unhappy years as though they had endured only minutes, black birds long ago dissolved in night. Gone for all time. He had made too much of past experience, not enough of possibility's new forms forever. In heaven's eye he beheld a seeing rose.

... But Levin had long ago warned himself when he arrived at this intensity of feeling—better stop, whoa. Beware the forms of fantasy. He had been, as a youth, a luftmensch, sop of feeling, too easy to hurt because after treading on air he hit the pavement head first. Afterwards, pain-blinded, he groped for pieces of reality. "I've got to keep control of myself. I must always know where I am." He had times without number warned himself, to harden, toughen, put on armor against love.

It snowed heavily.

The snow fell in buffeted veils. It bent shrubs and small evergreens and broke branches everywhere. There hadn't been such a snowfall in years, Mrs. Beaty said. Gilley's Marathon night passed and Pauline did not visit Levin. He accused himself, then blamed the snow, until after three warm days it vanished and she still had not appeared. Had his antics, while avoiding the bed, scared her away? He hungered to call her or write, but she had once asked him not to. Another Marathon night went by and Levin's desperation grew. He felt he had lost her.

When Pauline appeared in his room ten days after he had discovered he loved her, Levin was moved by the glow of her, the lovely form she achieved in being. How love perfects each imperfect thing. What she was was beauty. With breasts she couldn't possibly be the one he loved. I mustn't forget this, he thought, it's worth remembering.

Yet as she entered the room he knew at once—it smote him— that her detachment, almost unconcern—was something more than of the moment; and if desire, no more than that, the little she wanted from him, for which he castigated himself. She scanned his face and finding him fit plucked off her earrings. Hearing no objections to the contrary, she undressed for bed. When he embraced her she stiffened momentarily in his arms. When he spoke of love she whispered she had only an hour. Levin was thinking of forever. He felt he had loved her from the time he had laid eyes on her at the railroad station last summer—years ago. They had looked guardedly at one another. Had she guessed he would love her and turned away as though the thought was burdensome? Could she ever know that before meeting her he had loved the idea of Pauline Gilley? Didn't that make him worthy of her love?

But what had tilted Levin into love had not tipped her. In bed she dispatched the act with an easy cry. He loved her, wanting as he loved. She fell asleep as he lay awake thinking of the unyielding irony of his life.

Afterward she said, "You've been so strange."

He apologized. "I had some trouble but it's gone now."

"Is that the truth?"

"Pauline, the truth is I love you."

She said after silence, "How like a woman to want to love the one you sleep with."

"I do."

She held her hands to her ears.

He shut his mouth, eyes, his life. She dressed and quickly left. He wasn't looking.

Each day passed excruciatingly, he tried not to count. He fought thinking of her, a mockery—she was in every thought. He beat his brains to destroy her place in his mind without maiming himself. How to be, please God, not Levin? How to live loveless or not live? Once more he paid for who he was, a dirty deal.

Late one night she tapped on his window and nervously entered. Levin, putting down a book he couldn't read, faced her with what dignity he could muster, concealing love in his own defense, and the pain her presence invoked.

"I saw your light," she said.

He answered nothing.

"I tried not to come," Pauline said. "It isn't fair to you."

Fair or foul, he would settle for sex.

"Considering what I know about your life—what you've been through—I have no right to love you or expect your love, my poor darling."

He rose with an aching heart.

"I love you," she was saying, "although I try not to. I tried to be fair to you, to Gerald, and my children."

They embraced. She dug her nails into his back. He beat her with his heart.

"I love you, Lev. That's my name for you. Sy is too much

like sigh, Lev is closer to love. I love you, I'm sorry, you deserve better."

"I deserve you."

"I should never have let you that day in the woods. But I
love the kind of man you are, the kind I have to love."

"I love you willingly, with all my heart."

"Oh, my darling, we must do something with our lives."

My God, thought Levin, "What hath God wrought?"

It was easy to duck Gilley whether on campus or some down-town street. From afar his red head flared; Levin spun around and walked another way. In Humanities Hall he cut out tea to stay out of the coffee room. He could not avoid him at department meetings but didn't go near his office—hadn't since Albert Birdless. If it were possible to escape the sight of him, Levin escaped. Yet when they met at somebody's house, since Pauline was there he felt less self-conscious with Gerald than he thought he would be, guilt diminished because divided. (She glanced at him; he looked at her; she looked away.) Gilley and he sometimes talked shop, or the sportsman described how to wallop a little white ball across the grass or pull a half-dead fish out of water. He teaches me, thought Levin, and felt, in spite of all, a mild affection for the man, a sort of third cousin by marriage. But when he was alone,

Levin worried. He feared the HUSBAND of the wife, ashamed of eating his apple, spitting on his manhood, betraying him in a way the betrayer would have died to be betrayed.

Levin had only casually tied morality to sex, the act, that is. Sex was where it grew, where with luck he found it, manna when least expected. What was for free was for free so long as nobody got hurt. If the lady was willing nature approved. But the matter became moral when, in getting at sex, a man interfered with another's "rights." Though he loved Pauline he had no right to her at present. Gilley had staked his claim and she had agreed, the marriage contract. Destroy the value of that and every personal right lost value. And pretense to Gerald, at the moment he was sleeping with his wife, that their relationship—such as it was—continued to be what had it had been, ladled hypocrisy on deceit. He was also ashamed of old-fashioned disloyalty to someone who had favored him with a job that pointed to a future. For which Levin (bearded witch riding Gilley's corpse) repaid him with kicks where it hurt most, once, God forbid, he knew he had been kicked.

Yet he tried to convince himself not to let his conscience weigh too heavily. Gilley was, after all, not guiltless; he erred too. Indifferent to his wife in vital ways, did he deserve her fidelity? His "rights" were formal, less than right because he hadn't used them very well, at the very least to keep her from sexual hunger; and rely on more than two adopted kids to hold the marriage together. He had flubbed his best chances. As to what Levin could do for her, what his chance amounted to (beyond love itself) he did not know for sure. Since she was not free it was a matter for the future; they would have to wait for the right time. Pauline, after confessing her love, had thus far said nothing that reached past present, suggested no startling changes in their lives. He would have worried if she had, was still bound by the plans he had come with. If they were to live together some day, it would have to be arranged with the greatest care; neither of them could afford to make the wrong compromises. He thought good must eventually come from their love, willy nilly Gilley; and when it came, would the ex-husband profit less from more in the world? Although such reflections induced no great peace, at least Levin knew where he stood, and wasn't knowledge a blessing, even when it weighed on the head like lead? So he continued to avoid Gilley wherever possible, a bit of a feat because they used the same classroom three mornings a week at contiguous hours. When the bell rang the instructor bolted but had twice managed to run into arms that had held Pauline.

One day, shortly after lunch, Gilley knocked on Levin's office door, the instructor fabricating a cracked smile as the condemned man entered. Levin felt an odd abashed gratitude to him for coming in, as though he were a dear friend (apart from the fact they shared a wife) who by his appearance in his office guaranteed his once and future innocence. By definition: a friend was not an enemy. Or as though the husband, present without a club to bash his brains in, was proof of innocence or, at the very least, of gentle pardon. The instructor, flipping open a folded handkerchief, hastily blew his nose, for he felt a tense discomfort until Gilley, visibly on edge, on noticing Levin's collection of sample textbooks in the bookcase, suggested it might be a good idea to call a meeting of the textbook committee sometime soon. Levin then felt a little relieved.

"We'll still be using *The Elements* in comp next fall," Gerald said with that innocence that made him seem so simple in a complex world, "but you could be thinking ahead about a new freshman reader since we do change that every few years or so."

Levin agreed to call the meeting, still concerned about what might have upset Gerald. An uneasy conscience plastered peril everywhere.

Gerald, red behind both ears and back of his neck, lingered a minute over the view through the cracked window before turning again to Levin, who could not help sighing.

"Haven't seen much of you lately, Sy. Don't you drink tea any more?"

"Once in a while," said Levin.

"You aren't sore about anything in particular?"

"Not me."

"About the Birdless boy?"

"Not any more."

"Good. I didn't think you'd carry a grudge."

"Can't stand them."

"I'll try to remember to get that window fixed," Gilley said absently.

"No hurry."

"But that's not what I came to say."

Levin, as though in a sudden blizzard, feared the worst until Gerald explained he had been upset by something that had happened in Professor Fairchild's office that morning.

"I started out to tell George about it, but he's gone so I thought I'd tell you."

Sunshine devoured blizzard; Levin cautiously relaxed.

"It was embarrassing, Sy, though I came in at the tail end, after Orville, who had borne the brunt of it, sent Milly to get me. What happened was this. The father of one of Dr. Kuck's girl students—he's a millhand in town—was waiting in Orville's office when he returned from his cup of coffee. The man was about fit to be tied. He shouted he wouldn't have his daughter reading dirty stuff even if this is a college. He was objecting to a Hemingway short story Leopold had assigned in his survey of literature class. Orville tried to talk sensibly to the man but didn't get very far. He pounded with his fist on Orville's desk and broke the plate glass cover. He also brought on one of Orville's high blood pressure headaches. Finally Orville promised to look into the anthology we've been using in that course. He asked me to do it and report to him. Then he left for home, looking like something the cat had mauled."

"What story was he objecting to?" Levin said, fiddling with his whiskers.

" 'Ten Indians.' Do you know it?"

"I don't remember anything wrong with it."

"They object—the girl and her father—to the sex parts."

Levin rubbed his nose. "I don't remember anything—er—particularly outstanding."

"It has a raw touch of subject matter. The boy in the story has been having intercourse with this Indian girl. The girl's father—the one in Leopold's class—her father—said his daughter came to him so embarrassed she couldn't look him in the eye when she asked his opinion of the story. After reading it he forbade her to open the book again. He told Orville if he didn't get rid of that book he'd go to President Labhart, and if *he* didn't give him any satisfaction he'd take it up with the governor, and I believe he would. That was when Orville called me in and it was all I could do to calm the man down. I read the story at lunch time and, frankly, I think we ought to drop the anthology."

Levin, suppressing excitement, hesitantly rose.

"You can't do that. Didn't you tell the man what literature is, why we study it?"

"There was no telling him a thing. He was absolutely enraged. I thought he was going to sock Orville, he was that sore."

"Maybe you should have asked him to leave?"

Gilley made a face. "The townspeople are just as good as we are, Sy."

"I wouldn't doubt it," said Levin, "but are ideas equal?"

"My policy with complaints is to hear them out, not antagonize anybody further."

"Fine—but—er—censorship is dangerous business."

"I'm not sure I'd call it censorship." Gerald had to clear a rough spot in his voice.

"Whatever you call it, that's what it is."

"I'd like to ask you what kind of budget you think this college would rate if this man's complaint reached the legislature? It's more than likely they'd see it pretty much as he does. We have to watch our step nowadays, or the next thing you know they'd be accusing us of something a lot worse than teaching sexy stories."

"A college is no place to show contempt for art or intellect. If you drop the book, you'll be making cowards of us all."

Gilley frowned. "Aren't those pretty strong words, Sy?"

Conscious of nervous knees, Levin sat down.

Gerald spoke mildly. "You sound as though I were out to hurt the institution, although what I was thinking of first and foremost was our welfare. Let me tell you what happened in one of our colleges of education last year. This art instructor they hired from some California college got a nude model to pose in his painting class, which nobody knew anything of till he exhibited the pictures they had painted of her. Well, the exhibition lasted about an hour, but that was long enough to raise a fuss and smell that the newspapers carried all over the state. The next thing everybody knew, it was reported in *Time*. Only last month one of my former students, who is now in oil in Venezuela, sent me a clipping of it in Spanish. But the worst of it was this. Although the art instructor was canned, in traveling around the state I still hear occasional smutty talk about what the students are learning in the Northern Cascadia College of Education. It wouldn't at all surprise me if their graduates are having trouble finding teaching jobs in the state, and maybe out. Now we can't afford to have that sort of thing happening here. The reputation of an institution of higher learning is sacred. That's why I did everything I could to pacify the man instead of antagonizing him, as you suggested. Besides, the girl was just nineteen, and you know how sensitive they are at that age."

"Maybe she doesn't belong in college," Levin said.

"Any Cascadia high school graduate is by law eligible to enter Cascadia College."

"If the course is too much for her she ought to drop it."

"That's not the point. All she does is object to a story I can't legitimately defend."

"If you'll pardon my saying so, I think you're wrong."

"Have you read it recently?"

"No, but I've never heard any criticism of it as an improper story."

"Leopold had gone through the anthology before he recommended it to Orville, who at that time was too busy to read it, but he admits he might have slipped up on that particular story. For one thing, the boy's father seems to have approved the son's illicit relationship with the Indian girl, even though he had told him—his son—that he—the father—had witnessed the girl having intercourse with somebody else in the woods. Now would you defend that as a story for classroom discussion?"

Though Levin felt hot under his beard and was contemplating a sarcastic remark, he had quick second thoughts. *In the woods?* For a wild minute he was convinced Gilley had followed Pauline into the forest that day and was leading up to a devastating accusation. The instructor felt tense and sweaty, but as he guardedly studied Gerald's face he knew his annoyance was for something less than a mortal wound. Again he felt secret relief.

"What would you have done if you were in my shoes?" Gilley asked.

Levin, limp, said he wasn't sure.

"I'll bet you'd have done pretty much what I had to. I've read *Aereopagitica*, too, Sy, but we have to be practical as well as idealistic. Suppose we kept on teaching the story and one of our Indian students, or somebody with Indian blood in him, objected to it as degrading the American Indians? They're pictured as drunks, even if there was a Fourth of July celebration in the story. It wouldn't be long, I bet, before we'd have the Un-American Committee here investigating us and making all sorts of nasty charges. Then where would we be?"

Staring out of the window, Levin noticed that the cracked glass resembled forked lightning. He drew a wavering breath but said nothing.

"It's a question," Gilley was saying, "of our bread and butter."

"Not of our immortal souls?" Levin laughed unwillingly.

Responsive to smiles and laughter, Gilley beamed. "I knew you'd see it my way. We may disagree here and there, Sy, but I think we value the same things."

In shame, Levin looked away.

After rereading Hemingway's innocent little story he felt faint, disgusted with himself for the ineffectuality of his protest.

Standing at the lone urinal in the second floor lavatory he tried to think what he could possibly do to save the anthology. The voice of Dr. CD Fabrikant penetrated the thin wall from his classroom, and Levin, as though staring the man in his hypnotic big eye, listened. He had on this spot previously heard portions of lectures on "The Noble Savage in James Fenimore Cooper," "Nightmare in Edgar Allan Poe," "Huck Finn's River Journey," "The American Past," and parts of other discourses. One heard in Fabrikant's dehydrated rumble a breath of excitement in the expression of ideas, perhaps his only emotion after too many dry years; still, he was able to communicate that ideas can excite, and Levin considered him a good teacher. He was at the moment lecturing on Emerson, and the instructor after a while listened with half an ear, still thinking of his upsetting talk with Gerald.

Particularly since the Birdless hassle, Levin had thought he would like to suggest an improvement or two in department principles and methodology, subtly or otherwise, if not to Gilley perhaps to Fairchild through some of the men on good terms with both. Since overcoming his drunkenness, perhaps as interest received on what he had accomplished, or what learned from what he had been through, he had from time to time felt the return of the courage of his convictions. As of old, Levin felt the human lot could be infinitely improved, but what was he doing about it? The true liberal, in his moral fervor, kept alive the visionary ideal, in the long run perhaps the

228

decisive thing, and fought at every opportunity to translate it into a better life for people; but not Levin. The ideal got no farther than the inside of his head. Although thoughts of "making things better" continued to arrive by inspiration, at Cascadia College he restrained them. He did nothing to resist the status quo. He was, after all, a newcomer here; of the same race as the Cascadians, true, but a distant relative. And if not abysmally timid, not terribly courageous. Too often, in the midst of discussions with those who found his liberalism distasteful, Levin—as though his nervous system voted conservative—broke into hot sweat and his knees softened; lockjaw set in.

He blamed this unwilled reaction partly on his personal history, partly it was the effect of the times. He had dragged through the past a weight of shame and sense of exclusion from normal life, engineered by his father, Harry the goniff, misfit turned thief—he stole from everyone and his own left hand—whose fantastic thieving was the talk of every neighborhood they had to move out of. Levin had his whole life felt imperiled. In recent years he had come to pity his father but was still influenced by his distortions. Add to a backlog of personal insecurity his portion of the fear that presently overwhelmed America. The country was frightened silly of Alger Hiss and Whittaker Chambers, Communist spies and Congressional committees, flying saucers and fellow travelers, their friends and associates, and those who asked them for a match or the time of day. Intellectuals, scientists, teachers were investigated by numerous committees and if found to be good Americans were asked to sign loyalty oaths. Democracy was defended by cripples who crippled it. At Cascadia College the American fear manifested itself, paradoxically, in what was missing: ideas, serious criticism, a liberal position. Levin remarked this only to Bucket, who nodded once. No one, for instance, disagreed with Professor Fairchild's daily dispraise of "Roosevelt socialism"; if one did, disagreement was silent. Levin's protective coloration was to pretend he thought like everyone else. The specter of Duffy haunted his head, beware his *fate*. You have only one life to live, the instructor counseled himself, why lose it here, cut down in your prime at a cow college in a backwoods town for bucking the petrified order? For who, after all, was Levin but a poor man trying to make an honest living, a tough-enough proposition for him in the best of times. Therefore be smart, mind your business, don't make trouble.

Yet because others were more timid than he (who was striving, as Chekov said, to squeeze the slave out of himself) perhaps Levin, mixing feelings of weakness with intimations of strength, was brave by default; for even as he whispered warnings to himself the word within sometimes was, "Speak up, do what you must to uphold the common good"—emphasis on the issues, Levin, conservative radical, loyal opposition, master of the gentle tactic, patient persuader, calm reasoner. He must *on principle* not be afraid. "The little you do may encourage the next man to do more. It doesn't take a violent revolution to change a policy or an institution. All it takes is a good idea and a man with guts. Someone who knows that America's historically successful ideas have been liberal and radical, continuing revolt in the cause of freedom. 'Disaster occurs if a country finally abandons its radical creative past'— R. Chase. Don't be afraid of the mean-spirited. Remember that a man who scorns an idealist scorns the secret image of himself. (Levin's notebook: "Insights.") Don't be afraid of names. Your purpose as self-improved man is to help the human lot, notwithstanding universal peril, anxiety, continued betrayal of freedom and oppression of man. He would, as a teacher, do everything he could to help bring forth those gifted few who would do more than their teachers had taught, in the name of democracy and humanity. (Whistles, cheers, prolonged applause.) The instructor took a bow at the urinal.

Such being his mood these days he felt the need to make an issue of the book censorship business, all but convinced that Fairchild and Gilley would retreat if they ran into unexpected opposition. But Levin though feeling free and energetic, remembered he was in love with Pauline Gilley and stood speechless.

If not I, who shall lead? he eventually asked. Listening to Fabrikant's voice, the instructor wondered if he ought to ally himself with the scholar, and if Fabrikant managed to come into power, become useful through him? There seemed no doubt that an election was on its way, though no one could say just when. Fabrikant, according to Bucket, was still eager to become the next head of department, and Levin thought he would offer his support, at least a vote added to Joe's and a few others' who seemed to take the scholar's candidacy seriously. Levin had considered this course of action before but hadn't made up his mind because he was still not entirely sold on Fabrikant. CD wasn't exactly the open type; he offered little of self. Sought out, he could be hospitable, laugh you his short laugh, even invite you to come again, but if you didn't he wouldn't miss you. He was not warm even to warmth. Scowers called him "soured—he has lost too many battles." Leopold Kuck had remarked that privacy represented more than a privilege to him. "He enjoys it as an exclusion of those he thinks don't appreciate him." Levin knew what they meant but tended to explain certain of Fabrikant's limitations as brought on or intensified by his hard life during the Depression, and, for that matter, his kind of luck. He was a man who had never run ahead of the life he lived. Maybe so, Levin thought, and he wears white socks, and his shoes squeak but what matters are his principles and record.

He knew George Bullock didn't think much of either. George had once said that CD had never fought a major battle. "Okay, he's got good marks for plugging for salary increases, more promotions, freer sabbatical rules, and a better retirement system than we now have on the books. He's also for academic freedom, but who isn't outside of Congress? I hear tell he did use to go see Marion Labhart every now and then and urge him to support this or that item, but once when he took a dim view of a policy of required attendance at department meetings, Marion blasted him out of his office, and, as I understand it, CD has never gone back in. If you want to know what's mostly on his mind, read some of the letters he's written in the past few years to the local rag and the college daily. On campus he's against reports in triplicate, fraternities, and student apathy in college elections. His letters to the *Commercial Budget* protest the inefficiency of county government. He's against indiscriminate garbage dumping and dogs that run loose and murder his chickens. He's also got no use for chlorine and fluorides in the drinking water. 'What this country needs is a pure glass of water.' If he's written one letter on that subject, I swear I've read five. Do you call that a record?"

On the other hand, Gilley, so far as Levin could learn, had fought not even for a pure glass of water. Beyond his good nature and lovely wife, he had little to recommend him. At the very least Fabrikant stood on principle. Gilley, totally congenial, was blown by every wind, in particular Fairchild's. Fabrikant, though maybe a little eccentric—give him credit—showed in his independence a strength of sorts. Gilley's strength was to persist in his weaknesses. Fabrikant might grow as an administrator as he loosened to life, once it had at last rewarded him; Gilley would remain as he was, gregarious, generous, ungrown. Of these two most possible choices it seemed to Levin the better was Fabrikant.

Through the wall came his dry voice reading Emerson: "'Whoever would be a man must be a non-conformist. He who would gather immortal palms must not be hindered by the name of goodness . . .' That is to say," said Fabrikant, "not 'goodness' but 'the name of goodness.' 'Nothing at last is sacred but the integrity of your mind.'"

"Amen," sighed Levin.

The bell in the hall rang. He checked his fly and turned to the sink. Standing there was Professor Fairchild, watching him with interest.

"All yours," Levin stammered.

On his way out of the building that afternoon he visited Fabrikant in his office and in a low voice told him the story of the censored anthology. The scholar, his thick brows pressed together, listened gloomily.

"It's been that way as long as I can remember."

"Couldn't you talk to Fairchild?"

"It wouldn't do any good. Once his mind's made up he's stubborn as a goat."

"Even if you talked to him?"

"Even if Teddy Roosevelt did."

"Shouldn't we at least try?"

"It wouldn't come to anything. I'd advise you not to worry about that book. One battle isn't the war."

"Unless it is," said Levin.

"It isn't. This isn't the time to fight each petty tyranny or idiocy that comes along but to wait and overthrow the tyrant."

"You think it's possible?"

"A lot depends on popular support."

Levin said quietly, "I would like to offer my—assistance in your campaign, in some way."

"Fine, but you must understand I can't show my hand just yet, though I will soon. I have one or two other irons in the fire. Fairchild has promised my long overdue promotion and I want to be sure that's gone through before I antagonize him again. I should know in a month."

"Don't wait too long," Levin advised. "Anyway," he said, "I'm your man. I meant to tell you before this." He felt not quite at ease saying it but said it.

"Call me CD." Fabrikant cordially offered a cigar.

Levin refused a light but to be sociable sat with the cigar in his mouth. Feeling foolish, he thrust it into his breast pocket. "I'd better be getting home. I have a load of papers to go through tonight."

"Feel free to come in."

The instructor thanked him. He almost walked into Gilley in the corridor. Levin tried to hide the cigar but failed though he crushed it into his pocket. Gilley nodded coolly, his expression suggesting suspicion. Levin, wondering which perfidy he knew, absently lifted his hat.

If Gilley were alive to political affront, he showed not the slightest sign he was aware of a situation that insulted his manhood; and Levin's passion for his wife grew, fed by the secrecy it lived in. His heart was a taut string played hard by love, one further note of longing and it would snap in its face. Secrecy was an intensifying component, another that he saw her rarely now, and lived much in images of desire. At the time of his deepest need (one way of tormenting himself was to imagine spending twenty-four normal hours in her company) Gilley's winter extension course ended and he did not reschedule it for spring. The trout season wouldn't open till April, and freshman recruitment was temporarily over until a last intensive week in May. Gerald was therefore either home with Pauline or out with her. She saw Levin for occasional short visits, but was now hesitant to give as her excuse for going out, non-existent civic meetings. A Mrs. Bowie, whose house she was supposed to be at, had called one night, and Gilley was mystified until Pauline (fresh from love with Levin) said she had remembered the meeting had been postponed and so had dropped in at Jeannette's. She had become again "deathly afraid." It's the town, Levin thought; too tight to maneuver in. Too much is visible to the naked eye. When they met it still took her a while to stop being afraid. She looked sometimes as though it were all too much for her. Levin said that one night but she denied it. "It's just that I sometimes worry what would happen to the children." He had not much thought of them, but now he thought, though not much. She made him promise faithfully never to mention her name to anyone.

Though the Gilleys entertained more frequently now, Pauline thought it best not to invite Levin. "It's hard to pretend no-love when I feel so much for you." Therefore though they made plans to be together more often, they saw each other less. As always he "had" again as have-not; hadn't bargained for this much longing, this much not having what was his to have. Missing her became work. He reveried a warm floral time when they'd be inseparably together, in various stages of dress or undress, bed or board. My God, if I could only walk in the street with her. He dreamed of her as his wife, but on her belly was tattooed "Mrs. Gilley." She wrote him suddenly, a spate of letters in official-looking brown envelopes, which he was not permitted to answer because Gilley made a point of going to the box after the mail delivery during the lunch hour; and Levin, after carrying it in his inside pocket, reading and rereading it, burned each letter in the fireplace because she had asked him to. The letters he couldn't write her were a further loss. He was in his heart a poet these days; each thought of her was crammed with beauty. It's what you don't say that counts. But she let him telephone if he made sure Gerald was either at his desk or in class. Levin went into a phone booth in the Student Union to make his call, his heart thumping like a hand on a bull fiddle. They exchanged endearment and hung up. On Saturday mornings she called from downtown, if she could. If Mrs. Beaty, deaf or not, was too close by, she could tell from his voice and said goodbye. If not, each praised the other and both praised love. Afterwards Levin walked unknown distances.

They had met rarely by chance before they became lovers, but in March, as though for compensation, he began to see her almost every time he left the house, and he left the house to see her. Walking downtown he would spot her driving the family Buick, tall in the seat, her straight hair touching her shoulders, nose pointing direction—where Levin must go. They met by accident in the post office, library, market. She greeted him vaguely and hurried the kids on. He would pass her on the street and tip his hat. Last fall, when they had met, she had stopped to exchange a word; he was the one in a hurry. Now her greetings were hesitant, formal. She hid love, a concealment painful to him. But there were times when for the slightest second her eyes were in love with him. Sometimes he saw her alone across the street; he liked her brisk high-heeled walk. Each noticeable new thing about her was an event: what she wore: a split skirt showing a bit of white slip against her leg. Long dark blue socks awoke forest memories. He knew when she had washed her hair. Once in a food market, Gilley and both kids waiting outside in the car, when Levin approached Pauline dropped a can of tuna fish she had just taken off the shelf. It rolled along the floor. He bent for it, remembering the casserole she had ladled into his lap the night they had met. As he gave her the can their fingers touched and his heart grew flowers. Leaving the store, she glanced back at him. He lived on that for a week.

One Saturday morning when she had not telephoned, Levin hurried downtown hoping for a glimpse of her. Wherever he went, she wasn't. At noon he was returning in disappointment to his car when he passed a photographer's shop displaying some enlarged shots of the Cascadia basketball team in its window. An intuition stopped Levin and he went to the window. Almost at once he discovered Pauline in a picture ("Profs and Wives Cheer Team"), nothing less than revelation. While the photographer was posing a bridal party in the studio at the rear of the store, Levin entered, plucked the picture out of the window, folded it once, and slipped it into his pocket. He drove home in a hurry and in his room cut out her intense, open, lovely face. Levin then tore up Gilley, the Bullocks, and the rest of the crowd he had extracted her from. He kept this little picture of her hidden among the best thoughts in his notebook and would often gaze at it.

Now and then he saw her at people's houses, a star, a flower amid the full-breasted faculty wives. What they lacked she had. What she hadn't nobody needed. It was high adventure for him when she walked in, even with Gilley, even if she hardly seemed to recognize her lover. Better that than not appear; that broke the night. At these social gatherings talk was small and wit rare, but hospitality and warmth were undeniable; Levin eagerly laid hold of any invitation that might produce her. He was surprisingly often invited where she was, almost as though people sensed romance and fostered it, though he hoped not. Whenever they met the action was as before: although they had talked together casually in the past, now, as on the street, she gave him little more than hello, how are you? She was no actress. He loved, therefore, behind the eyes; always conscious of what she was doing, when alone, talking to Jeannette, Alma or another woman, or to men and which men, when in the kitchen, on the sofa, or momentarily gone to the bathroom. He must know where she was. From where Levin observed, standing among others apart from her, sitting near her at a dinner table, trying not to stare, or watching from the next room, her face was gentle and luminous, sometimes a little sad; he created her quality as love created him; her loveliness enriching her clothes, the air around her. Once she drew back a lock of hair to adjust a barrette and revealed an ear pinned like a jewel to her head. Another time she was wearing her hair in a bun and he whispered, "Your neck is stupendous." Pauline, in spite of herself, laughed. Lord, thought Levin, how beautiful women are, and how hungry my heart is. But how short life, how soon gone. Where will I find the patience to go on hungering? Love entitled him to create her beauty but never to embrace it when he most desired.

They sat in circles and talked; or, depending on the specialty of the house, watched slides, listened to records, or acted charades. He was pleased when his play acting amused her. There was no mood to a party but Levin's own. Once after dancing with her at Bullocks, he followed her into a bedroom. Pauline returned his kiss then drew back. "Please don't when Gerald's around." She walked out as he wiped his lips clean. He felt there was no future in their love, until a few minutes later, when as they met in a momentarily empty hall, she took his hand and pressed it to her cheek.

Although during the evening he could blot Gilley out of his mind, what most tormented him was their leaving together, Levin locked out, a dirty trick on a lover. At midnight one of the women mentioned her baby sitter, her husband automatically stood up, and the whole company rose in a body. That ended the party, a blow to a bachelor who slept with his beard. Gilley gave his wife the eye and she went for her coat. They left for what lands, what voyages Levin couldn't make. He sometimes walked downtown and ordered a meal, to eat up his hunger.

One night at Bullocks she stayed as far from him as she could. She clung to Gilley, on her fourth drink without George's assistance. He recalled the time she had said she hoped for a revival of Gerald's love. He doesn't deserve it, Levin thought; but he felt she loved short of his love for her —his usual fate. Pauline saw him watching her and went into another room. She stayed apart from him all night. He was embittered, desolate. At midnight when the Bullocks served their elaborate buffet—coffee and cake was the customary nightcap elsewhere—Pauline filled up a plate and brought it to Gilley. He took it with a grin, placing a public arm around her. Levin, jealous of the years and substance of her Gerald had had, put down his glass and went out into the garden. It had begun to drizzle. As he was thinking he would leave from the garden and come around tomorrow for his coat, he heard footsteps on the patio. She was in his arms before he could turn.

"Forgive me, darling, Gerald's been awfully sweet, and I've felt very guilty. At times I hate myself."

"Don't feel bound to me."

"The truth is I do."

"Then don't feel guilty."

"If it were only that easy."

"Is that why you're drinking?"

"To forget you a little."

They kissed. "I'd better go," she said.

238

He took her hand. "You're so lovely."

"I feel lovely with you."

"My heart aches for you."

"I for you."

"When can you come?"

"I'll try tonight."

"Don't if you feel bad."

Pauline said she would try.

It was past two when she tapped on the glass. She had slept in Erik's room after Gilley had fallen asleep. When Erik called for his water she gave it to him, then changed the baby in her sleep and left. "I can only stay a few minutes."

"Did you take the car?"

"I was afraid of the noise it would make."

"I'll drive you back."

"Not all the way."

But she had not touched her earrings.

"Aren't you going to undress?"

She looked at him then looked away. "I can't tonight. Gerald wanted to and I couldn't say no."

He was struck by a grave sadness.

A few nights later she came in at nine. "I'm supposed to be at a late movie he doesn't want to see, and I've got to be home just after it lets out."

It was a time of fulfillment. Afterwards Levin said, "I hate to see you so scared. We've got to think of something we can do."

"What, for instance?"

"Whatever you say."

"What about your plans?"

"Sometime we'll have to tell him the truth."

"Not yet," she said. Then she said, "Let's wait till summer, then we'll talk about it."

"Why till summer?"

"To see how things go."

"Don't you think we have a future together?"

"Sometimes I do and sometimes not."

"When do you think so?"

"When it suddenly looks possible. I feel calm and see it that way."

"When doesn't it?"

"When I feel you ought to have someone with fewer problems to bring you."

"Forget that. How does it look now?"

"Possible."

"That creates the future," Levin said.

Before she left he asked, "Are you sure you love me?"

"So much it takes me time to think how much. Why do you ask so often?"

"All my life I've been engaged in wanting."

"Love makes a long journey in you."

"Your love inspires me. It always will."

"Don't make me cry, darling," Pauline said.

She left at midnight, it was raining. She had stayed longer than she had intended; but she had taken the precaution of dropping in at the Scowers before, to say she had been there too if Gerald asked anything.

"The lies shame me most," she said.

He lit her way down the stairs with a flashlight and watched her leave the yard, regretting her going. Tonight the room was empty after she had gone. Levin switched off the light and tried to fall quickly asleep. He was beginning to doze when he heard a knock on his door and roused himself.

The landlady, her gray hair in braids, held her battery box in her hand. She was upset.

"I'm sorry, Mr. Levin, but I have my self-respect to think of. I asked Mrs. Gilley not to come here again. I'm sorry for her and I'm sorry for you, but it's not right, and I have the reputation of my house to think of."

He listened with battered heart and stone ear.

"A few nights ago when I awoke to get my medicine I

thought I saw her coming out of the alley with you. Since then I waited up every night, and tonight I missed her going in but I heard her high heels come down your stairs. At first I was going to talk to you, but then I decided to talk to her. She isn't the right person for you, Mr. Levin, and you'll get into real trouble at the college if you go on with her. Whether you do or you don't, I don't want her coming here any more."

"It would have been merciful if you had spoken to me."

"I'm not sure that a married woman carrying on deserves much mercy. I feel sorry for Mr. Gilley."

"What did she say when you spoke to her?"

"All she did was run away."

Levin groaned.

After the old woman went downstairs he felt a furious desperation. What had happened now seemed inevitable. He dressed and left the house. Levin walked in the rain to Pauline's. Her house was dark except for the white tree on the front lawn. He stood across the street, wanting her through walls. Half the night he wandered in the rain.

In the morning he was impatient to call her but Gilley wasn't at his desk during his office hours and Levin did not want to risk it. Later he found a letter in his office mailbox, a blue envelope addressed in block letters. She had never written him here before.

"Just a word, dearest. I suppose you know?—I'm awfully sorry. I was afraid of something like this. I can't tell you how bad I feel, God knows how I'll get through the night. I'm writing this in Erik's room. Call me Thurs. between 9 & 10, no later. I just had to get in touch. I love you. I miss you so. Destroy this. Pauline."

He kissed the letter.

Thursday at nine he called. Hearing her voice made him feel as though they had been separated for years.

"When can I see you?" he asked.

"Lev, I'm frightened to death. Let's be careful. Not for a while is best."

"I could look for another room or maybe a small apartment with a private entrance?"

"If you move now she may tell people. If she lets you stay I doubt she'd talk. Has she said anything to you?"

"Just only what happened. She hasn't asked me to move but we ought to have plans."

"You have plans, Lev."

"I mean in case something happens."

"I don't want anything else to happen, nothing, nothing."

"Don't be scared."

"I was brought up to be."

"If I could just see you."

"Not for a while, please. Just call me Tuesdays and Thursdays, about this time. I may write but please don't you. I'm terribly sorry—I shouldn't have come so often. She wasn't nasty but I felt awful. I'm sorry I'm not somebody else, I mean someone not married. You don't deserve this."

"I deserve you."

"I'd better hang up. I don't want to cry on the phone."

Though he telephoned twice a week for a brief word of love, he saw her only in passing, in motion away from him. He thought of her with such intensity it was like waking when he stopped thinking. So Levin lived, famished, except for the sound of her voice on the phone and an occasional letter to the office, which he dutifully tore up. Beyond the word he lived on memory: her heart easing presence in his arms. Levin inspired, by her embrace, breath, beauty, the smell and feel of her, their consummation, and aftermath, when because of love's possibilities the previous minute's love was deepened. Otherwise hunger.

"I never see you," he said on the phone. "Where are you besides in my heart?"

"Here," she said, "at this end."

"We've got to meet."

"Where would we go?"

"I'll find some place," he said.

242

"A beautiful place, a forest."

At night Levin haunted her street. After a walk to river, or the hills, he came to her house when it was late and unlikely Gilley would step out with milk bottles or the cat. Levin stood across the street near the flowering plum tree thick with deep-hued pink blossoms. He watched for a touch of Pauline, a glimpse of her dress as she passed the half-shaded window, or whatever morsel luck would let fall into his empty hands.

In his thoughts he crossed the street and entered his house. She was waiting for him. They ate together, then when the kids were in bed, talked, read, listened to music. They went to bed and made love without ache or fear—was there ever such a life? Anyway, it was love and he had it, until he was standing alone across the street as she lay in bed with a stranger . . .

Levin was startled by a touch on the arm. A cop, staring at his beard, said a taxpayer had called and complained of a peeping Tom.

"Not me," said Levin.

"Could I see some I.D.?"

Levin produced his automobile license.

The cop looked at it and returned the card.

"Could you tell me why you're standing here?"

"Resting after a walk. Such a beautiful night."

"Right in the middle of the sidewalk?"

"I love this tree."

"The lady that phoned said you had been here more than an hour. She thought you might be casing one of the houses across the street."

"That long?" said Levin. He left, heavy hearted.

One early spring night when a brimming moon in the white sky gilded houses, trees, and spring flowers, a moon-drenched Levin wandered along Pauline's street and paused at the flowering plum. He crossed the street and stood, hat in hand, a few feet from her partly-open, dark bedroom window. Come to the window for a minute, my dearest, and I'll be content for a month. But no one appeared, though he thought of it often. In the stillness he heard the rhythmic creaking of a bed, and then on the night—a bird, catch it, hold it—the soft cry of a woman at the height of her pleasure.

Gilley had, in an inspired moment, satisfied her for him.

They made plans to be together but for one reason or another abandoned them. She was afraid they might be seen wherever they met. "It would be absolutely cruel if Gerald found out through gossip." "Am I never to be with you?" "Be patient, Lev." He cursed the day Mrs. Beaty had seen her in the alley. One morning when he was famished for a look at her, she let him watch from down the block as she entered the food market. When she came out, she looked in his direction for several seconds, then walked to her car. This can't go on, he thought.

Learning on Thursday morning that she was going with Gilley to a post-season basketball game on Saturday night, Levin hurried to the Basketball Palace and with luck got a reserved seat in the balcony, facing the faculty section. On Saturday night he was there early, amid an enormous crowd of students and townspeople. Levin spent most of his time scanning faces with his birdwatching binoculars. Once the glasses met a pair directed at him, a hard eye for an eye. A chill ran through him as he recognized the flushed half-bald dome and expressionless features of Dr. Marion Labhart. Levin had sulfurous visions of himself as Arthur Dimmesdale Levin, locked in stocks on a platform in the town square, a red A stapled on his chest, as President Labhart stood over him, preaching a hellfire sermon denouncing communist adulterers, the climax of which was the public firing of Levin out of the college. Next to the president sat Dean Lawrence Seagram of the Liberal Arts Service Division. When Levin first saw him in September the dean was a clean-shaven youngish type; now he was middle-aged and wore a grizzled Van Dyke but at least looked human.

Seeking Pauline, Levin located Gilley with an empty seat at his side, a gap for Levin. Above in the next row were both Bullocks. Levin, focusing on the empty seat, wondered what had happened to Pauline; he waited impatiently for the two-hour sight of her. From a man at his side he learned that Cascadia was playing Los Angeles for the Western Conference Championship. The floor of the court blazed with reflected light, practice went on, and two bands blared. Among the rally girls on the Cascadia side Levin recognized Nadalee Hammerstad. She shook red pompoms, danced and twirled, revealing her slim thighs and frisky black-tighted behind. She performed directly below Pauline's empty seat, and Levin was uneasy at how life related events and people.

When the game started, Pauline had still not come. He considered running downstairs to telephone to make sure she was all right but he was caught in the prevailing excitement and stayed. The L.A. band had antagonized him. Costumed in hard straw hats, red bow ties, shorts and hairy legs, it created a jazz uproar, drowning out the pep songs of the white-shirted Cascadians. If the strategy was to keep their own players hopped up, they did the same for all present, setting Levin's teeth on edge, and arousing in him a strong antagonism to the State of California. From the whistle Los Angeles broke into the lead, and Levin, realizing the home town was the under-dog, found himself cheering it. For a minute he studied himself with a sour eye yet went on as before.

Though he had not since college watched basketball, he was gripped by the game. More than once he jumped out of his seat to cheer a good play or boo a bad call. What a bad call was he left to the crowd. He shouted encouragement to the players, in particular Whitey Barker, a skinny, long-chested type, a solid C minus student in Levin's last term's class, but on the court, canny, alert, graceful, wise. He defended like a matador enclosing the bull, and on offense hit baskets with every kind of shot. His rebounding was outstanding. The instructor waving his hat, cheered himself hoarse for his former student—although he suspected the boy had complained to Bullock about the grade he had got, because George had been cold to Levin for a while at the end of the winter term. Peering with his binoculars at the faculty section to study George's face, he discovered Pauline sitting next to Gerald.

A little ashamed of having forgotten her, he focused his glasses and was moved by her drawn face. She had lost weight. He could hear the game going on, ten men thundering back and forth, pitching a ball at two hoops, but now he kept his glasses tightly on her, taking his excitement from her presence. Pauline seemed, after a while, to be squirming this way and that; he realized she had become aware of him and was trying either to shrink or hide from his magnified eyes. Levin lowered his glasses and absent-mindedly watched the last few minutes of play. At the end he did not know who had won.

As he was leaving the Palace he thought he had at least shared the town's big emotion. He would not, if he could, deny them basketball if once in a while the big emotion came from a good book.

Going down the stairs, he overheard one beanied freshman he knew talking to another.

"Did you see that cat with the black whiskers who had those binocks in front of us? That's my comp prof."

"So what?"

"He's supposed to be nuts about some dame. Maybe he could see her naked in those glasses."

When Levin arrived home, he snipped off his beard with scissors and shaved the rest.

When they met, on a street at the southern edge of town, Pauline looked at him in disbelief then wept, though Levin said it wasn't too bad. He had searched long in the mirror, felt ill but lived. Too much face, the eyes still sad candles, blunt bent nose, lips without speech telling all, but the jaw looked stronger, possibly illusion.

"Why did you do it?" she asked. "It had gotten to look so rich and silky. I hope it isn't bad luck."

He waited until she stopped talking about it.

They tried to think where to go to be alone. He suggested the woods or the riverbank but it rained every day and they had to settle for motels near outlying towns. This was during a time Gilley was beginning to go fishing again. Levin registered and she stayed in the car, her face averted. Alone, they kissed, he tasting on her tongue the Scotch she had had to relax her. She was still mistress of the quick lay, and once it was over he dozed by her side, dreaming of her. Longing was long, the consummation brief. Satisfaction bred quick hunger. It saddened him he couldn't be contented for more than minutes. Levin held her in his arms, longing for Pauline. The thought of all the time that would go by before he saw her again oppressed him.

She wanted, of course, not to be nervous but usually was. "I hate motels. Your room was so nice. I felt at home in it." He offered to move to Marathon, where nobody knew them. "That's not good either," she said. "You'd be miles away and I'd have less time to be with you. And after a while, no matter where you lived, somebody would find out I was coming to see you and this would start again."

One night when there was not much time and they had worked themselves into desire in Levin's car, parked by the riverbank, she joked about the back seat, then grew depressed. The result was nothing achieved, his loss, for she seemed soon to feel better, as though she had exchanged nothing for something. He had lost more than a lay. But loss enlarged love, or so they said. And part of the experience of paradise was when it was no longer paradise. This thought had come to him in a former time when he was struggling to accept fate without making less of experience.

She said, as he was driving her to the street where she usually got out and walked home, "I've been thinking if only something very good happened to Gerald it would be easier to think of leaving him. Please don't oppose him for the head-ship. I'm sure he'll be good at it."

"There are better men around," Levin said.

"Last night I dreamed he found us in bed and took the children away from me."

"That won't happen."

"I always knew I would fall in love again but I wasn't pre-pared to feel ravaged so soon."

"Love is life."

"I wish you hadn't cut your beard."

"What can I do to make things easier for you?" Levin asked her. "I could stay away for a month, even till summer if you'd feel any better. Then in the summer we could come to a decision."

"Could you stay away that long?"

"I could for you."

"I don't think I could stand it, I'd worry about you."

"What worry?"

"About how you were and if you still loved me."

"You know I would."

"No, I don't want that kind of worry. I'd rather have this."

Afterwards he wanted to send her something—flowers—but what would she say if Gilley asked her where they had come from? So he settled for a pair of gold hoop earrings which he bought for more than he could afford. But when could she wear them except with him, and where would she hide them later? He kept them for her in his notebook drawer.

The next time they talked on the phone she said, "Don't think of me as poor Pauline, think of me as rich. I may have fears but I have you. I have lovely thoughts of you. I want to give you what you haven't had. I want to make up for all you've been through in the past. I want to make you happy with me."

He said he was happy.

In bed, the next time, she failed to achieve satisfaction. Since this was twice in a row Levin was disappointed.

"Don't make anything out of it," she said, "I've been sleeping badly and I'm usually tired. The kids tire me, and it's not easy to live with one man and be always thinking of another. I worry he senses something is wrong. And I worry about the strain on you."

"Don't worry about me."

"Now you have her, now you don't is no life for a man. And I worry about a definite break with Gerald. I guess I was not passionately attached to him but I've never been able to unlove anyone I ever loved."

"We'll settle it in the summer."

"I already have settled it but my nervous system hasn't. That's what flopped just now—not me. But I'll be myself next time."

Next time was in a little hotel about thirty miles out of Easchester—she was insisting they not go back to the motels they had been to. After a while, Pauline, her brow wet, said, "Don't wait for me, I don't think I can."

"Are you sure?"

"Come without me."

Finally he did.

"I'm really beat," she said.

"Is that it?"

She said, "Gerald is ardent again. I think he senses something. I told you he might. Sometimes I get so tired of sex."

Now we have truly come to adultery, Levin thought.

"I would have skipped it if you had asked me," he said.

She caressed his beardless face. Her eyes were tired, her nose thin. "Please don't worry. I go through these periods. I was in a bad period with Gerald just before the first time with you. But he's used to me and doesn't seem to mind."

"I mind."

"Don't idealize sex, Lev."

"Not sex, you."

After the fourth fruitless, songless time, one end-of-April night, Levin lay awake while she slept, grinding her teeth.

249

She had looked imperiled. He felt he had to do something to help her or this might get beyond her. Since it was almost certainly too late to start writing around for a new job, if he could get an assistantship somewhere, and Pauline a part-time job, things might work out. But making new plans worried Levin; it was as if those he had come West with had been wrong to begin with. If that was the case would he ever in his life make the right plans? Yet he felt for her a deep tenderness and dreamed of a decent life for them. When he awoke it was almost six-thirty and Pauline was frantic.

They were racing through a thick fir forest. Levin had said he would take her to the Easchester bus station where she could get a cab, and she had in silence agreed, her face calmly locked in fright.

"What will you do if he's awake?" Levin asked.

"I'll lie."

"Could I go in with you?"

"No."

Above the trees the light brightened, yellow, then foggy gold. " 'Tis the rising, not the setting sun,' " he said.

"Who said so?"

"B. Franklin."

"He was wrong."

The fake forest, Levin thought.

As he was speeding out of it, a siren sounded behind them. A state trooper in an unmarked car waved the Hudson to the side.

Levin cursed. Pauline shut her eyes. Any minute he expected to see gray in her hair.

The trooper talked for ten minutes before handing Levin the ticket. Pauline stared ahead, her stomach rumbling. She bent to hide it but couldn't.

Finally they were off again at fifty.

"I'd better go in with you."

"No, please no."

They parted at the Easchester bus station. She hurried into a cab, forgetting goodbye, Until We Meet Again, or even to wave. He watched the taxi turn the corner on a dull gray morning.

Afterwards Levin sweated it out in his room. He had visions of disaster for all, particularly himself. Yes, she loved him, but she also loved Gilley and she loved the kids. If she had loved Levin as he loved her, she would already have made up her mind to leave Gilley. To go on as they had been, would prolong the torture and destroy what was left of the joy of love. He stayed in the house Saturday and Sunday, waiting for a word from her but none came. Only Pauline lived in his thoughts. He thought of her as she had been when they were first in love and how worn out and unhappy she had looked lately. Levin struck himself for the harm he had done her. He promised that if, by some stroke of luck she had got in without Gilley knowing it, he would not see her till summer. The rest would do her good.

When he went to work on Monday morning, after his first desperate glance at Gerald, Levin knew Pauline had got in safely. Out of love he gave her up.

May sunbursts flooded the windows, making the mourner invisible; he sat, when he came in, unable to move, even a breath unsettling pain. He secretly waited for a word, a sign she loved him, would never let him give her up. She had once seized his flesh: "I'll never let you go." He waited for her to redeem the pledge. Through long days he waited, loving her, giving her up, trying to forget the last hours with her, memory repeating memory. But when she appeared—through Mrs. Beaty on guard, thick walls, a ring of flame, the salt sea—he sneaked her home past her husband at indecent hours; then in his mind (to save her from this) parted from her forever, the worst place to part from anyone. The landlady left a plate of oatmeal cookies at his door.

He secretly waited. She did not write or phone; nor appeared in the universe. After relief at her escape he ate himself slowly; his heart like a vessel of pain against bare bones; the mourner attended his perpetual funeral. He had expected in the ruined aftermath a diminished misery, reason the shield, since he had himself brought the affair to its broken end; but a surgeon operating on himself does not excise the pain, and now he knew the majesty of his. Having betrayed his nature, his deepest need, he had surrendered something of life to death. In pain he mortified what he was attempting to kill, his short-lived love, self-created freedom. Ah, the soaring anticipation of Pauline Gilley; possessing her in feeling's fullness; dreaming of what he had had. Dreams dead by suicide.

Silence burdened ache. Why had she not told him she had got in safely, knowing how intensely worried he would be? He could only explain it that she had given him up at the same moment he had abandoned her, breaking off before impossible got worse, ultimately relieved to be done with an unhappy affair. It tormented him that he had left her, in the end, unsatisfied. Why does the last event condition the quality of the past? In his most desperate moments he felt a hatred of her that relieved the fundamental pain, but with such frightening other effects he preferred the pain. In the midst of which, in some shaded place within, dwelt Levin's Pauline, tender, lovely girl of the graceful shoulders and shapely can, their own fine art; the woman he had least expected to be in love with, source of his discoveries of her beauty (as when her hand or the wind touched her hair). Thoughts such as these made his loss unbearable.

After he had endured all he thought he could, there was more; he had in a former existence lowered the threshold of heartbreak. Ah, sweet mastery of life—if only Levin could. The more he suffered, no matter how frequent or pure his resolutions to change himself, the more he suffered. For whatever unknown or unpredictable cause. He did not kid himself, he was his own bad cause, causing what caused him pain ("Which way I flie is Hell; myself am Hell."); somewhere along the line he had erred, his life gone wrong, wronger. And when Levin erred the result was serious, no matter how often he promised to take life more lightly, less frantic seeking of a hold to throw it with. He laughed seriously and suffered merrily, miserere.

The sorrows of Levin: his mouth thickened with thirst. He hid a brown bottle under the bed, then slept with it. Ache turned at teasing times to prurience (original original sin) within which he imaged a bearded billy goat chewing Someone's pubic hair, the lady responding to the tickle and other jests in 167 satisfying ways. He plowed through the black pants she wore. Pricked with pins her bubless nipples. Clobbered her with sex, though she sobbed no, then begged for more, satisfaction levitating her a foot in the air. Amid such pleasures Mrs. Beaty's white cat fell in love with him, laying a broken-feathered bird at his door, fat headless robin. He asked the landlady to keep the cat out of the house but pussy in love was faithful, finding more ways in than he could block off, depositing another bloody-breasted bird. "Eat my heart," he cried and kicked the beast down the stairs. Ascending on three legs she delivered a mangled rat, then went into heat, her raucous cries sounding throughout the house. He considered taking off with packed bags, but to return where he had failed was failure. Depression dug a fast hole and in it he sat drowning. Alas, Levin, ever-drowning sailor. What had he done to his poor self? . . .

But time, though he hid from it, rained him in the face and change changed against the will. He rose once more to the surface, not the same man but who was? Apathy followed, worse yet. "A grief without a pang, void, dark, and drear,/ A stifled, drowsy, unimpassioned grief,/ Which finds no natural outlet, no relief,/ In word, or sigh, or tear." This went on too long, till he was ready to secede from the world; until a fissure appeared in the windowless wall and he wriggled through. No-feeling, purged, left mildewed melancholy. Each day introduced its own variation and quantity of ache. He felt sadness for every living thing. Even a tree, when Levin looked, looked sad. He was his own pathetic fallacy.

The bright flags of loneliness unfurled and flapped in the breeze. He knew it in every size and shape, hard, soft, black, blue, concrete city-type recalled; and woodsy-leafy country-kind. He had lived in dark small rooms in anonymous tenements on gray streets amid stone buildings crowding the sky; loneliness tracked him in the guise of strangers. In the country it dwelt in the near distance under vast umbrella skies. In the city, compressed; spacious in the country. Space plus whatever you feel equals more whatever you feel, marvelous for happiness, God save you otherwise. God save Levin. He longed for her to share the burden of his incompletion, the cheat of being human; longed for a past that was now memory pickled in regret. The unhappy clever purpose of the disease was to compel him to expel it. It would never succeed. Despite all his exertions to forget her, Levin remembered and desired; the town was small and she lived nearby. He had one day seen Erik scraping the sidewalk in her long shoes.

To get away from what he could not escape he drove his car on dusty country roads leading nowhere. Sometimes he stopped and shouted in the stillness. Lonely crows flew up from the fields. White farmhouses and rain-stained barns were lonely, cows and horses, every living thing. Trees were lonely, fences, so was the horizon. That somehow was the worst. The dust blew up behind him as he sped home. He knew that the only way to fight his sadness of spirit was to be among people but he did nothing to be. Throughout these weeks he managed to teach students, then escaped his office. Though an occasional invitation to someone's house came his way he did not accept, not to see her. He was certain she didn't want to see him; this made him deathly lonely. He often doubted she had truly loved him. He was at times desperately moved to write her but wrote nothing. If she wanted it ended, he would keep it ended. He would help her resist him if she were resisting.

Levin resisted with the same arguments: She was, for the thousandth time, a married woman with a family. She had caused herself to love out of discontent, although her discontents were tolerable. Gilley was good to her; she had a better than average home, kids she loved. Maybe she was bored but she wasn't desperate; she probably could go on living with him forever. If diversion was what she had wanted, a little love on the side, she wasn't made for it, the pleasure butchered by anxiety and shame. She wasn't the type who could give "all" for love. And he doubted he could inspire such love, the limits of her passion conditioned by the man he was. He might awaken love but not madness, although maybe it was mad to chance what she had chanced; maybe she understood he too was unwilling to give "all." He had lived through too much, become wary to the frazzled ends of his nerves of too many "lessons." He was, in love, not Seymour Gordon Lord Byron, but a modest man and would not complain if all he got was no more than he gave. He left to Casanova or Clark Gable the gourmandise, the blasts and quakes of passion. He wanted love like a fountain in the wind. He wanted in a woman loveliness and feeling, of course, but character, constancy. He wanted someone free to love so he could freely love.

Whenever Levin saw Gilley he thought of his treachery to him; it was wrong to have continued to see his wife under the circumstances. Sneaking love in his room, in motels; the hiding and guilt had hurt them both. He would have done better to have kept his door shut against her; only if she were willing to give up Gilley was the way. If she were, there might have been no problem. If she were that willing he might have run from her, over the hills and far away; at least tipped his hat and backed off. In the street they would nod to each other, a lanky lady and a bearded gent, and hurry by. He would not then have been incapacitated before her husband when there was an issue to fight for, a principle to defend. Somebody should have fought for the retention of the short story anthology; he was the coward in that affair. Now, if he expected to be of any help to Fabrikant he had to quit wanting to duck whenever he saw a red head in Humanities Hall. That was no career for a man with a future, future as man.

Morality—awareness of it—perhaps in his reaction to his father's life, or in sympathy with his mother's, or in another way, had lit an early candle in Levin's. He saw in good beauty. Good was as if man's spirit had produced art in life. Levin felt that the main source of conscious morality was love of life, anybody's life. Morality was a way of giving value to other lives through assuring human rights. As you valued men's lives yours received value. You earned what you sold, got what you gave. That, if not entirely true, ought to be. Our days are short, thought Levin, our bodies frail. The universe is unknown, remorseless. We have no certain understanding of Nature's intentions, nor God's if he intends. We know the meagerness, ignorance, cruelty of too many men and too many societies. We must protect the human, the good, the innocent. Those who had discovered their own moral courage, or created it, must join others who are moral; these must lead, without fanaticism. Any act of good is a diminution of evil in the world. To make himself effectual Levin must give up Pauline, or what was principle for? The strongest morality resists temptation; since he had not resisted he must renounce the continuance of the immoral. Renunciation was what he was now engaged in; it was a beginning that created a beginning. What an extraordinary thing, he thought: you could be not moral, then you could be. To be good, then evil, then good was no moral way of life, but to be good after being evil was a possibility of life. You stopped doing what was wrong and you did right. It was not easy but it was a free choice you might make, and the beauty of it was in the making, in the rightness of it. You knew it was right from the form it gave your life, the moving esthetic the act created in you.

I must give her up, he thought, if I haven't.

He had for half his life in wintertime yearned for spring. In the East, as early as February he woke sniffing the breeze for the first vernal fragrance still locked in a future month. Yet when spring burst into life he continued to hunger for it as though it weren't there, secretly knowing that what he desired did not grow on trees. In the Northwest this year spring had leapfrogged over winter's back before habit could rouse the spirit's hunger. And when he became aware of spring he was already involved with Pauline and spring made little difference. But now the green and floral season overwhelmed him, for with all its beauty it could not return to him an iota of the happiness he had lost. Sitting in his room on the very day they had parted (an act in aftermath) he watched the cherry tree blossom outside his window. In the morning sunlight a single moldy branch broke into flower and by evening the whole tree wore white. Up the block the hawthornes surprised: a flood of rose-hued blossoms capped the tiny dark-green leaves. And the chestnuts raised their white flambeaux. Everything was in flower around the corpse; and the corpse flowered in desire. Unable to resist the beauty of this spring night, love still tormenting despite all his exertions, he left his dreary room and walked in the direction of Pauline's house.

He had seen her downtown that day, a slim, pale woman with a distracted lovely face. Torn by the sight of her he had turned away, dizzied, drunk from seeing, desiring her from every pore. He ached beyond belief, famished, struggling to steel himself before he was overwhelmed. Levin cursed his particular body, inept apparatus; nothing brought relief. He prayed the night would, but it appeared in profuse beauty, a perfume of new flowers stirring pain. As he walked, a tree came alive with chirping birds. Bullfrogs were noisy in the distance; beyond that, the lowing of a cow. Realizing how close he had come to where he wasn't going, Levin halted. Was a man no more than a pawn to the season's mood? Why had he suffered if not to be his own master?

A woman in a light dress was coming toward him in the dark. Good God, it's Pauline. What will I do?

He waited for her to approach, or on recognition run the other way, but it wasn't Pauline. . . . It was Avis Fliss, her baggy chest stiff in a pink cotton dress stained by sweat around the armpits. She looked as lonely as he felt. Have I invented her? Levin thought.

"Why, good evening, Seymour. I almost didn't recognize you without your beard. Congratulations, if I may. If you hadn't been staring at me I would have walked right past you. Isn't tonight out of this world?"

They had returned to first names after being thrown together at people's houses during the winter, the old maid and lonely bachelor. She had lately shown signs she had forgotten her irritation with him.

"Are you enjoying an evening stroll?" Avis asked.

He nodded, watching her like a hawk, suspecting she was waiting to see which way he would go. He had noticed, when she was present at parties, Avis' livening of attention when he had stood near Pauline or their hands had brushed in passing.

"Were you by any chance going to the Gilleys?"

He said nothing.

"I wasn't meaning to pry," she said. "I thought I might save you a trip if you were, because I'm just coming from there and they're about to go out. I walked this way after supper to give Gerald a little thing I had just finished writing on teaching remedial grammar. I have copies if you'd care to read it. Gerald was delighted to have it. He offered to drive me home but I preferred to walk. When I was a little girl in Louisville, on nights like this everybody walked. Daddy often used to take me and sister Cora out and I can recall many young couples courting, holding hands in Charity Park. I realize the automobile is necessary to our economy, Seymour, but don't you think it has caused something gracious to leave our lives?"

He grunted. Avis' eyelids fluttered. "Are you bound somewhere in particular?"

260

He had no particular place in mind.

"Would you care to continue your walk with me? I—I've wanted to say something to you, Seymour."

Levin walked with her. They went toward the campus. It seemed to him that all he could smell of the night now was her overpowering orange blossom. He would walk another block or two, then ditch her and go back.

They passed Humanities Hall, all dark for once. Under the maple tree Avis turned to him breathlessly. "Mr. Levin—I mean Seymour—I shan't allude to this again, but I do want you to know I am most sincerely grateful to you for—for your self-control that time. It isn't often a gentleman will assist a lady to preserve her virtue."

Levin laughed badly.

She said quickly, "But that isn't what I meant to say. I've wanted to discuss with you a matter that concerns the welfare of our department, something I'm sure you'll be discreet about for obvious reasons. Let's just walk out of the campus, shall we? Voices carry here."

He went with her across the quadrangle and lower campus in the direction of the river. They came to a wooded area by the water, to a stone bench dimly lit. Two students who had been necking got up and walked off. She had brought him to Lover's Lane.

Lighting a cigarette, Avis crossed her legs. She puffed without inhaling, Levin motionless. She glanced at him nervously, then said in a low voice. "Just how much have you been told of the past?"

"Whose?" he asked drearily.

Her eyelids were in action. "Specifically, Leo Duffy's and, frankly, Pauline Gilley's."

"Specifically," he said slowly, "I know she liked and sympathized with him."

"Yes, that's true, but did you know?"—her strained breathiness broke—"that they were lovers"—she wet her lips—"actually?" Avis stared in another direction.

Levin sat there with a splitting headache. Though his impulse was to choke Avis he lived through torment to a clear understanding of Pauline's anxiety and fear: she had been through it before. Amid the rocks in his heart he silently groaned. What hurt most was the realization there had been in his relationship with her more than he knew, something that explained the end it had come to. What he had assumed to be the unique truth of their love was less than that. That she had had a lover before him he might forgive, but to keep from him that he had followed, under Gilley's nose, smack in another man's footsteps was deceit. He felt a rage of helplessness, again the victim of a lying life.

It changes nothing, he desperately thought. At the same time he knew it changed everything, even the past.

Avis, squirming on the bench, apologized for her news. "Please understand I tell you this only because it has some reference, more than indirect, to the future of our department." She spoke with eyes shut.

It took Levin a minute to speak through his misery, a complex self-renewing institution. But he hid what he felt so that he could learn what was left to know, afraid to be ignorant of anything that concerned him.

"Gerald knew?"

"Yes." She stepped on her cigarette and sat very still. "It all came out when he—when he developed the picture."

"What picture?"

She was restless again. The sweat marks around her armpits spread.

"Hadn't—hadn't you heard of it? I was sure Dr. Fabrikant had told you."

"No."

She hesitated, then quickly said, "Gerald took a photograph of them on the beach one day at the coast. They were both naked. I assumed you knew, or I—I wouldn't—"

He lived through a nauseating sense of having been here before.

"He—he had followed them. It was when Pauline and he were seriously considering divorce and he was collecting evidence—as he had every right to do. He took it with a certain kind of lens, from a distance. They had been in the water and as they were coming out, Gerald snapped."

"Was there a mess?"

"Not quite. Although he had consulted an attorney, Gerald did not file for the divorce. And once Leo was discharged from his position by President Labhart, that's what people talked about. Apparently they hadn't been seen together. Shortly after Leo had left, Gerald and Pauline dropped their plans for divorce, mainly because their adoption of Erik had come through. I assume Pauline had discovered that her heart was in domestic life after all, and that helped bring them together."

"Was the picture the only proof they were lovers?"

"I believe," Avis answered, "that Pauline had admitted that fact to Gerald."

"He told you that?"

"I'm not really at liberty to say."

"Did you see the picture?"

"It was described to me. You ought to know that Pauline has not seen it. She doesn't know of its existence, Seymour. Gerald was going to show it to her but when she confessed she loved Leo, he did not have to. It would only hurt her to know about it—that's why it's so important to be discreet."

"Who knows about it?"

"Not many. Counting—ah—you, about a dozen people. The wonderful thing was that everyone closed ranks behind Gerald to protect him and Pauline from further embarrassment, although perhaps that was more than she deserved."

Levin asked her if Bucket knew.

"He may possibly have heard from Dr. Fabrikant."

"Who told him?"

"Gerald, I believe."

He now understood.

"We've all been careful not to talk much about it," Avis said uneasily. "But I was certain you had heard, or I would never to my dying day, I assure you, have told you. I felt you ought to know the truth, since there are one or two people who have criticized Gerald for having taken the picture. I give you my word of honor that was my one and only reason for revealing this to you, Seymour, otherwise I would not have under any circumstances. I was told that Dr. Fabrikant—to be perfectly honest he told me himself—he said that he considered you to be one of those supporting his candidacy for department head, and I assumed, though perhaps I should not have, that he had won your confidence by telling you about the picture without describing the extenuating circumstances." She was unable to sit comfortably on the bench.

"I honestly did not wish to impugn Pauline's reputation," Avis went on. "I was thinking of no more than the welfare of our department, as I've said. If you knew Dr. Fabrikant as well as some of us, you'd understand he is not the most suitable person for head of department. He may indeed be a scholar, and I personally have nothing against him, but he's barely civil to other people. I'm not asking you to support Gerald—I wouldn't presume to—however, I thought it wasn't fair for you to go around with a wrong impression."

After a long, hopeless silence, Levin got up. Spring was gone, an interior army had murdered it with hammers.

"If I had to know," he muttered, "I had to know. I don't hold it against you."

"Against me?" she said hotly.

He wandered off.

"Mr. Levin—" she called after him.

He went without hearing, without judgment of her, or memory. He had saved her virtue and she had preserved him as a moral man.

When he attempted, after a period of renewed misery, to grow a beard, the stubble, to his horror, was sprinkled with gray, so he abandoned it.

Q. "What have I done to deserve my fate?"

A. "I am worthy of no other."

He saw in the strewn garbage of his life, errors, mishaps, ignorance, experience from which he had learned nothing.

He was as a man inadequate, in the sense of being powerless to achieve the most meager happiness. He had been left far behind by Purpose—those chances for self-fulfillment that spring up around the man who is not fortune's fool.

Whatever strayed into Levin's orbit wrecked it. He could not make happen to him what happened to all but the poor bastards of the world, a use of the better choices of life; with, sooner or later, some sense of accomplishment—however slow if visible.

And love, for Jesus' sake, so that he have not lived in vain.

He was not ambitious for power, wanted no extraordinary rewards; he wanted most to break through the hardened cement of self-frustation, to live in the world and enjoy it.

He felt, as always, the need of change—in and of himself, but no longer knew where to begin. His life was a sad hash of beginnings.

He could not understand why he chose so badly, why he invariably wound up with just that woman who was most clearly wrong for him, verboten, bound to bring him to broken bloody knees.

But as the days passed, there were whole hours in which he no longer thought of her, and though she still appeared, deviously, trickily in the mind, her image was thin, abstract. Yet it wearied Levin that he should be aware of her so continuously: open an eye in sleep and she was pallidly present. Close it and she trailed across a dream. He had locked himself behind a double-barred door—her rejection of him and the revelation of her true tie to Duffy, consequently, of his own; namely that he was a dead fish to begin with. Her easy way out: she had loved him to repeat Duffy, or possibly forget him, both reasons amounting to the same thing. She appeared and

disappeared, hiding behind her transparent skirts Gilley par-
boiled before the second cuckoldry. God knows what else.

If in his thoughts she failed him, in fairness, in the same
country he failed her. Levin, pipsqueak coward, who had not
loved no matter what. "Love alters not with his brief hours
and weeks,/ But bears it out even to the edge of doom." He
could say, as he often did, I quit to help her, for her, not me;
but Duffy, exposed by Avis, made fast the trembling quittance.
He had therefore left her for what she had withheld, the Irishman and his aftermath in her life. Aftermaths breed aftermaths. "Strangers are welcome," the magicians of love who
pass in the night. Bearded and beardless whoremasters. He felt
for a time a corrosive self-soiling jealousy of a ghost; Levin,
contaminated substance of Duffy's shade. He endured to be
unhaunted, the last of love in its rotting coffin.

After an oppressive time, the hours few but endless, his
"spirit" a foggy mishap, as if he were in perpetual sleepwalk,
Levin found himself looking for something to do in his "spare
time." "But tasks in hours of insights will'd,/Can be through
hours of gloom fulfill'd." Not that he could will or fulfill
anything, but he hoped to transform the mind from the
vinegar-soaked sponge it had become, or broken bottle full of
broken glass, once more into a functioning instrument. He
secretly meant to prove there was reason to be alive although
he scarcely believed it. In working, one at least worked to an
end. With luck some small purpose might come to something
larger, possibly a purpose to live for. At this he snickered for
he was repeating himself. Still, one sought a task to escape the
impoverishing richness of time. Every minute made Levin
poorer. If I were a poet, he thought, my miseries would have
value; but what does a teacher teach if he can't teach what
he is? He considered a philosophy project, to work towards a
unity of Plato and Aristotle? Or maybe learn Russian and read
Pushkin in the original? Or take up the guitar or recorder,
Bach on both? Maybe paint weekends, not that he could
weekdays. He had no heart for any of these things, then

wondered if he could begin to collect material for a critical study of Melville's whale: "White Whale as Burden of Dark World." "Moby Dick as Closet Drama." He liked the idea of an intellectual task, the whale on his head, relief through balancing the weight on the heart, a disguise and punishment in perpetuity, a means of keeping his poor ego from shattering into bits. Under a burden some found freedom. It had happened to slaves.

Levin began to read and make notes but gave up the whale when he discovered it in too many critical hats. He wrote down possible other titles for a short critical essay: "The Forest as Battleground of the Spirit in Some American Novels." "The Stranger as Fallen Angel in Western Fiction." "The American Ideal as Self-created Tradition." Levin wrote, "The idea of America will always create freedom"; but it was impossible to prove faith. After considering "The Guilt-ridden Revolutionary of the Visionary American Ideal," he settled on "American Self-criticism in Several Novels." Limiting himself, to start, to six books Levin read and reread them, making profuse notes. Almost with the first words he wrote, he was disappointed in how ill-prepared he was to evaluate ideas and express them. But he forced himself to keep on—if nothing else this might lead to a subject for a future dissertation. He wrote for a week, into the early morning hours, pushing himself, exasperated, suffering for having heaped punishment on punishment, yet ultimately producing a ten-page paper which Milly typed for him. After he had proofread it, the essay looked useless. He reread it with growing hatred, wanting to burn it, but decided to let someone else read it first. He thought of Dr. Fabrikant, thought no, then yes, and finally delivered it to the scholar, apologizing for taking his time. An hour or so later he found the paper in his mailbox with attached note: "I find this an illuminating insight and will be happy to advise where it might be sent. Am glad you have decided to publish. We sorely need that kind of thing in this institution. In the future I would hope to encourage it. CD." Levin thought of sending the paper out at once, but doubt lingered so he decided to try one more opinion. He considered Bullock but abandoned the thought and left the little essay on Bucket's desk. "Would appreciate any comment. No hurry. S.L."

After several days no word from Bucket, not even an acknowledgment he had got, or was reading, the paper; but Levin waited patiently. Two more days made him restless. He had come up with a new idea but did not want to work on it until he knew how good the first paper was. If Bucket agreed with CD he could see the article already in print. S. Levin, essayist and critic, the start of a new career. Patience, he counseled, knowing how busy poor Bucket was. His dissertation had been newly rejected and he had begun a "final" revision: Uncle Toby once more at his sorry fortifications. In a rare free moment he was still hammering boards on the addition to his still uncompleted house. Algene was pregnant. The little Buckets, Levin knew, had been trading illnesses since November. Joe himself had come down with chicken pox, "an humiliating experience." To pay doctors, medicine, and other bills he had added to his odd-job schedule several hours in a gas station where he had worked as a boy. (He had once lubed Levin's car.) And he still had themes, preparations, quizzes to take care of. Levin was now sorry he hadn't thought twice before wishing the article on him, even if only ten pages.

He considered asking him to return it, but then worried he might be offended—Bucket could be touchy—if Levin got in the way of his making up his mind what he wanted to do, or seemed to be pressing. The instructor had learned in the West that his Eastern timing was often on the tightly wound side for many of the people he dealt with. He was concerned with time even when he had on hand more than he knew what to do with; you couldn't knit with it or purl. None of his colleagues seemed to grow jittery about where time went. Perhaps it was the climate, no clearly marked seasons to make a man conscious of, and impatient with, passing time: Time's winged chariot walked. Such being so, best wait, Levin advised himself, till the assistant professor either returned the paper unread or indicated he had read it and was willing to express an opinion.

Although Levin saw him at least once daily, Bucket never alluded to the essay. By now the instructor felt he must do something about it, or he might not see it for years. There were that type; you didn't know who until you dealt with them. Since he had made the mistake of leaving Bucket the original copy, and not wanting to pay Milly for another from the carbon if it wasn't worth doing, Levin reluctantly decided to drop him a note. He would say he needed the original to send out but would gladly leave the carbon if Bucket had time to read it; if he hadn't Levin understood. But when he entered his office after his last morning class, the manuscript, somewhat worn—the first page looked as though it had kissed a lollipop—lay on his desk. He thumbed through hastily for comments and found none. Levin searched the floor, under the desk, even the wastebasket, for a note that might have fallen off but there was no such thing.

Seeing Bucket in the hall later he thought he would speak to him, but then it seemed to Levin that the assistant professor was pretending not to see him; Levin said nothing. He returned to his office, his heartbeat in his ears, but blaming his sensitivity lately, heightened by every sort of dissatisfaction. Have I done something to him that I shouldn't have? he wondered. Had he perhaps heard about Levin and Pauline and thus shown his disapproval? Ironic if so at this stage, yet not likely. If he knew something he minded his business, his virtue his fault. He wasn't a puritan, nor addicted to gossip. It must be something else—but what? He recalled a pleasant cup of coffee with Bucket in the Student Union the day after he had left the paper, neither mentioning it; still it was pleasant. Was he, despite that, secretly annoyed that his customary good nature had earned him an unwanted task when he had so much to do? If so, why not say it instead of putting on the mask of Fu-Manchu? Whatever the answer, from the look of the ms., he was certain Bucket had read it; yet he seemed not to have the slightest intention of saying what he thought of it. Levin, now greatly irritated, didn't know what to do next.

Maybe there had been a misunderstanding? No, his request for the man's opinion was clear; the least he could do was acknowledge he had read it. Or maybe Bucket was worried about something—he had his worries, all right. Could he, for instance, be ill? A secret cancer? Levin saw him later, in the hall, looking healthy as an ox. I don't understand, he thought. He's a nice guy, affable, honest; but isn't it just good manners to say something: "Sorry, I couldn't get to it," or "Sorry I did." Was he too timid to say the paper was bad, in fact, stank? If Bucket had a weakness it was his small-town timidity—the departmental disease, or how could they have lived so long with *The Elements* and the damned d.o., to say nothing of how Fairchild and Gilley, seemingly equalitarian, autocratically ran things? Climate or moral climate? "We all have our weaknesses," Levin sighed. But Bucket had never before held back criticism of his ideas, so why begin now? Could he have gone through some private crisis while reading the paper? Jealous because the instructor wrote not badly whereas he (evidence: the oft-returned dissertation) wrote like a clod? Professional jealousy?

He considered every possibility but none satisfied him. He often peeked into Bucket's office to see if he had a minute to talk, but his day was always booked solid with students. Standing unseen near his door, Levin had once heard him go on—he estimated twenty minutes—to a not fully awake fresh-man, concerning the uses of the semi-colon. For semi-colons he had all day, for a colleague's paper not a minute. Infuri-ating. Levin considered waiting downstairs on the porch until Bucket left for home, and walking with him a bit to sneak in a question or two. But pretense of this sort bothered him (his little moralities). So time went by without satisfaction. One day Levin had to speak to Bucket about a book committee meeting and the assistant professor seemed his cordial self, tempting the instructor to pop a question then and there. But before it popped, out of pride he swallowed, then chewed his bitter cud all day. From Bucket's behavior who would think he had ever seen the manuscript? Or had he in a former existence? or was he mesmerized when reading, or had been hit on the head by a brick and no longer remembered he had seen the paper? How else explain the mystery? Apparently what was important to Levin did not exist for Joe B. How far apart men are, strangers to each other's needs. In anger he thought, Be damned to the bastard, I swear I'll never say a word to him about that cursed article. Either he brings it up or he can go to hell. What could he have expected from a man who had not once in all these months invited him to his house for a little talk and hospitality? He had made not the slightest effort to be more than an acquaintance despite Levin's desire to have him as friend; the instructor had clearly shown this by his good will for Bucket that still—mind you—lived in his breast. He doesn't need me, so his theory is I don't need him. Knock on his door and you knock on wood, nobody answers. I hate his small guts. Levin worked himself into fits of rage. Whatever he looked at looked black. Once he had to run home and take a cold shower to calm down.

When they passed each other in the hall he wouldn't look at the man, his skinny frame, oversize goggles, meaty ears. He envisioned punishment fallen on him, some sad misfortune: One day J.B. collapsed at his desk and died at home. Levin came uninvited to the wake. The former assistant professor was laid out in the still unfinished parlor, in wool sweater and brown socks, shoeless. He lay on a soft fir slab he had cut him-self, his trusty crosscut saw at his side. During the services, Levin, assisting wherever possible, held a dripping candle over his waxen face. As the five little Buckets prayed for their father's return he prayed with them, but Bucket had entered his last long silence.

The next morning Levin awoke with wet cheeks. He woke inspired: what a unique man Joe Bucket was! This was *he*, his personal quality, the only one in the world who could be Joseph P. Bucket. He had acted on his rights as a free man, the right not to say, for whatever reason, under no matter what provocation, what he didn't feel like saying. He did not care to say anything about Levin's paper, probably to save someone pain—himself, both, either. He wasn't talking, his natural and constitutional right. And it was his free choice as a man *not* to choose Levin, not to have him in, not to make a bosom buddy of him, not to utter a single syllable in his presence if he so pleased. And he pleased. Marvelous! "Man, the wonder of the world!" The instructor threw aside his covers and hopped out of bed. He found his article in a drawer, and gritting his teeth, read through it. He was slowly nauseated. He fought contempt for Fabrikant, but after tearing up and burning both copies of the paper, did not blame CD. Probably he was, in his way, trying to be kind. The article was trivial, not an original thought in ten typewritten pages. He had inflicted gratuitous punishment on a friend by asking him to read it, then worsened the situation because the poor guy wouldn't confess the agony he had undergone. The unpardonable affront was Levin's. He hated his sick pride.

I must be humble, he told himself. Humility is its own virtue, sweet, if true. I must be generous, kind, good. He wanted to embrace Bucket and ask his forgiveness. He vowed he would forever be his friend, no matter whose friend *he* was. This was Levin's own choice. He drove to town to buy Bucket a present. Sweet are the uses of humility. He left a potted white carnation on his desk. Without a word, nameless, for the wrong he had done him.

Levin was moved to discover he cherished what he had best cherished. For the first time since he had parted from

Pauline the world seemed home, welcome. He had, as men must, given birth to it; he was himself reborn. Proof: leafy trees stippling green of earth on sky. Flowers casting bright color everywhere. Vast fires in cosmic space—all nature flowing in Levin's veins. He felt tender to the grass. "God's handkerchief," Whitman called it. He watched with pleasure a flat-footed bluejay hopping up and down branches in the blooming cherry tree. He was amiable even to Mrs. Beaty's cat, licking herself on the lawn at night, her whiteness, light. And Levin wanted, still, to be closer to men than he had been. The good you did for one you did for all; it wasn't a bad way to love.

He had visions of service to others, the truest form of freedom, a secret he had unlocked. It stared him in the face like a crown of violets, diamonds, plums and wild pink roses. When he wore it on his head he created invisible miracles. He had become an extraordinary physician, S. Levin, M.D., F.A.C.S., an experienced man with a bony bald head, craggy face, kind eyes, sparse gray beard, and thin-fingered confident hands. He healed the sick, crippled, blind, especially children. When not practicing medicine he wrote, played the harpsichord, or spun his spinning wheel. In his tiny room only a cot, table, chair, and shelf of books. He lived on dried dates and goats' milk. He often fasted for days. Levin read and reflected to know for tomorrow. He lived everywhere. Every country he came to was his own, a matter of understanding history. In Africa he grafted hands on the handless and gave bread and knowledge to the poor. In India he touched the untouchables. In America he opened the granaries and freed the slaves.

Alas, the picture blew up in his face. What dreadful egoism, willed humility, inverse, ass-scratching pride. Saintliness was for his betters. Levin was a small man, constantly in error, and had to live practically.

He changed to his students. He had allowed his disappointment in their mediocre work, their sameness as people, to sour him against them, though this bothered him in afterthought. Levin's freshmen, when he met them, were eighteen and warm. Many were fine people, earnest, ambitious in uncomplicated ways, some obviously bright, but very few he knew were committed to ideas or respected intellectualism. They showed almost no interest in the humanities and arts ("electives"). They overvalued "useful" knowledge and confused vocational training with humanistic education. They consistently applied standards of technical efficiency to the values and purposes of life; so did too many of their professors. Even their fears were unimaginative: not that civilization was imperiled and might be destroyed, but that if their grades were not high enough they would miss out on the "good jobs" and have to settle for a "lower standard of living." They were badly informed about themselves and the world. Their intelligence, their lives, were absorbed in triviality. They had lost much without knowing it. They had not earned their innocence. This wasn't, of course, true for all, but it was true for too many.

Still they were human and possible. Although they were responsible for tomorrow, they had not invented the world or the values they had found in it. He could not blame them for being uneducated to begin with; he blamed them for their resistance to ideas they had not inherited. For their unexamined lives. Still, a teacher's job was patiently to teach them. It was the nature of the profession: respect those who seek learning and help them learn what they must know. So Levin, although now spending solid hours trying to catch up with papers he had neglected during the time he had felt so bad, opened his office to them. There he sat in full view of the multitudes in the corridor, WELCOME tacked on the wall above his head. Though he hadn't Bucket's forbearance in explaining punctuation rules, he had his students read them again and answered questions. Although their personal lives were none of his business he asked them who they were and what they were living for. He said the wealth of life lay within, keeping his fingers crossed because he hadn't learned all the lessons he taught. He advised the students he had not already frightened away, to study more of the liberal arts before they became technicians, even if it meant transferring to Gettysburg. He quoted Mill: "Men are men before they are lawyers or physicians or manufacturers. . ." He loaned out his best books and asked those who read them to come back for more. Once he caught a glimpse of George Bullock easing an ear close to his door. Levin suspected there had been complaints—that he was a communist propagandist, homosexual, corrupter of youth. But he continued to say: The liberal arts, you can't get enough. They teach what's for sale in a commercial society, and what had better not be. That democracy is a moral philosophy and can't be defended by lopping off its head. A man can find an ideal worth living for in the liberal arts. It might inspire him to work for a better society. It takes only one good man to make the world a little better.

Holy smoke, Levin thought, suppose *I* were head of the department?

One morning shortly after his avowal of service, humility, good will to men, after the wars in the soul had more or less subsided, Levin ran into his old self across the hall in George Bullock's office. Having knocked and got no answer, he had unlocked the door, to leave on George's desk a reader he had asked Levin's committee to consider for fall-term use. As he put the book down near the phone—Gilley's gift to Bullock— the instructor's eyes momentarily lighting on a picture of Jeannette in a bathing suit, fell on a typewritten list of names, among which, without trying, a second after sensing he would, he found his own. Stapled to the list was a note from George addressed to Lon Lewis, the head football coach: "For your personal information. These are lukewarm if not downright unsympathetic to athletes. I frankly can't advise your key men to take their classes. In fact I'd say lay off unless emergency threatens, and then not to unless they've talked to me first. Best ever, George."

After reading this twice and finding himself in a state of high excitement, Levin shut the door and studied the names on the paper, at the same time trying to think what he would say if Bullock walked in. With Levin on the list were Bucket, Fabrikant, O. E. Jones, Haddock, Scowers, Merdith Schultz, Sprinkle, and surprise—Farper. To rate inclusion, Levin figured, you had to be considered prejudiced to athletes, a tough marker, or an irritable pest like Farper. Conversely, those not listed, though not necessarily scoundrels, might be expected to give the boys an easier time and possibly a "break" if needed. What angered Levin was Bullock's gratuitous defamation of his colleagues, the harm a list of this kind could do—probably had done, no doubt there had been others. Since shopping for grades was endemic at Cascadia College, there was already a good amount of prejudging professors and courses in terms of grades given, on other students' say so; but George's document worsened the disease as it destroyed reputations. Levin now understood why, this term, he hadn't had one of the usual letters from the coaches asking how their boys were doing; simply, the athletes had avoided his classes. Alternating between flush and tremble, he felt feverishly eager to confront Bullock with his list. Levin began to copy down the names but had to stop. He tore up what he had written, picked up the book he had come to return and was about to leave when the postscript of a letter on George's paper-cluttered desk caught his eye. This, after a swift unsuccessful pushing match with his conscience, turned out to be a financial report from George's father: "Your personal worth as of today's date is $104,337.31." The telephone rang and Levin left.

Staring through his cracked window (Was Duffy cracked? flitted through his mind) he was unable to stop thinking of Bullock's dirty list, going to the P.E. department, surreptitiously to most of the football players—only a few were good students—then no doubt to their girls, *their* sorority sisters, and where not—everybody knowing who had been proscribed but the professors themselves. Something ought to be done and Levin tried to think what. He could of course speak to Bullock, but that had its disadvantages; Levin would be on the defensive simply in knowing about the list; and if Bullock said, "So what?" Levin was powerless to stop him. Somebody had strongly to tell him where he got off. Who? The instructor felt helplessly without a source of appeal. Gilley? He would find some way to defend Bullock. Fairchild? He would deny the list existed, then gently lecture Levin for having read George's correspondence. The list seemed to imply more than an individual act of Bullock's; it hinted at a way of life. Levin wasn't sure, if he made a public issue of it, that he wouldn't be jumped on by somebody in the administration "for impugning the integrity of the institution." Then he'd be the traitor and Bullock would assist at the funeral—Levin's. So he did nothing, unwilling to jeopardize his job—he shuddered at the chances he had taken with Pauline—a job that was more precious to him with every jeopardy. Here he had begun his career as college professor, sweet dream of his life; here, as a result of some miraculous batting of both eyes by fate he had gone almost a year without being kicked out. One more and he would have enough respectable experience to make a change to a better place. Therefore be prudent, the more the better. Easy does it, Levin thought, you've got to live with all kinds in this world.

But the decision to do nothing was like a bird imprisoned in his chest. A worrisome hour later he was in Fabrikant's office, relating in confidence what he had discovered, and urging the associate professor to give George some fatherly advice; if possible, get him to destroy his list before it went out.

CD, not the least surprised to learn of the existence of the paper, after several minutes of reflection, urged caution.

"As I said before on a similar occasion, the way to fight this is not piecemeal but by getting at the source of a rotten situation. In the meantime let's not tip our hand but keep our powder dry." He winked his big eye.

"But why hide where we stand?" Levin asked. "Everybody knows there's a contest between you and Gerald. Time's fantastically short if it's going to be held this term."

"I'm not so sure that it is," CD said gloomily. "So far as I am concerned it's still no more than a rumor."

"Gilley's positive it's coming off soon, so is Bullock."

"I've already indicated to you why I must proceed carefully."

"The promotion?"

Fabrikant nodded.

"Hasn't that gone through yet?"

"I understand it's in the president's office now."

"Avis told me you said I was supporting you. Surely you know she's for Gilley and anything you tell her will get back to him?"

"I may have been indiscreet," CD admitted. "I hope I didn't cause you embarrassment by speaking of you as a possible ally?"

"No," Levin said impatiently. "It would have to come out sooner or later. I hear there are others with us. Can I ask who?"

"Bucket, you, and I, as of now, but there are several who will join us when the time is ripe, Merdith Schultz and Jones, I have reason to believe, and others. As for tactics at present, we can keep a record of grievances, including this incident and the censorship of the textbook." He laughed dryly. "I can supply a lot more of a similar nature going all the way back to 1932. Once the dean announces the election, whether my promotion has come through or not, we can begin to discuss these matters privately with various members of the department. Then if word of what we're saying gets back to the higher-ups, as I don't doubt it will, no one can accuse us of muckraking, or fuss for the sake of fuss. We'll be engaged in the legitimate American activity of practical politics."

"I see the point," Levin said.

But the point—he didn't see it steadily or whole—gave way

to an inspiration that made Levin nervous. After leaving CD he spent an hour trying to get rid of it, but inspiration prevailed. Late that afternoon, after Marv Beal had swept up and left, and even Avis had gone home, Levin sneaked across the hall. The letter and list, though he wished them annihilated, still lay on Bullock's desk. Not allowing himself to think, the instructor slipped them into a folder and hurried to the library. There he had the papers photostated, then returned them to a memorized spot on the desk. "Practical politics," he told himself. He had, however, a brutal headache, and went early to bed.

The next morning he found in his mailbox a letter from Dean Seagram and a folded note "from the desk of Gerald Gilley." The dean's mimeographed letter officially announced an election for a new head of the English department. It was cosigned, as a matter of form, by Professor Fairchild, who had more than once stated in the coffee room that it was foolish to make a simple thing complicated—seniority was the most sensible means of promotion. "If a man's good enough to hold down a job for twenty years, he is good enough to advance to a position of responsibility. And if he's already done that, he should have first choice at something higher." The details of the election were at least simple. It was scheduled for the day after Commencement, in the office of the dean, by secret ballot. Nominations were open and would be received at once. If in the voting no candidate won a two-thirds majority (14 votes) after three ballots, a temporary chairman would be appointed by the dean and a new election held on the fifth of next January.

Gilley's handwritten note asked Levin to drop in to see him at his convenience. Levin, knowing the two communications were related, shuddered. The election, for so long no more than a possibility, was about to become an event. He had looked forward to it—always enjoyed a contest—but now felt no pleasure in the announcement, although the thought of

Bullock's list still irritated him and any even remote come-uppance for him, for instance through Fabrikant's election, was something to look forward to. Although he would gladly have skipped seeing Gilley—forever, without missing him—Levin ran into him in the hall. The director of composition was his tall, loose-figured self, and although a bit reserved, still friendly in speech. He said at once, "Why don't we just go into my office for a minute, Sy? What I have to say won't take so long." The instructor dumbly followed him down the hall.

Gilley looked uncertainly at Levin across his half acre of desk, covered with the apparatus of his picture history of American literature. On the desk lay a portrait of Henry Ward Beecher leering up at Levin. He shut his eyes. When he opened them, Gilley seemed tired to him and older by more than just the number of months that had gone by since they had met at the railroad station last summer. His face was motionless yet unsettled, the eyes mirroring Levin's own un-ease. Whether he knew it or not, he had lived through much since January. He showed, however, not the slightest sign of suspicion, or knowledge of betrayal, and Levin doubted he could have hidden his wound once he knew he had it. It was as if gossip, if any, had stopped dead at his ear—so much for her anxious fears of exposure. A curious thing about a small town: if it didn't destroy you, it protected you. He was of course glad she hadn't been found out. Her luck was still running strong. But had or hadn't, he felt shame before the man; yet when he thought of the picture he had taken of his naked wife, a betrayal perhaps worse than hers of him, Levin was conscious of renewed disgust, although who was he to measure sin? His own moral calipers were badly bent. In the end he boiled up a scum of sympathy for Gilley as victim—Levin's (his favorite sport since Albert Birdless); he felt almost affection for the vulnerable hackee, cheated by his wife and a man he had surely hired to vote for him in the election, a fellow victim, taken over the rocks by the same woman and somebody named Duffy; one's fate is long on the loom before he knows what has happened to him. I owe him something, Levin thought, for the harm I've done him.

Gilley, running his hand through his hair, spoke huskily, although pretending voice normal, relations unchanged, business as usual.

"Sy," he said, evoking cheeriness, "though we've had our small differences they're nothing I myself take too seriously, and I know that holds for you. You don't seem to me to be the type that goes around holding grudges against people for not agreeing with him. Not only that, but as time goes by I am sure we'll understand each other better and our occasional hassles will give way altogether."

He beamed tentatively as Levin, about to stroke his beard, found it missing, and smiled vaguely.

"Anyway," Gilley said, after a pause, "I thought I'd better ask you where you stand in the election we seem to be having in June. I suppose you've seen the dean's notice?" Having stated the question, he pulled his handkerchief out of his back pocket and blew his nose.

Levin admitted he had seen the notice.

Gilley brushed his nostrils both ways, carefully tucked away the handkerchief and buttoned his pocket.

"Have you made up your mind who you're going to support?"

Though the question basically insulted, Levin found it hard to look the man in the eye, although he attempted a decent approximation of the act after fighting down a suspicion that Gerald, probably through Avis, knew where he stood and was leading up to something else.

What shall I tell him? he thought. That I can't vote for him because he's a mediocre leader, no matter how many years he has coveted the job or been Fairchild's Friday to get it? Or that I can't trust him for the pictures he takes (my God, who can trust me?)? Or shall I say I can't vote for him because I've betrayed him with his wife?

"First let me ask you something," he said hesitantly. "Suppose you—er—had found out that somebody in this department had typed up a list of his colleagues he recommended for athletes to take; or possibly the names of ten people whose courses he told the boys to stay away from. And that he had sent these names to the P.E. department, specifically to one of the coaches, for distribution among the players. Could I ask you what you would do about that?"

"Is there," Gilley asked, his eyes narrowing, "that kind of list?"

"Suppose there was?"

"I wouldn't believe everything I heard around here. I don't listen to most of it myself."

"Suppose I saw it?"

Gerald leaned back in his chair. "I'm not for any such kind of list."

"Could I ask what you would do about it? Would you, for instance, talk to the one who had compiled it, tell him he had made a serious mistake and the best thing he could do would be to withdraw and destroy it? And would you firmly say he must cut out that kind of thing in the future?"

"I might," said Gerald, reaching for a ruler on the desk and absently measuring his hand. Glancing up, he said, "I may not be for that kind of list, Sy, but I'll tell you this. I frankly don't see anything wrong with anybody wanting to look out for the boys on our teams. They have their place in college as well as anybody else. You know what the Greeks said about physical fitness and the well-rounded man. Athletes set certain standards of perfection which is part of your liberal education. Sports mold character. Besides that, practically speaking these boys bring us a lot of exciting games and keep the town interested and grateful to the college. It builds good will all over the state and even intersectionally in some of the bigger games. You could say they're really playing for America. People appreciate that and are solidly behind our sports programs, even in the public schools. Just between us, one of the

Easchester school board members personally told me that if it came to a choice between funds for a further developed high school athletics program, or none for kindergartens, he'd vote to abolish the kindergartens. I say this not because I necessarily agree with him—Erik will be ready for kindergarten in '53—but you ought to know what people think. A lot of them in Cascadia give very loyal support to the state colleges because of our teams, and that's mighty important when it comes to funds for new buildings and raises for us all. Don't kid yourself that spectator interest in athletics doesn't influence legislators. The fact of it is that our athletes do a lot for all of us and we ought to admit it and be thankful. I know George tries to assist those who need some help here and there, but in case you don't know it he has more than once been personally thanked by President Labhart. And I suppose you know how fond of him Orville is?"

Levin slowly fanned his face with his hand.

"Let's face the facts," Gilley said. "People *should* be doing things for these boys who break their backs for Cascadia. Sure, most of them have their athletic scholarships for which they have to put in seventy hours a month in the off seasons, but just how far do you think eighty bucks a month goes in these times? And keep this in mind, Sy. The boys on the football squad are out on the field sometimes while you and I are snug in bed, practicing in every kind of dirty weather. They get hit hard, often landing in the mud under a ton of beef. And if they break an arm or leg, or something a lot worse, you never hear them complaining. Spring practice is already on. And when the boys get back in the fall, a whole month before everybody else, they'll be at it day after day until the season ends. By nightfall they barely have the strength to get their clothes off and hit the sack, yet there are plenty of them who keep up good grades. We need people to help them pick courses and advise them generally. Please note no one is asking you to do it."

"I'm not belittling what they do," Levin said, "only that we think they have to do it." He brought up the list again. "Wouldn't you say it was an unethical business?"

"Whose list is it?"

"Well," said Levin, "I'll tell you off the record, although we both know whose it is."

"Then what's the sense of talking about it? Unofficially I can't do anything."

"Not even talk to him?"

"I might do that."

"Tell him to cut it out," said Levin.

Gilley laid down his ruler. "Which brings me back to the original question I asked you before." He did not repeat it.

"I'm thinking of supporting CD," Levin said.

Gilley's expression was momentarily blank; he then shot Levin a look of genuine hatred. The instructor's scalp crawled yet by an act of will he kept himself seated. Gerald hadn't known he was supporting Fabrikant. Avis had probably kept her mouth shut, possibly fearing that if he confronted Levin with previous knowledge of his vote the instructor might say who had told him about the picture; but now Gerald knew and apparently couldn't believe that somebody he thought was in the bag, wasn't.

It then occurred to Levin he had done a foolish thing in saying who he was voting for. He ought to have answered, "Yes, I've made up my mind," and then mum, or just the simple statement that he would not reveal his vote. Gilley would have said no more than he hoped Levin would support him. That would have kept peace between them until the school year ended. Next year was next year.

I told him because of all I haven't told him, Levin thought.

Gilley said bitterly, "I assume that's in the nature of thanks for all I've done for you."

Levin, shoulders hunched, waited for a thunderous revelation of Gilley's service, gift, sacrifice—a statement that would unstitch his skull and destroy him.

"I got you this job—I gave you your office and other privileges—"

"You did more than that—" Levin's voice cracked. He bit his compulsive tongue.

Gerald stirred. "Fabrikant," he muttered. "What makes you think he's such a hot bargain? He doesn't know beans about administering any department, and he can't meet people. A fine mess of public relations he'd make. In no time he'd have us in a snafu so thick it'd take an act of Congress to unravel it."

"He wouldn't have sacrificed the anthology."

"God damn it," Gilley said, "I had Orville on my back on that. If I had been my own boss I'd've had a committee consider it."

"Committees can be cowards—"

"Who are you calling coward?" Gerald glowered.

"Excuse me," Levin said. "All I meant is that one determined man could have saved that book."

"You know," said Gilley, "I'm beginning to think you consider yourself some sort of fount of wisdom put on earth to tell us how to run our affairs. The next thing, you'll be advising the prexy to step aside so you can take over and run the college."

"Oh no," said Levin, perspiring under his clothes. "And don't think I don't appreciate your good qualities, Gerald—I do. But these are dangerous times, and since education is so important this college has to be more effective—"

"Who says we're not effective?"

"*More* effective."

"In the first place, this isn't Harvard, you know. There are thousands of places just like us. In the second, I already told you I expected to make changes in the department once I was in a position to."

"We'd need more than those changes," Levin said.

Gilley glared at him for a tense minute, and Levin looked around to see where the door was, but the director of composition sat back, shaking his head.

"You have a rare nerve to criticize, with no experience to speak of to back it up. You haven't even taught a full year in a college. How knowledgeable do you think you are, for instance? How much have you studied our practical problems— the budget, our mode of operation, the philosophy of the land-grant colleges, et cetera? Until you do, what's your big hurry to give out advice about changes *you* think we ought to make? Those of us with experience, who have faced problems of administration, know what we have to do and how much we can sensibly accomplish in any given time. I've told you more than once Cascadia is a conservative state. One thing you so-called liberals can't get into your heads is we *want* it that way. Also remember taxes are way too high. Rural people tend to be frugal and the state legislature is a rural power. We can do what they want us to do. If you don't start with that premise you are off-balance to begin with."

"New ideas cost nothing," said Levin. "Some things are easy to change. And sometimes the college has to lead the community."

"What do you think is so wrong with English?"

"With reference to composition, if you'll pardon my saying so, the course is half dead. We have to get rid of *The Elements* and those damn workbooks. We have to abolish the d.o. because everyone's teaching for it and not beyond it. And we ought to introduce some literature into the course so the students know that good writing means something more than good report writing."

"We have all the lit courses we need. Composition is writing, not studying the forms of literature."

"Just enough lit for inspiration, to liven it up, to ease the heart."

"We're not teaching comp for the sake of the instructor, I'll tell you that."

"Nor for the students, if you ask me. If we were we'd be giving a full liberal arts and science program along with the other stuff."

"If you know anything about educational trends you'd know that pure liberal arts programs are dying out all over the country."

"In that case we may die with them."

"What do you expect me to do?" Gilley then asked. "You know darn well I can't arrange the kind of program you want, all by myself. What about Dr. Labhart? I have heard him say that Plato, Shelley, and Emerson have done more harm than good to society."

"God save us all!"

"Don't underrate him. This place has just about doubled in size and scope during his tenure. He's a first-rate organizer. As a student he paid his way through graduate school by founding and running a successful used-car business that his brother still carries on in Boise."

Levin sighed.

"You know," Gilley said with renewed anger, "one thing I have never liked about you is the way you look around with an eye that says 'I've seen better.' If you took the trouble to check into figures you'd find that our kids on the average get more education per person than yours in the East. And we send a larger percentage to college than you do. Our literacy rate is one of the highest of all the states. I didn't expect you to know that because you have the New Yorker's usual cock-eyed view of the rest of the country. You are still an outsider looking in."

"I don't feel like an outsider."

"That has nothing to do with it. It's how you act here that counts."

Pushing back his chair, Gerald strode over to his long closet and pulled out a fishing rod, assembled and ready to strike. "This is a spinning rod," he said. "Do you know it from a fly fishing rod or an African spear? This is the reel, the line—monofilament, eight pound test which I use for steelhead—dropline, lure. I bet you thought we use worms."

Levin admitted it.

"You've been here for almost a year and have never once, so far as I know, gone fishing. If you did that now and then and a few other things I might mention you wouldn't be so dissatisfied. I'll bet you'd be less impatient with your students and colleagues. I personally don't think you enjoy your life, or you wouldn't have that pain-in-the-gut look you have gone around with in the past weeks. If you don't watch out you'll wind up with high blood pressure and will someday keel over while tying your shoelaces. You ought to get out into the open and tone up your muscles. We have some of the best fishing streams in the world in Cascadia. Ernest Hemingway has fished here. How will you ever teach Thoreau, once you have your Ph.D., without ever in your life having been to a wild place?—"

"I've been to Walden Pond—" Levin said.

"God knows I'm not against books," Gilley said, "but I'm against only books."

"I too," said Levin.

Gerald raised his rod and flipped it as if casting. "I don't think you can imagine what it means to wade into a swift icy mountain stream—"

"I can imagine—"

Gilley moved into the cold, fast flowing stream.

"The fisherman estimates the pull of the current from the froth on the water so he knows how deep he can go in without being knocked over and carried away. One wrong step could mean his life. He's got to be mighty careful with his footing when he jumps from one slippery scum-covered rock to another."

He raised his foot, jumped, and made it.

Bravo, thought Levin.

"Now he's in the water up to his chest," Gerald said, extending the rod over the desk, "his arms moving rhythmically as he searches the stream for a fish, pitting his sportsman's knowledge against the instinctive wisdom of the species. This is contentment, this is the good life."

Levin pictured himself in cold water up to his heart (ah the balm of it) enjoying the good life.

"Half the fun is knowing what to do," Gerald went on, "when to fish upstream, when down. He knows just where to drop the lure—or dry fly if he's a real afficionado—a steelhead coming up to a floating fly is a thrill he never forgets. He knows how far to wade in after a struck fish before he's close enough to land it. And when he does that's perfection. And even if you don't catch a single one, you are a better man for the day's work."

"All my life I've wanted to fish—"

"You have seen almost nothing of this country. In the winter and spring vacations you stayed home. What the hell did you buy a car for?"

"I drive into the country," Levin said. "This spring I saw Scotch brume for the first time in my life, pure gold in the fields—marvelous. In the sky the drama of the clouds never ends—"

"I'm not talking about what you can see in the city parks," Gerald said. "I'm talking about *nature*. I mean *live* in it. Camp *alone* in it. I mean *climb* a real mountain. Then you'd know what this country means. And the same holds true for Cascadia College. After you've been here five years you can think about reforming us."

Levin got up. "I wish you luck in the election, Gerald."

Gilley rose, still flushed. "I suppose I got what I deserve for hiring you, also overlooking the harm you've done here, including advising your students to transfer to Gettysburg."

"Did Bullock tell you that?"

"Never mind who told me. It's an act of disloyalty to the institution that pays you your salary. If the University gets ahead of us student-wise, they'll collect most of the budget and we'll get beans. You'd better cut it out."

Levin swallowed. "I'll do what I have to."

"Then you'd better keep this in mind. If I win the election, and I have a darn good chance to, let me tell you there won't be much of a future for you here. And when you leave, don't bother to ask me for a reference. I have nothing good to say about you." Picking up his shears he snipped a picture out of a magazine. "No more New Yorkers, goddammit."

Levin returned to his office. His knees were trembly as he stood at the window, watching his career fly off to a faraway world. Yet the day was serene, the sky blue to the mountains. Not a cloud anywhere but in his head.

A knock on the door. He expected Bucket but Gilley appeared. He had calmed down, though his eyes were still moody.

"Maybe I let myself get a little out of hand," he said, "though I still honestly think I will do a better job than CD once I am on my own here. Anyway, what I wanted to say is this. I just happened to come across a quotation in *Time*, that gives me a better understanding of the type you are." He read from a tiny clipping. "It's by George Santayana and says, 'Americans are eminently prophets; they apply morals to public affairs; they are impatient and enthusiastic.'"

Levin said, "He also said if you don't remember the past you were condemned to relive it." He laughed his broken laugh, and Gilley, once more in a benign ambient, smiled.

"What I thought I would suggest is this," he said. "Of course I'd still like to have your support—" he was gazing out of the window "—but if you can't honestly give it to me, at least don't vote against me."

But Levin said he couldn't do that.

Fourteen votes for Fabrikant were no small picnic to arrange, but since four or five were presumably on hand, nine or ten more, according to Bucket, "seemed not impossible." Levin for some time had had certain hesitations about Fabrikant, including one that really troubled him, but CD was the only candidate other than Gilley who evoked some expression of respect, and since Gerald was almost certainly (inevitably) his enemy now, Levin's situation in the department, so long as it lasted; and future, insofar as it depended on recommendations, would do better under someone else as head, if that could be arranged. He urged CD, now that the dean's notice was out, to carry on a vigorous campaign in the few weeks that remained before Commencement. There had been as yet little serious talk on anyone's behalf, for although Gerald had begun to sound like a candidate as far back as last September, nobody had felt the matter was especially pressing. CD told Levin that he would do what he could short of aping Gilley buttonholing people in the hall and asking for their votes. For that Levin couldn't blame him, but he asked for permission to speak to some of their colleagues in CD's behalf, Bucket to try others. Fabrikant consented. Since Joe felt he would be more comfortable on the second floor, Levin went upstairs among the young instructors, those whom Fabrikant called "the unknown quantities." He called on them with reluctance because a month of salesmanship had once harrowed him to the core. However he was received with the usual amicability, and was courteously listened to, except by Ferris Farper, who glowered as Levin nervously talked, then said he would never vote for anyone a buttinsky supported. But most of the other men seemed no more than mildly interested in what was going on. Either they hid their interest for reasons of their own, or it was a case of "whoever wins is good enough for me," equalitarianism at its most desperate. For good or ill no one expressed any fervid loyalty to Gilley; some lowered their voices or sneaked a glance at the door when speaking his name. Levin sensed more dissatisfaction with the director of composition than he had anticipated, although he was aware that any administrator was bound to annoy some people just in existing. Still it was good there was no strong feeling Gerald was a sure thing.

Levin suggested the department was in the doldrums and needed a shove by someone with a few ideas; it astonished him that several of the men wanted to know what was wrong with the way the department was being run. They weren't kidding.

The instructor was at first irritated; they deserved Gilley. Then, annoyed with his annoyance, he patiently explained what ought to be improved and they nodded and said nothing. He expected hot commitment but would have to get used to commitment withheld. He felt heavy-handed and big-booted among them, shaken by their blandness and reticence. Yet gently pinned down, they agreed the better the leader, the better the department. CD, they admitted, had merit as a candidate. He had in the past, they had heard, pushed faculty benefits. No doubt he would do things Gilley mightn't care to try. It was rumored CD would give each instructor a lit class to teach and would insist that everyone in the professorial ranks take a comp class. Levin realized he had started the rumor by talking of it as a "possibility." He hastily denied it was a plank in Fabrikant's platform. But almost everyone complained Fabrikant was not very sociable. He never went to anyone's house and invited no one to his; he never appeared in the coffee room; he practically lived in his office. "How the hell am I supposed to vote for him," Scowers said, "if I'm not even sure what he looks like?" Fitznogle remarked, "I have a hunch he might be stubborn in close quarters with anybody who didn't agree with him. I'd be afraid of that." And Purtzer said, "Wouldn't it be better to ask the dean to drop the election and bring a new man in from the outside? I've seen these elections before. They leave a lot of bad feeling and are more trouble than they're worth."

Levin went again to Fabrikant. "CD, I think it might pay you to talk to some of the men upstairs. I think they'd like to make your acquaintance and hear your ideas about what ought to be changed around here."

But Fabrikant was not so sure he wanted to visit the third floor. "Let them come down here," he suggested.

"I suppose you know Gerald's been up there twice this week?"

"That's his privilege. I don't think it's dignified to knock on doors and ask the instructors to vote for me. Furthermore, I don't like the antagonisms this competition arouses."

"A campaign is a campaign," Levin said.

"That may be," CD said uneasily, "but if Gilley wins the election I'll still have to live with him."

"Granted, as he will have to with you, if you win."

"He has his full professorship; I haven't. He doesn't need my assistance but I may need his cooperation in the future if the president turns down my promotion. It's been on his desk long past the usual time," he said glumly.

"Why would he turn it down?"

"I don't know but I don't want to encourage it. Gilley is one of his white-haired boys. They play golf and pinochle together. Things I can't and won't do." He looked unhappy.

Levin nodded.

"However, I'll see anybody who wants to see me."

"Fine, I'll tell them."

"One by one, please. I hate crowds."

Levin left him, troubled.

He still vaguely held it against CD that he had not told him his article was half baked. And what's he hiding from in his office—still the Depression? sex? the frustrations of life? Is he the best possible man around or can we do better? But what most troubled Levin was the old question why CD had dropped the defense of Leo Duffy.

He telephoned Bucket at supper time. "Joe, maybe this is the wrong question right now, but do you have any serious reservations about Fabrikant?"

Bucket laughed self-consciously. "I have reservations about everyone, not excepting myself."

"Do you think he'd make a better head than Gilley?"

"I would say so."

"Does he stand a chance to be elected?"

"It seems to me he does."

"Joe, why don't you run?" Levin asked. "I bet people would support you."

The phone was silent for a minute, then Bucket said, "That's very kind but I don't care for administrative responsibility."

Levin said it was just a thought. He had been about to ask if Fabrikant had told him about the picture of Pauline and Duffy, but if Bucket knew, the instructor wanted him to mention it first.

The next morning he found a sealed note in his mailbox, his first written communiqué from Bucket: "Although I genuinely admire CD in several ways and will unquestionably vote for him, I'd be less than honest not to admit one reservation—his withdrawal of assistance to Leo in the Academic Freedom sub-committee of our AAP. Having said that, I hope you will excuse me from further comment."

Levin hunted him up after the end of the hour.

"Excuse me, Joe—I hate to ask, but could you give me a little more information?"

Bucket refused. "All I will add is that secrecy in this matter is not merely willful on my part."

He knows, thought Levin.

"Thanks," he said. "I think I'll talk to CD again."

He had come to a reluctant decision and all day postponed doing something about it although he felt he must. In the late afternoon he knocked on Fabrikant's office door but he wasn't in. That evening, as the sun was setting, Levin drove to his farm and came upon the candidate on his horse in the meadow. The brown horse was a big-bodied animal on short legs, and Fabrikant resembled Napoleon with a cigar. Was he planning a new melon patch or a pitched battle? Austerlitz or Water-loo? Defense in front or rear?

Levin waded out to him through the knee-deep grass. The scholar, in a mellow mood, removed his cigar. "Nice of you to come by." He gestured at the twilit sky.

"So peaceful," Levin said, and paused, hat in hand.

Fabrikant waited, alert. The horse stirred in the grass.

"You recall," Levin began, "I once asked you about Mr. Duffy, why you gave up defending him?"

Fabrikant, chewing his cigar, remarked, "I recall."

Levin cleared his throat. "If you'll pardon me, CD, why did you?"

"That's a private matter."

"Wasn't it also a public one?"

After a silent minute the instructor said, "I'm not referring to the picture."

Fabrikant frowned. "What picture do you have in mind?"

"The one Gerald took of his wife."

The horse moved forward. Fabrikant checked her.

"Did he tell you about that?"

"No. Someone else did—not Bucket."

The scholar grunted. The horse whinnied. "Whoa, Isobel."

"Specifically," Levin said, "what I'd like to know is, was it just the picture that made you change your mind about helping Duffy, or was it something else—or both?"

Fabrikant let out a puff of smoke. A statement followed: "When the photograph was called to my attention I realized there was more to the mess than I had guessed. An ethical problem presented itself which, until then, I had no knowledge of."

"Did you tell the AAP committee about the picture?"

"I told them I no longer intended to defend Mr. Duffy."

"That killed the entire defense?"

"More or less."

"Wasn't that too an ethical matter? That his rights had been violated and no one did anything about it?"

"It was my opinion that the introduction of that photograph cast a different light on his previous trouble."

"All the picture showed—didn't it?—was that they were naked coming out of the water?"

"I wouldn't care to discuss that."

"I'm trying to understand what—er—actually happened."

"It was an indecent business."

"The picture, or the sex angle?"

"Call it what you will."

"Er—Did Duffy ever say anything—in explanation?"

"I don't know. You can ask Gilley."

"Did you tell Bucket?"

Fabrikant coughed. "He had sympathized with Duffy and asked me to explain my action. I afterwards promised myself I wouldn't discuss it with anyone again, nor have I until this evening."

"Excuse me for pursuing this," Levin said nervously, "but it's very important. Did Gilley say, when he showed you the picture, that his wife and Duffy were lovers?—that she had conf—admitted that to him?"

"He didn't say anything. He stopped in my office and handed me the photograph. I took one look and handed it back. There was no further communication on the subject, except his remark later that his wife didn't know about the picture and he would rather she didn't."

Fabrikant turned his horse and Levin had to step back. "I find this discussion unpleasant, Seymour."

"Excuse me for asking," Levin said, "but surely you must have assumed they had—they had been intimate, because there's no moral issue in going for a swim naked."

"What I assumed is my own business."

"I'm on my way," Levin said, "but I want to be clear about one thing. Before you saw the picture—correct me if I'm wrong—you were willing to stand up for Duffy, but then you changed your mind. The main issue, the one that influenced you to offer your help was that he had been fired publicly for being a trouble maker. He had not been given notice, which I understand is contrary to universally approved policy. There was no bill of particulars, or a hearing by any organization on campus, so far as I know. Anyway, what I'm specifically asking is whether the issue on which you decided the matter in your own mind—the reason you wouldn't go on defending him—whether it was based on the merits of the case or just on your seeing the picture?"

"I don't see how you can separate one thing from the other. The evidence was clear."

"Evidence of what?"

"Of his character, of their relationship—do I have to be franker?"

"But did you ask for—er—any other proof? I mean, could I ask whether you gave Duffy the benefit of a reasonable doubt— for instance that he might just have happened to go swimming in the nude with a woman—let's say on impulse—hers—and otherwise the relationship might have been perfectly innocent? It's possible." Levin ended with his voice off pitch.

Fabrikant testily answered, "I decided he was a pestiferous nuisance, not worth the fuss he had kicked up, and washed my hands of the whole annoying business."

"Ah," said Levin. He put on his hat.

Night had fallen. The fragrant warmth of late spring rose from the fields. A crescent moon and single green star glowed overhead as a garden of blue stars evolved in the sky.

Levin sighed. "I'm sorry, CD, but after thinking it over I'm not sure I can support your candidacy any more. I want you to know I like you personally but it's the principle involved."

Fabrikant's big-pupiled eye, reflecting a star, throbbed and sparkled. His horse moved restlessly as he tried to steady her.

"Mr. Levin," he said, cold, aloof, "as you grow older, and I hope wiser, you'll learn there's more to mature behavior than snap absolute judgments. Are you being principled in supporting Gilley?"

"Not him," said Levin.

"Then who?"

His dry lips parted. "Myself."

"That smacks of sickening pride." Fabrikant rose in his stirrups and flung his cigar away. He galloped thunderously across the dark field.

Why should an unlocked door make Levin itchy in his pants, prurient? To say nothing of how the heart throbbed in anticipation. He knew why but pretended not to, to stay put in his office. Coming in just before eleven, after hours of walking after he had visited Fabrikant, on going down the hall to the water cooler he had noticed Gerald's door ajar, his office dark; this rarely happened. Back at his desk, temptation tempted Levin. Gilley's lock did not respond to the common key so it was now or never. He knew that inside Gerald's office was a filing cabinet with a drawer marked "composition personnel." In it was Duffy's folder, probably his history and imperfections described, possibly with pictorial illustrations. This thought roused Levin's prurience. He decided to go home and be done with temptation, but once in the hall he walked the wrong way. For safety's sake he knocked first, softly, and listened to utter silence throughout the building. Levin's legs were so wobbly he had to trek back to his office. He rested his head on his arms on the desk. Go home, he warned himself. In the distance a church bell thinly tolled midnight. What's the sin, he asked, in knowing the truth? Is it ever wrong to know? He rose from his seat at the thought and hastened down the hall, non-stop into Gilley's office, leaving the door partly open in case he had to make a quick exit. I'm always breaking into something of his, he thought, someday he will justifiably shoot me. In the dark he tugged at the top drawer of the filing case. Locked. Good. Levin go home! But he stayed, ensnared in flouting verboten. A door, for some unknown reason, had been left open. You walked in if you were the type. A drawer was closed, you hunted the key. If he found it, what Pandora's horrors would he fall into? A boxful of doors, Levin. The nature of evil: one wrong door opened untold others.

He was feeling for the key in Gilley's drawer when steps going down the stairs froze him. He went quickly to the door and listened as someone walked slowly down from the third to the first floor. Then the footsteps moved in his direction. Yet they were going down the stairs to leave the building. He realized there were two sets of footsteps. Too late to escape,

Levin ducked behind the desk. If Gilley came in, what in God's name could he say he was doing there in the pitch dark? He pictured himself caught. Total disgrace as a thief, his father's fate, not unexpected. The steps stopped, the door slowly creaked open. A light played on the wall, filing case, desk. Someone waited, breathing heavily. Levin, cowering on the floor, pictured a cop. That was it, the campus police! He had forgotten their midnight inspection of buildings, putting off lights, shutting doors. He held his breath to the point of madness. When the door shut, for a desperate moment he thought the cop had closed it to prevent his escape; but as the lock snapped he felt he had exploded into freedom. Ten minutes later he dragged his mangled self to his office.

At one A.M., Levin opened Gilley's door, cunningly left ajar; he drew the blinds, put on the light, and located the key to the filing cabinet. In the file in his own folder was his letter of application and signed loyalty oath. Duffy's folder was empty.

Professor O. Fairchild, on his way home, bent to pick a daisy at the edge of someone's lawn. Levin, dawdling half a block behind, saw him stoop for the flower in a wavering way. Slowly rising, the professor tottered as though the daisy were too much for him. He paused to draw its stem through his buttonhole, smoothing the white petals; always meticulous, everything where it should be. Then he strolled on as though concentrating on a line drawn to infinity. Possibly the sidewalk boxes made the long line difficult to follow. When he walked off it, trying to get back, he put his foot in the wrong place. He stepped on the grass. This happened twice. The professor looked at the sky, loosened his collar, then neatly drew his tie tight. A passing car honked. His arm half rose in greeting; he almost turned to watch it go by. With his neatly folded silk handkerchief he patted his forehead. For half a minute he studied his watch and then walked on slowly. Could he be drunk? Levin wondered. Does he secretly tipple from an office bottle, his father's fate long since caught up with him? The instructor shivered. He had left the office late, and seeing the old grammarian walking on ahead, had not wanted to catch up.

A few days before, Levin had been summoned into the professor's office (Strangers are still welcome . . .) via a short typed note in a sealed envelope, sure trouble. He had knocked nervously, not because he had much of a career to lose (although he had foolishly been wondering would the old gent, in a burst of pre-retirement good will, write him at least a mild recommendation "to whom it may concern"?), but because he felt he had earned his displeasure. Professor Fairchild sat at his desk scanning galleys, the sun flaring his white hair; he looked as though he hadn't budged since the time Levin had visited him in this many-windowed room last August. He had the impression he had seen him then for all time. Since summer he doubted they had exchanged a hundred words. The old man, bags heavy under his eyes, laid down a galley page and focused on Levin a watery blue frown.

Maybe I should have worked up a little hatred of him, the instructor thought. If he had been strong we would all be stronger. He created the wrong past:

*Here Lies Orville Fairchild, Lost Leader*
*He Ran the Cheapest English Department on the West Coast*
*Requiescat and Please Omit Flowers*

Now the head of department was supporting Gerald Gilley for his place, as Gilley was grooming George Bullock, his man Saturday, for his. (Levin's Law I: Weak leaders favor weak leaders, the mirror principle in politics). He saw himself sternly accusing the old man of a lack of concern for those who came after him, the professor cowering as S. (for Savonarola) Levin lectured him.

Instead Levin stared at his shoes. The professor, after inviting the instructor to sit, said in his vibrant voice, not unkindly, "Mr. Levin, I have asked you into this office not to protest your enmity to my grammar text—which in its twenty-eighth year, thirteenth edition, and twelve hundred and sixth adoption, needs no defense; nor your disrespect for Dr. Gilley, your immediate superior, and the person most responsible, may I say, for putting you on here; nor because of your presumption in other matters which do not concern you; but to insist you show a decent respect for the opinions of mankind."

If he forgives me, I'll forgive him.

"And I advise you," the professor said sternly, "not to have anything more to do with the wives of your colleagues. They're married women."

All is lost, I lost it.

"Yes, sir."

"My wife tells me there's talk you've been seen with several faculty wives. Is that true?"

"Several, sir?"

"That's right."

"No, sir. I did—ah—see one but that's all past tense."

"Well, keep it so. I warned you very strongly against that sort of thing and I renew my warning. I am being tolerant only out of charity, to keep you from destroying your career at its inception. To subdue your passion to interfere with others as well as criticize everything in sight, you might profitably begin with some much-needed reforms of yourself."

"How true, sir."

"Remember the sad fate of Leo Duffy."

"I do."

"I speak to you as a father to a son."

Levin, choked up, had to blow his nose. "Thank you, sir."

"Be humble. We must all be, especially those who teach others."

Levin nodded.

"Be good—"

He promised faithfully . . .

The old professor, lifting his coattails, had without a backward glance, sat down on the grass. He sat in the shade of a leafy linden tree on a small round grassy island amid three intersecting streets deserted at the supper hour. A little girl in a red dress, on one skate, was watching him as Levin came by. The professor had lain back, his eyes watery, lips blue, nose shrinking.

"Oh God," cried Levin.

On his knees he loosened the old man's collar, his chest heaving as he gasped for breath. Levin ran across the street, frantically pushed a door bell and asked the woman to call an ambulance. He returned to tell her to call Mrs. Fairchild, then raced back to the island. The little girl had skated away.

Although he seemed not to know where he was, the old man appeared to recognize Levin. He hoarsely whispered something and Levin bent low to hear.

" '—Shot—an arrow—into the—air, it fell—' "

"Don't say a word," Levin begged. "I've called an ambulance. You'll surely get better."

He's dying, he thought. Where's everybody?

" 'All are—archi-tects—of—fate—' "

The old man smiled with wet eyes. His face was smaller now. His lips twitched as he tried to speak. Levin leaned very close.

"Try to rest."

"The mys—mystery—of the in-fin—in-fin—in-fin—"

"Infinite."

"In-fin-i-tive. Have—you con-sidered—its possi-bil-i-ties? To be—"

He paused, gazed intently at Levin, and muttered, "Poor papa." His mouth shut sternly. He died.

Gerald made all the funeral arrangements. Pauline, at the church and graveside on a coldish day clung to her husband's arm, a thin-faced mourner unable to look at an open grave. The department was present en masse, including all the young instructors and their wives who looked like girls. President Labhart, pink-skulled and grim-visaged, Dean Seagram, ex-Dean Feeney, small and unpressed after retirement, were present with their modest wives. Fabrikant and his sister came in white faces and dark clothes. Probably the saddest man present was Joe Bucket, who had lost an old friend and bene-factor. Gilley bore up. Bullock's face was serious but inexpres-sive. Pauline looked lost in the crowd, in black dress, small veilless hat, nose aimless, her hair dark gold in the afternoon sun. Levin gazing across the coffin met her sad eyes. He felt regret, a sense of loss beyond all loss, like death in childhood, that somehow passed. She looked away. His heart remained heavy. The professor was buried at the foot of two gnarled fir trees in a new section of the cemetery, not too far from the graves of pioneers with their weather-beaten wood, and eroded stone, markers.

Afterwards rumors flew that Gerald, Fabrikant, Leopold Kuck, George, and even Bucket were being considered for acting head; and Levin hoped for Joe or anyone who wasn't Gilley or Bullock; even CD. It turned out, according to Avis, who had got it from a reliable source, that although the dean was considering everyone, President Labhart, after reading a sealed letter left by Professor Fairchild, "in the event of my death before retirement," proposed Gerald because he knew the department from A to Z, where everything was and went. Gilley was duly appointed, Levin's hopes for a change for the better suffering a not unexpected blow. Almost at once Gerald moved across the hall. People going into Milly's office for a stencil or to get their mail could see him through a connecting door, closed during Fairchild's tenure but now always open, sitting at his predecessor's desk. He had got a haircut and new brown suit and was no longer visible in shirt sleeves. It seemed strange to see him where the old professor had been but Levin soon got used to it. Gerald's first official communication was a dittoed sheet in praise of the late head, followed by an announcement that department policy for the few weeks he was acting head would remain unchanged. He expected every-one would, of course, pitch in to keep things moving as usual. In a subsequent notice he announced that the departmental elections, contrary to false rumors, would take place as sched-uled. In the meantime he was at your service. "Feel free to come in."

Although department policy remained ostensibly as usual, Gilley himself showed an alteration or two, nothing serious. Though he looked smaller in a large room, he seemed to have gained weight in a matter of days, noticeable around the mid-dle and jowls; wore bright bow ties and button-down collars, and looked surer of himself, less preoccupied than in the recent past. He was healthy, happy, flourishing. His color had picked up, brilliant in the light that swirled around his red head. He still impressed Levin as everybody's boy, but modi-fied, as if events had proved his mettle, fait accompli, no hands on his part; for hadn't the mantle of office fallen smack on his shoulders? He strove less yet managed to campaign without seeming to do so, whereas Fabrikant, according to Bucket, hardly talked of his aspirations. Wasn't it politicking when Gerald sent out, more often than necessary, notices signed "Gerald Gilley, Acting Head"? He functioned with assurance, to be expected considering his long apprenticeship for the role. What he was doing he had done for years—per-haps a few more decisions to make, and his signed notices more prominently displayed on the bulletin board; otherwise his activities were as before, emphasis on freshman comp. He looked as if he were ready to stay forever where he was unless someone did something about it.

Things were the same only more so. A few days after Gerald had entered the new office, he had his own large desk moved in and continued to clip pictures for his book. He put in the usual time in the coffee room, alone meditating on the twists and turns of fortune; joking with instructors; or discussing the college baseball picture with Marv Beal and Doug Womack, Milly's husband, in cowboy hat and black windbreaker, who waited hours to transport her in his one-ton truck, wherever she had to go. Gerald was friendly as ever to anyone who approached him, the same congenial democratic soul, five-eighths affection for people, Levin guessed, three-eighths fear, as though his well-being depended on *everybody's* good will. Besides clipping and pasting, he read *Field and Stream*, liked to enter in his class record book the objective test scores of his students, which he also graphed; and sometimes read popular fiction to light music on the radio. On days it wasn't seriously raining he golfed during the lunch hour, napped after eating, and returned to the office raring to go. Whenever Cascadia College scheduled a home baseball game he was there as official scorer, reward for years of perfect attendance.

The acting head made no attempt to hide his dislike of Levin. Apparently he told Avis, who told someone who slipped it to the instructor, that he was annoyed with him for "campaigning for Fabrikant behind my back." As a result of Levin's underhandedness, Gilley seemed to have grown doubts of his honesty. The doubts were valid if grown in truth; he was admittedly dishonest but not in the small, ratty ways Gilley seemed to think. For instance, when in Milly's absence Levin extracted a three-cent stamp from the cigar box in her drawer, a customary procedure when she was not at her desk, Gerald watched him hawk-eyed through the open door to see that he paid three pennies. When the instructor came in for paper, pencils, chalk, the acting head, peeking out, noted on a pad what supplies Milly gave him. And Gerald once sent her to ask Levin if "he had happened to see" two missing rolls of scotch tape. Levin was often reminded he was a chip off his father's block.

Gilley's suspicions of the instructor were perhaps evidence of an increased sensitivity to him as implied "chief critic of everything," particularly when the acting head was diddling at something that wasn't work. At times Gerald seemed nervous in Levin's even momentary presence. He became conscious of his cup of coffee if the instructor happened to be

307

passing while he was imbibing. Once at Levin's approach to the water cooler Gerald, standing in the hall, quickly thrust into his pockets some film negatives (Pauline in the bathroom?) he was showing Leopold Kuck. Even Kuck seemed embarrassed. The next day Gerald hurriedly removed his feet from his desk when the instructor walked into Milly's office to inspect his generally useless mail. In a further complication of cause and effect Levin had a sudden desperate feeling he was Gilley's unwilling nemesis. (Levin's Law II: One becomes his victim's victim. III. Stand for something and somebody around will feel persecuted.)

The cold war between Gerald and himself, plus the hot between his conscience and natural timidity, was exhausting Levin. One morning he went very reluctantly into the acting head's office to report the selections of the textbook committee at their final meeting. Gilley slipped a magazine into his top drawer, locked it with a key, and glumly faced Levin.

"I just came to tell you," Levin said, aware of the thick beat in his breast, "that our committee has voted to recommend the use of *The Elements* in the 'Grammar for Teachers' course. In the comp classes we'd like to substitute Smith and McGinnis' *Composition and Handbook of Grammar*. We also suggest a better—more suitable reader, Guffey's *Experience in Fact and Fiction*."

"Where do you think that'll get you?" Gilley asked sarcastically. Without waiting for an answer he said, "You might at least have waited until Professor Fairchild's corpse was cold in his grave."

"I'm reporting the committee's decision."

"I'll bet you led them by the nose."

"Our decision was unanimous. You can poll Bucket, Jones, Scowers and Carson Fitch if you don't believe me."

"We'll see about that."

He had flushed darkly and Levin felt his stomach flip. "Gerald," he said, trying to keep his voice steady, "if you countermand these recommendations I'll have to go to every-

308

body and tell them about Bullock's shit-list that you did nothing about."

"Don't you use that kind of language in this office." Gerald looked indignantly to see if Milly had heard but she was in the lavatory.

"I will also tell them, if they don't already know, that Bullock invites the outstanding athletes into his own classes so he can look after them personally, and no one has done a thing to discourage that either. On top of that he tutors those who are too stupid to get a C, and gets paid for it by the P.E. department. That's twice for the same student. How do you think the Cascadia taxpayers would feel about that?"

Gerald got up and shut both doors.

"Are you trying to blackmail me?"

Levin denied it.

"Nothing is being done that the President doesn't know about. It's all on the up and up, so don't try to make it sound like some kind of secret conspiracy," Gerald said, his fury subdued but showing. "George had the initiative to start this tutoring program on his own. The P.E. department insisted on paying him for his time, he didn't ask for it, he doesn't need the money. I personally mentioned it to the president and he didn't think it important enough to comment on."

"Have you told him about the list?"

"Nobody has any proof of that."

"Why don't you ask George if it exists? If he admits it you can then tell him to cut it out. You could also ask him to stop tutoring those he teaches."

"I don't see what difference it makes who tutors them," Gerald said, "so long as he's qualified to do it, and I'd like to point out to you that George, who is three years younger than you, has had his Ph.D. for the last two years, the youngest man in this department with the degree. He is eminently well qualified to teach or tutor anybody. Now I want to tell you that you're not fooling me with your complaints. I know darn well that you and Fabrikant, and Joe Bucket, are playing these things up because you want to discredit me and win the election for CD. But I'll tell you this: it won't work because everybody in the department knows that things aren't as bad as you try to make them out to be."

"They're a lot worse."

Gilley sat down looking miserable. "Sometimes I curse the day I brought you here. You're not fit to be a college instructor."

"Why did you?"

"I was a damn fool."

"To get my vote for giving me a job?"

"If I did I don't want it any more. Listen, Levin, why don't you go back where you came from—to the stinking goddamn New York subways?"

"I'm here to stay." Levin barely believed it.

"That's what somebody else thought who is no longer with us. We'll get rid of you just as we did him."

Though the instructor had borne up fairly well till then, Gilley's threat made him wilt. He might have discovered his ass on the floor, had he not then heard the acting head's desperate voice asking him to be reasonable. Afterwards he felt a dark sense of isolation. He was meant for a peaceful life.

He tried again to persuade Bucket to run, but the assistant professor said he had already committed himself as far as he could.

"If Gilley wins," Levin said, "I'll be kicked out for sure."

"Not without good cause."

"I've given good cause."

"And I've given five hostages to fortune," Bucket said, "not counting a presently pregnant wife, a not unsizeable company to consider."

"I am my only hostage," Levin sighed.

Home, he lay on his bed for hours, staring at the wall.

That night, while picking up a box of crackers in the neighborhood grocery, Levin spied Dean Seagram hefting grapefruit at the fruit counter, and his heart skipped a beat. With his Van Dyke and pinched nose he looked slightly aristocratic but Levin suspected he was approachable. Though the dean had brought nothing particularly new to the Liberal Arts Service Division, he had at least upset the English department with his plans for an election. Levin had more than once seen him in this store; usually they nodded and each went his way, but tonight the instructor felt a desire to talk to the dean. Lately he had been thinking of discussing with him Bullock's concern with athletes but it was too much like snitching. Tonight something else was on his mind.

He waited outside the store and when the dean appeared carrying a huge paper sack loaded with grapefruit, Levin lifted his hat.

"Good evening, I'm in the English department, S. Levin." This took an effort but less than he had imagined.

"I recognized you," the dean said. "You've cut your beard—a pity."

"Oh that." Levin laughed in embarrassment. He fell in step with the dean; they crossed the street at the corner and walked on.

"Do you live this way, Mr. Levin?"

"No, sir, the other. I—ah—thought I'd like to speak to you about an idea I have."

He laid his hand on his chest to calm the galloping organ. It had occurred to him that the dean might have had a bad report of him from Gerald and he now regretted having approached him. Still, here he was, so he spoke.

"I've been wondering if this mightn't seem like a possible good idea to you: to introduce a Great Books program here, something we might carry on at night in the college library? I would be willing to do whatever running around is necessary, et cetera, to get it started."

"I don't understand," said the dean. "Do you mean a Great Books course for our students?"

"No sir. They could come if they want to—everybody welcome including townspeople—but I had the faculty in mind mostly. That is if you think the idea is practicable. What I've been hoping is to get a mixed group together—liberal arts people, scientists, technologists, and business school people— so we can explain these books to each other. Most of them are classics of literature and the rest are from science and the social sciences. What I've been thinking is this: After we've talked about some of the books maybe the others would understand us a little better, at least what the humanities are and why they're necessary to our existence. I realize," he went on quickly, "understanding is a two-way street—some of us know dismally little about science, but in Cascadia College it's obvious who the second-class citizens are, as Dr. Fabrikant calls them. The technologists barely know we're alive and hardly seem to care. Our people have almost no status and accept their fate; some, as I understand it, don't even defend the importance of the subjects they teach. How can they when we're so service-oriented, if I—er—may ask? One can guess the effect of this on their students—"

The dean nodded.

He was about to remark something but Levin hastened on. "I figure if we could keep the program going for a while it might eventually create a climate of opinion in favor of the return of the liberal arts to this college. And maybe this group could become a sort of nucleus of a faculty forum? That is— er—if nobody objects."

Shifting his grapefruit bag, the dean looked intently at Levin.

God damn me for a miserable fool, thought the instructor, why do I never learn?

"Now there's an interesting suggestion."

"You think so?" Levin drew a jagged breath in relief.

"No doubt about it, if we could get the right sort of group. Maybe the approach should be to ask the Council of Deans informally to sponsor the project so that it doesn't look like a propaganda job of the Liberal Arts Service Division? I'll tell you what, Mr. Levin, why don't you drop up to my office some time shortly after Commencement and let's talk about it? We might make a stab at getting such a thing started next fall. I have my doubts as to what the response will be but it's worth trying. Even if we can't get any technologists to join, it'd do some of our people no harm to become re-acquainted with the Great Books—or should I say acquainted?" He laughed hesitantly. "If we could get half a dozen participants from all the other schools, we'd be doing unusually well. It's a unique idea. I congratulate you."

They walked on, Levin with light step. One more idea like that, he thought, and he'd give me a bang-up reference.

"Ah—there's something else I wanted to mention," he said after another block. "This election we're having soon—can anybody run?—I mean an instructor?" He was beginning to laugh hollowly and choked it off. "It may sound silly but all sorts of people run in elections. What would happen if—ah—an instructor won?"

The dean shifted the grapefruit bag to his other arm. "I haven't given a thought to that possibility. Generally the men at the upper ranks are the likely candidates; still if an instructor managed to win fourteen votes I imagine we'd commission him on the battlefield. I'd suggest he be immediately promoted to assistant professor, with all the privileges and emolument thereof—not much of either, I'm afraid. But there might be something additional for administering the department, though not so much as a man of higher rank would get. However, in the unlikely event an instructor won, just to be cautious I think I'd urge that the chairmanship be made rotating—say a new man every two years, at least for a while."

"Fair enough," Levin said.

"Are you interested in running?"

"I'm not sure." He aborted a mad snicker. "Is it—it isn't too late for further nominations?"

"Yes, it is. I sent out a poop sheet to you people this afternoon, with the names of the nominees. However you were nominated, along with Drs. Gilley, Fabrikant and Bullock. The latter called me at home this evening and asked to have his name withdrawn."

"Me?" said Levin in joyful surprise. Bucket did it, he thought. Or Jones, or maybe Scowers. He wondered if the dean thought he had nominated himself, since names had been entered on unsigned sheets. He laughed nervously.

Dean Seagram laughed too. An oncoming car separated them in the street, Levin waiting as the dean ran ahead.

"Look out," he yelled.

The dean, glancing back to see what had become of the instructor, was heading into a phone pole. He stopped short of it but not before his grapefruit bag had hit the pole and split apart.

The grapefruit went rolling into the street. Levin, clucking, rescued an armful. At the dean's insistence he piled a few on those he had in his arms but what he couldn't carry Levin did.

In fine fettle for being so helpful, almost without thinking he asked the dean how much notice anyone who was not going to be re-hired usually got.

"Well, sir," said the dean, hugging his fruit, "the Administrative Regulations require us, after the first year, to give twelve months' notice to faculty members without tenure. But if you're referring to someone serving his probationary year, he's got to have notice in writing by the latest at the beginning of the spring term that we won't be renewing his contract for the fall."

I've had nothing in writing, Levin thought with elation. Though he realized he had asked a foolish question he could not help thinking that a man had no true idea of his possibilties until he had investigated them. Even with Gilley as head of department, in another year, given a break or two, he might recoup his fortune at Cascadia College if he played it right. Therefore, no further questions.

"But dismissal is summary," the dean went on cheerily, "on

any sort of morals charge. I understand that that, ultimately, was the justification for getting rid of Mr. Duffy."

In a minute they were scrambling after grapefruit after Levin had walked into a tree.

Am I worthy? he asked himself. Me, jailbird's son, ex-drunk, unfrocked idealist, sinner re-sinned, mistake-maker-of-every-kind? How can a man who has so often failed in obedience think of himself as a possible leader? Do I dare, with my nature, weaknesses, history of failures, seek any task other than that which fosters humility, cleans conscience, and/or balances the mistakes of the past? Levin had never before even remotely considered running for office, had never been a candidate for anything but punch-ball captain at twelve, and later for a couple of college degrees. A worthy leader means man of virtue and wisdom, virtue embodying courage; he had not much of either, mostly he had good intentions. Still a good-intentioned administrator who was not afraid to try a worthwhile idea once in a while might do all right. Of course it was a hell of a nerve for an instructor with so little experience in a college, an Easterner not long in the West, until recently a stranger to most of his colleagues, to ask them to elect *him* head of department. Yet maybe that sort of shock was what they needed here. If that happened, anything might.

He reveried accomplishment, Levin the leader; foresaw an effective if necessarily short career. What mightn't he achieve at Cascadia if he devoted himself to the task: a hundred needed reforms—raising the department from mediocrity to excellence. And while at that, who knows if, working every which way, he mightn't succeed in starting a campaign to bring back to Cascadia a liberal arts majors program? Easchester would flower. One good thing led to another once somebody dared. Good institutions proliferate good deeds. They might, in town, build a concert hall and public forum, start an art gallery, theatre group, show foreign films, even open a bookstore that sold books. An enlightened public opinion!

Easchester, Athens of the Northwest! And when Levin left to take up a new career (Why leave if he had created the conditions of his survival? A woman one was bound to meet sooner or later.), the good people of the town, inspired to communal gratitude would parade him up and down Main Street amid Lions, Elk, Women of the Moose, Odd Fellows, the Easchester Taxpayers Association, cheers, tears and a brassband. Levin, benefactor, Culture Hero, Seymour J. P. Bunyanseed, Fautor et Cultor Bonorum, American Patriot! He had to slap himself to leave off.

Though he detested asking people for their votes, to raise himself above them, hated the indignity of campaigning, it was what he had to do. He counted, three, maybe four, votes in hand, but there was a way of inducing a half dozen others, even more if he could do the dirty thing he contemplated doing. If he did, it was doubtful he could make fourteen votes, but possible. If not, the trick was to prevent Gilley's election in the hope that somebody neutral would be appointed acting head, though the instructor had doubts of that too, since Gerald was already serving. Still, Levin's plan was to keep him from certain power until he had landed a job in another college. What happened after he left was their business; if they voted Gilley in, they deserved to have him. Gerald was sure he had the inside track but Levin, upstart shmo, had a photostat of Bullock's shit-list; and since there was little time, began—an uneasy Machiavelli—(I'm telling them for their own good; ignorance is not bliss) to show it cautiously around. He had cut off from the letter Bullock's signature. When people guessed who had compiled the names, he neither affirmed nor denied it, saying only that he had called the paper to Gerald's attention but he had refused to take action against the perpetrator of the list, the original copy of which now reposed amid the football coach's papers, a filed defilement. No one particularly hit the ceiling in surprise or indignation but several people were disturbed, Bucket and O. E. Jones to the point of quiet misery. One or two were frightened to see their names on the list. "How can I get off?" they asked Levin.

As if to compensate for the first document, he produced another, mimeographed in secret late at night: "S. Levin, PLATFORM: To maintain our self-respect, OUT with *The Elements* (as recommended by the composition textbook committee), ALSO the d.o., ditto the policy of unwilled favoritism to athletes; and censorship of responsibly selected texts; fear of the public and distrust of staff; the composition room and assorted gadgets. IN, a writing-centered comp course; one literature class to each man insofar as possible; the ideal of the humanities—foundation of democracy." He went on, in talk, almost without meaning to: held these truths to be self-evident: there is more to democracy, even in the American West, than equalitarianism. Equality means equal justice under law, equal suffrage, equal opportunity through free education; it doesn't mean every man is as good as the next—that there is no such thing as aristocracy of mind, spirit, attainment. Jefferson (his italics) to Adams; to Levin: "There is a natural aristocracy among men, the grounds for this are *virtue and talents.* The natural aristocracy I consider to be the most precious gift of nature, *for the instruction, the trusts and the government of society.*" Equality is not achievement of the identical average. Nor are "ideas" equal in value because they were thought up by friendly people. A man seeks excellence through education and accomplishment. When its leaders are great, democracy is. Levin, his armpits sizzling, was at this point usually stammering, on the verge of disconnected sentences, the felt disjunction of his worth with what he must say. When he was asked why he no longer supported Fabrikant he said he thought the department needed a stronger man, and when his auditor inspected him with a critical eye, in a canny moment the instructor offered to quit his candidacy if the dean would appoint as head a capable man from the outside. O. E. Jones said he and Ed Purtzer would at once suggest that to Dean Seagram.

Levin stirred up, during the last days of the term, a terrible discord. He was, and knew it, the subject of much talk and rancor. He lived on the edge of things, on edge, his nerves ragged, yet forcing himself to push his campaign to get himself elected. Those who agreed with his criticisms and suggestions for improvement of the department, seemed to be as much annoyed with him as those who disagreed, who thought *The Elements* was fine, Gilley's policies fine, the way things went, fine. He was accused of starting trouble and disturbing people's peace. He was accused of exaggerating, lying. He was called to his face by Leopold Kuck, usually a mild sort, "the main victim of your own presumptuous desire for power." He quoted Lord Acton and informed Levin he had never trusted him. "You don't understand us," he all but yelled in his office. "You have no idea of decorum. You're as bad as Leo Duffy, without his virtues. You oughtn't to be teaching in a college." Ferris Farper—Levin had been expecting this—called him a "lousy goddamn un-American radical." I'm a poor substitute for one, Levin thought, but here a little goes a long way. He felt like a viper. His heart palpitated when he was doing nothing. He feared the name-callers, satisfied with what they had, wanted more of the same, three cars in every garage. Anyone who suggested that to be too contented with one's life or society was a subtle form of death, was clearly off his rocker, alien, without doubt a Red.

A few days before year-end exams began, George Bullock, his sharp face florid, encountering Levin in the hall, threatened to knock his block off. "Where the hell do you get your fat nerve copying my private correspondence and showing it around?"

"I cut your name out of the letter," said Levin. "I didn't mention whose list it was."

"You mentioned it to Gerald."

"The list, not your name. He guessed whose it was."

"You can't make a crime where none was intended," Bullock said angrily. "The athletes are the only ones around who achieve anything worth talking about. I have every right to protect them from the likes of you. Jesus, what a sucker I was to invite you to my home. You betrayed my hospitality."

"I'm sorry—I was grateful for it."

"Like hell you were. You and that foul beard, the minute I laid eyes on it I knew I couldn't trust you."

"Don't blame my beard—"

"You won't get a single goddamn vote more than your own."

Gilley, listening down the hall, smiled grimly; Fabrikant, on his way to the men's room, glowered.

Levin's isolation deepened. He was weary of making enemies, sick to death of fighting alone, living alone, of his lonely mind. The battle had become more than he could stand; he wanted desperately to quit.

But that same day Bucket came to him and said he had, after much contemplation, decided to support his candidacy.

"Ah," sighed the instructor, "only don't do anything you'll be sorry for."

" 'The more my uncle Toby pored over his map, the more he took a liking to it.' " Bucket cackled a bit. "I'll do what little I can to help."

As Levin, moved to celebrate the acquisition of an ally, was sitting in the men's room later, a voice from the next stall asked, "Mr. Levin?"

"Speaking."

"I thought that was you talking to yourself. This is Merdith Schultz." Levin had seen him, other than at department meetings, maybe twice during the year although their offices were next to each other.

"I've been following your career with great interest," said Merdith Schultz. "You have more friends than you know."

Levin went home in an improved frame of mind.

During final-exam week some of the animosity seemed to evaporate from the air. Now and then people passing Levin in the hall, smiled. He had the feeling he might make it; it was "not impossible."

319

On the Saturday night before finals Levin went to his office to average grades and after a few minutes became restlessly conscious of a scent he recognized. He put his head out of the window and breathed the cold air, then sniffed inside and was convinced the warm odor was orange blossom. His scalp prickled; he had lately got the feeling he was being watched—ridiculous. He had blamed it on his nerves—now he suspected Avis had been in his office. He quickly went through a mess of papers in his top drawer and was moved and frightened to find among them a letter of Pauline's he was positive he had destroyed, the one she had written after running into Mrs. Beaty. The paper seemed alive in his hand and he sensed Avis had read it. Levin tore it up and burned it in the wastebasket. Then he opened a book and waited.

In about an hour he heard Avis shut her door and walk up the hall. She hastened past his office. He listened to her crooked heels clacking down the stairs, gave himself seven minutes, then let himself into her office. Her desk drawer was locked but he pried it open with a screw driver he had got in Marv Beal's closet. In her perfumed, neat, old-maid's drawer, he found several notebooks labeled "Lesson Plans." Flipping through them one by one, Levin discovered that a portion of the most recent book had been converted into a rough diary of his "movements." Avis had for the last month been listing his comings and goings. She had recorded the number of girl students who had entered his office, and whenever possible, the length of time each had stayed. She had also listed the names of colleagues who had been in to see him, Bucket's name most often but at one time or another everyone on Bullock's list. The last entry, dated tonight, was Pauline's letter copied in Avis' girlish hand.

"Just a word, dearest. I suppose you know?—I'm awfully sorry. I was afraid of something like this. I can't tell you how bad I feel, God knows how I'll get through the night. I'm writing this in Erik's room. Call me Thurs. between 9 & 10, no later. I just had to get in touch. I love you. I miss you so. Destroy this. Pauline."

His impulse was to rip up the notebook, but he rolled it up and slipped it into his pocket. Pulling the drawer out as far as it would go, he discovered several packs of letters bound by rubber bands, arranged chronologically within the pack, going back to Avis' first year in Cascadia. Levin sat down and looked through them. They were for the most part from her family and Louisville friends, reporting local chitchat. But among the letters he found an unstamped yellow envelope addressed "Avis" in strong, thick-stroked writing. Inside were two thin sheets of papers, short handwritten notes. The first, dated 18 October, 1948, read: "Dear Avis—I am most grateful for last night. Yours, Leo." The second, 3 April, 1949, said: "Dear Miss Fliss: I'll thank you to keep your nose out of my business. Leo Duffy."

Levin returned both notes into the envelope and pocketed it. From Milly's office he dialed Avis, saying he wanted to see her. She answered, after a short pause, that she had already hung up her dress but would be pleased to see him in the morning.

"Put something on," said Levin. "I'm coming over."

"Have you been drinking?"

"Not yet."

She hesitated. "All right, you may come."

She was waiting for him on the porch in her pink—he thought at first, nightgown—but it was a summer dress though the night was cold. She gave forth orange scent and her bosom was quietly agitated.

"Avis," said Levin, "I would appreciate the truth. Have you already told Gerald about the letter you copied into your note-book tonight?"

She stamped her foot. "Oh, you are vile." Her hand went to her chest and her knees buckled but as he reached out to help her she grabbed the porch rail. Her eyelashes fluttered endlessly. At last she moaned and lowered herself into a chair. When she spoke her body was rigid, voice expressionless.

"No, I haven't—"

"Good," said Levin.

"I won't promise not to. You both betrayed Gerald. I suspected it. I felt you were hiding something and when you began to take George's letter around I thought you deserved a similar treatment. Not only do you want Gerald's job, you want his wife. Your inhumanity knows no bounds—"

"The notebook," said Levin, "also contains the names of some of our colleagues who have nothing to do with Pauline or me, and who might seriously object to being spied on. I also have two notes from Leo Duffy to you."

Tears filled her eyes. "You contemptible, perfectly awful person, don't you dare show them to anyone or I'll have you arrested."

"I have no intention to, but I ask the same consideration from you. The lady and I no longer see each other. She's reconciled with her husband. It would help nobody if you told him about her letter."

She sat motionless.

He said gently, "You were in love with Duffy?"

She seemed to come to after a while. "For a short time," she said. "However I retained my virtue though he tried endlessly to persuade me to bow to his will."

"Later he became interested in Pauline?"

"She threw herself at him," Avis said bitterly. "She enticed and seduced him."

He hadn't the courage to deny it.

He beheld her through the musty curtains of the front door, his hand resting on the knob. How can it be? he thought; that's in the past. It was a cold early morning; he had been getting up at five to work on a paper about a white whale. It was an awesome burden and woke him in the dark every morning. At a quarter of eight he had drunk his coffee and was about to leave the house to give his first exam when he saw her through the curtain, standing across the street. The day was overcast, intensifying color. Behind her were purple irises and a flaming azalea bush. She stood at the curb under a tree and he thought at first she was waiting for someone to give her a lift, though why at this hour, or why here, or where she might be going, he didn't know. He was, however, moved to see her and memorized this picture of her standing across the street alone.

May, in its middle, had turned disappointingly cold. June came in as bad. Heavy vaporous clouds, on the move from the Pacific, hid the sun except for unexpected minutes of light. It rained on and off. In the late afternoon the sun bloomed gold but give it a welcoming cheer and it sank in a red sea. Mrs. Beaty recalled many a wet cold summer. She wore long underwear, thick around the ankles under heavy stockings, and often drank hot tea. They decided to continue the furnace full time, for a while had been using no more than a half hopperful of sawdust each morning to flush the chill. The chill was there especially because it wasn't supposed to be, less than three weeks to summer.

He watched her from deep within, his hand still on the knob, nothing new about her that he could see. She wore her raincoat and black headscarf. Though she was a plain woman he could still see wherein she was lovely. It was this thought that had momentarily moved him. Also a sense of the waste of life. Of experience lived to what purpose? He knew she was waiting for him.

Levin went up the stairs and out by the back way. He climbed the fence, crossed a muddy yard, then over another wet fence to come out on a side street. He hurried to Humanities Hall by a roundabout route. All morning he wondered how long she had waited. He stayed in his office, grading papers. When he got back to the house, toward six, there was a note on the hall table, that Mrs. Gilley had called. He was both surprised that she would and that Mrs. Beaty would tell him so casually. Upstairs on his bureau lay a blue envelope addressed in Pauline's writing; it had been mailed yesterday. He put it into a drawer. Later that night, after returning from a walk he hadn't particularly wanted to take, Levin got out the letter and tore it open. He read it with spy glass from a distant planet. Then, by an effort of the will, he read it in his room. "I must see you—*please*. Can you call me? Pauline." An overwhelming sadness settled in him. If suffering was for something what had he suffered for? Levin burned her letter.

What renunciation was supposed to do he assumed it had done. Occasionally there were still unexpected moments of warm recall—his first sight of her in the forest, their falling in love, the bed at its best; but remembrance of the bed invariably led to thoughts of their last failures, nature uncooperative, hers. What he felt now—felt?—was abstraction, no more than the memory of memory. She stayed in the mind in the act of dropping into his unwilling lap the hot contents of a tuna fish casserole, mopping same with baby's diaper; he thought of her as the small town lady who talked of a new life but had been consistently afraid of it, never daring beyond the frontier of sex. He was at times harsh in judging her, Avis Fliss once removed. Wasn't that renunciation?

At his worst he blamed her for Duffy. Not that she had invented him; the man had an existence in history that Levin, almost from the moment of hearing his name, had in self-love been drawn to. But he blamed her for having used the Irishman against him, as it were, in a sense negating Levin's value as Levin. What she had probably wanted was someone like Duffy at a Duffyless time, so she settled for him come disguised with a beard. He held against her her never revealing the repetition she had fabricated, never told him whose carbon copy he was. She had not once whispered of her wild Irish lover, who, although he hadn't created it, had most recently lived the myth Levin fell into, or was dragged into assways. She had caused him to believe he was her first true love, Gilley not qualifying beyond somebody who had married her in a desperate moment (hers), although Levin had seen in her picture album also a Guggenheim scholar she had girlishly given her heart to, who had given it back. Before that, innocence; after, Duffy. Once he had heard about Leo from Avis, during the bad time he was having Levin thought he had lost the will to be Levin; that he was, so to say, the extension of Duffy's ghost. This sort of thing could become dangerous if it went too far. What most enraged him was clear evidence of the continued weakness of his old self.

He was thus affected until, as events developed, he had reason to distrust Avis as informant and began to wonder at some of his recent judgments of Pauline. From nothing to speak of he had more than once in his life erected fantastic structures, complicated Babels on stilts, overwrought constructions that collapsed under a single cold fact, or in whiff of sober sense. In talking with Fabrikant that night in his melon patch, Levin had realized doubts of his own suspicions that Pauline and Leo Duffy had been lovers. He knew only circumstantial details of an affair between them; her rumored confession to Gilley, authored, however, by Avis, author of the spying notebooks and the story of a picture she hadn't seen but could describe. If the photo existed, and Levin assumed it did, all it proved was that Pauline and Duffy had once gone swimming bareass together. End of evidence. What it proved about Gilley was a jackass of another color. From the supposition of the existence of the picture it was of course no trick to infer an affair between two discontented adults; yet a man of more than ordinary imagination, with good reason might infer nothing of the sort. Two and two was sometimes not two and two. If they had been lovers it would somehow have come out. She spoke openly of her life even when trying not to.

Having arrived here, Levin, explorer, ventured farther. Suppose there had been something between them—love, affair, love affair, what did that subtract from *him*, appearing on the scene two years later, Duffy, if not forgotten, long since gone? Nothing, if the mind stopped overreaching itself in creating analogies. As for telling or not telling him, so she hadn't—out of modesty, shame, pain—who knows how many motives lead to a single omission. Had he, for instance, told her about Nadalee Hammerstad, for all her knowledgeability in bed not much more than a kid? Must Pauline confess who first had slipped his subtle fingers under her skirt; or he go back to age five, when he had packed earth in a little girl's backside through failure to think boldly? All this plus and minus in a long long world was nobody's business if privacy had any meaning. What Levin dwelt on was this: Was her love for him when it was love, less true because she had once loved Duffy, if she had loved Duffy? Why the obsessive linking of himself with the fabricated protoytpe, no more than just another guy trying to run into the meaning of his life, raising a little Cain in the process, and, in the nature of things, disappearing for good in all but name. There was enough in life to sneeze at without sniffing in dusty time. Let's admit— wherever Levin had been, someone had been before (no Chingachgook he, even in the primeval forest, even forest of the night). Two men with similar temperaments, possibly backgrounds and ideas, showing up after a short interval at the same all-but-unchanged locale, would see the same birds and flowers, walk the same streets, create similar adventures, and, not impossibly, love the same woman. What was wrong with my head? he asked himself. He blamed his overworked emotions and resolved to forget the long-departed Duffy.

Where did all this involved thinking leave him? It left him, a week before the election, electioneering. It left him much where one is left, he thought, who had suffered and renounced. Wherever he was he was left; if Levin, still in doubt. Recalling how deeply, tenderly, fervently—to the twisted core of his being—he had loved her, he could not understand how he had brought himself to give her up. Was it cowardice calling itself reason, or a true, even talented, reading of the hopelessness of the situation? It was hopeless; he had fled love to dispel her anxiety and misery. He had suffered to free her from suffering. He felt he had done the right thing; he sensed she had willed their break; he had carried it out for her.

Therefore, when he saw her through the front door he left by the back.

She was there, the image in the curtain, the next morning. Watching, he tried to feel something for her but felt nothing. I get this way, he thought. Levin escaped the back way, tearing his pants leg on a nail as he climbed the fence. A man in the neighboring house shook his fist at him. In the office a blue letter—guess who?—lay on his desk. He tore it up. Simply hopeless. Then he regretted what he had done, then tried not to.

Mrs. Beaty that afternoon nervously reported two phone calls. "She asked me if you knew she had been trying to get in touch with you and I said I thought you did. She said nothing after that, just hung up the phone."

"Thanks," he said. The old woman waited for more but got nothing.

Another call came while he was lying in bed, watching the rain. He had told her if it was Pauline to say he had gone out.

She walked slowly up the stairs and said through the door, though he pretended to be sleeping, "I told her what you told me to say, Mr. Levin, but please, you'll have to tell her yourself if she calls again."

He asked, after minutes, if she was lowering the drawbridge; she wanted to know what he meant.

"Aren't we still protecting the honor of your house?"

"Please don't be sarcastic with me, I'm an old woman. I'm sorry for her and I'm sorry for you."

"I'm in an election. I have my future to think of."

"Tell her yourself."

He tried to think what he could tell her but told her nothing. He reveried his life as a drunkard. He had suffocating dreams of walking miles for a bottle but when he got to the store he had no money. When he had got the money the store was closed. When the store opened he dropped the bottle on the sidewalk. Then he lay in a dank cellar watching his shoes burning. He woke apprehensive.

Looking out early on Wednesday he spied her coming up the back stairs. Like old times. Levin slipped out the front way as she was knocking upstairs. He called himself nasty names but saw no profit in the chase. The time to have come was a month ago.

Glancing out of his office window later he saw her, with Erik and Mary, in front of the Student Union. She waved, he retreated. She's surely mad. He stayed out of sight till she had left. Home, he tacked a sheet of heavy wrapping paper over the back door window, long overdue. Levin ate on the run and ran to a movie. He had considered leaving a note: "What can I give you? For Christ's sake, let's keep it quits." He lived in fear she would pop in at night, he would wake to find her in bed pumping his organ. But she did not appear; maybe Gilley kept a wide-open eye on her now.

Though he hungered to stay in bed the next morning, because he had slept badly and had no exam, he was dressed early to be out of the house before she appeared. He figured another day or two and the chase would end. He had waked heavy-hearted, a weight of sadness in every movement. He had felt this way, on and off, since the day she had reappeared. For three days he had tried to beat the mood but couldn't; he was uneasy that it persisted. Lifting the wrapping paper he looked cautiously out at one corner. Nothing but the wet world. He detested having to climb wet fences. At half-past seven Levin went downstairs and looked through the front door. She was standing in the rain under the dripping sycamore, with both kids. His teeth were on edge.

He went up to his room. It's useless, he thought. I can't outrun her.

Mrs. Beaty labored up the creaking stairs. "It's raining hard. The children are getting wet."

"Have you talked to her?"

"Just for a minute."

"What does she want?"

"She'll have to tell you herself."

For five minutes he listened to her breathing at his door.

"Ask her to come in," said Levin.

He heard her go down and open the front door. Then he heard her speaking and Pauline saying something to her, and they all came in.

Levin looked at himself in the mirror and looked away. He went to the window and gazed at the back fences but returned to the mirror. He did not remember going to the stairs, only going down them.

Pauline, holding Mary on her arm, ground her teeth. The little girl began to cry.

Mrs. Beaty took her. "We'll make coffee." She took Erik's hand and they went into the kitchen.

When they were alone Pauline said, "I'm sorry, I wanted to leave them but I couldn't get anyone to sit at this hour."

She looked weary, harried, lonely. Her face was taut, small, her dark eyes, restless. "Why did you run from me?" she said bitterly. "Why didn't you call when I asked you to?"

"Does Gerald know you came here?"

"No. He's always at the office early during exam week."

"Come inside."

They entered the small parlor off the hall. She sat in one stiff-backed chair at the wet window, he in the other at the wall opposite. The clock ticked above his head. She had removed her wet raincoat and scarf; her hair hung in dark rattails. Turning her head away from him she wiped her eyes with her fingers. Outside it was raining steadily. He listened to the sound of the rain.

"Not much of a spring, I guess." She had slipped off her shoes, twisting one long foot behind the other. "I hope you don't mind, my shoes are damp."

The depression Levin felt, hung in him like a dead animal. Where's my love gone? He wanted to warn her something was wrong; instead he hid it.

She asked, then, why he had stopped seeing her.

Levin, after long silence, spoke. "At first to help you. After a while I felt you no longer wanted to see me. I got used to it."

"It's true," she said. "I didn't."

"I figured that, I tried to help you."

"If you had written once at least."

"I hoped you would, it had to be by your choice. What could

330

I do under the circumstances? You didn't let me know how you had got into the house—or if you had got in though you knew I'd be sweating it out. Not hearing from you I felt you wanted to call it quits."

"I didn't call purposely. I did it for *you*, not to involve you further in my confusions. I ate myself about you but I was terribly unhappy about Gerald and the children. I had got into the house without the least trouble. He wasn't there, he had left at four to go fishing with George. He thought I had come in and gone to sleep in Erik's room, and didn't want to wake me—I'd been sleeping so badly. The kids were alone in the house from four till almost eight. There were signs Mary had waked and cried herself back to sleep. Erik had gone looking for me and then began to play with his toys. When I got back, he cried as though he had found out for all time what a bitch I was. That I wasn't his mother and never would be. What if there had been a fire? I would have killed myself. That was my state of mind for most of a week and I decided I must give you up—my love for you. I imagined you would know, when you saw Gerald, that I had got in safely."

He said he had known.

"I swore to myself I'd be a better mother, and wife. I did everything I could to suit myself to him, to be less critical, to enjoy life with him. I did everything, short of cutting my throat, to forget you."

"Ah—" said Levin.

"The more I tried—I hope you don't mind hearing this—the less I could. There were days when I almost didn't think of you, when I felt I had killed you in me, but the very thought renewed my feeling of loss so profoundly that sometimes I felt I had left drops of blood where I was standing when I had thought of you last. But I kept trying to end you in me, and I was, bit by bit, until I saw you at Orville's funeral. When I saw you then, your face so lonely without the beard you had cut off to protect me, what was left of my heart beat itself silly trying to get to you. I realized then how much beyond recall

I was in love with you. If you had come over to me and said I was to go with you, I would have gone. Afterwards I fought against myself for your sake—to save your plans—until I no longer could. Then I thought, I must go to him, and that's what I did."

Levin sat like a broken statue. The destruction of love she could not commit he had accomplished.

The landlady brought in two cups of coffee on a silver tray. Pauline had her handkerchief to her eyes.

"I'm sorry for your trouble," Mrs. Beaty said.

"And I to trouble you."

"There's none at all. The children are playing with my pots and pans."

"We'll be leaving soon—"

The landlady set the coffee cups on the small tables near each chair and returned to the kitchen.

Pauline held her cup in her palms.

Levin did not touch his. He grew desperate to leave.

"When we got home from the funeral," she was saying, looking at the cup in her hands, "I went upstairs and tried to sleep. But I thought about Gerald, about all the kind things he had done for me. I found myself thinking that my character had deteriorated with his. I overlook too much in both of us that I oughtn't to. I try to be honest and I'm not when I want most to be. He knows I no longer love him but he can stand it so long as I keep my mouth shut and we go on living together. He gives me little, I give him less. I try but fail with him, we fail together. I don't want to any more. I want a better life. I want it with you."

He listened in petrification.

"Lev, I love you. Be my love again."

He muttered what of her husband.

"I've made up my mind to ask for a divorce. I feel I'm entitled to my love for you. I've worn out the obligation—if it is that—of living half a life. I want to be your wife."

He rose hastily, upsetting the cup on the table. Levin

watched the stain spreading on the rug. He ran to the kitchen
for something to mop it with.

Why don't I keep on running?

But he returned with a cloth and dabbed at the rug. She
wanted to do it but he wouldn't let her.

When he came back from the kitchen again she was standing
barefoot at the window, watching the rain. She turned to him
with eyes like sad flowers.

I've got to be honest with her, Levin thought. That may be
all I have left to give.

"Pauline," he said heavily, "I'm sorry for the way I am now—"

"Don't you feel well?"

"I'm not myself—"

"Have I upset you?"

"To tell the truth, I wasn't expecting this—"

"That I would come back?"

"Yes—" She went to him, put her arms around him. "Hold
me, please hold me."

He held her.

"Hold me tightly."

Levin tightened his arms. She gazed at him as though he
had just returned from a long voyage and she was trying to
remember what he was like in a former time.

"Don't you love me any more?"

"Love—" he said with a heavy heart. "Who knows what I've
mangled—"

She seemed to shrink, then held him harder. "I love you, say
you love me. Say it the way you used to."

Holding her, he strove to say it, groping from one obscure
thought to another for an explanation, the secret of what
afflicted him, anything that might free him to love her. At last
Levin said, "Why didn't you tell me you and Leo Duffy were
lovers?"

She pushed him away. "Oh God, is that what's bothering
you?"

"I don't know—"

"I thought you knew, that Avis or someone had told you but you never mentioned it to be kind to me. If I loved him what difference would it make?"

"I want to know the truth—"

"The truth is we were lovers, sexually, once. I slept with him the day he was publicly fired. If you want to know where, it was in his car that night. I've had that experience too—"

"Did you love him?"

"Not then, but I fell in love with him after he had gone. Now you know what I'm like—"

"Are you sure you still don't love him?"

She smiled sadly. "Leo's dead."

Levin shuddered. "Dead?"

"He died last year. His mother wrote in the spring that he had killed himself in January. I don't know the circumstances and couldn't bring myself to ask—"

"I'm sorry—"

"He left a note: 'The time is out of joint. I'm leaving the joint.' "

Levin sprang to her and they desperately embraced.

He packed both bags and drove off along a lonely road lined with black cypresses, past a railroad crossing, full granary, and deserted farmhouse. He was making good time when the car gave out with a clunk. Abandoning suitcase and valise, he took off on foot, the dust of the road settling on him. He had run through the day and was on night's tail when an obscure figure appeared on the road, coming at him from a mirror, the opposing self or its spitting image.

QUO VADIS, LEVIN?

Towards freedom.

Loud laughter in the wings.

He awoke clammy, and spent half the night wandering amid the crosses row by row in a graveyard of mangled hopes, purposes, schemes. Hadn't he planned—it said in his notebook —to be a college professor? To Straighten Out His Life?

334

Come To Something? He hadn't planned to be entangled with a married woman. To be anyone's second husband before he was somebody's first. To be this unsettled, confused, tormented, at this time of his life. He suffered from Unfinished Business. He wanted to win the election. Now that classes were over, he was moved by an oppressive desire to rush to Humanities Hall and teach all who would listen, the mysteries of the infinitive.

Flight flew in him. He wasn't fleeing yet fled, unable to determine whom he was running from, himself or her. He blamed the flight, paradoxically a pursuit of feeling, on the fact that too much had happened in too short a time. He couldn't cram it all in, experience leaked out, confusing subjectivity. He had, since their separation, harbored a secret belief that they had through love marked each other for future use; he hadn't expected the future to explode in his face, shattering all he had to think, decide, do. The responsibility was terrifying —taking away another man's wife, the miserable mess of divorce, having to fit himself to her, all her habituations and impedimenta, to suit to her clutter his quiet bachelor's life, needs, aspirations, plans, which though more than once destroyed and replaced, remained essentially what they had been, except that their fulfillment was farther in front of the nose with every step he took. He was distended by the fast thrust of events, of too many revived possibilities—where would he put them all? He feared his destiny had been decided apart from him, by chance, her, not him. She called the signals and he awoke running in the play. He had grave doubts, if he took her on again, that he could be master of his fate to any significant degree; he had already lost—the terrible thing—his freedom to feel free.

Levin beat himself into a concrete frenzy to resuscitate his love for her, but try breathing green, purple, rose. He tried every way he could, by every use of the imagination, to recapture love as it had been in fullest flower, as though the mind could recreate what it apparently rejected. Memory was a dark door leading through dark doors floating in space to Orpheus always descending. Levin a whirlwind of enraged impotence at what had become of him. In love he had unwillingly pulled the stopper, ug glug, no further feeling. This though he told himself he *must* still love her. Love for her was in him as experience, as valued idea, pleasure received, which he wanted to repeat. Except it wasn't where it had been, or should be. He had had and hadn't it. What in Christ's name had he done with the love he had only a month ago felt for her? Had he butchered it in the vize of will, sublimated it beyond repair, or recall, like a magician prestidigitating a girl into a tree, then forgetting the hocus pocus so that when he wanted a woman he embraced wood? Was such a thing even remotely possible? These thoughts drew others equally unhappy into their orbit. Was it love murdered or love imperfect, less than love to begin with? Had he loved her for the lay and not much else, giving it a tainted reciprocity of feeling? Was it a guilty response to experience he should have accepted as one accepts sunlight? Why must he forever insist on paying for being alive?

And with the lay as good as gone—he had believed—had he then, after a show of self-castigation to make himself look decent in the mirror, stopped loving the little he had loved? Or would this, in time, have happened anyway, out of boredom, without the necessity of a sudden decisive surrender of her? Or was his interest in Pauline basically that she belonged to someone else—life's initial tease—and once he had her as far as she went, when her thing broke down in various motels, best send her back to daddy, the lover's gut glutted? Who knows the answer? Not Levin. But why scratch sores to see what lies under them? "Thought is a disease of the flesh." T. Hardy said it, not the diseased Levin. Levin couldn't stop scratching: if it was none of these things then wasn't it really as in the past—the thought returned—the suffocating quasideadness (alas poor Duffy) of going through more than he could stand, nervously frazzled to the point of immobility?

Can I give out with only three pints of feeling before the well runs dry? Is it nerves, glands, the broken machine itself? What's to blame: the poor quality of his love, how beat to death, or the imperfections of an imperfect man? Or, please God, that he had simply gone through her, she no longer interested him as a person—perfectly normal and he was making a sickness out of it? Conscience the rotting onion in the mind's stomach. Whatever the answer or answers, the doubt most in his mind was What to Do: Was it best to stall for time—wait it out and hope to approach her again with a full heart, to which she was entitled; or must he commit himself now, no matter how bad he felt, or couldn't feel? In her mind she had parted from Gilley and was alone in his house, possibly frightened at all that lay ahead to be done. He felt for her a blunted compassion, not enough to give relief but at least a response.

Everdrowning Levin saw the thirsty world from under the sea. It wasn't the world, it was more of the sea. He was a lone fish poking its snoot into bursting bubbles. On the bank sat Gilley with hook, line, sinker. The poor fish fled. Levin in watery flight followed confused currents. Every way out was his way in. He fantasied self-destruction, fish hooking self, funny for a fish. (Duffy, proud bird, had blown his coop.) ... He woke in terrible thirst and frantically searched for a bottle in the bottom drawer until remembering he had long ago dumped it into the garbage can. He tried drowning thirst in water, drinking glass after glassful until his stomach bloated. He bathed in Mrs. Beaty's tub, thirstily soaping himself six times over but still was thirsty, thick as toothache, fire in the mouth, boiling lead dripping down his salted gullet. Levin dressed in the dry middle of the night and walked in rain till the rain stopped. He stood on the riverbank watching the thirsty-fingered dawn on the surface of the hidden water. For hours he wandered in downtown streets, his eyes glazed as he gazed through glass, thirsting to dive into a whiskey bottle. What sweet relief to feel the searing stuff go through his tortured throat. To feel the sodden spirit soar. To be in peace not

337

Levin. To lie pickled thirstless, satisfied. Wandering, he cast love-sick glances at both brown-bottled tavern windows, drunk with emptiness, wrenching himself along in rectangular circles, until broken by weariness he pushed through a door and stood solemnly at a bar.

"What'll it be?" said the hairy bartender.

"Love," Levin said, and as the man looked for the bottle, fled.

Hiding under the rattling boards of the old river bridge as the sun set, dust sifting into his hair whenever a car rumbled overhead, Levin, the machinery of his existence creaking, in a private place in the mind put things together thus: that he, S. Levin, the self again betrayed by the senses (if not vice-versa), did not presently desire her, in no way diminished her as one worthy of love (his), and what is worth loving is worth love, or the other way around. What I had from forest to last frustration was worth having—I respect what it was. If I could have it again, I would. I have no cause now not to love her, granted I loved; I grant. I loved her; we loved. She loves me still, I have never been so loved. That was the premise, and the premise you chose was the one you must live with; if you chose the wrong one you were done to begin with, your whole life in jail. You cheated yourself of the short freedom you had in the world, the little of life to be alive in. He craftily told himself time alters everything, premises wear out, change produces incompatibles. He sniffed out reasons to escape, go where he pleased, unbound, unburdened, where fancy fancied and the feet followed. . . . Then by devious ways he returned to the premise: She was his love, changed by it only as he by hers. What had changed beyond that was badly willed, now unwilled. A man sentenced to death may regain freedom; so may love. It was possible, it surely had happened. No matter what he had suffered or renounced, to what degree misused or failed feeling, if Pauline loving him loves; Levin with no known cause not to will love her. He would without or despite feeling. He would hold on when he wanted terribly to let go.

Love had led him, he would now lead love. Having reasoned thus he cursed reason.

They talked that night in his car, parked on a country road, black fields on both sides. He had for an hour felt relief at a decision made, had begun, he had thought, to anticipate seeing her. But after picking her up on a street not far from her house, he knew it still wasn't right. The feeling he had tried to feel, had in her presence disappeared like a flight of birds sucked into an underworld; or maybe blown the other way, scattered and lost in the sky. He once more hid imprisonment.

It was a cold spring night. Fog drifted in patches across the road. Gray clouds hung low; the quarter moon when it momentarily slipped through, looked lusterless, odd. Levin was his stiff, numb, shattered self. Pauline rubbed her cold nose against his rigid jaw. She teased him to kiss her. More than once he told himself he was no longer in love with her. The reason didn't matter, the condition did. Having thought it he denied it, weary of denial.

She was bright with plans for them. He had his own: delay, let her say nothing to Gilley, forestall any final commitment. He must see the election through. Win or lose, he wanted another year at the college. He hoped for the dean's recommendation. Next year would be soon enough to talk of marriage.

But when he suggested that, she asked whether he expected her to go on living with Gerald.

I'm sure you understand I can't. And when I move out of his house what sort of recommendation do you think you'll get once he lets it be known why we have separated?

She urged him to let her tell Gerald tonight—she could no longer stand keeping it from him. They would settle things, and when Levin had his grades in, would leave. She spoke of a Nevada divorce so they would not have to wait a year to get married. She had a little money that her father had left her, and the divorce could be got comparatively cheaply if she stayed with a college friend in Carson City, the girl she had told him about, with the mismatched breasts. He could live, meanwhile, in San Francisco, more beautiful, less overpowering than New York City. After she got back from the divorce, if he had decided to return to graduate school in the fall they could get married and go. They would somehow get along. The references he needed he could get from the professors he worked under. If he would rather give up teaching, her uncle in San Francisco would help him find a job.

She's got it all planned. He wrestled a rage against her, answered nothing.

Then shall I tell him? she asked. He senses something's wrong but doesn't know what. He tends to wait for a situation to disappear and this one won't. I feel sorry for him. I think we ought to tell him.

The moon had gone again, the fog risen. He felt spasms of irritation and self-disgust.

What's the matter, darling? You're so quiet. Aren't you well? He denied it.

Don't keep anything from me, like that time you had the pain I didn't know about.

Though Levin craftily warned himself to keep his yap shut to protect his undiminished pride, to keep whole her image of him as a man, he at last confessed how tormented he still was.

I feel as though I no longer can love, as though all feeling were buried in me under a rock. I'm in that again. I told you about it that time in the woods. It's a hellish thing.

In the dark she turned pale, embraced him tightly, blamed herself for his trouble, for not knowing her own mind.

I should long ago have agreed to leave Gerald. Her eyes glistened. Don't you feel anything for me?

I'm worn out. It's a terrible emptiness.

Suppose the truth is you just don't love me any more?

He said, after long hesitation, he had no reason not to.

Then maybe you ought to see a doctor?

No, said Levin, I've been through it before. I know what it is.

What will you do?

Wait it out.

How long did it last the last time?

Months. Maybe a year. I'm not sure.

It needn't again.

No?

You're not alone any more.

He had forgotten.

Are you afraid? Pauline asked.

More of the world than anything else.

My darling, she said. They held each other.

Levin recalled their fruitless nights in motels. Should we go somewhere? he said.

Go where?

To my room, or maybe in the field now. We both have our coats.

But she said no. I've thought of that but decided not to. If we get married—if we ever do—I'd rather not till then. I want to come to you with a little innocence saved up.

Abstaining makes you a virgin?

I'm withholding it from myself. Help me to a little virtue, Lev.

Virtue lies between the legs?

It's a way of being despite what you've been.

Then she kissed him with cold lips. I'll sleep with you if you have to prove something to yourself.

No.

Please love me, she said. Don't not love me. Please protect me. I'm afraid to be alone. She began to cry.

Don't cry, Levin said. I love you.

I'm crying for the way things are.

He let her cry.

She wiped her eyes with a handkerchief. If we broke up

you couldn't be sure, could you, that it would be what you really wanted?

No.

I believe in you, do you in me?

He said he did.

Then hadn't I better tell Gerald?

He said the hard thing was to make decisions without confidence in his feelings. Couldn't we wait till the end of summer? I might have it licked by then.

It will take till then till I get my divorce. I think we ought to do what I suggested before. I'll leave Gerald and we'll go to San Francisco. After that if things turn out well, they turn out well. If they don't, we won't get married.

Her eyes misted again.

Secretly relieved, he sat in silence.

Only I don't believe in that kind of end for us, do you? She asked.

He said no.

Then shall I tell Gerald?

He said yes.


He woke in the dark, both arms flailing. A light blinded him. Papers fluttered in the room as a cold wind blew in through the open door. I got to lock it, Levin thought, struggling to sleep.

A figure emerged at the foot of the bed.

Levin sat upright. "Don't shoot."

Gilley stood there in shirt sleeves, his face agitated, eyes lit in hatred of the one in bed.

"You goddamn two-faced, two-assed, tin-saint hypocrite, preaching reform all the while you were committing adultery with my wife!"

Levin lay back, groaning.

"Don't deny it, you slimy do-gooder, false pretender to virtue. You ought to be strung up—"

"I confess I loved—do love—her—"

"Preach one thing, practice the opposite, a dirty thief throwing up a filthy smoke screen while stealing a man's wife from him."

"We were in love—"

"You're two of a kind—"

Levin slowly sat up. "Are you so innocent?"

"What do you mean?" Gilley thundered.

"You drove her to it, a man not above taking a picture of his naked wife and showing it to a dozen people."

Gilley's jaw sagged. He raised his arm as if to defend himself and couldn't. Looking wearily around he located a chair but didn't get to it. His eyes had turned glassy, his mask of misery fitted his face.

"CD told you?" he sighed.

"Your pal Avis—"

"She shouldn't have. She gave— You haven't told Pauline, have you? She doesn't know about it."

"I'd be ashamed to."

"I was desperate."

"I'll bet you look at it every day."

Gilley shook his head miserably. "It's been destroyed. Not by me, I'll admit, though I would have by now if he hadn't. Duffy did it. I hid the one print I had developed, and the negative, in his folder in my files. One night he sneaked into my office—I'll never know how unless he picked my lock—I wouldn't put that past him—and he stole everything in the folder, all his incriminating records, and the picture of them, and burned it in my wastebasket. I found the ashes the next morning."

"Bravo!"

"She drove me to it," Gerald said heavily. "First she took up for him, then with him. I suspected something was fishy and watched her, as I ought to have done with you around if I hadn't been so stupid in underestimating what you were capable of. One day I got wind they were going to the coast and I followed them. My Leica was in the glove compartment of the car. I always keep it loaded—"

"It was loaded so you snapped."

"Spare me, for Pete's sake. Both of my ears hurt. You're in no position to be preaching to me."

"My error," muttered Levin.

"I admit that taking that picture was a mistake, although I thought I might need it for a divorce, but that certainly doesn't excuse you for all the harm you've done here. I want to warn you about one thing, don't bet on her love for you, if that's what it is. All she sees in you is a certain resemblance to somebody else."

"Explain that one."

"I will," said Gilley. "A few months after she found out Leo Duffy had bumped himself off, or however he did it, she picked your application out of a pile I happened to be studying. I had my strong doubts about that but in a minute of foolishness let her. She was still in a funk about him and blaming herself for his suicide. I felt bad myself, though I honestly had no reason to, so I let her."

"Let her what?"

"Pick your application as the one we would take. I had brought home a pile half a foot high from people looking for jobs. We had had a man renege out of his appointment because he had got a better offer, and I had to replace him on very short notice. I had previously put you in the discards as unsuitable, but Pauline was reading the newspaper at the dining table where I was working and her eye just happened to light on your picture among the discarded applications. She picked up yours and read through it. The next thing I knew she was advising me to hire you, a thing she usually keeps out of. I was suspicious right off but wanted to show I was sympathetic to how she was feeling, so I said I would. What a cockeyed mistake that was."

"Why did she pick me?"

"She said she thought your experience was good and liked

the letter you had written about your ideas of teaching composition, which I thought was pretentious when I read it. I guess it also appealed to her that you were from New York. Duffy was from the East."

"Chicago?"

"That's East out here. There were other resemblances between you both."

"Why did you let her if you didn't trust her choice?"

"Frankly, I didn't think she could be interested in you after seeing your picture. Yet I admit I did feel that if I took her suggestion I'd live to regret it."

"Was Duffy a handsome man?"

"In his way. But that was a good trick of yours coming with a beard."

"Trick?"

"Pauline has always had odd tastes."

"I tricked her and she tricked you?"

"She'll do the same to you. She's a discontented woman and I could tell you more. If you were to marry her you'd find that out soon enough, and I'd pity you when you did."

"If that's the case why do you want to keep her?"

"I love her," he said miserably.

Levin socked himself hard on the chest.

Gilley then came up with a proposition: "We've both made mistakes, though I wouldn't have done to you half of what you did to me. What I have to say is that I'm willing to forgive and forget if you will resign and leave. I promise you good references."

But Levin sadly shook his head.

"She's all I've got," Gerald said brokenly.

The instructor lay back with both eyes shut.

On Monday the acting head let it be known through Avis Fliss and George Bullock that he and his wife were separating, with an assist by Mr. S. Levin. The halls were thick with talk as department members came in to hand in their grades and get on their gowns for the Commencement ceremony. People

345

avoided Levin and he avoided them. The next day the election was held in Dean Seagram's office. Levin did not attend. Neither did Bucket. The first and final vote for head of department was Gilley 17, Fabrikant 2, Levin 0. Though he had expected nothing less, Levin, poor man's Parnell, somewhere in his buried self felt shame and loss. He might have led.

In his mailbox was a note from Gilley. "I am willing to let you stay on for one last year, provided you promise not to see my wife again, or otherwise interfere in our lives. G. Gilley, Head of Dept. P.S. In thinking it over we will use the books your committee recommended. G.G."

Levin did not reply. Later in the day he received by messenger an official communication from President Marion Labhart, terminating his services "as of today, in the public interest, for good and sufficient cause of a moral nature." He referred to the ex-instructor, among other things, as a "frustrated Union Square radical."

Levin put his fist through Duffy's bloody window.

He awoke with Pauline in his arms. She had kissed him awake. "Mrs. Beaty let me come up when I told her I was upset and had to see you."

Levin, realizing it was no dream, sat up slowly. She moved back on the bed, looking worn, tired, lonely. She was hastily dressed and in doubt.

"How's your hand?"

"Better."

He lit a cigarette with his bandaged hand.

"I never saw you smoke before."

"I go back to it sometimes."

"What else do you go back to?"

"What do you have in mind?"

"Nothing really. I'm sorry I'm nervous." She asked, "How do you feel?"

"I slept badly, thinking of the job."

"But you knew you would lose it. Even if you had won the election you would have lost your job once people knew why I was leaving Gerald."

"For a short time in my life I felt I was able to say what would happen to me next."

"There are other jobs," Pauline said. "But if you think you're sacrificing the right thing for the wrong woman, you can call it off. Don't be too proud to admit defeat."

He said he wasn't.

Pauline said, "Gerald left last night and went to the hotel until I leave the house. We had a nasty argument about the children. He said he'd contest my divorce and not let me have them. He accused me of deserting them in spirit long ago. I said the truth was I had long ago deserted him but hadn't the courage to say so. Our marriage was in shreds after Leo left, but the children kept it together until I fell in love with you."

She got her handkerchief out of her bag. "I've never seen him so hurt and unyielding. He asked me not to leave him, and when I said it was for the good of us all he got very bitter and said if it was a question of whose good it was, he would keep Erik and Mary."

She blew her nose. "I'm blowing my nose," she said. "He has been an affectionate father but I've always thought of them as more mine than his. I was the one who really wanted them. He made me wait almost six years before we put in adoption papers. After he left I kept waking up every hour and wanting to look at the kids. I went upstairs several times. I've been so positive he would let me have them and I almost died when he said no. Please help me get them, Lev."

He had always known she would want them. I'm in so far already, he thought.

He said he would help her.

"I hate to burden you further," she said. "But you really don't have to marry me."

"We've gone through all that," he said.

"Why are you then?"

"I've told you."

"Tell me again."

"I love you."

"Without feeling?"

"As I am."

"You love me on principle?"

"Yes."

"Is that all?"

"No."

"How else?"

He was silent.

"I get afraid," Pauline said. "It's so easy to make a serious mistake." She said, after a minute, "Will you talk to him? He wouldn't listen to me."

"Would it be so bad to leave them with him?"

"What would he do with them? Either he'd have to bring someone in to take care of them or send them to his parents. I don't want strangers bringing up my children."

"Couldn't he take one and we'd have the other?"

"I couldn't do that, they both need me. They're still babies."

"Suppose I said I didn't want them?"

"I don't think you would."

Levin asked, "What do you want me to do?"

"Talk to Gerald and persuade him to let us keep them."

"What makes him think he could take them from you?"

"He said he would tell the court I wasn't a fit mother."

"Don't cry."

"I wouldn't if you put your arms around me."

He did that, thinking he hadn't planned to see Gilley again, either.

Pauline waited downstairs while he shaved and dressed. It took him longer than usual, partly because of his bandaged hand. When Levin came down, they were all in the kitchen, the kids playing with Mrs. Beaty's pots. Pauline was having a cup of coffee with the landlady.

"Good wishes if I may, Mr. Levin," Mrs. Beaty said.

"Lev want to marry Mama," said Erik.

"Would you like a cup of coffee?" Pauline asked, reddening. "Mrs. Beaty very kindly made a fresh potful."

"I'll eat later."

"You can now, there's no rush."

"I'd rather go now."

Levin called the office but Milly said Dr. Gilley was staying at the Covered Wagon Hotel. They drove downtown in Levin's car. Summer had come, the day was warm. They said little.

In the hotel lobby Levin asked, "Are we all going up?"

Pauline, tense, shook her head. "I'd rather not. I will though if you want me to."

"Wait here," said Levin.

"Tell him I want Erik and Mary and mean to have them. If he wants to go to court that's all right with me."

Then she said, "Maybe you'd better not say it that way. Speak to him nicely. Maybe he'll relent. Do you think he will?"

"I don't know."

"Try not to make him angry—any more than he is."

He said he would try.

She pressed his hand.

In the elevator he thought: I've slept with his wife and here I come asking for his kids. He felt he wanted to give Gilley back everything he had taken from him and more.

Levin stood in front of the door five minutes before he knocked.

Gerald, in a seersucker robe, unshaven, dark half-moons under his eyes, opened the door.

"Oh, it's you."

"Sorry to bother you again," Levin said, "but there's one last thing I have to see you about." He was ready to step back if Gilley slammed the door in his face.

"Come in," Gerald said. The magazines and newspapers he

had been reading were strewn around the armchair and base of the lit pink lamp in the darkish hotel room.

He looks like a misplaced bachelor, Levin thought, and I feel long since married.

"Pardon the small room," Gilley said. He sat in the armchair, crossing his long red-haired legs. "I was hoping you'd show up."

Levin sat on the edge of a hard chair. "I'm sorry I've been such a thorn in your side, Gerald."

"More a pain in the ass," Gilley said. "And if you're so goddamn sorry, why don't you close up shop and go haunt some other neighborhood? Why did you have to pick on me? I've worked doggone hard in my life and don't know why I shouldn't be allowed to live in peace with my wife and kids and enjoy the fruits of my labor."

"The reason I've come," Levin said, "is to ask for the children. They'll miss their mother. She says they'd only be in your way."

"If their mother wants them so much why didn't she act like one? Why didn't she consider their welfare before breaking up their home?"

He was haughty, embittered, so unhappy Levin found it hard to look at him.

Neither of them spoke until Gerald, uncrossing his legs, said, "I thought you'd be more than glad for me to take them off your hands, but if you're asking to have them for her, that shows you don't really have any true idea what you're in for. Up to now you've had a free ride on my back, although I can't blame you entirely, I suppose. I know darn well it wasn't all your fault, and that's why I opened the door to you just now instead of punching your eye. But the way you're acting convinces me, if I haven't already been convinced along other lines of the same thing, that you are a very inexperienced person. I mean with women as they really are and not as they pretend to be, or as they are when it's a question of going to bed with them. I don't doubt you're in love with my wife.

Duffy was too, but that's not the whole of it. A lot you don't know will pop up the minute you begin to live as man and wife under the same roof. Up to then the picture might as well be something you think you're seeing whereas the real thing is something else again after it's been developed. That's why I thought I ought to talk to you before you go on with this."

"I appreciate it," Levin said, "but I know what you mean."

"You can't," said Gilley, "unless you've been married to her for years. First off, she has some qualities that would drive even the most patient man, and I am one of them—crazy. If you want to know why I want her back if that's the case, and after she has twice deceived and humiliated me, the reason is understandable. I'm used to her and know what to expect. She can't surprise me any more, good or bad, though this would be her last chance with the bad. I've had it. Yet I'd be a liar not to admit there are some wonderful things about Pauline or why am I bothering to talk to you now? But as somebody thinking of marrying a woman who has been married a dozen years, the best and freshest of her youth, you are due for some unpleasant surprises, and I wouldn't be surprised myself in the least to hear that you and she break up within six months if you are so foolish as to marry her. In order to save you unforseen trouble I'll give you some idea what she's like."

"I know what she's like—"

"You think you do. I've already told you she is never contented, but I don't think you understand what that means. She was born dissatisfied, as some people are—Fabrikant comes to mind, and I could mention others—or maybe she was brought up that way. Whatever it is, even when as a student she turned in some very good term papers to me, which I gave high A's to, she never was satisfied. She always said she felt she should have done better. Not that she *could*, mind you, but that she *should* have, as though all you have to do to execute a better performance is to wish for it. I blame her old man for this, to some extent. I understand he was a fine physician and a nice thoughtful person—I've suffered myself from his virtues—but it's plain to me that he gave her a blown-up idea of herself. She was an only child, too, be that as it may. If you make the mistake of tying yourself to her, more than once—I guarantee—you'll wake up at six A.M. to hear her already going on about her life and how it didn't pan out as she wanted it to. When you ask her what she had expected, all she can tell you is that she wanted to be a better person than she is. And this, as is obvious, from a woman who admits to two extra-marital lovers in the last three years. Then you will hear in long detail everything she thinks she has done wrong, or those things she tried to do and had to give up, or everything she now does and does badly. She will never once tell you what she does well, which can get pretty monotonous. After that she'll blame you for as much as she blames herself, because you married her—in my case when she was twenty— and didn't do what she calls 'bring me out,' meaning make out of her something she couldn't make out of herself though you may have broken your back trying to think up new ways to do it. I've suggested courses, taken her on trips, kept her on a decent budget even when I couldn't so well afford it, given her a position in the community, a car, fine home, children just as real and lovable as anyone else's, although adopted, and in general tried everything I know to make her happy. And when she's through with that complaint she will have worked herself up into a nervous jag, so that unless you get out of the house early you'll be having an argument with her that may run through the day and into the night, just to the time, let's say, when you might be thinking of a little natural satisfaction. The next day it'll take her half the morning to wake up because she hasn't slept well, which happens more often than you would think. I'm not saying I hold these things against her, and I'm willing to bet that if you asked her right now she'll admit I've always been considerate. Maybe it's just the way her nervous system is built. It might be what used to be called 'delicate.' Almost anything can throw off her balance and start you both being miserable."

Levin shifted in his chair.

Gilley went on: "If you happen to want someone who is a good housekeeper and will keep the house as neat and orderly as I've seen your office—I'm not talking about those fireballs who do canning, baking, gardening, civic activities, refinishing furniture, bean picking in summer, and play tennis besides keeping up the usual household chores—I am talking about a reduced scale of domestic efficiency—well, you'd better forget it. She has her periods of efficiency, I admit, usually in the spring and early fall, but there are times when for one reason or another she can't get organized enough to clean the toilet and I have to do it after a full day's work, especially on a day she has spent most of the time with a pile of cookbooks around her, cooking a dinner that should take two hours to prepare instead of seven, and is not anything super-special anyway. That's why we don't entertain as much as I would like. She doesn't care for housework—it bores her, and even on days she is concentrating on getting it done, her resistance to it cuts down on her accomplishment. That's why I frankly thought we were better off not adopting for a while because I knew she'd be more swamped than ever. As soon as I could afford a cleaning woman for her twice a week I agreed to having the kids. I know how finicky you are to order and punctuality, but if you marry her you can bury your clock for all the good it will do you. Not only does she resist time, she makes it her enemy."

"I'm not such good friends with it either," Levin sighed.

"What I mean is that for years—this started in her twenties— she has been keeping track of her wrinkles and lamenting the passing of her youth, which, I take it, was from eighteen to twenty-five, and I can't convince her otherwise. With me around she has the advantage of my forty-five years as a comparison to her thirty-two, but with you and your thirty or thirty-one, you can imagine what that might do to her morale.

She'll be older with you than she is with me, older at every age and, believe me, you won't find any advantage to it. Living with Pauline though it can be pleasant is generally no bed of roses."

"I have never slept on flowers."

"And then there are her health problems."

"I'd rather not hear—"

"It won't take a minute. I won't call her health bad but she has her problems that you'd better know about. After thirty a woman doesn't get any younger. She sometimes has constipation, which I won't go into, but the real nuisance is her female troubles on and off. When you least expect it, she goes into her nine-day-or-so period that is caused by what they call anovulatory cycle or some such name. The doctor says that with her it's more a nuisance than anything serious and could clear up on its own, which it sometimes does, but the result is that you never know where you stand when your instincts are up. No doubt she saved her best times for you but you'll be making a mistake if you take her for a sexy babe. Once you're married to her you can bet your boots that many times when you are looking forward to your satisfaction there is nothing doing that night. You might just as well beat your brains out then as argue with her to go to see a doctor. She's afraid of them and resists till she gets so wound up from worry that when she finally does go, your bill is twice as high as it should have been. Think of that on your salary."

"Excuse me," Levin said. "What I came about is the children—"

"I was getting to that," said Gilley. "They also have their troubles, as all kids do. Little Mary is generally healthy but has eczema all summer, and the pediatrician has warned Pauline she could go into asthma overnight—it's some kind of strong allergic condition. She gets shots that are costing me over a hundred dollars a year. And Erik never stops having colds he can't shake off, that either go into bronchitis or ear infections. One month this past winter his antibiotics bill alone came to sixty dollars. He's also had strep throat three times and the pediatrician is always testing for a possible low-grade rheumatic fever as a result of the streptococcus. He doesn't think Erik is such a sick kid but Pauline has yet to stop worrying about him, and when she worries, brother, you worry."

Levin, fanning himself with his good hand, continued to listen.

"I said before there are some wonderful things about Pauline —I wouldn't in the least call her a flop. Though you mightn't guess it she plays a good game of golf. She also began to learn how to ski a few years back, but I can't, so we don't go often. She's also good around the garden. She reads a lot, listens to music—I built her a hi-fi—and she has knitted me some nice sweaters and socks. She has wanted to go to work but I'd rather have her at home because that's what needs the most attention. It all boils down to what I said before, that she is dislocated by nature, and in the end there is a better than even chance she will tell you what she has told me, that maybe the cause of it is she didn't really love me when she married me. I'll tell you this," Gerald said with bitterness, "I know love in a woman when I see it, and believe me, I saw it in her. I have her letters to prove it. Once she begins to question herself, nothing is sacred any more. And to top it all, at times she'll get so low and unhappy that more than one night I've had to comfort her, as for instance after she had deceived me with Duffy. You may be doing the same with her some day over some other third party. Don't think your situation will be much better than mine."

"It's the chance you take—"

"The odds are not in your favor."

Levin again mentioned the children. "She'd be miserable without them. We could work out some sort of arrangement so that you could have them part of the year—maybe the summer."

Gilley stared at him. "You expect to go on with this after what I've told you?"

Levin laughed badly.

Gilley snapped off the lamplight and rose. "In that case she can't have them. When she deserts me, she deserts them."

Levin sat humidly on the hard chair. "How can you hurt her if you say you love her?"

"The same way she hurts me. The way you do. The way I want to hurt you."

His eyes were dark with distaste and anger. "If you want so much to have the kids, there's only one way—"

Levin, in pain of anticipation, leaned forward.

"Are you willing to give me your promise you will give up college teaching?" Gerald said.

Levin jumped up in rage. "Are you crazy? That's a fantastic blackmail."

"Take it or leave it."

"It's unconstitutional," Levin shouted. "Inhuman, barbaric, immoral."

"And what is it when you steal a man's wife and children from him?" Gilley thundered. "Is that so g.d. moral, since you use the word so much?"

"Pauline is a free agent."

"Can you say the kids are, or that she deserves to have them, a woman who had two lovers?"

"Will you use them any better than you used her?"

"She used me. She played me for a sucker."

"How am I supposed to support them if I can't teach?"

"I didn't say you couldn't teach. I said not in any college. You can go back to a high school. They generally pay better anyway."

"What's the difference whether I teach in a high school or college?"

"You'd do less harm in high school. You're not fit to teach at the college level."

"What a low form of revenge."

"It's your own fault. I want to get at least something out of this mess."

"I won't agree to it. We'll fight for the kids in court."

"You won't get anything in court when I testify she engaged in adultery with Duffy, then with you—during which, as she has admitted to me—she sometimes left the kids unattended. She isn't a fit mother."

"You're not in your right mind if you say that."

"I'll argue about it when the time comes."

"You'll have no evidence. She won't testify against herself."

"I have all the evidence I need—on tape."

Levin groaned from his shoes up. "You mean you took a tape of her talking, without her knowledge?"

Gilley blanched. "So would you."

"These goddamn gadgets will destroy you. I'll testify as to the kind of pictures you took of her."

"Picture, damn it, and *she* was naked in it with a man, not I. I wish now I had had the sense to print more than one copy. As for whatever evidence you have to give, I'd advise you not to or the judge might be interested in hearing a lot more about you. I don't want to bring this up just yet because I haven't finished investigating it, but one of the boys at the Alpha Zeta fraternity, which I am the faculty adviser to, recently became engaged to a girl who told him one night in his car that she had had intimate relations with one of her English profs, who she didn't name. Out of curiosity I looked up her record and found that three people in the department had taught her, Avis this spring, Leopold Kuck last winter, and you back in the fall. Both of them gave her C's. You gave her a C first, then petitioned to change it to a B. I remember that business very well and was suspicious when you wanted to raise her grade. Her name's Nadalee Hammerstad."

Levin felt as though Gilley had broken a lead pipe on his head; but the bleeding was internal.

"The grade she got was the grade she earned," he muttered.

"You are now shown up for the first-class scum you are."

What else could I expect, Levin thought, given who I am?

"Well, take it or leave it," Gilley said.

"I'll speak to Pauline."

"Tell her how goddamn moral you are."

He descended three flights of stairs in a stupefying daze. Pauline was sitting on the lobby couch, Mary on her lap, Erik by her side, turning the pages of a picture book.

She looked at Levin in fright. "What happened?"

He told her Gilley's terms and she was furious. "Oh, that's awful. We'll see my lawyer. I'll sue for the children."

"You may not get them," Levin said. "Why did you tell him you had left them alone while you were with me?"

"It slipped out as we were arguing. I was afraid to tell you I had told him."

"Suppose his lawyer asks on the stand if you had slept with Duffy. What would you say?"

"Please lower your voice," she said, lowering hers.

"Would you deny it?"

"No."

"And with me?"

"I lie so badly."

"You'd never get the kids."

She hugged the baby.

"Under the circumstances are you willing to give them up?"

"No."

Erik, still looking at the pictures, began to cry.

"Don't cry, Erik," Pauline said. "Lev wants me to have you and Mary."

"Suppose the court doesn't?"

"I'd die."

Erik continued to cry and the baby began.

"Then we have no choice," Levin said.

"I can't ask you to give up your career for us. The whole thing's mad. It's Gerald's revenge against me. Isn't there some other way?"

"Not that he offers."

"What will this get him? When he's himself again I don't believe he'll hold you to it."

"When he's himself will he let you have the kids?"

"I'm afraid to take the chance. But I don't want you to hate me all my life for bringing this on you."

"I brought it on myself."

She opened her purse.

"Don't cry."

"I have to."

Levin climbed up the stairs to Gilley's room.

"I agree to your terms."

"You're batty," said Gilley. "You're cutting your throat."

"You're cutting it. Do you want me to sign anything?"

"I'll take your word, you're a fanatical type."

"Isn't there some better way?"

"Yes, go away and leave my wife and family alone."

Levin opened the door.

"Goodbye to your sweet dreams," Gilley called after him.

"I hope yours are sweet."

"An older woman than yourself and not dependable, plus two adopted kids, no choice of yours, no job or promise of one, and other assorted headaches. Why take that load on yourself?"

"Because I can, you son of a bitch."


They drove to the house. Levin went unwillingly in, the signs of the husband still around. Pauline fed the kids, then put them down for naps. She made sandwiches and they sat in the kitchen. Levin ate, looking at the stump of the leaning birch tree in the back yard; Pauline said Gerald had chopped it down in the spring.

After coffee she said, "He gets the house and car and I get a cash settlement. All I'll take are my clothes and the children's things. I'll send the crib and Erik's bed, my two trunks, some books and records, to my uncle's, and we'll have three bags for the trip, plus yours."

"How long will it take to get there?"

"Two days without rushing. Three if we want to look at things along the way. Don't worry about the driving. I'll spell you."

"Let's make it two days. I want to get there and look around."

"You'll have weeks while I'm in Nevada."

"I want to get started."

"How do you feel now?"

"The same."

"Please take my hand. My feeling for you is an ache."

He took her cold hand across the table.

"It makes me sad that you're still this way," she said, "but now that you're with me I feel you'll want me again. Maybe not so intensely but so long as it's love I'll have no kick."

He said nothing.

"My maiden name was Josephson," Pauline said. "Think of me as Pauline Josephson. Joseph was my father's name and he wanted a son but I was his best-beloved daughter."

She was looking out of the window. "Imagine, we've never been for a walk together."

Afterwards Levin asked her why she had picked his application out of the pile Gilley had discarded.

"You had attached a photograph," Pauline said, "although you weren't asked to."

"It was an old picture. I wanted them to know what I looked like."

"You looked as though you needed a friend."

"Was that the reason?"

"I needed one. Your picture reminded me of a Jewish boy I knew in college who was very kind to me during a trying time in my life."

"So I was chosen," Levin said.

That night, after packing his few possessions, he caught sight of his doubtful face in the mirror. Am I in my right mind? He sat in a chair, head in his hands. His doubts were the bricks of a windowless prison he was in, where Gilley's voice endlessly droned the reasons he ought to quit. Every reason was part of the structure. The prison was really himself, flawed edifice of failures, each locking up tight the one before. He had failed at his best plans, who could say he wouldn't with her? Possibly he already had and would one day take off in the dark as she lay in bed. Unless the true prison was to stick it out chained to her ribs. He would look like a free man but whoever peered into his eyes would see the lines of a brick wall.

He left the house and walked to the river. What if he beat it now, sneaked back, and when the old lady was snoring away with her ears turned off he would lug his suitcase and valise down to the car and drive away? He could head north to Canada, and then east. No one would know where he was or was going. He would leave a note, "Sorry, I don't think it will work. Too much has happened. I do this for you as well as myself. Sincerely, and with regret, S. Levin." He would slip that under her door and fade away. All she had to do when she found it was unpack and call Gilley at the hotel. She would cry a little but could say, "He wasn't worth your little finger. I made a dreadful mistake. The children miss you—please take us back." And Gilley, the forgiver, would hotfoot it home, holding flowers. They'd go on as before.

Or if she were really sick of him, she could take the train to SF and stay with her uncle. She would feel bad for a while but sooner or later some middle-aged gent would show up who would want to marry her; she was that type. Let somebody else marry her, Levin thought. He had from the first resisted becoming her savior, or victim. She had in a moment of unhappiness after the death of a former flame picked him by chance from a pile of discards. She had marked him x in a distant port and summoned him across the continent. Did this casual selection make him responsible for her for life? Was he forever bound to the choice she had made? That was stretching kismet too far. Who was a man if he surrendered freedom in a prior time?

The town was quiet as he walked, all but deserted since the college students had gone, the houses dark, silent. He met no one. At the river, after watching the moving water, he turned back, avoiding downtown and his reflection in store windows, still roaming, after so many years, the stone streets of the past. The city haunted him tonight. While others were sleeping Levin, in stinking clothes, had sneaked out of the bug-infested room he hid in during the day and wandered along long dark streets, peering into the houses of strangers for drops of light. Many a night he had walked in anguished desire of a decent future; failing that, another bottle. He drove the seasons away after hounding them to appear: winter, sniffing the icy wind for the scent, the breath, of spring; yet a time of flowers drove him wild; amid summer foliage, in ascetic heat, he obsessively hunted dead leaves and found them under every bush; autumn inspired his own long death. This went on for too many years to remember.

He came by a roundabout way to her house and stood under the ornamental plum tree across the street. The house looked already empty, except the lit living room where, through a half-open window, he could see her packing. She wore a shapeless shirt and her toreador pants, and with a cigarette in her mouth, was putting kids' things into a suitcase. Who is she? Levin thought. What do I really know about her? He thought if after she got back from Nevada he was still not sure how it would work out, he would call it quits. That would finish the promise to Gilley and he would, after a year in graduate school, try again to get into a small liberal arts college and teach there. With luck he might make it.

Pauline was holding a yellow dress against herself to see how it looked. She put it down and with a cloth, rubbed something on the table. When she picked it up and placed it under her chin it was a violin. She tried the bow, then played. Levin listened till he recognized the music.

Overslept, he awoke with a bang and was splashing cold water on his face when the landlady knocked. "Mrs. Gilley called and said to come right over, it's very important."

This could go too far. He hurriedly dressed, shaved, and left the house, leaving behind both his bags for protection.

When he drove up, Pauline, watching at the window, opened the door for him.

"What's wrong?"

She seemed not to want, or be able, to look at him. A massive excitement seized Levin.

Meeting his eyes at last, she murmured, "I'm about two months' pregnant."

He remembered then to remove his hat. The blood in his brain gave his head the weight of a rock.

"Mine?" he asked.

She smiled wanly. "Not Leo's."

"I mean Gerald—no, I guess I don't."

"I suspected something last month," Pauline said, "but thought no because I had a slight flow at the more-or-less usual time."

"I didn't think of the possibility of conception those last times."

"You want the right feeling for every event?"

"Don't you?"

"Yes," she said. "I called you as soon as I knew for sure. I happened to think last night that my period was late. Then I checked the calendar and it was very late. I called the doctor and was examined this morning. There isn't any doubt I'm pregnant. I didn't want you to think I had come back to you because of that. I thought I'd tell you before we left in case you want to call it off."

"What would you do if I did?"

"I frankly don't know. I could try to abort."

"No."

"Are you saying that with your steely will or pity for the human race?"

364

"I want the child."

Pauline said, "I'm so relieved. I wasn't sure how you'd take it." Then she said, "Touch my breasts, they're beginning to grow."

Levin touched them.

"They'll shrink after the baby is weaned but at least you'll know how I look with little ones."

He returned for his bags, passed up eating from the cherry tree and said goodbye to Mrs. Beaty. On the way back he saw Bullock in a new red station wagon. George had expected to be director of comp but Gerald, Pauline had said, was combining that job with his own.

Pauline was ready with both kids but instead of three bags she had four, a duffel bag, and a violin case. Levin, in a sweat, was thinking of a luggage rack for the roof of the car, but then the Buckets came along, Algene heavy-bellied in her ninth month; Joe helped Levin get five bags in the trunk, and two, with the violin case and his umbrella, they put in the back of the car.

"No rack needed yet," Bucket said. " 'A penny saved is a penny earned.' "

"It's the earned penny that worries me," said Levin.

" 'God tempers the wind to a shorn lamb.' "

"Lev's no lamb," said Pauline.

"I speak for myself," Bucket said.

Levin lifted Erik into the back seat. "I'm your father now."

"I want my real daddy."

When they were in, five counting Pauline's baby, Levin started the Hudson and the Buckets waved them off. What if I had bought a seven-passenger car? Levin thought.

Mary sat in the baby seat, in front, the sores on her arms covered with ointment. Pauline's hair, brushed bright, was drawn into a bun. He thought she would be wearing the yellow dress he saw last night but she wore the sleeveless white linen he had first seen her in. When they drove off she gazed back at the house, then turned away.

Levin drove to the edge of town for a last look at the view to the mountains. The clouds were a clash of horses and volcanoes.

"Beautiful country."

"If beauty isn't all that happens."

They drove through the campus, the trees in full leaf, arched above the narrow streets, shading the green lawns.

"I failed this place," Levin said.

"You got *The Elements* kicked out after thirty years."

"A hell of a revolution."

"Gerald is also thinking of offering some of the instructors doing graduate work a literature class."

"I still want to teach," he said.

"Don't undersell yourself."

"It's what I do best."

"What else have you tried?"

"Too much."

They saw Fabrikant, a stogie in his mouth, hurrying to the office.

"He's growing reddish whiskers," said Pauline.

"I hear the dean asked him to handle the Great Books program."

"That was your idea," Pauline said. She said, "Gerald wouldn't keep that promise if he had made it to you."

"That's the point," Levin said.

She rested her head on his shoulder. "Trust me, darling. I'll make you a good wife."

Her body smelled like fresh-baked bread, the bread of flowers.

"Wear these." He gave her the gold hoop earrings he had kept for her.

She fastened them on her ears. "God bless you, Lev."

"Sam, they used to call me home."

"God bless you, Sam."

Two tin-hatted workmen with chain saws were in the maple tree in front of Humanities Hall, cutting it down limb by leafy limb, to make room for a heat tunnel. On the Student Union side of the street, Gilley was aiming a camera at the operation. When he saw Levin's Hudson approach he swung the camera around and snapped. As they drove by he tore a rectangle of paper from the back of the camera and waved it aloft.

"Got your picture!"